CHARYBDA

Worldstrait Book I

A.L.S. VOSSLER

Cover art © Koltryin Alexander, used under license from Shutterstock.com. Cover design by A.L.S. Vossler. Map design by Beth Seethaler.

Published by Imaginescence Imprints, McFarland, Kansas

ISBN-10: 1-947955-00-4
ISBN-13: 978-1-947955-00-4

For Virgil and Corles, who encouraged my creativity.

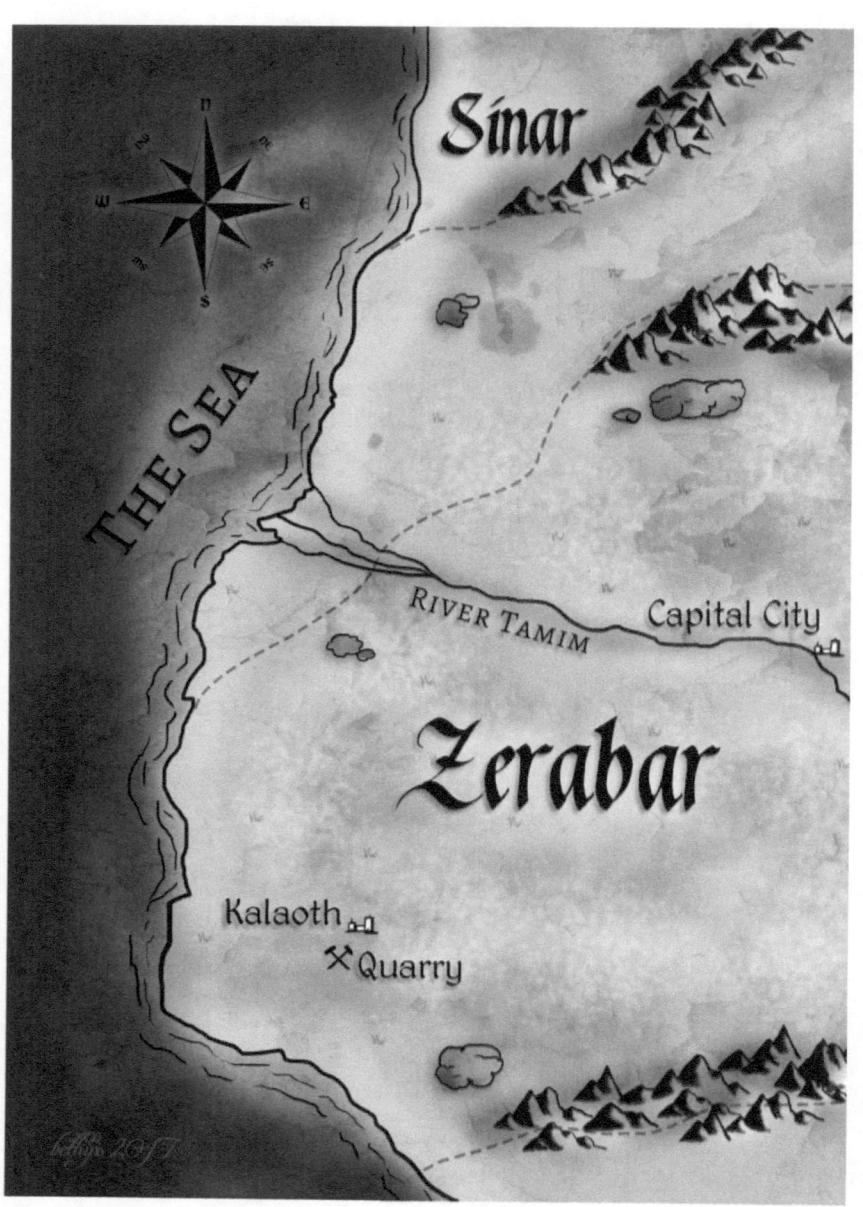

CHAPTER ONE

"Violent prisoner entering! Beware, beware! Abomination!"

The dank and mildewed halls of the dungeons reverberated with sound.

Nivin tilted her head, listening to the shouts of soldiers and the jingle of mail. She could hear them even from inside the small kitchen her father had set up for her in the dungeons. Moans and roars punctuated the customary wet, dark quiet. Whatever abomination they were bringing, it sounded huge. Thunderous footsteps echoed through the passages. Nivin could feel the vibrations through the cold, damp stone under her bare feet.

Making a mental note that this prisoner might need a larger meal than usual, she turned her attention back to her cooking. She reached for her long wooden spoon, which she always kept in exactly the same place so she could find it easily. It was how she organized all of her utensils. Not a thing could be out of place, especially if anyone might come in and watch her. If she had to fumble around, patting the surfaces until she could find what she searched for, people might suspect her secret.

Sometimes, she wondered if they already did.

After she stirred the stew, she carefully replaced her spoon and left the kitchen to investigate what manner of abomination they had brought to the dungeons this time. She gently dragged a hand along the damp walls of the corridor as she walked, listening carefully to the echoes for guidance.

Her father's footfalls, lightly marked by a shuffle, hurried down the corridor. When he passed her, he gave her long braid an affectionate tug. "Go back to your cooking, Nivin. You know I do not like for you to see the prisoners come in."

"Well, there is no danger of that, now is there?" Nivin whispered.

"Shh! Do not say things like that—do you want to be found out? It's a miracle you have made it to seventeen, as it is."

Nivin hung her head. "Yes, Father."

Her father heaved a sigh and continued down the hall. Nivin waited for a few moments before quietly following after him. She knew the dungeons well and could navigate them with ease. It was only on those few occasions she left the dungeons that she had trouble finding her way around.

She lingered behind a bend in the passage, listening intently. It sounded like a large crowd of people were around the corner.

Her father gasped and swore. "An abomination? You said he was an abomination, not a boulder. Where exactly am I to house this *thing*?"

The prisoner moaned indistinctly in response and her father shuffled back a few steps.

"That is your problem, Jailor Benin," barked one of the soldiers, his voice haggard. "Now, you and your men solve it quickly, before he breaks his bonds."

"All right, all right," her father said. "I have a cell that can hold four men—perhaps that will work." His footsteps went further down the corridor, and he unlocked the more spacious cell. "Bring him down here."

There was a moment of silence, followed by the sound of several feet shuffling away from the prisoner.

"Well, come on then!" her father shouted. "Do you want him to break loose from those ropes, you worthless idiots?"

Finally, the guards took over for the soldiers and goaded the prisoner down the hall. Bolstered by the prisoner's compliance, they grew rougher and laughed as they drove him. As soon as the prisoner was inside, Nivin heard her father leap forward and slam the door shut, then go to lock it.

Nivin listened as the soldiers walked down to the cell. She guessed they still held their weapons at the ready, in case this "violent prisoner" decided to escape. She imagined they all looked into the cell, marveling at whatever they saw.

"You think this cell alone will hold him?" said one of the soldiers, his voice filled with skepticism.

"Better than those ropes will," her father snapped. She heard the distinct sound of a key in the lock.

"He could still break those ropes should he get a mind to," said the soldier with the haggard voice. "The lock might not be strong enough. Get him in those manacles while he's still docile, or you will regret it later."

With a huff, her father unlocked the cell again. "Do it," he said sharply.

The guards once again reacted with silence.

"Just do it, you cowards," said another of the soldiers. "I've seen what this abomination can do."

"Then why don't you go in and shackle him?" said one of the guards.

There was a tense moment of silence.

"Oh, fine, I'll do it, you useless lot," her father growled. He hurried into the cell, and tried to place the manacles around the prisoner's wrists. He sighed in exasperation. "They won't even fit." Chains rattled. "All right…just join them in the middle…there! That will have to do."

The loud *click* of the lock was met by sighs of relief from the soldiers and guards.

"Don't you think for a minute he won't put up a fuss, now," said her father. "He might be strong enough to break those chains."

"He is still bound," replied one of the guards. "Maybe together it will be enough."

"He makes me nervous, nevertheless." Nivin could hear the fear and tenseness in her father's voice. "I want a close watch on him."

The prisoner, however, simply moaned softly.

Nivin hugged herself. What manner of abomination was this? Surely it was no ordinary man, brought in for the crime of a typical deformity. He must have been huge and incredibly powerful.

"Well, that is all your responsibility now," snapped one of the soldiers. "We have to tend to the families of our dead."

"Dead?" her father said. "I suppose that shouldn't be surprising. How many?"

"Three," the same soldier answered, his voice tense with anger. "They were completely brutalized. This abomination practically crushed every bone in their bodies. Like they were nothing more than bothersome beetles."

"Save the king," her father whispered.

"This is one abomination that truly deserves to die," said a young, angry voice. Nivin did not recognize it. It must have been one of the soldiers, and by the way his voice broke, she guessed he was just old enough to serve.

"Silence, you fool!" said the soldier with the haggard voice. Based on the volume and direction of his voice, he had turned around. "All abominations deserve nothing but the death set for them by our king! Watch your tongue, lest you be hanged for treason!"

"Ah, yes, all abominations," Nivin's father said. "But surely you must agree—well, not all are as perverse corruptions of nature as this one."

Nivin balled her fists.

"Indeed," replied the soldier with the haggard voice. "And there are some who are more abominable still."

"Yes," her father said, clearing his throat. "Of course, all of them deserve death, whether more perverse or less."

"Indeed," the haggard-voiced soldier said again.

Nivin's eyes stung with tears for a moment. She forced them away. It was not as though she could truly expect her father to say anything different—if he did, then both of them would die. But every time she heard him say something like this, Nivin wondered if he did, on some small level, actually mean it. After all, he still held his position as jailor—he had not given that up for her sake. His role in Zerabar's twisted justice system remained the same.

She knew this was why he hated for her to be present during prisoner intake. Because she would have to hear him say this kind of thing as though he believed it.

Maybe he wondered whether he believed it, too.

"My thanks, lads," he said, a little too heartily, with a slight chuckle. "You have done honorably in bringing this piece of hideousness to justice. I'm sure his execution will be finished on the morrow."

Presumably catching the tone, the soldier with the haggard voice instructed his men to leave. He turned around again toward the youngest and murmured, "Perhaps another abomination shall be dead ere then." Raising his voice, he continued. "Neither of them deserves the courtesy of a last meal." With that, he turned and proceeded out of the moldering halls of the dungeons. The rest of the soldiers followed behind him.

As she listened to their footsteps fade, Nivin drew a deep breath and tried to quiet her stomach. It was no secret to her that people hated her activities, but something in the haggard soldier's tone made her afraid.

Her father laughed nervously and turned toward his guards. "Keep a sharp patrol, lads."

The guards dispersed. One of them came toward Nivin. His footfalls paused in front of her, and he murmured her name by way of acknowledgment. She turned her head toward the sound of his voice and nodded. He continued without another word, the sound of his clothes and equipment following him.

Once again, the halls of the dungeons were filled with

damp quietness. She heard her father sigh softly and walk toward where she hid. For a moment, she thought about running, but he would spot her before she could make it back to her kitchen.

When he rounded the corner, he drew a sharp breath and cursed. "Nivin, how long have you been standing here?"

"The new prisoner sounds massive," Nivin said, folding her arms across her chest. She was not about to back down under whatever upbraiding her father was preparing for her.

"Yes—he's hideous. His face is all misshapen, he's nearly twelve feet tall, and has a girth as wide as three of you. I have heard of gigantism, but not until today have I ever witnessed a man deformed by it. I cannot believe he has survived as long as he has—he looks almost forty, if I had to guess. With his strength, it's a wonder they did not kill him instead of going to the trouble of bringing him here."

"Doubtless, a spectacle like this will help King Temere keep the public afraid and on his side. After all, how can the people of Zerabar disagree with a man who slays monsters? It makes it easier to justify the slaughter of innocents."

"Watch your tongue, child. Do you want to be on the other side of these bars?"

"Why not put me behind bars, then, if you are so dedicated to your cause?"

Her father put his hands on her shoulders. "There are days you tempt me, little one." He chuckled and laid a gentle kiss on her forehead. "You know I love you more than life itself. I will keep you safe, whatever the cost."

Nivin balled her fists again, drawing a deep breath to steady herself. "I am going back to my kitchen."

"Wait. Do not bring that monstrous creature a last meal. You heard what the captain said. It could be the final straw for my men—I do not know what they would do if you treated this thing like any other condemned man."

"But all abominations are equally monstrous, are they not? The Law of Condemnation is universal and impartial."

"Please." His voice was pained. "Just listen to me this one time."

With an exasperated sigh, Nivin turned and walked back down the familiar dungeon passages to her small kitchen. She went in, shut the door, and slid to the floor, leaning her back against the door. She drew her knees close to her chest and rested her head on them.

Silently, she wept.

Gurgle. Murmur. Moan. Even from where she sat, she could hear the giant man's noises punctuate the quiet once again. But this time, they were softer, almost mournful. She heard the jingle of mail and keys as guards walked their patrol.

No.

She was not going to let her father stop her from what she had come to consider her purpose. It was who she was: she, who labored over her deep copper pot. She, who sweated as she kneaded bread and baked it in her clay oven. She, who pared away the spoiled bits from old root vegetables, who simmered into tenderness the toughness of least choice meats.

She, who brought the savory food to the prisoners in a solemn solitary funeral march.

She could not save them, but she could soften the

harshness of their last hours. That included even this man—however grotesque others might consider him.

Her purpose called her.

She rose from the floor and went over to her cooking station. It was small, since the only food she prepared was for the prisoners' last meals, but to her, it was the altar of her mission. She stirred the stew and tasted it. It had been simmering for most of the day already and had turned out nicely. After easily finding her knife, she sliced off a large chunk of the bread she had baked earlier and placed it on a tray. Then, she ladled the thick stew into a large clay bowl, adding an extra spoonful for good measure. Once the tray was prepared, she braced herself for whatever consequences might come and exited the kitchen.

As she approached the giant's cell, she heard the soft sound of someone moving. She thought she heard a sniff, as if someone stifled tears. Unsure who it was, she decided ask a question she might ask someone who knew her. "What are you doing here?"

"Pardon me, Mistress. I am in your way."

It was the young soldier's voice. He must have remained after the others left. "No," Nivin said, "not unless you determine to deny this man his last meal."

"He does not deserve it," the soldier said, his voice choked. As he turned to face her, something scraped along the floor—most likely, a spear. "He killed three of Zerabar's finest men, soldiers with families and young children!" He took a deep breath. "But I am not here to stop you."

"Why are you here, then?"

There was a long pause. "I...am making sure this monster does not escape."

"He is bound and chained. You have done your work already. Leave it to the guards' care."

"I must do this."

"Why?"

The soldier sighed. "I did not...had I been...braver, some of the men need not have died." Pain filled his youthful voice.

Nivin felt a pang of sympathy for him, despite his clear hatred for abominations. "Be brave now. Help me give this man his last meal this side of living."

"What, and break Eschewment?" His voice cracked. "If you were any other man's daughter, you would be put to death for doing so!"

"Breaking Eschewment?" Nivin gave a forced chuckle. "Giving a little meal to a condemned man is hardly breaking the spirit of the law. He will still die." She crossed over to the cell and briefly probed for the small horizontal gap in the bars of the door. Fortunately, she had a good idea of where it was and found it quickly. Otherwise, she would have given up and returned when the soldier was not there to watch her. She wondered whether she ought to do that anyway, since her father had cautioned that giving the giant a meal might be the last straw.

No. She was not going to let her father—or anyone else—stop her. She gently slid the tray through the gap and waited.

The giant did not even acknowledge the food's presence.

"Eschewment requires that no comfort or quarter be given to any abomination," the soldier said emphatically. "How can you say you are not breaking the law?"

"We don't always slay them on sight. We put a roof

over their heads while they wait for death. That is quarter, now, is it not?"

The soldier drew a breath as if to reply, but was silent. Nivin suspected he could not think of any retort for her. She smiled at the thought.

"Eat," Nivin said, nudging the tray in somewhat farther.

"You know he cannot reach that, don't you? Not the way he is bound."

She should have taken that into consideration. They had even said the giant was tightly bound. "Then take your spear and push it to where he can reach it."

"I? I will take no part in this."

Nivin folded her arms. "How strange. Jailor Benin usually demands his guards do whatever I ask them."

"I—I am not one of your father's guards," the soldier said, his voice wavering.

Nivin smiled. She had him on the defensive now. If he had suspected anything based on her failure to notice the giant's restraints, it was driven from his mind. "Yes, but surely our king, whom you so *loyally* serve, would not wish for you to disappoint his jailor. Need I remind you who the most favored men in our king's court are?"

"I will not—"

"The jailor and the executioner. Two men you mustn't cross."

The soldier sighed. He came over to the cell and used his spear to slide the tray along the ground. "There. Even bound, he should be able to reach it and eat it like the animal he is. Are you pleased, Mistress?"

Two dungeon guards passed by. They began to mutter to each other quietly. Nivin did not need to hear them to know what they were talking about. Either it was about her, or it was about the fact that the soldier was there with her. Normally, she would have simply ignored them, but she did not want to put the young soldier in danger, particularly since he had just aided her.

"Silence, you! This man is not breaking any laws. I ordered him to assist me, by my father's authority."

With a scoff of disgust, the two guards departed.

"There," Nivin said. "Now they shall have no cause to think you are doing this of your own will. I should hate for them to think you are freely associating with me. Much like you, they despise that I give last meals to the prisoners."

"As I said," the soldier said, "were you any other man's daughter, you would be put to death for doing so."

"So I have been told." Nivin leaned up against the bars of the cell. "Come now, eat," she urged the giant.

The giant did nothing but moan softly.

"His mind is void," the soldier snapped.

"You cannot know that," Nivin said.

"I saw him kill in mindless violence."

"Someone loved him."

"That makes no difference."

Nivin clenched her fists. "It makes all the difference!"

The giant erupted in gurgled shouts. "Murm! Hurt murm! Kill murm! Mu-u-urm!"

Nivin jumped. Gasping, the soldier grabbed Nivin by the arm and clung to her like a frightened boy.

The giant fell quiet again.

Nivin shook free of the young soldier's grasp. "Are you sure he can reach the food? Push it in farther."

"Are you mad?"

"Just do it."

With a grunt of assent, the soldier slid the tray in a bit more.

The footfalls of two men pounded down the hall. A spear whistled through the air. It tore into the young soldier. He let out a strangled yell and collapsed to the floor.

Horrified, Nivin stumbled back.

The footfalls drew closer. "It wasn't enough that you failed us in the fray?" It was the haggard-voiced soldier. "You had to help this abomination-lover, too?" A sword rang as it was drawn from its sheath.

"No!" Nivin ran forward to interpose. "No! Stop! Leave him alone!"

The soldier grabbed her arm and pulled her away. Another man immediately seized her. A sword swished as it swung through the air. There was the sickly paper-tearing sound of flesh parting from flesh and then metal scraping against the stone floor. The air grew thick with the reek of blood.

"No, no, no!" Nivin fought against the man who held her.

"And you!" bellowed the haggard-voiced soldier. He grabbed her by the collar of her dress. "You seek to comfort this abomination? You have evaded the Law of Eschewment for far too long!" He dragged her forward and threw her onto the hard stone surface.

She tried to scream for help, but the soldier clapped his hand over her mouth. He knelt down over her, pinning her to the ground with her arms behind her back. "Kill the abomination," he growled to his comrade. "I will teach this abomination-lover a lesson."

Laughing, the other man wrenched the spear out of the

dead young soldier and advanced toward the cell.

"Death is too good for people like you," the haggard soldier said. He reached his other hand down toward the buttons of her dress. "Someone should have done this to you a long time ago." With a fierce yank, he ripped the buttons open. He ran his fingers across the fabric of her undershirt, then grabbed it tightly at the neckline.

Nivin screamed against the soldier's hand.

The giant bellowed. Shreds of rope went flying and chains clattered as the giant tore the metal restraints from the wall. He attacked the bars of the cell, bending them open. The metal creaked as it gave way to his force. Nivin heard the other soldier scream, and not a moment later, her captor was lifted bodily off of her and slammed into the wall. His bones cracked from the impact. She scrambled up from the ground and ran, so disoriented that she was not even sure which way she was going.

The other soldier shouted for help. The echoes of charging armored feet filled the halls. The giant roared. He lifted the soldier and threw him down on the ground. Metal scraped and the soldier let out a strangled yell.

The smell of blood intensified.

Massive footsteps thundered after Nivin. The next thing she knew, the giant reached down and hoisted her up. When he stood up, Nivin's head banged against the ceiling. The giant barreled down the hall with her slung over his shoulder.

Struggling and fighting, Nivin cried out for help.

Prison guards arrived from around the bend of the passage, but the giant's momentum knocked them over and his massive form collapsed on top of them. Nivin flew forward from the giant's shoulder, slammed into the wall, and slid to the floor. Dazed, she pushed herself up, squeezing tears of pain from her eyes. The air had been forced from her lungs. She gasped to catch her breath. As she tried to get her legs under her, the sounds of the fray assaulted her. She heard the crunching of bones and the tearing of flesh and the screaming of grown men, magnified a thousand times by echoes. Crying out, she clapped her hands over her ears and fell back to the floor. But there, the sounds pulsed and vibrated through the rock. She was lost in a world of violent auditory. The sounds echoed so loudly that she could hardly hear herself screaming *stop*.

The giant broke free of the soldiers and grabbed her, dragging her back up onto his shoulder. More soldiers awaited them at the foot of the steps, but a swing of the giant's massive arm knocked them aside.

Twelve feet tall, the giant ran up the stairs and out of the dungeons.

Nivin lapsed out of consciousness as she lay dangling from his shoulder.

CHAPTER TWO

Nivin drifted in and out of consciousness. She was vaguely aware of shouting, but eventually it faded away, replaced by the rushing of wind and the singing of crickets. When she finally came to her senses, she realized she was lying on soft grass.

She had no idea where she was.

Panicking, she got up and scrambled backward, trying to make sense of her surroundings. She backed into something hard and yelped.

"Murm," said a voice in front of her.

Nivin started at the sound. It was the voice of the giant who had taken her from the prisons. "Where are we?"

"Murm. Hurt murm."

The giant clearly did not understand what was going on, or if he did, he could not explain it to her. "Is anyone else there?"

Only the wind answered her. The strong breeze made it sound like a river rushed by them. It was a sound Nivin had only heard a few times before, when her father took her on their rare excursions outside.

It was the sound of leaves blowing in the wind.

She ran her hands across the surface of whatever it was she had backed into. She remembered the feel of tree bark beneath her fingers from years ago.

This was the same.

She began to make sense of her surroundings. So she was outside, beneath a tree. A fairly large tree, she discovered, as she tested its girth by wrapping her arms around it. She could not make her fingers meet.

It must have been night, too. She had always been able to tell the difference between light and dark, and she remembered the brilliance of the light on their trips outside in the daytime—so bright it hurt.

She summed up her situation. She was under a tree, at night, completely alone with a violent prisoner. The soldier had said the giant's mind was void, and that he killed in mindless violence. But maybe, there was a chance she could reach him.

What other choice did she have?

"Please. Where are we?"

There was a moment of silence, during which the giant seemed to be considering the question. "Murm."

No use.

Nivin squeezed her eyes shut. Trembling, she pulled her knees to her chest and wrapped her arms around them. She leaned her blood and dirt-smudged face against the tree trunk and tried to make sense of what had happened to her, longing for her father's strong hand and reassuring voice.

"Trees," the giant said.

Startled, Nivin lifted her head up. "Trees?"

"Trees. Lots trees."

"Are we in a forest?"

"No, trees. Trees food," the giant said with a tone of exasperation.

"I don't understand. Please, where are we?"

"Trees!" The giant grabbed her chin and forced her head upward. "See trees? See food?"

"No." Nivin drew a shaky breath. If she could make the giant understand, maybe he would not hurt her. "I cannot see. I'm blind."

"Bline? No see?"

"That's right. I'm blind. I don't see."

The giant let go of her chin and gently stroked the side of her face. "Hurt?"

"No. I was born this way."

"Born?"

"Yes. I've been this way forever."

"Bommation," the giant moaned sadly.

"Yes." Nivin reached up and took the giant's hand—a massive hand nearly the size of a plate. Clearly, he was not mindless, and he was surprisingly compassionate. "I'm an abomination. My father managed to keep it a secret."

"Me bommation too. Murm try save me. Kill murm, murm hurt."

"Murm." Nivin finally understood. "Your mother?"

The giant made an odd noise of assent. "Hurt murm."

"You accidentally hurt her?"

"No! Never hurt, never kill!" the giant bellowed, leaning forward and slamming his fists on the ground.

"Men! Men kill!"

Nivin jumped and threw her arms around the tree again. "The men who put you in prison?"

"Yus," the giant said. "Solshers hurt murm. Try save murm." He paused and sobbed for a moment. "Kill solshers." He started pounding the ground again. "Never hurt, never kill!"

"You were protecting her."

"Murm save me. Keen Tuh-mere hate bommation. Keen solshers kill Murm. No save Murm."

"I'm so sorry."

"You bommation. Me bommation. Frens?"

Nivin choked. Really, this giant was not so different from herself. He was only violent and dangerous because the soldiers had driven him to it. "Yes. We can be friends."

"Frens," the giant said. "Food. Take."

Nivin was unsure of what to do for a moment, but then the giant bumped something against her hand. She opened her palm and took the thing he was giving to her. It felt like an immature apple. "Thank you."

"You give food," he said. "Thanks."

Nivin took a tentative nibble. It was so hard she could hardly tear a piece out of it, and it was sour. When she puckered, the giant chuckled gleefully.

"Frens!"

"What is your name?"

"Name?"

"Yes. What did your murm call you?"

"Anek."

"Ah-neck?" Nivin hesitantly sounded out the word, hoping she had heard him correctly.

"Murm," Anek said happily. "You call?"

"My name is Nivin."

"Vin." Anek stroked the top of her head gently. "Save Vin. Always save Vin."

At that moment, Nivin realized exactly why the giant had taken her. She had been in danger—threatened by the same soldiers who had attacked him and killed his mother. He did it to save her because she had been a friend to him.

What would have happened if he had done nothing? She shuddered at the memory of the soldier's touch, how he had torn her dress. All of the buttons had been ripped off, leaving her dress open down to below the bust. Fortunately, her snug undershirt was still firmly in place, so she was not exposed—even if it felt a bit immodest. If Anek had not acted when he did, the soldier would have torn that too, and done worse.

Pushing the thought from her mind, Nivin focused on the present situation. She took another tiny bite at the apple's skin before deciding it would be impossible to eat. "Anek, thank you, but I'm not hungry. Here." She held up the apple for him to take.

Anek snatched the fruit from her hand. At first, she thought she had angered him, but then she heard a loud crunching sound as he chewed. He must have popped the whole thing straight into his mouth. With a noisy swallow, he clapped his hands excitedly.

She sniffed at the air. The whole world smelled fresh—what her father had once described as a 'green' smell. "Anek, do all of the trees here have food on them?"

"Food."

"There are lots of trees with food, then?"

"Lots trees food."

Nivin searched her memory. "We are in an orchard, I

think. I know there is one outside the city. You should go. Run away. I will wait here, until my father comes for me."

"Frens?" Anek sounded lost.

"Please, run away now. Let me go home."

"Vin bommation. Keen hate bommation. Save Vin."

"I'll be safe," Nivin said, tears welling in her eyes again. "Only you and my father know I am blind, but everyone knows you are an abomination." She cringed just saying the word. "You'll be killed. Just go."

"Go?"

"Leave! Don't you want to live?"

"Frens."

Pity surged through Nivin. Without his mother, Anek had no one. "Yes, we are friends. But you have to go. You have to hide."

"Hide?"

"Yes, hide."

"Can hide. Hide Vin, too."

Nivin heard the sound of men marching in formation. They were close, too—the rushing of the wind in the leaves had masked them from her hearing. "Anek, listen. There are soldiers. Hide, *now.*"

Anek's voice fell to a terrified whisper. "Solshers. Hide." The grass rustled as he moved away, his footsteps surprisingly light.

With a sigh of relief, Nivin climbed up from the ground. The soldiers would take her back to her father, where she could be safe again. Nevertheless, a pang of regret shot through her. What would Anek do without his mother to guide him? Would he hide and run away?

She fidgeted as she listened to the soldiers approach. Should she stay with Anek until she could help him find somewhere to live? Could he even live on his own? What was certain, however, was that if she stayed with him, she truly would be guilty of breaking the Law of Eschewment. Unlike herself, there would be no way to conceal Anek's imperfections. There was no way she would escape the death sentence Eschewment carried. This was not a simple testing of fate, like bringing meals to the condemned. She would be thrown away the life her father risked everything to save.

No, she had to go back to her father. Despite their quarrels, despite his hypocrisy, she loved him. And he was certainly the only person who loved her.

A pair of hands seized Nivin by the shoulder. "They sent me ahead to scout for the abomination and his captive," said a low, hissing voice. "Imagine my surprise to find two abominations instead."

Nivin's insides froze. "What?"

"I heard you. You said only you and your father know about your blindness."

"I said what that abomination wanted to hear."

"Oh? If that is so, then tell me how many fingers I am holding up."

Always guess two, her father told her once. *It's almost always two.*

Nivin forced her voice to be confident. "Two."

The scout's fist slammed into Nivin's face, knocking her back. Her head smacked against the bark of the tree, and she lost her balance and fell to the ground, where he landed a swift kick against her ribcage.

"I wasn't holding up my hand at all, you abomination."

Drowning in disorientation, Nivin rolled over onto her

hands and knees. "It's dark—I didn't—"

"Over here!" the scout shouted. He grabbed Nivin by the wrist and dragged her up from the ground. The other soldiers hemmed them in. "The giant is nearby—he went off in that direction." Several of the soldiers broke away and spread out to look for him. "The girl, however, is blind. And Jailor Benin has been hiding it. The whole city has been in uproar over her absence, and she is an *abomination.*"

Murmurs of 'traitor' and 'abomination' went through the company of men.

"The king has given us permission to kill the giant without ritual execution," one of the soldiers said. "What of her?"

"Why burden the executioner with another prisoner?" The scout pulled Nivin closer to him and twisted her arms behind her back. "Particularly when he will be so busy dismembering her father?"

Nivin winced in pain as the scout tightened his grip.

"I say we kill her," another soldier said.

"No," said an authoritative voice. Nivin guessed he was the commander of the unit. "We are to kill the giant and bring the girl back, so that is what we will do. With her father's status, they will undoubtedly want ritual execution. You two, take her back to the city. The rest of us will keep searching for the giant."

The scout released Nivin's arms and gave her a rough shove away. Desperate, she broke into a run, only to run straight into one of the soldiers. Several pairs of hands seized her at once.

Thrashing, Nivin struggled against their grip. "Let me go!"

The scout laughed. "You can't *run*. There are too many

of us, and you wouldn't be able to find your way, anyway." He spat on her.

Nivin flinched as the spray of saliva hit her in the face. Rage, humiliation and terror competed for precedence in her mind.

"Worthless abomination," said one of the soldiers holding her. "I hope you suffer as much as your father does." Two of them started to drag Nivin away.

Kicking and screaming, Nivin fought wildly against their grasp. Tears ran from her eyes. This was the day her father had dreaded for seventeen years. It had finally come, and it was her fault.

"Vin! No!"

Nivin jerked her head up at the sound of Anek's voice. His footfalls pounded on the earth as he came barreling into the soldiers, knocking several of them to the ground at once.

The leader's voice rang out amidst the clamor of soldiers' cries. "Defensive positions!"

The two men who held Nivin let go of her and ran to join the fray. Once free of their grasp, Nivin chose a direction and ran, holding her arms out in front of her.

"No." The scout caught her by the waist and pulled her back. "You're going nowhere. I'll kill you first."

"Anek!" Nivin cried. "Help!"

The giant let out a tremendous roar. Soldiers yelled and bodies hit the ground. Within moments, the scout screamed as Anek ripped him away from Nivin and threw him into a tree. At the sound of bones cracking, Nivin flinched.

"Save Vin," Anek said, panting. He snatched Nivin up by the waist, threw her over his shoulder, and ran. The soldiers pursued, throwing spears and launching arrows after them, but Anek managed to dodge their attacks. Nivin cringed as an arrow whizzed past them.

The soldiers could not keep up with Anek's enormous stride. The sounds of shouting and jingling mail gradually faded. Nivin's disorientation grew. She was already dizzy with fear, and the way Anek kept ducking and swerving to avoid branches made her nauseous.

Perhaps half an hour later—Nivin had lost almost all concept of time—Anek finally stopped ducking and ran erect. They must have come out of the orchard, and sunrise was approaching, based on the way the world gradually grew lighter. Anek came to an abrupt stop.

"Solshers see here." Anek set Nivin down on her feet. "What do?"

Still dizzy, Nivin stumbled and grabbed onto Anek's arm for support. "I don't know." In less than a single night, her entire world had been turned upside down. Without the familiar confines of the dungeon, she struggled to hear what was ahead of them.

If she wanted to live, she could never go back.

She swallowed, trying to fight her disorientation. "Are they behind us still? I can't hear them anymore."

"No see solshers," Anek said. "See field. What do? Fight?"

"No. Don't go back and fight. Isn't there anywhere to hide?"

"Hill."

"There's a hill?"

"Yus. Hill far."

"You can run fast—run to the hill, maybe we can hide on the other side."

"Run, then," Anek said, still panting from his previous sprint. "On back." He crouched down and put Nivin's arms around his neck.

Nivin hesitated for a moment, catching the smell of blood on his back and worrying that she might hurt him. There did not seem to be another option, however, so Nivin jumped up from the ground and wrapped her legs around him, only just able to get her feet secured around his sides. She felt like a little girl riding piggy-back on her father.

She would never feel the warmth of his embrace again.

"Hold on," Anek said. "Run now!" He drew himself to full height and began to run. No longer constrained by the orchard branches, he stretched his legs out to their full length. The massive limbs, each as solid as a tree trunk, thundered into the ground as he sped across the field. Some kind of tall grass covered the whole field, which rustled noisily as Anek lumbered through it. Every now and then, the grass was deep enough that it tickled the bottoms of Nivin's feet.

The rush of wind in her ears disoriented Nivin even further. Nevertheless, she concentrated to the point of pain on the sounds around her. She tried to think about anything other than the life she had left behind, and what would happen to her father now that their secret was known. For one of King Temere's own high officials, being tortured to death would be the kindest sentence available for breaking the Laws of Condemnation and Eschewment. She shuddered. It was easier to think about her own quick demise at the hands of the soldiers than what awaited her father, so she strained to hear any hint that their pursuers had spotted them, strained for the sound of voices on the wind.

Birds sang and the wind whipped through the long grasses, but she did not hear their pursuers.

Though it seemed Anek possessed an almost inhuman amount of stamina, after an hour or so the running caught up to him. The pitch of his stride changed; Nivin suspected they had begun their ascent up the hill. He slowed to a walk and continued on in this fashion for a while longer.

"Vin," Anek gasped. "Rest." He came to a stop. "Rest."

Nivin slid off of Anek's back and plunged down into a sea of grass that came up past her waist. "I think it's safe to rest. I don't hear anyone following us."

Anek abruptly collapsed onto his back. He lay there for several moments, gasping at the air. The grass was probably deep enough to conceal his supine form. If anyone could see him at all from a distance, he must have looked like a boulder amongst the grasses.

Nivin ran her fingers along the blades of grass. There were stalks with fat heads of grain at the top. Curious, she plucked off some of the grains and nibbled at them. It was definitely wheat, and as it was midsummer, she suspected it was nearly ready to be harvested. Nivin cautiously made her way forward to Anek's side and sat down on the ground next to him. Her head just crowned above the heads of grain. The sunshine made her black hair hot.

"The smells here are amazing," she said softly, inhaling deeply. The grainy fragrance of wheat and the green and earthy smells of the outdoor world seemed like new life to her. She had only breathed in the odors of mold and damp, intermingled with the urine and feces of miserable people, for most of her life. She felt invigorated and renewed for a moment, but then she remembered the full implications of the situation. Her heart ached for her father. Fear for her own life seized her intestines. "I can never go back now."

Anek had no reply for her but the wheezing of his strained lungs.

"Are you all right?" Nivin could almost hear beyond the wheezing to the groan of his muscles and exhaustion of his frame; she could almost hear the grief for his mother that still moaned out within his soul.

But Anek covered all of his pains with one word. "Rest."

Sighing, Nivin pulled her knees up to her chest and rested her aching head on her knees.

They had been resting for a while when she heard it.

Angry voices on the wind.

CHAPTER THREE

Nivin jerked her head up. "Listen! Do you hear that?"

All of the sounds vanished as soon as the words had escaped her lips. She strained to hear them again, but her hearing was clouded by the sound of the wheat rustling as Anek sat up to listen. "No hear," he said. Fear entered his voice. "Solshers?"

Nivin swallowed hard, trying to quell the panic that writhed in her stomach at the thought. "Be quiet. Let me listen." She stood up, holding her breath, and slowly rotated so she could hear from all directions. When she turned around, her stomach turned to ice.

There were swirling lights flickering in the distance, distinguishing themselves clearly against the customary blankness of her optical perceptions. She had always been able to distinguish light from dark, but this was beyond anything mere photosensitivity had ever allowed her to recognize. It seemed the flickering lights were pale threads snaking in a circular pattern—they vaguely reminded her of the flashes of lightning that danced in her perception when she struck her head, but these moved in a clear pattern, swirling elegantly and not fading.

And they were coming closer, as if drawn by her presence.

"Anek," Nivin breathed. She pointed a trembling hand in the direction of the flickering. "Do you see that?"

"See what?" Anek replied.

The sound of voices returned, but they were not the same indistinct sounds she had heard earlier. They were close. They were clear.

They were the sounds of soldiers shouting battle cries.

Anek cried out. "Solshers!"

"Abominations! They will die!" shouted a voice Nivin recognized from the prisons.

"You!" Anek bellowed. "You kill murm. You hurt murm. You die!"

"Anek, no!" Nivin cried, too late. Anek had already started charging across the shrinking gap between them and the soldiers. She was about to call out again when the vague, mysterious sounds returned, and the lights grew brighter. Entranced, she listened to the voices, wondering if perhaps they originated from the strange pale flickering.

But the voices did not seem to originate from there. They seemed to be all around her, engulfing her. They grew louder and then fainter, as though they were being pulled in closer and then sucked away, like a vicious mouth was opening and closing and letting the foreign voices through.

The voices and sounds became stranger and stranger.

Roaring and screaming reached her ears. There was the sound of ocean breakers. But one of the voices grew more distinct: a young male voice, shouting barely intelligible words. The lights drew closer. The sounds grew louder. Words just beyond perception danced outside her grasp.

A terrible sense of recognition assaulted Nivin. She was held captive with fascination and terror. The sounds continued to swell and fade, swell and fade, moving in cadence with the snaking of the pale lights.

She could hear the soldiers shouting as Anek crashed into them. She was desperate to flee, desperate to help him, desperate to cry out, but something immobilized her. Other voices, more subtle, pulled at Nivin's heart. Something inside of her she did not recognize was responding to them—when the strange word tumbled clumsily off of her tongue:

"Charybdon."

At that, the tendrils of light flashed and leapt toward her, surrounding her as though she was the center of a vortex. They crept in on her more and more until they began to twist themselves around her ankles and calves.

In an instant, the tendrils tightened like ropes and a great force pulled against her.

She tried to shout for Anek, but she could no longer hear the sounds of his rage as he fought off their pursuers. Instead, the sounds of roaring and screaming and the young male voice crying out took over her hearing. The tendrils of light grew painfully bright in Nivin's mind, and a cold, clammy hand grasped at her ankle, as though it was trying to pull her through the ground.

The force became stronger and stronger, then suddenly stopped. All of the strange sounds culminated in a burst like a thunderclap and ceased immediately, leaving only rumblings of thunder throbbing through the earth.

Without delay, there were shouts of terror from the soldiers.

"What is it?"

"Witchcraft!"

"Retreat!"

Nivin barely heard the soldiers' retreat or Anek crying her name. She was paralyzed with fear. The hand was still around her ankle. It seemed to tighten and then slacken its grip on her. She was deafened and isolated by the thunderclap that had concussed her whole body, leaving it numb. It seemed as though the whole world had vanished.

Everything but the hand.

"Help! Vin! Vin—help!"

Slowly, she came back to herself as she heard Anek calling her name again and again. She tried to move toward him, but she stumbled and fell face down on the soft earth—the hand had caused her to trip. She had prayed the hand's grip was only an illusion, which would subside just as everything else had. Terrified, Nivin shook her leg free, scrambled upright, and ran toward the sound of Anek's voice.

He lay on the ground over twenty paces away from her. After bumping into him with a toe, Nivin fell to her knees and reached out to touch him. He was hopelessly entangled in a net, and his hand was the only thing between the delicate tissues of his throat and the tight cord of a garrote. "Help, Vin," he whimpered.

Nivin explored the lines of the net with her sensitive fingertips, but the strands were inextricably tangled around each other. She felt along the line of the garrote, and pulled back her hands sticky with blood. The cord cut into the flesh of his hand, and his struggling had only deepened the wound.

"We need to get you out of this," she said.

"Knife," Anek replied.

"We don't have one."

"Knife!"

"We don't have one!"

Anek groaned. "Bline, Vin bline. Knife, ground. Solsher knife. There."

"Oh." Nivin was embarrassed and angry as she patted the ground around them. Anek could not give her directional instruction, so he simply cued her as she got closer to the knife.

Finally, her groping hands found it. It was a small, extremely sharp throwing knife. Nivin smiled grimly at the passing wish that her kitchen knives could be whetted so finely. Then with a deep breath and a swallow, she left that thought behind her and went to cut Anek free.

Anek was quiet as Nivin carefully sawed through the cords of the net and the garrote, but he yelped when the knife slipped and scored the flesh on his arm.

Nivin gritted her teeth. "Sorry."

Anek quietly moaned what sounded like "Murm."

After several minutes, Nivin had disentangled Anek and he clambered upright, breathing heavily and wheezing.

"Are you hurt?" Nivin asked, tenderly laying a hand on Anek's hip.

"Hurt some," Anek answered. "Not bad," he added, after a moment's consideration.

Nivin had a feeling Anek did not fully understand the

extent of his own injuries. Even before this fight, she thought she smelled blood on his back, probably from the fight that resulted in his capture. And even if his injuries were not severe, the risk of infection was always a looming threat from even a minor cut. They at least needed to find water to cleanse his wound, as herbs for a poultice were almost certainly out of the question. She brushed loose strands of hair out of her face. "Can you go on? We should try to reach the hill before the soldiers come back, and see if we can find water."

"Yus, go. Vin hurt?"

"Not bad."

"Good," Anek said. He reached down, took her hand, and the two of them moved forward—Nivin had to trot to keep up with Anek's slow stride, wincing at the sharp terrain beneath her bare feet. After only a few large steps, Anek stopped.

"Who?" he asked.

"What do you mean?"

"Man. Boy."

"Boy?" A shiver went down Nivin's spine as she remembered the sound of a young man's voice and the clammy hand that had clung so desperately to her ankle not even half of an hour ago. Her voice dropped to a whisper. "What boy?"

"Boy ground."

"There—there's a boy on the ground?"

"Yus. Boy hurt, too."

Nivin took a deep and steadying breath. If he was hurt, she had to help him. "Take me over to him."

Anek guided her to the boy's side and put her hands on his prone form.

"Is he hurt badly?" she asked. Her compassion overwhelmed her fear as she groped at his body until she found the back of his head. Based on his build and the timbre of his voice—if the voice Nivin had heard was in fact his—he was not a young boy, like a child. He was probably somewhere between the ages of fifteen and twenty. She patted at his curly and matted hair, which was as cold and sopping wet as if he had just been pulled from the water. The thought triggered the memory of the sounds of breakers on the ocean.

She tried to push the thought away and kept exploring the boy's head. She found his ears, and reached around until she felt the front of his face. It too was wet, but a different texture—warm and somewhere between sticky and slippery.

It was blood. There was a lot of it. Too much of it. Her shaking hands were covered with it. She forced herself to sound calm so her own voice would not panic her even more. "Help me turn him over."

Anek reached down and easily flipped the young man over. Anek groaned. "Hurt bad. Bad, Vin, bad."

Nivin gently probed the wound on the young man's forehead. Deep, it poured blood. She took another steadying breath and tried to think. They needed to find water, and fast. A cut that deep was bound to become infected. "How far is it to the other side of the hill?"

"Far. No run. Tired."

"I can walk. Can you still walk?"

"Walk," Anek replied, though he did not sound as though he relished the thought.

"Do you think you can carry him? We have to keep moving."

"Yus, can carry." Anek's tone was resigned.

"All right," said Nivin, taking a few more deep breaths. She mentally went through the steps for treating injuries. "First we have to bandage him." She cast about for what she might use to dress the wound. "Anek, can you cut off some of the hem of my dress?"

"Hem?"

"The end," she answered. She held up the edge of her skirt. "A big piece." She handed him the throwing knife.

Without reply, Anek bent over and tried to cut the fabric, but the small knife was useless in his hands. He tossed the knife aside and tore the fabric with his bare hands, with incredible strength and ease. Instead of tearing along the hem, however, he ripped upwards until he had reached about halfway up her thigh, then horizontally until the piece was nearly a foot wide, and then back down. He handed the strip of fabric to her. "Good, Vin?"

In the midst of the strangeness of the whole situation, Nivin could not suppress a smile at his misunderstanding of her instructions. At least she had short leggings on underneath her dress. "I did say a big piece. Yes, it's good."

Anek clapped his hands together excitedly.

Nivin folded the piece lengthwise into thirds. "Hold up his head for me."

Squatting even lower, the giant cupped his hand behind the boy's neck and lifted his head a little off the ground.

Tenderly, Nivin wrapped the cloth around his head twice and then tied it tightly at the back of his head. "Let's go. We need to find water as soon as possible, so we can clean it out." She placed her hand against the boy's cheek, feeling for fever. "Pick him up now—gently, like a baby.

Understand?"

"Unnerstan," Anek said. He picked up the youth with a grunt of exertion. "Go now."

"Head for the hill. I'll follow you."

Anek immediately plowed forward through the wheat field, not even giving a moment's consideration to the fact that Nivin would not be able to see him.

Nivin did not need to see him, though. He made crashing noises as he stomped forward, and she focused on listening to the sound of his footfalls and the crackling of the rustling wheat. Briefly, she wondered how this noisy giant could be the same Anek who moved so lightly when hiding from the soldiers.

Shaking her head, she followed after him. This would be difficult. She could navigate the halls of the dungeons by years of memorization and listening to echoes. Uneven terrain and waist-deep wheat, plus the fear of rocks and pits in the earth, plagued her with anxiety. The soles of her feet, in their customarily unshod state, tore despite their thick calluses.

Nevertheless, she forged on, trying to keep all emotion from her face. She feared if she thought about the true nature of the situation, she would be totally swallowed up by terror and madness. So, she rebelled against her inner fears and kept her thoughts focused on listening to Anek's thundering footsteps. She had to run to keep up with his walk, and even then she could hear the sound of his passage gradually getting farther away. She ran with all her strength, wondering with each step whether she would trip and fall. She ran until her lungs were burning. Sharp seeds from the tares that hid among the wheat caught themselves in her dress, and buried into her exposed leggings through the large gap in the fabric.

But she did not relent. She ran as if running was all she had left.

It seemed like they had been traveling for an eternity, and the sound of the giant's footsteps had become so vague that Nivin could not discern their direction, lost in the wind rushing through the wheat. She froze in panic, tilting her head this way and that, trying to ascertain the direction of her large companion. She could hardly hear anything over the sound of her heart pounding in her ears and her rasping breath.

"Vin, why stop?" came Anek's voice from a considerable distance.

"I can barely hear you, Anek!" she gasped between breaths. "You know I can't see you. Please, please, come back!"

Without verbal response, Anek walked back to her. She listened as the footsteps became louder.

"Rest?" Anek said, when he finally stood next to her.

"No—no," Nivin panted. "We have to keep moving." She took a few steps forward, but her foot caught on a rock and she stumbled. A smirk twitched across her face. After all that running, it turned out to be walking which tripped her.

Anek caught her with an outstretched arm and steadied her. "Carry Vin." He shifted the boy so that he was draped gently over one of his massive shoulders, then scooped Nivin up in his other arm.

Nivin was too exhausted to utter her thanks. She clung to the giant's massive frame as though she were in the shielding, loving arms of her father.

Anek continued to plow forward at a steady pace. As

they drew closer to the hill's crest, however, the grade of the ascent became steeper. The giant's breathing grew more labored, and Nivin, hugging tight against his chest, could feel his heart thumping furiously.

Occasionally, she thought she could hear the sound of soldiers in the distance. How far they were, she could not tell, but she felt sure that as long as they kept moving, they would not be in any imminent danger.

As strong as he was, however, Anek would not be able to keep up the strenuous pace forever.

The wheat field came to an end a short distance from the crest of the hill, but the ground became more rocky and uneven. Anek's footsteps became far quieter after he was out of the wheat, but his steps became more weaving, as if he were stepping around things.

"Where are we?" Nivin said. "Are we on the other side?"

"No," Anek rasped.

"Where are we now?"

Anek hesitated. "On hill."

Nivin was unsatisfied. "What is around us?"

"Rocks. Big rocks. See top."

"We are close to the top?"

"Yus," said Anek.

"Do you see any soldiers?"

Anek stopped for a moment. "No?"

"Can you see them or not?"

Anek grunted. "No...no." His voice became more certain. "No."

Nivin could not hear any sound of soldiers, but the wind whipped across her ears and deafened her to distant sounds. Anek's answer assuaged some of her concern, and for the first time, she began to hope they might actually reach safety—whatever safety could be called in this nightmare of a situation.

Their progress grew even more laborious. Nivin's mouth was parched, and Anek's clothes were soaked through with sweat. She could only imagine how thirsty he was. Periodically, Nivin could hear the gurgling of Anek's stomach as it contracted with hunger pangs. His strength was obviously waning, and he struggled to keep his footing on the increasingly uneven and gravelly terrain.

"Rest, rest!" he said, after stumbling forward.

"No, we have to keep going until we find shelter," Nivin said, feeling cruel for saying so. "I'm sorry, Anek."

"Keep going," Anek grunted in response.

"I can try to walk," Nivin said.

"No, Vin. Not safe. Rocks."

Based on the light and temperature, Nivin guessed it was late afternoon when they finally reached the crest of the hill. The rocky ground radiated with summer heat.

Anek stopped, panting heavily. "On top. Rest now?"

"Not yet," Nivin said. "Let's go down the other side just a little bit. It will be easier going down than up."

Anek heaved a sigh and grunted his general assent. He started to go down the hill. The descent was far steeper than the climb up, and he had to pick his footing carefully.

Suddenly, his feet stepped into a patch of scree. He reeled forward and pitched down the hill, dragging Nivin and the boy with him.

Finally, after what seemed like forever, the three of them came to a stop. Nivin lay trapped under Anek's body, gasping as his weight bore down on her. Anek had been knocked unconscious. She struggled and struggled to escape from beneath the massive body pinning her to the ground.

She could not breathe; his weight pressed her down too much. His beating heart would be the last thing she ever heard.

Anek, she thought. *I'm sorry.*

The burning in her lungs overtook her senses; she forgot the crying out of her bones under the giant's mass. Her whole world was burning.

Then her world snuffed out as unconsciousness took her.

CHAPTER FOUR

Nivin woke to the sounds of night, the sound of low voices murmuring. The sensations of reality came back to her slowly. For a long time she lay still, convinced she was dead. But the sounds persisted, and eventually she struggled up into a sitting position. Her bones protested the movement; her whole body felt covered in bruises, and the unyielding ground beneath exacerbated her pain.

"She's awake," said a strangely familiar male voice.

"Vin! Vin!" Anek's heavy footsteps thundered over to her side.

"What happened?" Nivin asked, dazed. She tried to orient herself. They were still outside, and a cool night breeze caused strands of her hair to tickle her face. She winced as she moved her sore arm to tuck the loose strands behind her ear.

"We fell," said the voice. It came from somewhere in

front of her.

"Down the hill?"

"Yes. Anek said he slipped he as carried us down. When I woke up, you were trapped under him. I was just barely able to pull you out."

"Think kill Vin," said Anek, with a pathetic sob.

As Nivin's memories slowly seeped back into her mind, she finally placed the voice. "You're that boy we found. And you're hurt. Are you all right?"

"I will manage, thanks to you two," the stranger replied.

"Who are you?"

"Bran," Anek interjected enthusiastically.

"Bran?"

"Me," said the young man, with a hint of amusement in his voice. "My name is Brand. And you're Vin?"

"Nivin," Nivin replied. "My name is Nivin."

"Nivin," Brand corrected himself. "I'm relieved you woke up. We thought you were dead at first."

"How long was I out?"

"Hours. The moon was rising when I woke up, and now it has set again. It's past midnight. At least, I think it is."

"And where are we now?"

"About halfway down the hill. You must have fallen a long way."

Nivin reached up and rubbed a sore spot on her head. "Brand, where did you come from?"

There was a pause. "Anek told me I came here through 'bad magic.' I have heard of great sorceries, but I never heard of any magic powerful enough to bring me from the ocean shores to the inlands. I was hoping you could explain this to me." His tone was polite but tense—Nivin guessed from his injuries that he had been through a huge ordeal. He sounded disoriented and maybe even a little desperate.

Nivin hesitated. The memory of the flickering lights still haunted her; she wished she could deny it altogether. However, there was no way to deny that Brand's voice was definitely that of the young man she had heard earlier. "There was—a force. A whirlpool of sounds—and lights." She felt her face grow hot, knowing how incredible this claim must sound to him. "Then, there was a hand. Grasping at my ankle. The whirlpool was gone, and then you were there, still holding fast to me."

There was a short period of silence, during which Anek interjected "Bad magic" in a fearful mutter. Nivin expected at any moment that Brand would laugh, or be angry.

After the pause, Brand asked in apprehensive and serious tone, "Did you bring me here?"

"I did not bring you!" Nivin said, recoiling. "I am no sorceress. I was attacked by this—force!"

"I have never heard of a force capable of doing such a thing. Not only have I gone from sea to far inland, the constellations here look nothing like what I know. You are not telling me all you know, are you?"

Nivin hesitated. "I think the force might be called a 'Charybdon.' I mean, it might be. I have only—heard of them."

"And you did not conjure this—'Charybdon?'"

"No, I told you!" Nivin replied, though she found herself wondering the same thing. The subtle voices in the Charybdon seemed to have called out to her in an intimate way. The thought raised the hairs on her arms.

Brand was quiet, as though calculating in his mind all of the possibilities of the situation.

"Please, believe me," Nivin said.

"Thank you for bandaging my head," Brand said, as though he had not heard her. "It was kind of you. I would like to think it means you do not serve my enemy."

"Your enemy? Who is that?"

"First tell me with whom you stand," Brand said, with calculating intensity.

"I don't understand," Nivin said, just as carefully.

"Who is your ruler? Who is your king?"

Before Nivin could say anything, Anek burst out, "King want kill me. Kill Vin. Kill murm. Kill bommations."

Brand turned toward Nivin. "What is he talking about?"

Nivin took a deep, steadying breath as she prepared her answer. She was afraid to say it, afraid to admit what had become her reality. "Anek and I are fugitives. Our king, Temere, has sentenced us to death, and had Anek's mother put to death also."

"I have never heard of Temere."

"Well, he is the king of Zerabar."

"I have never heard of Zerabar, either."

"That's surprising, considering you speak Zerabari perfectly."

"Zerabari? But we're speaking in the Common Tongue of Libertas."

"I don't know what you're talking about. I have never heard of Libertas."

Brand let out a short laugh. "You make me wonder if I am going mad. I suppose I may as well ask you plainly for the information I want. You must forgive my caution—I too am a fugitive of sorts. Does Temere pay tribute to Scyllorin?"

"Sillrin?" Anek said. "Who that?"

"I have never heard of Scyllorin," Nivin said. "Besides, Zerabar pays tribute to no one."

"Good enough," Brand said. "As long as you are not in league with Scyllorin, then you are not my enemy."

"Frens?" Anek asked excitedly.

Brand chuckled lightly. "Why not? I'll take all the friends I can get."

Anek clapped his hands and laughed uproariously. "Frens! Two frens, Vin and Bran!"

Nivin could not help but feel a surge of warm affection for Anek. How could he have been condemned to die as a violent prisoner? Nivin suspected he had never been violent in his life until the soldiers attacked the mother he loved so dearly. Likely, he had never even had friends—no one but the mother who hid him from the law. They were much alike in that respect, she thought. Now they were both left to fend for themselves, without the parents who had loved and sheltered them. Like Brand, they needed all of the friends they could get.

The three companions rested quietly for a long time. After a while, Brand shifted positions. "How did I come to be here?" He turned toward Nivin. "If you did not bring me, then maybe Scyllorin sent me. But I've never even heard it hinted he might be able to transport someone so far—let alone change the layout of the stars, or translate foreign tongues. Besides, why would he send me here, when he was so close to killing me?"

"I don't know," Nivin said quietly. "How is your head?"

"It hurts. Badly." Brand stretched out on his back. "Do either of you know where we can find water?"

"No. I've never been outside the city, and I've only heard a few things about rivers and landmarks from my father. I think we are to the east of the city, because I know there is a section of hilly plains there. The city's main water source, the River Tamim, is to the west of the city. I don't know about any bodies of water to the east, except that there are supposed to be springs and brooks here and there."

"At least there is hope, then," Brand said, propping himself up on his elbows. "What about you, Anek?"

"No wadder," Anek sighed.

"You can't have been out here long without water."

"Less than two days, I think," Nivin said. "We left— abruptly."

"To escape your death sentence?"

"Yes."

"If you don't mind my asking, why does your king seek your deaths?"

"Bommations," grunted Anek in reply. "Keen hate bommations."

There was a long pause, as if Brand was waiting for further explanation. "What are 'bommations?'"

"Abominations." Nivin sighed. "Our king demands all who live in his land be free from flaw at their birth. Anek, as you can tell, is not a normal man. Hence, the king sought his execution, since the Law of Condemnation demands all abominations die. His men also killed Anek's mother."

"Was she also"—Brand's voice became uneasy—"an abomination?"

"No," gurgled Anek. "Not bommation. Love me." He

sniffed loudly.

Nivin choked back a sob. "Any and all who would shelter an abomination must die also, according to the Law of Eschewment."

Brand was respectfully silent for a long time. "Nivin, it's good of you to befriend this man. Is that why they seek you also?"

"No." Nivin clenched her fists. "I too am an abomination. Surely they are tormenting my father as we speak, if he even still lives."

"You?" Surprise filled Brand's voice.

"Vin no see," said Anek.

Nivin emitted a half-scoff, half-sob, and buried her face into her hands.

"You're blind?" Brand said.

"Yes, bline," said Anek. "But Vin good. Vin bring food prison. Vin, me—frens."

Nivin lifted her face from her hands. "They will most certainly kill my father, and his death will not be swift." She almost choked on the words. "It is one thing when an ordinary man resists the king's statutes, but for a state official..." She swallowed back grief. "He will be charged with treason. No mere execution for him. He will be tortured to death."

"What was your father's position?" Brand said.

"He was the jailor. He and the executioner are the most favored men in the king's court."

"And yet he sheltered a blind child in his own house? How could he aid the king in putting these men to death— knowing you would face the same? How could he claim to love you when—"

"Enough!" Nivin shouted.

"I am sorry," Brand said quietly. "That was out of turn."

Nivin hugged herself, blinking back angry tears. "Yes." The worst part was that it was something she herself had wondered for years.

"I'm just trying to understand. Please. Tell me more about you—both of you—while we rest. Dawn is not far off, and then we will seek water and food."

With a deep sigh, Nivin pulled her knees up to her chest. "What do you want to know?"

"Well—I admit I am confused. Not that I agree, you understand, but I can see how Anek could be considered an 'abomination.' But you? Your only flaw is that you are blind. How is that abominable?"

"I told you—all citizens of Zerabar must be free from flaws. Abominations are not just those who are as—strange—as Anek. Any child born with defect, however slight, must be killed or left to die—that is the Law of Condemnation I spoke of earlier. Anyone who refuses to comply and who saves an abomination must also die, which is the Law of Eschewment."

"The Freemen believe all life is valuable," Brand said, anger entering his voice. "How could someone kill a child just because it is not perfect?"

Nivin laughed bitterly. "'Imperfection is aberration,'" she recited. "Dwarfism, harelip, deafness, blindness, limbs misshapen and defective, gigantism, the stupid and slow of mind, and so on—but it doesn't stop with only those *born* with flaws. Temere, like his father and his father's father, is especially zealous. He even counts those who are deformed later in life by accident or dismemberment."

Brand sputtered several different syllables as though

he could not choose what to say. Finally, he found his voice. "So—a simple cut or broken arm is a death sentence?"

"No—only deformations such as a missing limb, or having one's eyes put out, or the like."

"What about your soldiers, wounded in duty? They fight for your king!"

"To be maimed is no different than death. Those who do not commit honorable suicide are put to death as criminals. Temere is adamant: 'There is to be no imperfection in Zerabar!'"

"Your king almost makes Scyllorin sound merciful. At least he rewards those who serve him. How could any man be willing to die for a cause like Temere's?"

"They think they are healing the world, making it a better place."

"Is that what your father thought he was doing? Is that what he told you?"

"Don't you dare talk about my father! You don't know him. He risked *everything* to save me."

Anek flapped his hands nervously. "Frens fight! No frens?"

Brand heaved a sigh. "Very well. Forgive my boldness. I'm shocked by what you've told me."

"Well, what about you?" Nivin said, prickling. "Who is this Scyllorin who is so much better than Temere?"

"I never said he was better." Brand picked up a small rock and chucked it out into the distance.

"Sillrin king want kill Bran?" Anek asked.

"He is not my king."

Anek scratched his head. "Oh."

"So who is Scyllorin, then?" Nivin crossed her arms

tightly across her chest. "Why does he want you dead?"

"Scyllorin is the king of Verderbera, who has been at war with us for generations. My people, the Freemen, are the last nation to resist his reign. In order to stand against him, our Council has selected Champions to fight against him. I was sent out as a Champion—"

Anek exploded up from the ground. "Oh, no, no no!"

The faint sound of voices echoed in the crisp early morning air.

Temere's men had caught up to them.

CHAPTER FIVE

Brand followed Anek's gaze up to the top of the hill, where the silhouettes of at least twenty men stood out against the slowly lightening morning sky. Suppressing the instinct to panic, he stood up from the ground. He grabbed for his sword, only to remember he had lost it miles before he had reached the sea.

Nothing made sense. How he had come to be here baffled him. How the stars were changed baffled him. The impossibility of the situation should have been enough to tell him this could not truly be happening. His eyes—and his instinct—told him otherwise. While it was possible, perhaps, Scyllorin had cast some kind of illusion on him, tricking the senses, Brand could not bring himself to believe it. Knowledge of Scyllorin's power was limited, at best, but in centuries of history, there had never been reports of something like this.

No. This was something different altogether. What was happening to him was real, and the soldiers swarming the hilltop were just as real as his two new companions—companions who were in danger.

Anek turned to Brand, his face twisted up in fear. "Solshers! Fight?"

Brand swept his eyes over his companions. Anek, while he was twice Brand's height and girth and probably twice his strength, he could not possibly fight off that many men. Besides, he was already hurt—bruises blossomed across his forearms and misshapen face, and the light shirt he wore was torn and stained with dried blood. Nivin too was injured; a deep purple patch along her cheekbone stood out against her pale skin. The dark dress she wore was torn open, revealing more bruises across her collarbones. Her expression was pure panic. None of them had weapons.

Fighting was not an option.

Brand did his best to take charge of the situation. "With any luck, we won't have to fight them. It will take them a while to pick their way down the sharpest part of the slope, so if we hurry, we might be able to outrun them."

Anek slumped forward. "Run again." The thirst in the utterance was palpable.

Brand grimaced. Anek was barely in shape to run. "We absolutely must find water. If you two have been this long without, then you're going to die whether the soldiers kill you or not." He glanced up at the peak of the hill, and then surveyed their surroundings. The vista was largely flat and barren. In one direction, however, the ground grew rough and rocky, and boulders sprang up out of the earth like dense shrubbery. The other directions stretched out in coarse untamed heath for miles and miles. In some places, the wild grasses were brown, dry, and thin. "Temere's men will be on us within half an hour if we stay here."

"They sound closer than that," Nivin said.

Brand shook his head. "Luckily for us, sound carries farther in the morning air. Our only chance of survival is to go—now."

"Do you think you can run again?" Nivin asked Anek.

"Yus." Without further hesitation, Anek lumbered over to Nivin and scooped her up in his arms. He then moved over to Brand and tried to pick him up.

"No," Brand said. "You are already too weak. I can walk."

Anek did not protest. He simply released Brand from his grip and started forging his way toward the heath.

Brand trotted after Anek's hulk. "Wait. Not that way. We should make for those boulders to the"—he looked at the sun's rising to verify his position—"south. There'll be more hiding places, and maybe, if we're lucky, a spring."

Anek looked at the boulders in the distance and changed his direction with a sigh.

Their progress was sluggish. Anek alternated between a walk and a shuffle, moving slowly even though the downhill slope favored them and the footing was far more stable now. Even with Anek's slow pace, Brand had to maintain a brisk walk to keep up. Anek's labored breathing was painful to hear—each ragged wheeze made Brand cringe.

Brand glanced over his shoulder. The soldiers were definitely making progress down the hill, but his assumption that they would have to move slowly was correct. Already, one of the soldiers had fallen into the same scree field Anek had, and the man lay motionless on the hillside far below his companions. Walking as fast as he could without breaking into a run, Brand pulled ahead of Anek. "I know you're weary and hurt, but if we're going to get out of this, you need to move faster."

Panting, Anek forced himself to match Brand's pace. Brand did not have the time or energy to pity him—not now, not while the danger was so near. Nothing mattered beyond their survival. There would be time for pity and sympathy after.

There would be time for everything after.

The heat of the morning slowly rose as the sun crawled past the horizon. Wherever Brand found himself, it was midsummer here, too. That much, at least, had not changed. It would not be long before the sun's full heat would beat down on them. Already, beads of sweat rolled down Brand's face and his heart pounded from the strenuous pace he had set for them. A hot summer day would make it almost unbearable, especially if they could not find water.

Brand glanced over and saw Anek and Nivin hardly sweated at all, despite the mounting heat. Their skin was matte where it should have been glistening with sweat. Without question, their bodies were hoarding what little water they had left. Brand had heard of such things happening before—it would be only a matter of time before heat prostration took Anek from consciousness, and Nivin might not be far behind him.

Water. The word pounded through Brand's head. The likelihood of finding water near the boulders was good—if there had been any recent rainfall, the moisture would pool on rocky grounds whereas the heath would greedily suck it up. But there was no guarantee there would be water, and even if there was, there was no guarantee such water would not be stagnant by now. And even if they had such miraculous luck, it was doubtful Anek would make it that far.

As their progress wore on, Brand started wondering whether he himself would make it that far. The searing pain in his forehead dizzied him. The heavy pulsing of his blood had reopened the gash, soaking through the makeshift bandage. Trickles of blood mingled with the sweat running down his face.

A sense of hopelessness started to set in. Even if they could make it to the rocks, there was still a good chance they would have to contend with the soldiers— dehydrated, weak, and outnumbered.

Brand pushed the hopelessness away. He did not have to luxury to allow such thoughts. The soldiers were further down the hill, moving more quickly now that their footing was more stable.

"Stop!" Nivin's hoarse voice rang out. "We have to stop."

Anek followed Nivin's order without hesitation.

Brand kept moving, turning around and walking backwards as he gestured to them. "No. We must keep moving. We don't have a choice. Come on!"

Mumbling, Anek stumbled into motion again.

"Not this way," Nivin said. She raised her arm and pointed to the southwest. "We have to go that way."

Slowing his pace, Brand looked where she pointed. It was right into the midst of the most withered portion of the heath. "No. There won't be water there, and there's no shelter either."

"We have to go that way."

"Listen to me, Nivin. I have years of training in survival, and I can tell by looking that going that way is a death sentence. Trust me—you can't see what I see."

"But you can't see what I see," Nivin snapped.

Dumbfounded, Brand came to a stop. "What are you talking about?"

"There are lights over there. I think it might be...it might be a Charybdon. Maybe it can take us back to where you came from, and we can escape Temere's men that way."

"Absolutely not. Scyllorin's men would be waiting for us on the other side."

"Maybe they have moved on."

"We can't risk that."

"I don't care. I just know we have to go to the Charybdon. At least we know there will be water."

"Salt water! You would die sooner drinking that than nothing at all."

"Well, make for your precious rocks if you will. Anek and I will make for the Charybdon."

"Sharbdon," Anek said loftily. Obediently, he changed direction to follow Nivin's pointing.

Brand glanced back at the soldiers. "No! We can't afford the delay. They are already too close!"

Anek and Nivin ignored him and kept moving. Brand cursed and took after them, running to catch up. Anek seemed more resolved than ever, and he walked faster than before.

Brand had to trot to keep up. His injury screamed at him, and the throbbing in his head made him woozy. He stumbled when his foot caught in a low-growing weed.

Anek only paused long enough to help Brand regain his balance.

Nivin's silence was impenetrable.

The sun climbed along its arc as time passed them. They finally reached the flat plain and began their trek into the heath. The soldiers drew closer, now running down the hill—it would not be long before they caught up.

"Nivin," Brand said, "how much further to your Charybdon?"

"I know we can make it," Nivin said.

"The soldiers are almost on top of us."

"Run!"

Anek broke into a run.

Brand was soon left behind, stumbling from blood loss and dehydration. Anek wheeled back, grabbed Brand by the middle, and threw him over his shoulder.

The gap between them and the soldiers closed even further.

"Run, run," Nivin urged, in a tense whisper.

Anek gasped for breath as he increased his speed. He would collapse in a matter of minutes if he kept up this pace.

The harsh twang of a bow sounded and an arrow flashed through the air. Its tip plunged into the flesh just above Anek's ankle. With a roar, Anek collapsed forward onto the ground, throwing Nivin and Brand out in front of him as he did.

Brand thought his head would break open from the impact. He lay on the ground for a few moments, stunned. More arrows whizzed through the air above him. The soldiers would be on them in less than a minute.

The world spun as Brand pushed himself up from the

ground. He stumbled back to where Anek lay on the ground, moaning in pain. "Anek! Can you walk?"

Anek could not even articulate a reply.

"We're almost there," Nivin said, gasping. She scrambled up to her feet and continued forward. Anek crawled after her.

Panic and fear threatened to send Brand reeling back to the ground. But fifteen years worth of training to be a Champion allowed him to draw a breath and steady himself. His path became clear to him. He had to protect Nivin and Anek's retreat. Unarmed and injured, he would only delay the soldier's advance by a minute at most before they killed him, assuming one of their arrows did not strike him dead where he stood.

One of the soldiers cocked an arm, ready to throw his spear, obviously aiming for Anek. Brand readied himself to intercept the blow.

Thunder pounded through the earth beneath his feet, nearly stopping Brand's heart. He knew that sound.

The soldiers stopped short and stared. Their faces went white.

Brand turned and followed their gaze. A vortex of shimmering air swirled around Nivin. Every one of her loose hairs stood on end as if charged with electricity. A faint murmuring ebb and tide of foreign voices flooded the air.

Anek covered his head like a frightened child. "Bad magic!" He huddled close to the earth and trembled.

Chills ran down Brand's spine. Was *this* what had brought him here?

Like the calm in the eye of a storm, Nivin walked slowly over to where Anek lay curled on the ground. The bizarre forces swirled around her viciously, and the shimmering air seemed to flash with invisible lightning. The ground around her seemed to ripple as though she was a drop plunged into the surface of a lake.

"Come to me!" she shouted.

Stumbling backwards in fear, Brand lost his footing and fell.

He never hit the ground.

Instead, he seemed to fall through it as if he had fallen into water, sucked into the whirling force focused around Nivin.

The forces collapsed in a seismic thunderclap.

Everything went black.

*

Brand opened his eyes to the dark green canopy of a forest. Judging by the light, it was drawing near to evening. He could not move; it was as though he had fallen to the ground from a great height and his body responded to the shock by shutting down all movement. Eventually, the temporary paralysis faded, and he struggled up from the ground.

Dizzily, he surveyed his surroundings. Nivin and Anek lay motionless a few yards away from him. Unsteadily, he started walking over to them, but he stopped as he recognized a sound sweeter than music in the distance.

It was the sound of running water.

Delirious with pain and thirst, Brand almost forgot his companions, but he paused long enough to ascertain they were still breathing before chasing after the tantalizing sound. He stumbled over the uneven mossy forest floor, ignoring everything around him except the sound of water. He cursed as he lurched into a patch of nettles, and again when he tripped over a fallen branch. Finally, he stumbled into a narrow clearing.

He groaned aloud in relief at the sight before him. Tumbling over a shelf of glossy wet rocks, a noisy brook cut through the clearing. A short foamy waterfall splashed into the pool that had collected at the shelf's base.

Brand staggered into the clear, rippling pool. Within a few steps, it came to just below his waist and he gasped as the cold water lapped against him. Without further hesitation, he tore off his head bandage and plunged his head into the water, allowing the intense cold to rinse away the crust and ooze from the vicious cut in his brow. His wound stung ferociously, and when he stood up again, eddies of blood swirled in the water before being whisked downstream. Red water dripped from his chin.

He waded further into the pool to the waterfall, where the depth rose to his armpits. His limbs now almost numb from the icy temperature, he thrust his mouth under the flowing water and gulped it down until his insides seemed frozen.

Shivering, he waded back out of the pool and collapsed on the bank.

He lay there for some time, lapsing in and out of consciousness. It was not until the dark green canopy became tinged with the red of sunset that he remembered his two companions. Struggling to his feet, he walked back over to the pool's edge for one more gulp of icy water and then turned around to retrace his steps.

He realized with a pang that he had hardly paid any attention to his surroundings on his trek to the stream. In the fading light, picking his way back to Nivin and Anek would have been difficult even if he had marked his path somehow.

His pain amplified his fear. Welts had formed on the skin that had brushed against the nettles, and though his forehead had stopped bleeding, it seeped a clear yellowish liquid that crusted around the edge of the wound. He had lost the bandage in the stream. His clothes were still damp in places, and in the evening breeze, he shivered. Miserably wrapping his arms across his chest, he chose the direction he thought he had come from and made his way through the brushy forest.

Too soon, it grew darker. Only the faintest remnant of daylight remained, and Brand still lumbered through the woods aimlessly. In the distance, he could just barely hear the sound of the tumbling waterfall. It was so faint that he knew he was nowhere near his companions—he had strayed too far, and perhaps they had wandered away in search of water or in search of him. With a despairing groan, he collapsed against the trunk of a tree and sat with his knees pulled into his chest.

In the increasing dark, the resolve that had steeled him earlier gave way to his youth. He was in pain. He was afraid. He was only a boy, not even sixteen years of age. Exhaustion, hunger, and the unknown had robbed him of all of his courage. Even though he was cold, his face burned with heat. As he huddled against the tree, tears began to form in his eyes. He tried to blink them back—the struggle for bravery made his brow tense, and his wound protested the movement.

The tears won. Silently, he bowed his head to his knees and wept bitterly.

He spent the next several hours in a fevered semiconscious state, drowsing, intermittently jerking awake to the rustling of leaves when a gust of wind passed through.

It must have been nearing dawn when the sound of snapping twigs ripped him into full, adrenaline-charged consciousness. Faint light tinged the sky. Brand scrambled up and found the sturdiest fallen branch he could. It was long as his arm and thick as his wrist, but the wood was aged. Splinters broke from the end and wormed into the flesh of his already abused hands.

The sounds drew closer; snapping and rustling, snapping and rustling—a definite pattern of steps. The sounds increased until they seemed to be only a few feet away. Brand raised his makeshift weapon, straining his eyes in the dimness to see his adversary.

The sounds stopped. Brand's heart pounded. His foe was surely only a few feet away. Perhaps it was one of Scyllorin's men—or worse, one of his minion creatures.

A fawn stepped into view.

His shoulders relaxed slightly. A fawn was traditionally a symbol of good luck, and there were dozens of legends about fawns giving blessings to weary or wounded travelers. However, some of Scyllorin's spawn could control animals. A fawn would be the perfect tool for deceit.

The fawn froze when it saw Brand standing there. Its spots had begun to fade as summer wore on, but its timidity had not been diminished. Ears perked high, it regarded Brand with rapid breathing.

Brand shouted and swung at it. "Spawn or beast?"

The fawn turned and bolted away.

Relief mixed with guilt flooded Brand as he collapsed back down against the tree trunk. He had spurned a fawn, and along with it any blessing it might have given him, but he was free from Scyllorin's sorcery and deception. Besides, he had long suspected the legend of fawns was likely taught to young hunters so they would not kill the little deer before maturity. Nevertheless, he still felt ashamed for having scared away the poor thing. Shivering with fever, he laid his head against the tree trunk and closed his eyes.

When the crackling of twigs resumed, he was not sure if he was awake or dreaming. The fawn had returned, and it moved toward him step by timid step, until its nose was only a few inches from his. Delirium and astonishment overwhelmed him. Was it possible the legends were true?

"Forgive me," Brand whispered.

In response, the fawn tilted its head slightly and touched its nose to Brand's. Its warm breath seemed to soothe the wounds on his face. Abruptly, the fawn licked the tip of Brand's nose. He laughed at the tickle of it, temporarily forgetting his fears.

There was sudden crackling through the underbrush. Someone was making a great racket, blundering through the woods.

The fawn bolted away.

"Come back." Brand's fear returned. He looked around in a panic, stumbling along the line between consciousness and unconsciousness, terrified by both. Too weak to stand, he stayed on the ground, cradling his makeshift weapon against his chest.

A huge figure lumbered into view.

"Anek!" Relief surged through Brand.

"Brand, I'm so glad I found you! Come with me. We found water, and Nivin is waiting at the stream for us." Anek's voice was strangely transformed. His speech was clear and precise.

Brand's relief died immediately. It had to be a trick. One of Scyllorin's spawn had found him. Had he really come all this way just to fall right back into Scyllorin's clutches?

Heart pounding, he struggled to his feet and took a defensive stance, trying to seem threatening. "You're not Anek—you're here to deceive me!"

Anek jerked his head back in surprise. "Brand, it's me! You're hurt bad—you need to come with me. I'll explain everything on the way."

"Liar!" Brand cried, flinging the branch at Anek.

With a jump, Anek held his arms up and deflected it. "Brand, I promise it's me."

"Scyllorin-spawn! You are not who you say!"

Anek stood quietly for a moment, shaking his head. A look of shame crossed his face. "Bran hurt. Vin wait at water, Bran."

"But—but—your speech," Brand panted. "You were— not speaking—you didn't sound like yourself."

"Bran hurt," Anek repeated in his gurgling voice. "Come. Vin wait at water."

Hesitantly, Brand staggered toward Anek. Light-headed from his injury, he collapsed after only a couple of steps and fell into unconsciousness.

CHAPTER SIX

A sensation of vague familiarity faded as Nivin came to her senses. For a moment, she could remember nothing at all.

Then she remembered. The lights, the voices...

The Charybdon.

"Vin? Vin, wake up. Please." Panic filled Anek's voice.

Stiffly, Nivin sat up in the near darkness that surrounded them. "It's all right, Anek. I'm awake." Thin and dry air surrounded her, and a cool breeze made her shiver. "Where are we?"

"I don't know. Brand's gone, and you've been out for a while."

Nivin jumped to her feet and stumbled back a step. "What did you say?"

"Brand is gone, and—"

"You can talk."

"I could always talk," Anek said. "But not right. Not

like this. I don't know what happened. I woke up, and...everything was different. In my mind, I mean. Everything." There was a pause. "I'm scared."

Nivin grasped for words, trying to find something that could both comfort him and abate her own fear and shock, but she could think of nothing to say.

Anek inhaled sharply. "Nothing makes sense. We were on the plains, and there was the"—he struggled over pronouncing the word—"Charybdon, and wind, and lightning I couldn't see, and thunder, and then...then...this forest. And no Brand. And you asleep. And me...*understanding.* No, that's not the right word. I don't understand anything that's going on. Nivin, I don't understand!"

"I don't either." Nivin slowly moved back toward Anek. She reached out and found his massive arm and gave it a squeeze. Finally, the right words came to her mind, and a tiny smile crept onto her lips. "But it's nice to hear you say my whole name."

"What?" There was a pause, and the muscles in Anek's arm relaxed. "I did say your name, didn't I?"

"You did." In the following silence, Nivin felt as though she ought to say something else, but a faint sound of running water distracted her. "Do you hear that?"

"Hear what?"

"Water."

"Maybe."

Nivin tilted her head and listened closely. The faint trickle of water was almost lost against the breeze whispering through the trees. "You said we are in a forest?"

"Yes, but...the trees are strange. They don't have

leaves."

"Like trees in autumn?"

"No. They have little sticks instead of leaves."

Nivin was nonplussed for a moment, but then she remembered her father talking about trees that grew high in the mountains, trees that stayed green even when the weather was cold and the snow was thick, that had needles instead of leaves. He had once bought a sprig of needles from a traveling merchant and given them to her. Maybe these trees were the same. "Can you bring some to me?"

Anek took several limping steps away from her and rustled around in the trees. He came back, took her hand, and gave her what he had found.

Nivin's hands explored the long, flexible needles. They certainly felt the same as the ones her father had given her all those years ago. When she broke one of them in half, it yielded a sweet, spicy scent that filled her nostrils.

"Pine," she said. "These are pine trees—the leaves are called needles. They don't grow around the capital."

"Where do they grow?"

"The mountains. We must be in the mountains."

"Do you think Brand got left behind?"

"No. I know he went through the Charybdon with us. I could feel it."

"Maybe he went to find water. I think I hear it, too, like you said." Anek took a few limping steps before stumbling and crying out.

Abruptly, Nivin remembered that Anek had been injured in their retreat from the soldiers. She cursed herself for forgetting.

"Anek!" She hurried to his side. "How badly are you hurt?"

"There's an arrow in my leg. I tried to pull it out but it hurt too bad."

"Why didn't you say anything sooner?"

"I—was distracted. By everything else."

Shaking her head and wondering how anything could be more distracting than an arrow in one's leg, she knelt down next to Anek and felt around for his ankle. He winced as she probed around the wound. Part of the arrow's shaft protruded from the back of his leg, while the head of the arrow had just emerged from the front of his leg. It seemed to have missed the bone.

Nivin grimaced. "Do you think you can walk for a distance?"

"I don't know. Maybe if you pull it out?"

Nivin hesitated. "I don't think you are supposed to just pull out arrows. The arrow itself stops the flow of blood."

"How do you know that?"

"My father talked about his days in the military before he became the jailor. He talked about the kinds of injuries—"

Anek shrank back. "I forgot you said your father was the jailor. I didn't really understand when you said it." Disgust entered his voice. "He chained me. He was going to keep me locked up until they killed me. Now you tell me he was in the military, too? What did he do? Hunt abominations? Kill their mothers?"

"No!" Nivin said, even as doubt filled her. "At least, never that he told me. All he told me was he fought against the Rashaan invasion." Nevertheless, it occurred to her that a position like jailor was probably not awarded simply for fighting against foreign enemies, but more likely as recognition for fighting against the domestic threat of abominations.

The thought made her sick.

"Anek, we don't have time for this. We have to go find Brand. If we can break off the shaft, it should keep it from catching on anything as you walk and injuring you even more. It might hurt, though."

"Do it."

Nivin snapped the shaft of the arrow an inch or two away from the back of Anek's leg. He whimpered as she did it, and was panting with pain by the time she had finally finished.

"Let's go," he said hoarsely. He sighed. "I'm sorry for what I said. You aren't your father. Anything he did is his own fault."

Anek took Nivin's hand and they walked toward the sound of water. The forest floor was scattered with dried pine needles that jabbed at Nivin's already torn and sore feet. She stepped on a pinecone and nearly turned her ankle. Anek tried to keep her from going down, but she slipped out of his grasp and fell to the ground.

"Let me carry you," he said.

"No, you are already hurt. I can manage."

"Please. I don't want you to get hurt any more than you already are."

Nivin had to admit the idea of being carried sounded more pleasant than walking, so she agreed. However, when Anek tried to pick her up, he could not. He grunted and strained but could not manage to get her more than a few inches off the ground.

"I don't know what's wrong with me," Anek said. "I'm so weak."

"You're just tired. Don't worry. I can walk."

The two of them limped the rest of the way as Anek guided Nivin to the side of the stream. They had to walk through a patch of sharp gravel, which was excruciating. Finally, they reached a group of large smooth rocks banking the stream. She put her hands in the freezing water and drank. Once she had finally alleviated her thirst, she stood up. Anek continued drinking.

Nivin listened closely. She did not hear the sounds of anyone moving around the area. If anyone was there, the sound of rushing water blocked out the subtler sounds.

"It seems to be getting lighter," Nivin said. "Do you see any sign of Brand?"

"It's hard to tell in this light. Everything mixes together. Should we call for him?"

"No. If we're still in Zerabar we don't want to attract attention. And if we somehow went to the place Brand came from, we don't want Scyllorin's men to find us."

"We're not going to find Brand, are we?" Anek asked softly.

Nivin sighed. "I don't know. Maybe we should just wait."

"Let's sit beside this pool," Anek said. "We can soak our feet." He guided Nivin over to a mossy rock on the water's edge, where she sat down and dangled her feet in the frigid water. The cold had something of a numbing effect, easing her pain slightly. Anek did the same, sitting down next to her and splashing his injured leg into the pool.

They sat quietly for a while.

"I like the waterfall," Anek said softly. "It sounds like Murm making water hot over the fire. Bubbling...no, boiling."

Nivin smiled. "Well, boiling water does bubble."

"She sang when she boiled water." Anek choked back a sob. "My favorite song."

The pain in his voice tore at Nivin's heart. She could not keep tears from welling in her eyes. Nivin's father had been her only friend, and it was no different with Anek and his mother. Anek probably had never even spoken to anyone but his mother. She was gone, now, brutally murdered by Temere's men. Nivin hoped her death had been swift.

"Sing it for me," Nivin whispered.

Anek sang haltingly, as though saying the whole words seemed foreign in his mouth. The light and spirited tune had a cadence that reminded Nivin of stirring a pot.

Oh, bubbly water, boil and sing
It's time to cook a tasty thing
A tasty stew or tasty soup
A tasty chicken from the coop...

Anek burst into sobs. "She's *gone...*"

Nivin scooted over to Anek and embraced him, unable to get her arms around his massive torso. "I know. Everything is gone for us now." She sniffed. "Even Brand."

"No!" Anek pushed her away. "Not Brand. I'm going to find him." He stood up, accidentally splashing Nivin with water as he did. "You wait here."

Panic seized Nivin at the thought of being left alone. "Anek, don't. You have no way of knowing the way he went."

"I have two friends in the whole world and one of them is missing. I'm going to find him."

"But what if you cannot find your way back?"

"I'll leave a trail to follow so I don't get lost."

"You said you can barely see in this light!"

"It's lighter now. I think the sun'll come up soon."

"You're still hurt—what if you fall? Anek—"

"I'm going, Nivin," Anek said, with a tone of finality in his voice. He started away from the brook back into the trees, leaving Nivin cold.

"Come back!" she called.

"I will. I promise." Anek's voice was softer this time. He limped away from the stream.

Cocooned in fear, Nivin listened as his footfalls and rustling through the trees grew fainter and fainter. Soon, she was totally alone, kept company only by the bubbling of the waterfall. She pulled her nearly numb feet from the water and hugged her knees to her chest and waited, distracting herself by quietly singing Anek's song and trying to make up more words for it. The world grew steadily lighter, and with it, sounds began to stir in the woods.

Nivin stopped singing and listened, her heart racing with fear. It was probably just animals—it was far too quiet to be men, but animals could be just as much of a threat.

She jumped when a bird started singing.

She could barely remember the last time she had heard birdsong. Usually she and her father rose so early to leave their comfortable house for the damp of the dungeons that it was before the birds began to sing. They spent such little time in that house anyway. Nivin knew the layout of the dungeons better than her own home.

This bird was unlike any she had heard before, a cheerful whistling loop interspersed with loud chirps. As the light grew, so did the number of birds. Different kinds joined in, too. Some birds laughed, while others repeated the same note over and over. One made a beautiful noise Nivin was hard-pressed to describe, a unique sound that started high and swooped low. She immediately decided it was her favorite kind of bird.

As she sat enraptured by the birds, sunlight finally crested whatever horizon had been hiding it and hit her full in the face. A horrible realization hit her. The sun had risen, and Anek had not yet returned. The fear that had fallen asleep while she listened to the birds re-awoke in full force. When she heard a loud rustling in the woods behind her she yelped aloud, only to realize it was Anek returning. His lumbering footfalls were unmistakable.

"Nivin!" he called, his voice still somewhat distant. "I found him!"

Nivin jumped up, wincing as her weight shifted onto her torn feet. She flexed her knees, working out the stiffness that had gathered there while she sat. Hesitantly, she stepped down from the rock, unsure of what the sole of her foot would find. She was relieved when her foot came down on a spongy patch of moss. Her next step, however, landed in the sharp gravel. Grimacing, she forced herself to take the next step and limped toward Anek.

She met him several paces from the stream. "I can't believe you managed to find him."

"He's hurt bad," Anek said, panting. "I hope I didn't hurt him more bringing him back. I couldn't lift him all the way. I had to drag him."

"Never mind that," Nivin said. "Put my hands on his face."

Promptly, Anek placed Nivin's hands on Brand's

cheeks.

As she feared, Brand's skin was hot—far too hot. "He is burning up with fever." She moved her fingers up to his forehead, only to find his makeshift bandage was gone. Gently, she probed around the edges of the wound. "Is there anything in the cut?"

"Dirt. Maybe pieces of bark or leaves."

"Help me drag him to the water. We need to wash it out."

"This is my fault," Anek said.

"How is it your fault?"

"If I could've carried him, then his cut wouldn't be dirty."

"You did the best you could. You're hurt too."

"I was hurt before, too! Why am I so weak now?"

"I am sure it's only exhaustion."

Anek heaved a sigh. "This is different. It feels like I've always been weak. That strength is just a memory."

They each took an arm and dragged him over to the stream. Nivin squatted down next to Brand, carefully scooping up water and pouring it into the cut. With a thud, Anek sat down on one of the big rocks next to them.

After several rinses, Nivin lightly probed the wound itself. "Is there anything still in it?"

"Not that I can see."

"Good." Nivin leaned in close and sniffed. Again, her fears were confirmed by the tinge of foul odor emanating from the wound.

"What are you doing?"

"Checking to see if it's infected."

"Is it?"

"Yes," Nivin said, sitting back up. An infected head

wound could easily spell a death sentence, drawn out in days of fever and suffering. She swallowed. It was likely all of their injuries would become infected, likely they would all meet the same fate.

"You can tell that by the smell?"

"Infection smells like rotten meat."

"You amaze me," Anek said. "How do you know these things?"

Nivin smirked bitterly. "I practically grew up in the dungeons. I know what infection smells like—and nearly every other bodily odor you can imagine. "

"Oh," Anek said sheepishly.

Nivin swatted away a fly that landed on the back of her hand, and it started buzzing around Brand's head. She frowned. She had heard of a certain type of fly in Neishar whose maggots cleaned away rotting flesh and aided healing, but she suspected this was not that kind of fly. The last thing Brand needed was for the wound to become infested with maggots which might worsen his condition. "Did you find his bandage, too?"

"No. He didn't have it anymore."

"Tear off another piece of my dress, then. We need to keep the flies out somehow."

Dutifully, Anek tore off another piece of her dress, this time from the bottom as she instructed him. Still too weak, he had to use the jagged edge of a rock to help tear through the fabric. "Wish I hadn't tossed away that knife we found." As Anek handed her the strip of fabric, he sighed. "Oh, Nivin. You look terrible."

Nivin smirked. Doubtless, she did look terrible. Her once long black dress was torn nearly up to the thigh and missing a foot of fabric, revealing the scratches she had sustained during their journey. With the top torn open too, it was a tailor's nightmare. Her undershirt failed to protect the delicate pale skin across her collarbones, leaving her sunburned and covered with grime. She reached up and swept a hand over her hair. Much of her hair had fallen out of her customary neat braid and was now frizzled and matted, probably acting as a perfect frame for her dirty, bruised, sunburned face. "Well then, I suppose it is fortunate I am in no danger of seeing myself." Nivin picked out the sharp seeds that had caught in the fabric of her dress and washed the cloth in the stream before folding it and re-bandaging Brand's forehead.

Anek held up Brand's head for Nivin while she worked. "He looks different."

"What do you mean?"

"His hair—it's a different color. It's red now. I thought it was brown. His skin is a little lighter, too. And he has freckles on his face. He still looks like himself, but different."

Nivin finished tying Brand's bandage in a secure knot. Colors held no true meaning for her—red and brown were nothing more than abstract words, though she understood they were distinct from each other. She considered explaining this to Anek, but decided she did not want him to feel embarrassed for failing to realize it. "Maybe he changed, too."

"Do you think it was the Charybdon that changed him? That changed me, my mind?"

The thought made chills run down Nivin's spine. "It's possible. What other explanation is there?"

Anek chuckled. "Bad magic, I called it. If it's your magic, it's not bad."

"It is not *my* magic!" Nivin said. "Something about these Charybda does not feel *right*."

"What do you mean?"

"That's the worst part. I feel like I know things about them, but I don't know anything about them at all. It is almost as though the Charybdon itself told me its name. Or maybe I always knew it. I can't tell." Nivin fell silent for a moment. "It scares me."

"But what happened at the Charybdon? Did you call it up?"

"No. It was already there."

"Then why did you look the way you did? Like there was lightning, but I couldn't see it?"

The thought she was somehow responsible for the Charybdon filled Nivin with a vague sense of disgust. "That was not me causing it. Didn't it look the same as when Brand showed up?"

"Well, there was the lightning. And the sound like thunder."

"There you have it."

"But how did you know it was there?"

Nivin threw her hands up in the air in exasperation. "Please, Anek, just stop! I don't know anything for certain other than the fact we are going to die out here!"

Anek made an odd noise in his throat. "I'm sorry. This is my fault. If I hadn't taken you—"

"Then you would be dead and I would have been raped and murdered." Nivin shuddered at the memory of the soldier tearing her dress. "No, this is better."

Anek sighed. "At least we would have faced a faster death."

Nivin's mouth fell open. "Do you really wish you

would have died on Temere's butcher block rather than a free man?"

Anek was silent for a moment. "No. Any death would be worth suffering for this. I've never had friends before. And I've never experienced such—clarity! I feel as though I was blind and my eyes have been opened."

Nivin smiled wryly.

"Er, forgive me," Anek muttered. "But I really would rather die with my new mind, here with you, than die a stupid brute in Temere's custody."

"A stupid brute? Is that what you truly think you were?" Tears began to pool in Nivin's eyes.

"It doesn't matter."

"It does! You were no better or worse then than you are now." The tears spilled down her cheeks. "You are my friend."

With a sad quiet laugh, Anek ruffled Nivin's hair. "Thank you, little Vin. I'm glad I don't have to face this long ordeal all alone."

"It might not be so long. We are all too badly hurt. It's just a question of whether we will have a chance to starve to death before our wounds infect us with fever, too." Nivin reached over to Brand and patted his cheek with the back of her hand. He shivered violently in his unconsciousness.

"Is there anything we can do for him?" Anek asked.

"We can keep him warm and comfortable."

"I can gather up some of these needles and lay down a bed for him."

Nivin cringed at the thought of how prickly it would be, but she had certainly heard of people doing such things. "That will do. Are you sure you can manage with that arrow still in you?"

"Of course. I might as well limp around while I still can."

As Anek's massive form stomped off into the brush, Nivin sat back down at the edge of the pool with her feet plunged into the icy water, splashing it at her legs. Every now and then she would raise her head and listen more attentively to the sounds of Anek's rustling around. She smiled when his noise disturbed a group of birds that took off chattering angrily.

But mostly, she focused at splashing water on her hurts. She was lost in thought, wondering exactly what had happened at the Charybdon, and if it did indeed somehow have the power to change the people who passed through it, and if she herself had been changed somehow. Even though thinking about it frightened her, it was easier than wondering whether she and her friends would die here on the stream's bank.

By the time she realized the sounds of Anek's foraging had stopped, she had no concept of how long it had been since she last heard him. She jerked her head up, tilting it this way and that, intently listening for any sign of him.

"You seemed so...mysterious, just then." His voice came from some way to her left. "So full of power. I don't understand it."

"Please, Anek," Nivin said. "Let's rest."

Anek grunted his agreement. He helped her up and guided her over to the beds of fallen pine needles he had made for them. Then, with tremendous exertion, he dragged Brand over and collapsed beside him, panting and wheezing.

Nivin had to admit, the makeshift tick was not nearly

as uncomfortable as she feared it would be, even if some of the needles prickled at her.

Soon they were all asleep, lulled into slumber by the sheer exhaustion of their bodies.

CHAPTER SEVEN

The sun had passed its zenith by the time they woke, and the full heat of afternoon beat down into the clearing. As she stood up and stretched some of the soreness out of her muscles, Nivin marveled at how the air had gone from so cold in the early morning to uncomfortably hot.

"It's so hot and dry," Anek rasped. He rose from the ground and limped over to the stream, where he drank water noisily. "This whole time I've felt like I can't breathe."

Nivin drew a deep breath. Anek was right. Even if she filled her lungs to the bottom, it still felt like she was breathing shallowly. "If we are in the mountains, we must be high. Father told me how the air in the mountains grows thinner the higher you climb." She slowly walked toward the stream, using the sharp gravel on the ground as a guide to remember the way. When her feet found moss, she sighed in relief and took a few steps more until she climbed back up onto the rock she had sat on earlier. She leaned over the water and scooped up a few handfuls to drink.

"Your father told you a lot of things," Anek said.

"Everything I know." Nivin sat down on the rock. "He almost never took me outside of the dungeons. We hardly spent any time in our house, even. He didn't want to risk anyone seeing me in full daylight, since they could have an easier time spotting my blindness." She was silent for a moment. "When I was a little girl, he only took me outside three times, and even then, only for a few hours. I have never been outside for this long before. Birds, the air stirring the trees, and the running brook...it's all so strange and wonderful to hear. It's almost as though—as though I'm free for the first time in my life, like I'm reborn."

"I understand." Anek reached over and plucked a pine needle out of Nivin's tangled hair. "I feel like I'm free from a prison in my own mind."

"We have been denied this our whole lives." Nivin bit her lip. "It's a bitter thing to have it now, just as we are about to die."

"Better than not at all. And at least we're free from Temere."

"Yes. It's the only thing that sweetens our death."

"Well, our death isn't certain yet. Maybe there's something we can try."

"There is nothing we can do." Nivin buried her face in her hands. "Nothing, Anek."

"Don't give up," Anek said, choking slightly. "I—we— need you. Earlier this morning I was about to give up too, but you gave me hope. Don't take that from me."

"What did I ever say that gave you hope?"

"It was nothing you said. It was just that mysteriousness I saw in you."

"Anek—"

A noise like a thunderclap sounded in the distance, rumbling through the earth. Brand woke with a shout, clambering up from the ground and scattering pine needles everywhere, by the sound of things.

"Brand!" In a few short strides, Anek ran to Brand's side. "Are you all right? What is it?"

"Scyllorin," Brand panted.

"No, you're safe here," Anek said. "With us—Nivin and me."

Brand sank back down to the earth, rustling the pine needles as he did. He rolled gently back and forth, muttering *no* over and over again.

With a little grunt of pain, Nivin pushed herself up from where she sat. "Safe is an exaggeration, don't you think?" She stepped down from the rock, hurrying over moss and sharp gravel and pine needles until her extended arm bumped into Anek.

"Safer than with Scyllorin, as far as I can tell," Anek shot back, lightly cuffing Nivin on the shoulder.

Nivin squatted down beside Brand and laid her hand on his face. His fever was even worse than it had been before. "Brand, can you understand me?"

Brand only murmured a few indistinct words in response.

"Help me get him over to the water, Anek," Nivin said. "Come, Brand, you need to get up now." Nivin and Anek each took one of Brand's arms and hoisted him up off of the ground. He was unsteady on his feet, but with their support he managed to stumble over to the bank of the stream. He fell to his knees and drank water from the creek like an animal.

As she listened to Brand's slurping, Nivin could not quell the rising panic inside of her. No amount of water could aid his fever. The hot, puffy wounds on her own feet were surely infected too, and no matter how much she tried to tell herself the aches in her body were only from exhaustion, she knew fever was not far off.

Anek said she had given him hope. She groaned inwardly at the thought. His hope was founded on her appearing mysterious and powerful, when all she had been doing was nursing her wounds and thinking of their imminent demise. Brand was already beyond hope. All that could be done for him was to give him comfort, and there was none to be had in the wilderness. As for Anek, he still had half of an arrow shaft embedded in his ankle. It would continue to reinjure him every time he moved.

Her despair was already set. She had always one way or another defied the rules set over her, but that spirit of defiance seemed to die a little more every time she thought of their predicament. She simply could not rebel against the mandates of her own mortality. The rich and earthy fragrances of the woods that promised so much life were nothing more than embalmer's perfumes for her.

Brand finally sat up from the water's edge, hiccoughing from the quantity he had just guzzled. Anek patted his back until the fit subsided.

"Steady, Brand," Anek said, trying to be encouraging. "Do you think you can stand on your own now?"

Brand moaned in response and unsteadily clambered up to his feet, grabbing Anek's hand for support.

"There you are," Anek said. "What do we do now,

Nivin? It seems he should be able to walk for a while."

Nivin bit her lip for a moment. "What is there to do?"

"Well, either we do something or we die."

"We are going to die no matter what."

"Die?" Brand burst out. "No, no. No. Scyllorin can't triumph. Must not."

"Then we do something anyway," Anek insisted. "Nivin, you say we're going to die no matter what. So we choose a direction—any direction, and we go. We may as well die looking for some way to survive, rather than die here."

Nivin took a deep, steadying breath. "You're right. Brand, do you have any idea where we are?"

Brand was silent for a moment. "A forest."

"Do you know this place? Do you have any idea where we should go?"

"A stream."

"Brand," Anek said, with matronly patience, "we are by a stream already. Does it have a name? Do you know any of this area?"

"This forest?"

"It's useless, Anek," Nivin interjected. "Let's just pick a direction and go, like you said. Maybe we will find a settlement out here."

"Let's go back the way we came," Anek said.

"No," Brand said. "Stream. Follow it. Downstream."

"Even better. Nivin, what do you think?"

Nivin cringed at the thought of the gravel that would surely line the stream's banks. "You two lead the way, then."

"Wait," Anek said. "Shouldn't we try to make something for your feet?"

Nivin thought for a moment before dismissing the idea. "No. I have always hated shoes. They make me feel out of touch with everything." Too much of her life had been spent in the dungeons—she was not about to die with her feet in miniature prisons, no matter how much it might hurt to go barefoot.

"But—"

"We need to go."

Their progress along the stream bank was painful. Anek's limp grew more and more pronounced, and Brand stumbled often. While there was less gravel, the underbrush became denser the further they moved away from the clearing. Scrub and vine impeded their every step forward. Anek warned Nivin of the upcoming obstacles as often as he could, but it seemed the most he could do was to keep her from walking directly into a tree. Every time he spoke, his voice was tense with pain.

Eventually, Nivin slumped forward with her hands extended in front of her. Random stands of nettle attacked her skin; branches and thorny bushes bit into her as she stumbled along. Her chills continued to get worse despite the warm sunlight that filtered down through the canopy.

They had only been walking for about two hours when Brand stumbled badly and cried he could take no more. Anek started to protest, but Brand went limp and slid to the ground, stretching out prostrate on the cool pine-scattered forest floor. After a couple of pathetic efforts laced with cursing to lift Brand up again, Anek resigned.

"I guess we'll have to rest." No sooner than the words left Anek's mouth, there was a faint *whoosh* in the distance.

Nivin stood up straight and tilted an ear toward the sky. "What is that?"

The sound grew clearer and more rhythmic. There was a thunderclap, unnatural and horribly familiar. It was the same sound that accompanied both Charybda that she had experienced, only this time cracking through the air instead of rumbling through the earth. But as far as she could tell, there was no Charybdon nearby, no swirling of lights or whispering of voices. The *whooshing* drew closer and closer.

Brand gasped and pushed himself up from the ground. "It's Scylla."

"Scylla?" Anek said, his voice filled with confusion.

A horrendous shriek split the air from above them. Nivin clapped her hands over her ears and ducked her head. A reek like disease and smoldering sulfur permeated the forest air. Something massive blocked out the sun for a moment. The temperature plummeted. As it passed, another thunderclap cracked through the air. The earth seemed to tremble in reply.

"A dragon," Anek whispered. "Murm said they didn't exist."

With a horrible realization, Nivin lifted up the crown of her head toward the sky. Whatever that thing was, it seethed with power and swirling lights. "That thing—it's almost creating a Charybdon." Inexplicable instincts tugged at her. "We have to follow it."

"Follow?" Brand cried. "Follow? You don't understand! Scylla—that dragon—she…Pock…"

"She is our only hope." Misgivings swarmed around Nivin's head like buzzing flies, yet against her better judgment, she knew following Scylla was the only option. After all, her instincts had saved them from Temere's men.

"Can hope come from death?"

"We have to trust Nivin," Anek said softly.

"You!" Brand said, his youthful voice cracking at the top of the word. "You—Scyllorin-spawn—you would follow after your mother to lead us into her vile jaws!" He picked up a stone from the earth and chucked it at Anek. It fell several feet to Anek's left, and from the sound of it, it was fairly sizeable.

"We're not here to hurt you, Brand," Nivin said. "Trust me—the way you trusted me before. Anek and I are your friends, remember?"

Brand mumbled something in response.

"Come now, stand up," Anek said. "Let's go."

Nivin listened as Brand climbed up from the ground and stumbled forward a few steps.

"Take my arm," Anek said.

Brand shuffled toward Anek, whimpering slightly.

"There you go. All right. Lead the way, Nivin."

Without another word, Nivin set off after Scylla, forging through the underbrush. The dragon's trail was not difficult to trace. Preternaturally cold air followed its wake, and the earth seemed to tremble, as though it had shrunk in fear from the beast's passing.

After several minutes of running, guided only by temperature and smell and instinct, Nivin tripped over a branch and fell to the ground.

In a moment, Anek was at her side. "Nivin! Are you hurt?"

Nivin winced. The heels of her hands stung with pain. "I think so. My hands caught the worst of the fall."

"Let me help you up," Anek said.

Nivin reached up a hand. Anek clasped his massive hand around her wrist and forearm. He heaved and strained, as if Nivin were an impossibly heavy weight.

"You needn't pull so, Anek." Nivin pulled back against his grasp and easily got to her feet.

"Too weak," Anek muttered. "I can't help you up—I can barely help Brand keep his footing."

Nivin breathed in through her nose. The stench of disease had faded from the air, and the warm sun began to drive the unnatural cold away.

"Oh, no," Nivin whispered. "The trail is gone." A sense of despair washed over her. The dragon had held their last hope—she was certain of it.

"It's all right," Anek said. "I can lead us back to the stream."

Nivin was about to tell Anek it was useless when something cut through her despair, registering in senses she did not even know she had. Something called her. As she turned toward it, she saw the faintest of swirling lights. It was too small to be the same kind of maelstrom that had sucked them all down through the earth and brought them to this forest, yet it seemed to be composed of the same strange flickering energy. Nivin sensed it had indeed been created by the dragon, as if some of the forces had congealed and fallen from the sky to the earth in a raindrop of pure power.

Slowly, she walked over to it, ignoring Anek's questions. Before she could even realize what she was doing, she knelt down and scooped up the cluster of energy. The forces danced across her palms, feeling like writhing hot ribbons. She transferred it from hand to hand, and began stroking it as though it were a small animal. A bizarre sensation of familiarity crept over her.

Her lips moved wordlessly, and the lights began to swell. As the swirling lights grew brighter, it became obvious this thing was a Charybdon—perhaps only the seed of one, but a Charybdon nevertheless. As she continued mouthing the foreign words, she began to hear the faintest of sucking sounds, the swelling and fading voices. Faint thunder echoed through the earth.

Its power was growing.

But not too much, her instincts told her. Carefully, she transferred the swirling energy into one hand. The lights seemed to cling to her—she could not have shaken them away if she wanted to. She had no idea what she was doing, only that a maddeningly strong innate impulse drove her to do it. Lips still moving silently, she moved over across the ground, shuffling on her knees, to where Brand and Anek stood. Brand released his grip on Anek's arm and sank to the ground.

Nivin reached out with her empty hand and touched Brand's cut. He flinched at her touch with a small cry. Then, as if against her own will, she brought up the hand filled with the Charybdon's swirling forces and slammed it directly into his wound.

Brand screamed like a man under torture.

"Stop!" Anek cried. He tried to shove Nivin away from Brand, but she was an immovable object. Anek tried to pull Brand away, but he was also fused to the spot. "Nivin! Nivin, please!"

Brand's screaming, strangely magnified, reached an unbearable volume.

As if through the sound of his screaming—or perhaps the power of the Charybdon itself—Nivin was able to sense the entirety of Brand's being. She saw the multitude of hurts he had sustained beyond the injury on his forehead: the bruises and scrapes on the surface, and the deep grief of loss that stabbed into his soul. She became aware of the outline of his face as if she had run her hands across it a hundred times, as intimately as she knew her own father's face.

She sensed it as a trickle of blood leaked from Brand's wound. In an ethereal swirl, it disappeared into the flickering lights. As if time had been sped up, knotted scar tissue crept across the injury, replacing the blood and exudates that seeped away into the sucking mouth of the Charybdon.

The ground beneath them rumbled. Brand continued screaming. His voice was hoarse and raw.

As Nivin worked, she tried to ignore the agony that tore from Brand's throat. This was the only way he could survive. The swirling lights expanded. At first, she was afraid, but then the foreign instincts took over. Nivin stretched the lights out like yarn and wound them around Brand's form. Soon, every cut and scrape on his body was replaced by fresh scar tissue. She held her hands stretched out over Brand, whose screams had been reduced to pathetic childlike moans.

She slammed her hands together in front of her chest. The percussion of a thunderclap rumbled in the clearing as she and Brand were tossed away from each other, landing several feet apart.

Neither of them moved. Brand was silent. Nivin lay huddled with her hands clasped together in front of her heart.

" Nivin!" Anek ran to her side. "Nivin, what—"

Nivin panted with exhaustion and struggled to her feet. "I have to do it to you now. We don't have much time left before the Charybdon collapses!"

"What?" Anek took a step back. "No!"

"You have to let me!"

"What about Brand? Is he all right? What happened?"

"I—I healed him. The pain is excruciating, but you have no choice. It's the only way to help you. Please, trust me!"

Anek stepped back again. "It's not the pain. A Charybdon gave me clarity. What if this one takes it away again?"

"That doesn't matter!"

"I can't—I can't risk it!"

"Then you'll die!"

"Nivin—"

Nivin sprang forward and pushed the seedling Charybdon into Anek's arrow wound. He roared like a primitive beast. Nivin nearly burst into tears at the sound of his agony, but she clasped her hands tightly around his leg, forcing the Charybdon deeper into his flesh. He cried out even louder. Nivin cursed the instincts that had led her to torture her friends. Where had they come from? Why were they so overpowering?

How was she so certain this would not kill them instead?

She sensed Anek's being every bit as intensely as she had with Brand, felt his many hurts and grief just as strongly. The arrow shaft in Anek's leg disintegrated into ash and vanished, and the wound turned into hard scar tissue. It was enough to disperse her fears for the moment, and when the swirling lights began to swell once again, she knew what to do. As she stretched her hands out, allowing the strands to wrap around Anek's body, eddies of light flickered brightly in his other injuries before snaking back into the cocoon of writhing energy.

The Charybdon was almost too big for her to control now. With a gasp, Nivin slammed her palms together again. The cocoon vanished from around the giant's body as the lights receded into her hands with a thunderous percussion. She was thrown onto her back by its force, and Anek's body crashed into the ground.

The lights were suddenly too weak. Without hesitation, she sat up, opened her hands, and let the foreign words dance voicelessly across her lips again, coaxing the Charybdon back from its flickering out. When her instincts told her to, she clasped her arms across her chest, pushing the Charybdon into her own body.

She was deaf to the sound of her own screams reverberating through the forest.

CHAPTER EIGHT

As Brand came back to his senses, the trees shook and the ground rumbled. He sat up and gasped at the sight in front of him. Screaming, Nivin sat on the ground, enveloped in energy that looked like heat waves shimmering around her. Her hair seemed charged with electricity. Her face writhed in agony.

Brand stared, his heart racing.

In a deafening thunderclap, the shimmering energy vanished and Nivin collapsed onto her back.

The following silence was equally deafening.

Brand could not hear anything over the pounding of his heart against his eardrums. Dizzily, he looked around. Anek was a massive heap on the ground a few feet away from him. Brand hastily crawled over to him and checked his pulse. His heartbeat was steady.

"Anek!" Brand rasped. He shook Anek, but he did not

respond. Fighting dread, Brand scrambled over to Nivin and checked her for signs of life.

She was alive, but like Anek, he could not rouse her.

Kneeling, he sat back on his feet and observed his surroundings. Survival instincts cemented by a lifetime of training took over his thoughts. The blue, partly cloudy sky suggested weather was not an immediate concern, and the sun-golden green canopy of the forest sheltered them from heat. He noticed the trees around them were a kind that only grew at high altitudes, and the rarity of the air taxed his lungs.

First in the ocean, then in heath-covered flatlands, then in the mountains? As Brand dazedly tried to patch together an idea of his whereabouts, he was startled by another swift thunderclap—and the faint *whoosh* of colossal wings approaching.

Scylla!

The trees around Brand and Nivin might be dense enough to disguise them, but Anek lay in a clear patch of sunlight. If Scylla was hunting—or worse, drawn by whatever Nivin had done—her keen eyes might well be able to see through the small gap in the canopy.

Brand rushed over to Anek's side. "Anek. Anek, wake up!"

Anek did not move.

There was another thunderclap, this time closer.

"Anek!" Brand slapped both sides of Anek's face. "Anek!"

Anek moaned softly and opened his eyes, squinting at the light.

"You have to move. Here, under this tree. Hurry!"

Slowly, Anek sat up. "Whuh?"

"Move!" Brand tugged at Anek's hand. "Now!"

The *whoosh* of wings grew clearer. An earthshaking roar of thunder crashed.

The noise jolted Anek into action. He scrambled under the tree and ducked down as low as he possibly could in the underbrush, covering the back of his head with both hands.

Brand hastily followed, desperately hoping the dense forest's shadows would be enough to conceal them from Scylla's eyes. "Be quiet," he whispered to Anek. Even if she could not see or hear them, however, he dreaded the thought that she might smell them—or worse, have other senses which they could never hope to fool.

Through the patchwork frame of tree branches, Brand watched as Scylla slithered through the air high above them. The color of jet, her massive wings stretched out from her serpentine form. Cruel spikes and horns riddled her silhouette, and even at this distance, her body seemed to bristle with black human fingernails. The sun dimmed as she swooped over their position, and the temperature dropped. Her horrid stench filled the air. Brand held his breath as she circled back, flying over them again. Anek crouched lower until his face touched the ground.

She stopped circling. Beating her wings and hovering right over their position, she hissed. Brand's stomach tied itself in knots. Sweat ran into his eyes. He glanced around—there was absolutely nothing he could immediately use as a weapon against a man, let alone Scylla.

Thunder shook the ground, and with a final hiss, she turned back to her original course. Her shadow vanished and the sun once again freckled the forest floor with light.

Brand nearly passed out in relief. "She's gone."

Anek sat up, uncurling his spine with a groan. "Was that Scylla?"

Brand's eyebrows shot up. "You know about Scylla?"

"Well, when that thing first passed us, you said it was Scylla."

"When did—I thought you couldn't speak properly."

"I couldn't," Anek said, scratching his head through his mop of curly hair. "When I woke up here, I could suddenly talk and think clearly. I can't explain it."

"It doesn't make sense." Brand's mind swam with confusion. "I'm not even sure how we got here."

"You were burning up and mad with fever. We thought we were going to lose you." Anek reached out a massive hand and touched the knotted scar tissue on Brand's forehead. "Nivin managed to heal you."

At that moment, Brand realized for the first time that he no longer felt the searing pain in his forehead, and that the delirium of his fever was completely gone. He probed at his forehead. "I don't believe it."

"She healed me too," Anek said, examining his own hurts.

"Is that what she was doing to herself?" He shrank internally at the memory.

Anek crawled over to Nivin's side. "It must have been," he said. "All of her injuries are healed up, too."

"Can you wake her?"

Anek shook her slightly, but she made no response. "Maybe she just needs sleep."

"I hope so." Brand came over and checked her pulse again, then pulled back one of her eyelids. She did not stir.

After several more attempts to wake her, Anek sighed.

"What do we do now?"

"Well, I have been trying to figure out where we are," Brand said, looking around. "All I can tell is that we're in the mountains somewhere. If we wait for nightfall, I might be able to guess from the stars—assuming that they're the stars I know."

"You can tell where we are just by looking at the stars?"

"Not exactly where we are, but a close guess, anyway."

"How did you learn to do that?"

"The Scholars taught me as part of my training to be a Champion," Brand said, "but I can tell you more about it later. Right now we're wasting daylight. Stay here with Nivin, and I'll see if I can find a place with a better view of the sky."

"Will you be able to find your way back?" Anek said, his face taut with worry.

Brand smiled. "Don't worry. You'll be surprised at how good I am at this when I'm not insane with fever."

Anek flashed his crooked toothy grin in reply.

It was not long before Brand located a good spot, a sandy-floored clearing surrounded by sparsely needled conifers. One of the trees in particular looked like it should be easy enough to climb if he needed a better vantage point to see the sky. He busied himself with preparing the site for the evening, gathering twigs, fallen leaves, and needles for makeshift shelters. Even though it was not cold now, if they were in the mountains like he suspected, the night could be frigid. Accordingly, he decided to set up under the trees just outside the clearing so that they could sleep in a place more sheltered from the weather—and unfriendly eyes.

After he had found enough twigs and sticks, he loosely wove them into the low hanging branches above the place he had chosen, and then he covered the improvised roof with a layer of pine needles. Beneath this, he spread a thick layer of more pine needles on the ground.

Briefly, he considered gathering wood for a fire, but the chance that Scylla still lurked nearby was too great. What would be warmth for them would be a beacon for her—it would be better to freeze to death than attract her.

Satisfied that the site was properly set up, Brand hurried to get Anek and Nivin. He had spent at least two hours preparing the site, and by the time he was done, the sky had already started purpling into evening. As long as there were no delays, however, there would be enough daylight left for all three of them to get to the camp safely.

It only took about half of an hour for Brand to find his way back to where he had left his companions. Half-camouflaged by scrubs and brush, Anek sat on the ground with Nivin's head resting in his lap. He hummed an indistinct tune and tenderly stroked her hair.

"I found a good place, Anek," Brand said, clearing his throat. "It's not too far from here. How is she?"

Anek did not look up. "The same."

"That's good. At least she is still alive."

"She's the first friend I ever had," Anek said, shaking his head slightly. "What if she never wakes?"

Brand's throat tightened involuntarily as he tried to suppress the memory of his fellow Champion—one of his oldest friends. He had fought so hard to keep thoughts of it from his consciousness, to keep it from distracting him from his purpose. Had it really only been days ago, when it seemed like years had passed? Pock's death was so swift, and his body was gone so suddenly. Brand would have given anything to be able to cradle and comfort him as he lay dying, to lay him to rest, to mourn him properly.

But he had no way then. He had no way now. He had to face what was at hand.

"We don't have time to worry about that now," Brand said, somewhat more harshly than he intended. "We should head for that clearing I spotted."

"I can't carry her," Anek said. He finally looked up at Brand, his face utterly defeated. "I tried picking her up, but it's useless. My strength is gone."

"Gone?" Brand raised an eyebrow. His situation seemed to grow stranger and more unpredictable by the minute. "How does your strength just disappear?"

With a sigh, Anek shook his head. "It must have been the Charybdon."

"Never mind that for now. We'll carry her together, all right?"

Brand hooked his arms under Nivin's and Anek supported her feet. In this fashion, they carried her to the place where Brand had set up shelters for them. When they arrived, they gently laid Nivin down on one of the makeshift ticks. Her pale skin, though healed of sunburn, nevertheless glowed pink in the fading evening light. The world grew cooler and cooler as the last vibrant orange sliver of sun disappeared beyond the horizon.

While Brand and Anek waited for the stars to come out, they periodically checked on Nivin. Except for her breathing and pulse, she lay as still as a rag doll—and even though they began to shiver, she did not. Her skin was becoming cool to the touch. Worried, they covered all of her but her face with a thick layer of pine needles to keep her warm.

"Do you think she'll make it?" Anek asked, holding his gooseflesh-covered arms tightly around his body.

Brand said the first comforting thing that came to mind. "As long as she is breathing, there's hope."

CHAPTER NINE

Brand and Anek were silent as the stars began to come out one by one. There was only a dim, waning crescent moon, and the stars were as clear as fiery sparks against the black of the sky. Once all of them had emerged, Brand got up from the ground and walked out into the clearing to examine the constellations. With a surge of relief, he saw they were his own constellations—those he had known his whole life, not the strange scattering of lights he had seen over Zerabar. He wondered if maybe his injury and fever had caused him to imagine the unfamiliar stars.

"Anek, come here," Brand said. "Look at the sky."

Anek rose from the ground with a bit of a grunt and walked stiffly over to Brand's side. He craned his neck back. "What should I look for?" he asked.

"Do these stars look familiar to you?"

"I don't know." Anek shrugged. "I never could see that

clearly, and so I never paid attention to the stars."

"But you can see them now?"

"I can," Anek said, realization dawning on his face. "How—all of these changes that are happening to me! I can think clearly, I can speak clearly, I can see clearly!"

"None of this makes sense," Brand said. "Why would you change so much, when Nivin and I haven't?"

"You have changed."

"What? How?"

"You look different. Your hair is reddish and you have freckles, and your skin is lighter, too."

"My hair has always been red, and I have always had freckles."

"Not when I first met you."

"Are you sure it wasn't your poor vision?"

"Absolutely," Anek said. "My vision was better up close than far off."

Brand shook his head. "Well, none of this is as confusing to me as the constellations changing. No matter where a person is in the world, the stars are the same stars, just in a different position. Not even the darkest sorcery could change that. I had never even seen stars like yours, so how was that possible?"

"Could it be because of your injury?" Anek asked.

Brand sighed. "Perhaps, but I'm not sure. The memory seems completely clear."

"So," Anek said. "Now that you recognize the stars, what do they tell you?"

"It's midsummer," Brand said. "And since I know we are in the mountains somewhere, that gives me a general idea of what to look for in the stars. Let's see—there's the Compass...give me a few moments."

Brand spent some time examining the sky, and he ended up needing to climb the tree to get a better view. Finally satisfied he had determined their general whereabouts, he climbed back down, jumping from the lowest hanging branch onto the ground with a soft *thud*. Anek, who was sitting at the edge of the clearing, looked up expectantly at the sound.

"We are probably somewhere in the southern Guardian Mountains, the range that skirts the west border of Verderbera, closer to Scyllorin's stronghold," Brand announced. "It only makes sense. Scylla doesn't usually fly far abroad."

"So we are right back where you came from?" Anek asked.

"No—that part doesn't make sense. Scyllorin had driven me to the ocean, miles and miles south of where we are now. I have no idea how we wound up here."

"Are we worse off, then?"

"Actually, this is far better. Libertas is on the other side of this range, though Council City is further north."

"Libertas?"

"Yes. It is my nation, the nation of the Freemen. If we can get to the other side, we will be in friendly territory."

"Will that be difficult?"

Brand sighed. Difficult hardly seemed like an adequate descriptor. The challenges of crossing a high mountain range would be dramatically increased by inexperienced traveling companions anyway, and Nivin's blindness would impede them even more. Furthermore, if she did not wake soon, they would have to carry her. They simply could not afford to linger this near to Scylla's hunting ground. "It won't be easy. How is Nivin?"

"Still the same," Anek said, shaking his head. "I tried waking her several more times while you were up in the tree, but she's still completely unconscious."

"Blast," Brand muttered.

"She hasn't gotten any colder, at least, and her breathing is slow and steady. Maybe she'll wake up in the morning."

Brand stared at the ground. "Maybe."

After a few moments of silence, Anek yawned. "Should we try to get some sleep now?"

"We may as well."

The two of them retreated back under the trees and slid under the temporary shelter Brand had constructed. As he settled down into the crackling bed of needles, Anek chuckled when his feet protruded past the crude roof.

"Forgive me," Brand said, sitting crouched near the edge of the roof. "I underestimated how large you are."

Anek waved his hand in dismissal. "It's nothing—I'm used to it. Aren't you going to lie down?"

"Not yet. I'm going to keep watch first. I'll wake you when I need rest."

"All right," Anek said. There was the sound of more rustling needles as Anek scooted a little closer to Nivin and put an arm around her to keep her warm.

Drawing a deep breath, Brand settled into a more comfortable position and stared resolutely out into the darkness.

*

The rest of the night passed uneventfully. Brand occasionally rose to stretch his legs and walk around the campsite. His mind was restless, teeming with confusion over what had transpired in the last few days. It would be pointless to wake Anek, since nothing could lull Brand's troubled mind into sleep. So, he decided to let the giant sleep until sunrise, and instead spent his anxious energy gathering any tightly closed pinecones that he could find.

By the time that Anek woke, he had collected a sizeable pile of them.

"You should have woken me," Anek mumbled, sliding out from beneath the shelter.

Brand shrugged as he cracked open the flaps of a pinecone. "You needed rest, and I couldn't have slept anyway. How's Nivin?"

"Still unconscious."

Brand sighed. "Here, help me with these." Reaching between the woody flaps, he carefully removed the tiny nut inside and held it up for Anek to see. "There are several of these in each cone. They aren't much, but a little food is better than none." He tossed one of the cones to Anek, who caught it deftly.

After struggling with the pinecone for a few moments, Anek hung his head and handed it back to Brand. "My fingers are too big for it."

Brand smiled. "These are hardly worth it anyway." He gave the small handful of the nuts he had already removed to Anek.

Anek slowly ate the tiny pine nuts one by one while Brand continued to shell a few more. "Brand, what exactly is this Scylla?"

"A dragon. You saw her, didn't you?"

"Well, yes, but you talk about her like she's something more. In your fever, you kept calling me 'Scyllorin-spawn,' and you said Scylla was my mother."

"I am truly sorry for that," Brand said, chucking away

an empty pinecone. He shook his head. "I must have been confused—all of it was a blur; I hardly remember any of it."

Anek chuckled. "I wasn't offended. What did you mean by it, though?"

Brand chewed on a few pine nuts as he considered how much he wanted to tell this outsider. They had proven themselves as allies, to be sure, but in the existence he had always known, only Freemen could be trusted.

However, his life had abruptly changed. Strange stars and countries and impossible sorceries had become a reality, and these two new companions along with them. If he was to survive, he would have to trust them.

Brand drew a deep breath and let it out slowly. "Scylla and Scyllorin. How should I explain it? It is an abomination of nature, a perversion of the natural order. Scylla is a dragon, as you saw, but—Scylla—is Scyllorin's *bride*." He spat the last word as though it was a curse.

Anek's eyes widened. "Scyllorin is also a dragon?"

"No. He is a man, practiced in the darkest sorceries known to man. How he came to be wedded to Scylla is a mystery, though there are many legends. I can tell you, though, their union is unnatural and evil. Their offspring—their foul *progeny*—form part of their legions. They are devious, cunning, and dangerous. They are too much like demons to be called anything else."

"And Temere calls the lame abominations," Anek muttered, shaking his head. "How can a dragon and a man have offspring?"

Brand shrugged. "No one knows for certain. The Scholars say she is a dragon of old, like one of those the fabled Knights of Ardor slew, and that Scyllorin's sorcery

116

gave her sentience. A very few people say she is the offspring of the demon that ate out the center of the earth, though that demon himself is just a legend. However, they suppose when the shell of the earth could no longer contain her and her father, she broke free to feed upon the earth's inhabitants." He paused. "Some even say it was Scyllorin who broke her free. But all of that is legend, which the Council of Scholars has denied as fact."

Anek wrinkled his brow. "I don't know your legends," he said.

"Well, you hardly need know anything to understand she is a scourge on the hearts of my people. You saw her. That in itself is enough." Brand smiled grimly. "However, it will take at least a week to cross this range, if we are lucky. I'll have time to tell you all the legends your heart desires."

Anek smiled in reply. "I would enjoy that. And you can tell me about your Council of Scholars, too. "

Brand stood up and stretched. "We should get started, then. I was thinking we could go back to the stream and see about following it as far northwest as we can."

Anek rose from the ground and brushed dirt and pieces of pinecones off of his tattered clothes. "Lead the way."

Unceremoniously, they lifted Nivin from her bed of pine needles. She did not even flinch or give any indication she was aware they were carrying her. Anek supported her legs as best he could, and Brand carried the weight of her torso with his arms hooked under hers. They started to move roughly northwest and back toward the mountain brook. The forest floor was uneven, and carrying Nivin between the two of them was cumbersome. Much to

Brand's irritation, though he had anticipated it, their travel time back to the stream was nearly doubled. By the time they found it, his mouth seemed filled with cotton, but when he saw the glistening flow of water cutting between the trees, his mood lightened. Not only could he quench his thirst, he would be able to use the brook as an additional guide as they traveled.

Gently, they set Nivin down near the bank and went to get a drink. Tiny silver fish glistened in the shallows. Brand could not suppress a smile when he dipped his hands in the water and the silvery cloud darted away into deeper waters. After Brand and Anek had drunk as much as they wanted, they propped Nivin up. They held her mouth open and poured a little water into her mouth, which she reflexively swallowed. After administering several small gulps, they picked her up again and continued on their way, following the brook upstream.

Brand kept a close eye on the sun's position as they went. The stream did not always flow the exact direction he wanted to take, but the bends and diversions canceled each other out enough that Brand suspected the water generally flowed south-southeast. Following it upstream might not take them far enough west, but for now it was more important to stay near a water source. The exertion of carrying Nivin made them sweat heavily in the warm sun.

Anek in particular wheezed and sweated excessively; he was not acclimated to such high altitudes. Brand tried not to show frustration when Anek needed to rest so frequently, since it would not benefit them if Anek succumbed to severe altitude sickness.

During one of their many rests, Brand could not quell his impatience at being idle, and so he decided to scout the immediate surrounding area. He relaxed somewhat when he realized the only signs of life in this vicinity were of animals—he passed a badger's burrow and several patches where deer had crushed the vegetation into a flat bed. When he startled a deer and watched the white flag of its tail disappear into the trees, he wished he had chosen to spend his time crafting a makeshift spear or bow and arrow.

Still, with so many animals around, there hopefully would be a source of food. After exploring a little further, Brand's heart leapt when he saw a stand of lamb's quarters growing in a sunny spot up ahead. Many of the plants were unfortunate victims of cervine foraging, but Brand had no trouble gathering two massive fistfuls of undamaged leafy stems. He tucked them into his belt and headed back to the stream.

"Well, I found some food," Brand said, walking up to his companions.

Anek turned around eagerly. "What is it?"

Brand extended a handful of the plants to Anek. "Lamb's quarters. It should stave off our hunger at least a little."

Anek looked at the plants, his brow furrowed. Taking them from Brand, he held one of the stems close to his eyes and squinted as he examined it. "Are you sure this isn't poisonous?"

"Of course it isn't. It's a favorite of sheep—and shepherds. It tastes better in the spring when the leaves and stems are tender. It's also delicious in stews, but we can't exactly expect luxury."

Anek wrinkled his nose. "For some reason I feel like I've seen this before. I thought it was poisonous."

With a shrug, Brand started pulling the leaves off of a stem with his teeth. "Trust me," he said, with his mouth halfway full. He swallowed. "I have eaten this more times than I can count."

Still frowning, Anek started to gnaw on one of the plants. Once he had finished it, he greedily set in on the others Brand had given him.

They sat on the shore of the brook, chewing on the tough stems and strongly flavored leaves. The weather was pleasant; a gentle mountain breeze and warm sun on the boughs of evergreens fragranced the air with the sweet scent of pine. The water bubbled cheerfully as it flowed along its course, and jays and squirrels squabbled in the trees above. The tiny fish glittered as they darted back and forth, and snails climbed with contented leisure along the blades of rushes.

Anek leaned over the brook for a sip of water. "It's beautiful here." He wiped droplets of water from his lips, then smeared his hands across his tattered shirt to dry them.

Brand glanced at Anek out of the corner of his eye and tore off another piece of lamb's quarters with his teeth. He shook his head. Beautiful? Beauty did not matter when they were in enemy territory. Beauty did not matter when they were close to starvation and their unconscious companion would grow more and more emaciated with every day. Nature's beauty more often than not meant obstacles and dangers.

He was about to tell Anek they needed to move on when he looked directly at his large companion, who was reaching out to touch one of the snails creeping along the rushes. Anek's childlike curiosity reminded him of Pock.

Even though Pock had learned to take the wilderness seriously, he would still take nearly every opportunity to see how many times he could skip a rock across a body of water.

Rocks. While they were stopped, gathering a few would be a good idea. Brand had a fairly good arm, and he might be able to take out a squirrel or a bird with the correctly sized stone. Brand stood up and stretched. "Here, Anek. Help me find some good throwing stones." He found a suitable specimen in the brook and held it up. "About this size—nice and smooth."

The water grew muddy as they collected the simple projectiles from the stream bed. After a few moments, Anek held up a smooth, flat stone. "Look," he said, grinning. "This one is flat like griddle bread."

In spite of himself, Brand felt a smile creep onto his face. "Let me show you something." He took the rock and rinsed the silt off of it. Then, with a flick of his wrist, he spun the rock toward the water's surface, where it skipped all the way across the narrow brook to the other side.

Anek's mouth fell open and his malformed face glowed with delight. "Incredible!"

At that, Brand gathered up the stones they had collected and stowed them in his trouser pockets, putting his personal memories away at the same time. "We should move on," he said, his voice somewhat hoarse. "We might still put in another mile before sundown."

"Will you teach me to do that?" Anek asked, still pointing at the brook.

"Perhaps later."

*

Over the next two days, their progress grew more and

more difficult. Still, Nivin would not wake up. Her heartbeat, breathing, and reflexive swallowing all indicated she was still alive, but they started to fear she would starve to death before she woke up. They felt a sense of guilt as they ate wild plants and the small game Brand was able to take down, but they could not feed her without the risk of gagging her. Anxiously, they proceeded while she seemed lighter to carry by the hour.

The uphill grade became steeper, and obstacles of boulders or slope forced them to deviate from the increasingly narrow stream often. Near the middle of the third day, they reached the stream's source—a spring that trickled from a small fissure in the stony mountainside. Immediately below the spring was a small rock shelf protruding from the surrounding trees. The place offered an excellent vantage point to see eastward. They were high enough that they could see the foothills below them, and a glimpse of the plains of Verderbera beyond.

"We may as well stop here," Brand said, "and get our fill of water before we move on. Oh, for a water skin."

While they were resting, Brand relieved a squirrel of its perch with one of the few remaining stones. He lit a small fire, and while he waited for the blaze to grow hot, he skinned and dressed the squirrel. "You can have most of this one," he said to Anek, skewering it on a stick. "I can make do with just a mouthful."

Anek grinned. "A mouthful is all that's on those rodents."

"Better than pine nuts," Brand countered.

"This is true."

A faint rumble of thunder sounded in the distance. Brand jerked his head up, looking out over the landscape.

The only clouds besides the wispy cirrus puffs above them were leagues away, barely visible on the horizon. Even those did not appear to be a suitable explanation for the sound. Anek glanced around nervously.

Straining his eyes, Brand scanned the sky. For a brief moment, he thought he saw a black speck in the distance, but he could not fix his gaze on it. Perhaps it was only one of the motes that always swam through his field of vision. He blinked rapidly and searched the sky again.

There was no sign of it.

Brand turned back to Anek. "I think we are safe."

A clamorous percussion of thunder shook the mountainside.

Nivin sat bolt upright, screaming.

CHAPTER TEN

Nivin drowned in thunderous confusion. She heard screaming—it might have been her own. It felt like thunder echoed inside her head. Voices said her name and told her to be quiet again and again.

A sweaty hand clapped over her mouth. In terror, she tried to push it away.

"Nivin, please! It's us. Calm down!"

Slowly, Nivin's awareness of the physical world trickled back into her consciousness. The screaming stopped. The internal thunder faded. Her senses began to feed information to her confused mind. She felt the hand move away from her mouth.

"Nivin?"

The deep voice was familiar. "Anek?"

"Yes, it's me." Anek laid his monstrous hand on her shoulder.

She had to be sure. She reached her hands up and felt his misshapen face. "I was swirling in nothingness," she whispered, lowering her hands back down to her lap.

Nivin recognized Brand's voice, hushed and tense. "You're safe now. Are you all right?"

"We thought you were gone," Anek added, his voice choked. "I feared you would never wake."

Dizziness assaulted Nivin when she tried to recall what had happened. She vaguely remembered healing Anek, and then she had turned the powers in on herself. Everything had gone black, turned to nothing. "I didn't even know I was unconscious. All I knew was nothing." It was a lulling nothingness that had cradled her like a newborn, and she had clung to it like a child to its mother's breast. She shuddered at the thought. "The nothingness—felt familiar somehow. Like it had consumed me—like I was it and it was me." A brief moment of panic seized her, and she grabbed Anek's hand like it was an anchor in reality.

"Don't let the nightmares frighten you," Anek said.

"They weren't nightmares. I was nothing."

"Nivin, you never stopped existing. You were just unconscious," Brand said, a slight waver to his voice. "You've been with us this whole time, I promise."

Anek chuckled. "Yes, and we have the sore backs from carrying you to prove it."

"Carrying me?" Nivin said, her mind reeling. "Where are we?"

"Higher up in the mountains," Brand snapped. He seemed completely unnerved. "That thunder was so close. Was that you?"

The thought made Nivin dizzy again. "I don't know."

It had felt as though the thunder was screaming inside of the confines of her skull, but had it not come from outside? Was that not what woke her, what drew her out of the void?

"Well, I can't see any signs of Scylla," Anek said. He patted Nivin's shoulder gently. "Do you think we should move anyway, Brand?"

Brand heaved an exasperated sigh. "If nothing changes, I think we can afford to wait as long as it takes for the game to finish cooking. But we are leaving as soon as the meat is done. It shouldn't take long."

While they waited for the squirrel to be done, Anek helped Nivin over to the spring, and she gratefully thrust her cracked lips into the water. The frigid water revived her mind somewhat. Brand and Anek took turns quietly explaining what had happened while she was unconscious. Her mind continued to clear, and she began to notice the environment around them. The thin, pine-fragranced air played lightly against her skin, and the smell of smoke and roasting game tickled her nostrils. Bright sunlight strained her sensitive eyes.

Brand paced around uneasily, keeping watch for any kind of trouble. Whenever his shadow passed over Nivin, the world flashed dark and then back to bright when the full sunlight hit her face again. The continual changing of the light made her head ache. Finally, she closed her eyes, put her hand over her face, and tried to listen to what Anek was saying.

"I think it might be done now," Anek said. An upward inflection in his voice indicated this was more of a hope than a statement.

Other than his voice, the only sounds were Brand's

footsteps, trickling water, and the popping of the fire.

A shiver shot through Nivin. "Hush. Why aren't there any birds?"

There was a pause.

"Maybe the thunder that woke you frightened them," Anek suggested.

As they listened, another faint rumble of thunder pealed through the earth. With a yelp, Nivin covered her head with her hands and cowered at the sound.

"Nivin," said Brand. He seized one of her hands and held it between his own. "You need to be quiet. We are going to move back to where the trees are thicker, just to be safe, all right?"

His grip on her hand steadied her.

"What about the squirrel?" Anek said.

"Grab it," Brand ordered. "I'll stomp out the fire."

"You can have the squirrel, Nivin," Anek said. "You must be starving."

"Thank you," Nivin said. Despite her hollow stomach, she could not even think about eating. The thunder had filled her with an irrationally overwhelming desire to hide.

Brand must have felt the same way. "Later! We have to go now." Their fire popped as Brand ground out the last of the coals. "Follow me."

Stooping over, Anek helped Nivin up. He held her hand as they followed after Brand, carefully guiding her around as many obstacles as he could. Pine needles prickled at the soles of her bare feet, and even though her thick calluses prevented any of the rocks from drawing blood, they still hurt. Moreover, the dizziness from days without eating made her head spin. She felt like she was going to faint, and that thought terrified her. Nothingness might still be waiting for her on the other side of consciousness, hungry to swallow up the essence of her being.

Fortunately, Brand found a secluded stand of trees before too long. One they were hidden, Brand let out a sigh of relief. "We have to wait and listen for a while, but I think we'll be safe here."

"There you go, Nivin," Anek said. "Here, I'll find a good spot for you to sit down."

Nivin did not share in Brand's relief. The sense of foreboding still plagued her as Anek led her over to the base of a tree. Sitting down with her back against the trunk, she huddled her knees close to her chest and rested her head on them.

Anek tapped lightly on her shoulder. "You should eat."

A faint murmur of thunder sounded, almost too soft to be heard. Nivin clasped her hands over her head again and whimpered. She hated the thunder. It was unnatural.

Worse, it resonated in her consciousness with implied meaning that lay beyond her grasp.

"It's all right," Brand said. "Whatever it is, it seems to be far away now. I have heard these sounds before. Scylla's thunder is the loudest, but her demon offspring sometimes cause it as well. As far as the Scholars have ever been able to surmise, it's an after-effect of their power. You don't need to be afraid of the sound. Lightning is dangerous, but thunder is harmless. This is no different."

"No," Nivin said. "That sound is more. It's evil. It's power."

"Even so—it can't hurt you here. Now please, eat."

Anek took Nivin's hand and pressed the squirrel into her grasp and chuckled. "Don't make us force you."

Finally overwhelmed by her extreme hunger, Nivin began to eat. Nearly feral, she tore off strips of meat with her teeth. She had no awareness of anything around her until she had picked the last shred of meat from the bones.

As she wiped grease off of her face and hands with her tattered sleeves, she weakly thanked her companions. Then, with a deep sigh, she leaned her head back against the tree and closed her eyes. She wished she could sleep to close her mind to the unanswered questions plaguing her, but the nothingness still lurked at the verges of her thoughts.

"How do you feel now?" Anek asked, sitting down next to her.

"Better," Nivin said. She knew she needed to keep thinking to keep the nothingness at bay. "But I am still so confused. Where are we?"

"We are in the mountain range to the southwest of Verderbera," Brand said.

"And that is the country your people are at war with?"

"Yes."

"Well, you know how Anek and I got here. How did you wind up getting in this situation?"

Brand snorted. "My story is a bit longer than yours."

"Please, Brand." Nivin was desperate for something to focus on, desperate for answers. "We hardly know anything about you. You've said things about Scyllorin and dragons and councils and champions, and we have had to guess to fill in any blanks."

"And if I recall correctly, you said you would tell me all the stories I could possibly want," Anek added.

Brand sighed. "I suppose we won't be moving for a little while." Finally, he ceased his pacing and sat down on the ground.

"Then you'll tell us?"

Brand chuckled wearily. "Yes. But there is a long and complicated history behind how I came to be sitting here with you.

"As I have said, I am a Champion of the Freemen. My people consist of a network of city-states spread across the nation of Libertas, but our capital is in Council City, which is where I am from. For centuries, our people have been the only ones to resist Scyllorin's reign."

"Is that why you call yourselves the Freemen?" asked Anek.

"No, it's because of our system of government. Each city-state is represented by a Lord, and the Lords vote to choose our Chief Councilor. We have no monarch; hence, we are free. All of the lands around us were their own sovereign kingdoms at one point, until Scyllorin conquered them. Now their kings are little more than ineffectual vassals who pay tribute to Scyllorin, both monetary and human."

Nivin felt a sudden chill. "Human?"

"Yes," Brand said. A touch of resentment colored his voice. "Scylla demands human flesh. Scyllorin rewarded those kingdoms who gave into him immediately by only exacting a tribute of one person per city per year. Those who resisted—well, that horrible dragon has free reign to hunt whenever she will. They also must pay a far heavier tax to Scyllorin. They are impoverished, pitiful nations.

"But the Freemen resisted. Not only were our armies strong and powerful, this mountain range made Scyllorin's invasion more difficult for him. Finally, the cost to him became too great, and he gave up on his war against us.

Out of bitterness he still sends his demon offspring to torment us. Every now and again one of his spawn will demolish a village or terrorize our cities.

"Even after Scyllorin abandoned his attempts to seize control of Libertas, the Freemen knew we could not abandon our efforts to stop him. We don't have the military strength to invade Verderbera, and so we developed a different strategy: the Council of Champions. Every year, a Champion is sent to challenge Scylla and Scyllorin. Hardly any of them return, but those who do bring back new knowledge with them, which is taken to the Council of Scholars.

"We now have centuries of accumulated knowledge. Every year we have grown closer to finally putting an end to Scyllorin's reign of terror. Now, we know we are closer than ever."

"How?" asked Anek, his voice tense with curiosity.

"Because—" Brand seemed to choke on the word. He drew a long, deep breath and let it out slowly.

When he spoke again, Nivin could hear suppressed pain in his voice.

"We became too great of a threat. Just over ten and a half years ago, Scylla herself attacked Council City. Over half of the Councilors were killed. She savaged the Champions in training. Only two of us survived—the yearling just brought to the Council, and me. I was only five at the time."

After several minutes of silence, Anek shifted. "I am sorry."

"It does little to be sorry for the past," Brand said. The tone of his voice suggested it was a platitude he had heard many times over. "But Scylla's attack had one positive effect. It doubled the Council's resolve. Even the Council of Scholars, traditionally resistant to change, decided we must increase our efforts. So it was decided that we must send out two Champions each year rather than one, to show Scyllorin that we are not so easily cowed."

"I mean no disrespect to you," Nivin said, "but you haven't even seen sixteen years?"

"I will have in autumn."

"Were you sent out so young because all of the other Champions were — gone?"

"No. All of the Champions are sent at fifteen."

Nivin was silent for a moment. She thought of the young soldier who had lingered in the prison, who, from the sound of his voice, had only just passed his eighteenth birthday. All of Zerabar's soldiers were required to be eighteen years of age before they were permitted to go into combat, though they could begin their training earlier. It was thought that anyone younger would be unable to face the trauma of combat. In the case of the young soldier, perhaps even eighteen was not enough.

Guilt wracked her. In a way, hadn't he been deemed an abomination for his association with her as well as his failure in battle? Was his death on her shoulders?

Anek's voice saved her from her thoughts. "Why so young?"

"Youth has the advantage of resilience," Brand said, though he did not sound overly sure. "And we have been trained in all we need to know. More time would not do anything other than delay the cause."

"Still, there is something to be said for simple maturity," Nivin countered, thinking again of the young soldier. "Maturity guides wise decision making."

"Only one thing guides the decisions of a Champion," Brand snapped. He stood up and began pacing feverishly; everything in his manner, from his voice to the weight of his footsteps, told Nivin he was agitated. "That thing is the knowledge that Scylla and Scyllorin must be destroyed, no matter the cost. Nobody understood that better than—" Brand's voice broke and he made a choking sound. He sat down again and was silent.

"Brand," Anek said gently, "what happened to the Champion who was sent out with you?"

When Brand replied, Nivin could hear the youth in his voice. Though he was only about a year and a half younger than she, his voice shook like a frightened little boy's. "Scylla swallowed him whole."

In horror, Nivin imagined a person being consumed by a dragon. She had been taught they existed nowhere save legend. Her touch had explored detailed bas-reliefs of the creatures—hideous, snakelike things with wings and legs. Her fingertips had lingered on the gigantic mouths filled with spear-like fangs, but she had never imagined they would be big enough to swallow an entire person. She had never imagined they could be the size of Scylla, whose massive wingspan blocked out the sun. The closest thing she could think of to such a horrific thing was the small snake she had once caught slithering in the dungeons, its body swollen with freshly eaten rat.

Anek was respectfully quiet for a few moments while Brand regained his composure—either that, or he too was shocked into silence by the idea of such a demise. "I'm so sorry. What was his name?"

"We called him Pock," Brand said.

"Why did you call him that?"

Brand's voice suddenly grew harsh. "It doesn't matter now. We've spent enough time resting. Nivin, do you think you are all right to walk for a while?"

"I can try," Nivin said. She itched to move away, to leave behind the dark nothingness that had grasped her.

Still, she feared that it would follow her.

"Let me help you," Anek said, standing up. With some effort, he helped Nivin to her feet. Upon standing, she found she was still weak and dizzy, but moving was not nearly as arduous as it had been upon first waking.

"We should go back to the spring and drink our fill before we move on," Brand said. "We'll be moving uphill. It will be sweaty work."

Brand led the way as they weaved between the trees back to stream's bubbling source. Nivin could not manage without leaning heavily on Anek. Every step felt like a jolt to her sense of balance. By the time they had reached the spring, she was exhausted and ready to rest again. However, the site of her waking made her shiver with fear, and she could not forget the claps of thunder that had reverberated over the mountainside. After the three of them drank as much as their stomachs could hold, they started to move away.

"Wait," Brand said, coming to a stop. "Nivin, I think we ought to make some kind of covering for your feet."

Nivin shrank at the mere thought of her feet being enclosed. "No. I need to feel where I am stepping."

"It is dangerous to go barefoot. I have some skins from the squirrels, and we could use fabric from your skirt as wrappings."

"I said no."

"It's no use arguing with her," Anek said. "I already

tried."

Brand sighed. "Very well. Let's continue on, then."

CHAPTER ELEVEN

Brand led their way, trying to pick out the smoothest path the mountainside had to offer. Knowing neither of his companions was as agile as he was, he kept several paces ahead of them to ensure no obstacles caught them off guard. However, not even half an hour after they had started their ascent, Nivin's knees buckled and she stumbled with a yelp.

Brand whirled around at the sound. Nivin sat on the ground clutching her knee, and Anek hovered over her like a fussy mother.

Hastily, Brand slid back down the slope to where they were. "Are you hurt?

"I skinned my knee," Nivin hissed.

"Let me see." Brand knelt by her side and examined the injury. The fabric of her short leggings had been torn just over her kneecap. The scrape itself was not deep;

several pinpricks of blood dotted the wound and a bruise was beginning to form. "This is practically nothing. You'll be fine."

Nivin grimaced. "It doesn't feel like nothing."

"It's fine. I promise." Brand looked up at Nivin's face. Her eyes watered from the pain. He gave her what he hoped was a reassuring smile, and then remembered she could not see him at all. To encourage her, he patted the top of her leg just above her knee gently. Nivin shifted uncomfortably at his touch. At first, Brand thought he must have hurt her somehow, but then the awkwardness of the situation occurred to him. He had been thinking of her as a travel companion and not a woman—he had carried her while she was unconscious without giving a second thought to her femininity. In any other circumstance, his reassuring touch would constitute impropriety worthy of a slap. He yanked his hand back from her leg and heat rose to his face. He was about to stutter out an apology when she spoke.

"I feel too weak to go on. I don't even think I can stand."

"We're too exposed on the mountainside like this," Brand said. The trees were thinner along the steep slopes, where the soil was not stable enough to anchor their roots. "We have to keep moving. We'll find a way."

Nivin reached up, feeling for Anek's hand. "Oh, Anek. How I do miss your strength."

"*You* miss it?" Anek grumbled. "I couldn't even hold you up when your legs went out. How do you think that makes me feel?"

"I might be able to carry you for a spell," Brand said. He was exhausted already, but now that Nivin was not limp weight he might be able to manage it. "All you need to do is stand up. Can you try that?"

With a moan, Nivin started to push herself up from the ground. Brand and Anek each grabbed a hand and pulled her up. Brand had her put her arms around his neck and scooped up her legs piggy-back style, the way he had carried around the younger Champions before he had left the Council. Once again, her femininity made itself obvious. He could feel her chest pressing into his back, and the feeling of her legs wrapped around his arms and sides made heat rise all over his body. As they continued up the slope, however, frustration replaced the awkwardness of Nivin's body pressing against his. The sun was hot, and the warmth of her body combined with the extra physical exertion made sweat pour down his face.

The sun followed its arc, and toward the end of the afternoon it had slipped behind the mountains' crests, leaving the whole eastern slope covered in cool, relieving shade.

After three hours of carrying Nivin with only a few short breaks, Brand had to stop for a longer rest. His pulse thudded in his ears and his mouth seemed full of sand. The three of them rested in silence; Anek huffed and puffed from his exertions of climbing. Brand stretched his screaming back and shoulder muscles, wincing as he did.

After they had rested for a few minutes, Nivin's stomach gurgled noisily.

The noise reminded Brand how hungry he was, too. Soon, the clouds would become rosy and they would need to find a place to rest for the night. If they were to light a fire, they would probably want to do that before dark, as well. His muscles protested noisily as he rose to his feet.

"We need to find a place to pass the night."

"What about behind those rocks up there?" Anek said, pointing.

Brand turned around. The large rocky formation protruding from the hillside might provide excellent coverage indeed. In his struggle to bear Nivin, he had been more focused on his footing than on scouting out what lay ahead. "I'm impressed, Anek. You'll be a master survivalist in no time."

Anek beamed.

"You two rest here. I'm going to scout out the path ahead."

Brand took a moment to scrutinize the landscape before he picked out a path. The rocks stood higher up on the slope and a few yards north of their current position. Once they reached them, the slope would become far gentler, but the terrain standing between them and their goal was treacherous. Long slides of dirt and stone had etched themselves into the mountainside, belying any hope there could be stable footing.

Brand looked around, hoping to find a more easily attainable place for them to pass the night. There were too few trees on this steep part of the slope to shield them from unfriendly eyes, and the trees did not grow thick again until the shallower slope above the rocks.

He turned his gaze straight upward. There seemed to be something of a shelf not too far above them. It might be stable enough to offer them safe passage over to the rocks. Slowly, he started to work his way up the hillside. Once he had reached the shelf, he looked back down at where Nivin and Anek sat. "It is a bit tricky, but if you can make it, the footing is more stable up here. Do you think you can manage it?"

Anek grimaced. "I suppose I can give it a try, but what about Nivin?"

"I'll help her. Just worry about yourself."

Anek began crawling his way up to the shelf, muttering under his breath the whole way. He slid back a couple of times, but managed to make it to the shelf in a couple of minutes. He sat down, panting. "I think I miss the plains. I've had enough of hills and mountains."

"We'll make it." Brand clapped Anek's shoulder. "I hope."

Anek rolled his eyes. "Thanks for the inspiration."

Brand sidled his way back down the slope to help Nivin. "I can't carry you. The pitch is too steep. But I'll take your hand. As we're going up, do not try to stand up straight. Lean forward as much as you can. Are you ready?"

Nivin drew a lip into her mouth. "If I fall?"

"You'll only slide back down to where we are now. It will hurt, but you won't fall off the mountain."

"I don't know if I can do it. I feel so dizzy."

"That's just the altitude. You'll be fine. Take my hand."

Nivin chuckled. "Here you are, a year and a half younger than me, and I'm the one acting like a frightened child."

Brand tilted his head. "You're only seventeen?"

"How old did you think I was?"

Brand ran his eyes over her slender curves. Heat rose to his face and he looked at the ground. "Honestly, I've been more preoccupied with your safety. Let's go." Brand took her hand and they began their ascent. Nivin's face was white as they went, and her grip on his hand was so tight his fingers grew numb. When she stumbled and slid back about a foot, she let out a short scream.

Brand barely kept his own footing. "You're fine. Just keep going. We're almost there."

Once they had reached the shelf, it was a straightforward path to the rocks. Nivin was able to walk, but she still clung to Brand's hand tightly.

When they were only a few paces away, Brand stopped short and stared.

An even, precise rock stairway cut its way down through the mountainside, passing directly between the boulders and snaking in perfect switchbacks all the way down. The angles of the slopes had hidden it from their sight until they had reached this vantage point.

Anek tilted his head. "Are those stairs?" He laughed. "We should've taken them."

Tension gathered between Brand's shoulders as he looked at it. "Keep your voice down. Move quietly." They went forward until they were behind the rocks, right next to the stairs. "This was recently cut. There is hardly any weathering on the stone at all." Brand looked up the stairway, which stopped only a few yards above them, then looked back down along the mountainside. "There can't be solid rock all the way down. Some of that had to have been moved into place."

Nivin tightened her grip on Brand's hand. "Something is wrong."

"I know. There's only one thing that could have done this. We need to get out of here."

"No, I mean—"

Thunder rumbled through the earth beneath them and one of the giant rocks to their side started to crack open.

A clawed fist thrust out.

"Spawn!" Brand shouted. He pushed Nivin behind him and held his arms out to shield her. Instinctively, he reached for the sword he had lost long before waking up in Zerabar, his heart leaping into his throat as his hand grasped at nothingness. He swallowed back panic as he cast about for something—anything—he could use as a weapon.

The rock cracked open and fell away like the shell of an egg, leaving the creature in a heap of broken stones. With features of both dragon and man, yet a true likeness of neither, it was unmistakably one of Scylla's offspring. Manlike in form, it stood seven feet tall. Gray scales the color of rock covered its whole body, riddled with spikes. Cruel snakelike eyes glared from its flat scaly face. The claws on its hands and feet were like small scimitars, as black and shiny as polished obsidian.

Brand clenched his fists and glanced over his shoulder at Anek and Nivin. "Get away from here."

His eyes wide with fear, Anek took Nivin by the wrist and started to lead her away.

Brand picked up a sizeable rock from the ground. If he could not hurt the spawn with it, at least it would distract it long enough for Anek and Nivin to make an escape. He cocked his arm and lobbed the stone at the advancing creature.

The spawn screeched—a sound like rock scraping on rock—and waved its hand as though it was swatting away a fly. With a low rumble of thunder, the stone disintegrated in midair, turning into a cloud of powder that was swept away by the breeze.

Brand's pulse thudded in his ears as the realization

swept through him. Every spawn had its own peculiar set of powers, and this one had power over rock. How else could the stone staircase have been made so precisely and evenly? Anything Brand might have as a defense against the spawn was rock—the one thing it had total control over.

It leapt into the air with an unnatural frog-like jump and transformed into a cluster of jagged rocks at the peak of its arc. Brand dove out of the way, barely avoiding the sharp projectiles. Heart racing, he jumped back to his feet. As soon as the rocks hit the ground, the spawn rematerialized and took off running after Nivin and Anek.

It closed the few yards in seconds.

Obsidian flashed.

With a roar, Anek stumbled forward as the claws sliced across his lower back. He wheeled around, fists balled, and landed a blow squarely on the spawn's chest. Unmoved, the spawn retaliated with two fists to Anek's gut. Anek staggered back, almost toppling to the ground. Nivin scrambled backwards several steps, holding her arms out defensively.

The spawn turned its gaze to Nivin.

As if she could feel the cruel eyes upon her, she froze.

Brand charged the spawn with a yell. To attack it without weapons was as vain as an ocean breaker throwing itself against rock, but he had no other recourse. The spawn whipped around, extending its claws like a fistful of daggers. Brand ducked.

The claws missed the top of his head by an inch.

"Run!" Brand shouted.

Anek grabbed Nivin by the hand again and ran, dragging her after him.

Like a hound following a scent, the spawn gave chase. It leapt through the air, shifting into the deadly cluster of shrapnel. Brand watched in horror as the jagged rocks descended toward them.

In a blur of motion, a man emerged from behind one of the boulders and dived toward Anek and Nivin. He held up a large round shield, deflecting the spawn's attack. With a screech, the spawn changed back into its original form. Claws sparked on the shield as the spawn slashed at him. The man shouted and forced the shield against the spawn with a forward thrust, knocking it off balance. It stumbled back a few steps, hissing.

For a moment, the two stared each other down.

The spawn charged. It barreled into the man, throwing him to the ground. It raised its claws to tear the man's face open—but he heaved the shield up in time to block the strike. With a shout, he swung the shield upward, catching the spawn under the chin. A well-placed kick to the spawn's belly knocked it off him, and he jumped to his feet. Before it could get up, he bashed the edge of the shield down on the crown of the spawn's head. Screeching, the spawn held up its arms to protect itself as the man brought the shield down a second time. A sound like rocks breaking filled the air as the spawn's arm broke under the force of the blow. It shrieked in pain. The man lifted the shield and struck a final time, striking the spawn's head with such force it went limp and lay still.

Chest heaving, the man drew himself to full height and looked at Brand with an evaluating gaze. A dagger hung at the man's waist. Like Nivin, his eyes were onyx, but where her skin was pale, his was the color of freshly dug soil, rich and brown. He was tall and emaciated, and his dark beard and long hair were wild and unkempt. His clothes were tattered and threadbare, as if he had worn the same outfit for years. Freshly healed wounds and deep old scars covered his arms and face. He gestured for them to follow him and headed for the stone stairs.

Brand hesitated. The man's complexion marked him as a Thallan, which meant he was the best ally they could hope for—or a sworn enemy. "How do we know we can trust you?"

The man stopped short and turned around. "Because I just saved your lives, you pasty ingrate." His voice was hoarse, but his accent was unmistakably Freeman. "You *are* a Freeman, are you not?"

Relief swept through Brand. "I am. And by your speech, so are you."

"Then follow me. It won't be long before it wakes again." The man turned back toward the staircase and started down the steps.

"Wait," Brand said. "My friend is hurt."

"Not that badly," Anek protested, poorly disguised pain in his voice. The back of his shirt was striped with fresh blood. "Its claws only cut me the first time it got me. The second time, only its knuckles hit me."

"I have something that can help," the man said. "But we *must* leave."

Brand nodded. He walked over to Nivin and took her hand. She flinched at the touch. "It's only me, Nivin."

"That thing," Nivin said. "It—it was—"

"One of Scyllorin's spawn. We have to go."

Nivin in tow, Brand followed after the man as fast as he could. Anek took the rear. A short way down, the slope to the north of the stairs grew shallower, and trees covered the mountainside again. The man led them away from the stairs and into the trees.

Only a few moments after they had left the staircase, unnatural thunder pounded through the earth and a horrible screech rose high above them. Nivin tightened her grip on Brand's hand.

The man let out a short barking laugh. "Seems I've truly frustrated it this time."

Brand raised his eyebrows. "This time?"

"That thing and I have been trapped in a stalemate for two weeks now." The man paused and drummed his fingers against his shield. "At least, I think it has been two weeks. I...I lose track of time easily." He shook his head. "No matter what I do, I can't seem to get around it. I haven't yet found a way to kill it."

"It seems vulnerable to your shield," Brand said. "What kind of metal is it?"

"It isn't metal. It's granite of some kind. Remarkably light. Why the spawn can't affect it, I don't know. Other rock seems to be no trouble for it." The man paused and examined a vine as they passed it. He pulled away the bushy leaves to reveal fat green berries. "Pick as many of these as you can. Watch out for the thorns."

Brand looked at the plant more closely. "Bramblevine. I didn't know it grew this far south."

"Obviously, it does." The man turned his shield upside down into a bowl. He plucked berries from the vine and dropped them into the shield. "Hurry. That thing might be following us."

Brand released Nivin's hand and dropped to his knees, combing through the bushy leaves of the vine for berries. As he dropped a handful of berries into the shield, he glanced down at it, noticing a small ornate G cut into the rock. He was about to say something when Anek picked up one of the green globes between his thumb and forefinger.

The fat berry was minuscule in Anek's hand. "What are these?"

"Vinegar berries," Brand replied, turning his focus back to the vine. "Put on fresh wounds, they can stave off infection."

"You know your plants, I'll give you that," the man said. "What is your name?"

"I am Brand, Champion of the Freemen. My companions are Anek and Nivin."

The man let out a scoff. "A Champion. And how successful has your campaign against Scyllorin been? Because it doesn't seem to be going very well for you."

Brand chewed on the inside of his cheek, biting back a hundred stinging words. "My campaign against him lives as long as I do. And what about you, stranger? What is your name?"

The man stopped picking berries and stared at his hands for several long moments, as if the answer to the question was a difficult one. Finally, he took one of the berries and squeezed it until it burst. "I am Ordnance, Champion of the Freemen."

The answer hit Brand like a punch in the gut. He mentally combed through the list of previous Champions he had been made to memorize as part of his history lessons. "Ordnance? But he was—you were—sent seventeen years ago."

"Seventeen years," Ordnance muttered. "I wondered how long it had been." He shook his head. "That is enough berries. We should keep moving. I have somewhere we can all hide. The spawn hasn't yet found it, and I don't want it to."

"You were thought dead." Anger surged through Brand. "But you're a deserter! You survived, and you did not return to the Council."

Fire sparked in Ordnance's eyes. "A deserter? I have borne seventeen years of pain for the Council, and you think I'm a *deserter*? You don't even know the true meaning of sacrifice."

Brand clenched his fists. "I know the meaning of sacrifice."

Ordnance shoved an accusing finger against Brand's chest. "Not until you have spent half a lifetime in Scyllorin's prisons."

Anger turned to shame as Brand looked into Ordnance's face, a face hollow with pain, hunger, and exhaustion. "I—I didn't know."

Ordnance turned away and picked up the shield, being careful not to spill any of the berries. "Now that you are done levying accusations against me, we should go. Unless you care to insult me further."

"I am sorry."

"I don't care. Follow me." Ordnance led them deeper into the trees, until they came to a cave in the side of the mountain. He turned and looked at Anek as if sizing him up. "Go inside. It widens further in."

Anek gave Brand a questioning look.

Brand nodded.

Without further hesitation, Anek dropped to his hands and knees and crawled into the cave. Brand guided Nivin into the cave and was surprised to find how big the space inside was. It was not high enough for Anek to stand, but he could sit on the floor of the cave without scraping his head on the ceiling, and there was still space for Brand, Nivin, and Ordnance to fit in.

Ordnance lingered near the cave's entrance for a few moments. "I do not think it followed us." He turned his attention back to Anek. "You—what did he say your name was?"

"I'm Anek."

"And you, maiden?"

"Nivin."

"Anek, take off your shirt and lie on your stomach. Brand, mash those berries into a pulp. Nivin, there is a spring in the very back of the cave. I have left a water skin next to it. Bring water."

"She can't see," Brand said. "I'll get the water."

"I'm blind, not helpless," Nivin said, a touch of coldness to her voice.

A crooked smile crept onto Ordnance's lips. "The cave's floor is uneven, but that is the only danger. You should have no trouble."

"Is the water skin to the left or the right of the spring?"

"The right."

Nivin extended an arm and found the cave's wall, then followed it until she disappeared into darkness. Brand's stomach went cold as he watched her go. It had only been a few hours since she woke, and her steps were still a little wobbly.

"If she falls, we'll hear her," Anek whispered, as if sensing Brand's fear.

Only slightly reassured, Brand sat down and turned his attention to the vinegar berries. He found a small rock—a chunk of limestone that had broken away from the walls of the cave—and started to mash them up. Rosy light filtered through the trees into the cave, making the berries' bluish seeds look purple.

With a groan, Anek took off his shirt and lay prone on the floor of the cave. "All right. Now what?"

Ordnance walked over to him and examined his wounds. "Not too deep. Good. The vinegar berries should be enough to set you on the mend."

Brand finished mashing the berries and carried the shield over to Anek. "This is going to sting." He scooped up the pulp with two fingers and spread it over the stripes across Anek's lower back. Anek flinched and hissed through his teeth. While Brand applied the vinegar berries to Anek's wounds, Ordnance stood near the mouth of the cave, looking out into the twilight.

Brand silently chastised himself as he worked. Ordnance had saved them from the spawn, and Brand had called him a deserter. For a Champion, there was no transgression as deep or as shameful as desertion. It was a wonder Ordnance had chosen to continue helping them.

"There," Brand said, putting on the last of the mash. "That needs to sit for several minutes."

Grimacing, Anek nodded.

Brand looked over at Ordnance, who was nothing more than a silhouette against the fading light. He went over to Ordnance's side and bit his lip, trying to think of what to say. No apology he could offer would ever be enough to make up for the severity of his accusation. "Ordnance, I..."

"We are brothers," Ordnance said, not looking at Brand. "Our vows to defend Libertas against Scylla and Scyllorin unite us. Pain and fear and suspicion are what divide us."

Unsure of what to say, Brand simply nodded.

"Your companions are strange."

Brand let out a chuckle. "You hardly know the half of it."

"How did you come to be in the company of a blind girl and a giant?"

"To be honest, I'm still not entirely sure. I—"

"Brand!" Anek cried. "Listen!"

Ordnance jumped and snatched the dagger hanging from his belt, looking around with an expression of panic. "What? What is it?"

"Nothing like that. I think I hear Nivin."

Ordnance bit his lip and slowly replaced his dagger, eyes still darting around the cave. He muttered something to himself.

Brand strained his ears, catching a sound that echoed from the back of the cave.

Nivin was weeping.

CHAPTER TWELVE

"I'm blind, not helpless."

As Nivin spoke the words, she wanted nothing more than for them to be true. Since she had woken from the nothingness that had engulfed her for days, she had been completely dependent on Brand and Anek for everything. She could hardly even carry herself on her own feet, she was so weak. When she tripped and skinned her knee, she felt as though she was a child again, with her father helping her up from the ground. When she lost her footing and slid down the slope, she screamed like a little child. When the spawn had attacked them, she froze with fear when she realized it was looking at her. It took Anek's grabbing her by the hand to jolt her into motion again.

She still was unsure how she knew the spawn was looking at her, but she had known the moment it set its eyes upon her. Something about the way it moved while attacking them was disturbingly familiar. She had somehow sensed it was present even before it attacked, and from the moment Brand cried out she knew exactly where it was, as clearly as if she could see it. She knew it was manipulating rock and transforming itself, even though nobody had told her so.

She knew all these things, and was helpless to do anything about it.

But she was not about to let anyone save her from something as simple and harmless as fetching water.

"The cave's floor is uneven," Ordnance said, "but that is the only danger. You should have no trouble."

Nivin could handle uneven ground, and now that they were in a confined space, she was confident she could find her way. She could already hear the faint trickle of the spring. "Is the water skin to the left or the right of the spring?"

"The right."

Nivin extended an arm and found the cave's wall, using it as a guide to lead her to the back of the cave. She took each step carefully—the cave's floor was indeed uneven, and rough loose rocks littered the ground. As she progressed, the way sounds echoed told her the passage was narrowing. A sudden sensation of closeness made her hesitantly reach a hand up, where she found the ceiling was only a hand's breadth from the crown of her head. Crouching slightly, just in case the ceiling dropped further, she continued toward the sound of the spring.

Her feet came down in a puddle of icy water. Carefully, she reached out with both hands and found the wall of the cave only a foot in front of her. The spring gushed merrily from a crack in the rock and trickled down to the ground, where a fissure in the floor must have let the water out again, sinking somewhere down into the mysterious deeps of the mountains.

Now, all she had was the simple task of finding the water skin Ordnance had spoken of. She turned to her right and started groping along the floor of the cave, trying not to think about how she might disturb spiders or snakes in the process. After several minutes of searching, she still could not find the water skin.

Frustration boiled up inside of her. The accursed thing could be just an inch or two away from wherever she felt, and she would never know it.

She broke out sobbing, all of her fear and frustration and sorrow finally breaking through the veneer of calm she had forced upon herself. As much as she wanted to believe she was not helpless, she knew it was a lie. Outside the dungeons and her home, she was totally unable to perform the simplest of tasks, let alone climb mountains and fight horrific monsters.

"Nivin? Are you hurt?"

It was Brand. She smeared the tears away and cleared her throat. "No. I'm not hurt."

"What's wrong? Why are you crying?"

Hot shame rose to her face when she realized she was crying because she could not find a water skin, a simple problem that could have been fixed had she not been too proud to ask for help. *He will only think I am helpless if I tell him the truth.* "I—it's…it's nothing."

Brand laid a gentle hand on her shoulder. "I know how overwhelming…nothing…can be. I spent years training and all of this is almost too much for me. You were unprepared for everything that happened to you from the time you fled your city. That you are holding together as well as you are proves your mettle is a thousand times greater than mine." He chuckled. "That you're willing to walk deep into a cave without being able to see proves that."

Nivin's spirits lifted somewhat. "That's kind of you to say."

"It's true. I didn't mean to say you were helpless by offering to get the water. I only wanted to keep you safe. I hope you'll forgive me."

"Of course." Nivin bit her lip for a moment. "I can't find the water skin."

Brand laughed. "I don't know if I will be much help. It's so dark back here *I* can barely see."

"Ordnance said it was to the right of the spring." She took a couple of steps back, accidentally splashing through the icy puddle again. She hopped out of the puddle on the left side of the spring, shaking the cold water off her toes. Her heel came down on something soft. She reached down and picked it up.

The water skin.

"Apparently, he can't tell his left from his right." Nivin held up the water skin.

"At least you found it," Brand said, laughing even harder than before.

At the sound of his laughter, Nivin could not help but laugh too. She uncorked the water skin and held its mouth under the stream of water spilling out of the spring. Once the water skin was full, she drank as much as she could and refilled it. She handed it to Brand, who did the same.

"Thank you," Nivin said.

"For what?"

"For what you said. About my mettle." She sighed. "I have always hated that I need help with things. Living with my father, I had everything so well mapped out I hardly needed any help, except for when we were outside the dungeons or our house. I haven't been this needy since I was a little girl."

"If you had been raised in Libertas, you would know there's no shame in needing help. Especially when one has a difficulty like yours." Brand took her by the hand. "Come, now. Anek needs water, too."

They carefully made their way back to where the others were.

"Did you get lost?" Ordnance said.

"Only because you gave her bad directions," Brand countered. "The water skin was to the left of the spring."

Ordnance let out a short barking laugh. "Sorry. I was so preoccupied saving your lives from the spawn, I forgot."

Anek drank so much water that Nivin had to go back to the spring to refill the water skin, this time much more confident and able to do so without assistance. Once he had drunk his fill, he passed the water skin to Ordnance.

"I regret to say I have no food to share with you," Ordnance said. "And I even further regret to say we can't light a fire for fear of attracting that thing back here. It will be a cold and hungry night."

Anek chuckled. "I'm starting to get used to those."

"Perhaps we can distract ourselves by sharing our stories with each other," Brand said. "How does a lost Champion become found again?"

Ordnance was silent for a long moment. "It is not a pleasant tale." His raspy voice was tight with pain. "I wouldn't even know where to begin."

"I know your mission was different from that of the other Champions. The History of the Council of Champions says you were sent to seek knowledge, not to fight Scylla and Scyllorin."

"I never stopped to think that my name would be written in the Histories." Ordnance picked up a loose stone and threw it across the cave. "I suppose I should start with my departure. When I left the Council, I was not sure exactly which way to head. Since it is said that the Knights of Ardor slew many dragons and even prevailed against Scylla for a short time, I decided my first course of action should be to find out as much about them as I could. So, I departed Council City and headed for Sardraco."

"Nivin and Anek know nothing of our history," Brand interjected. He continued on in an explanatory tone. "Sardraco is where the Knights of Ardor are said to be from. It is one of the countries under Scyllorin's reign. Forgive me, Ordnance. Continue your tale."

"No trouble," Ordnance said. "Sardraco is a strange place, a land covered in mountains and dunes. I spent months there, asking as many questions as I could without raising suspicion. Since Sardraco shares a border with Thallas, I passed easily enough as a Thallan traveler."

"Thallan," Anek said. "Is that why your skin is so dark?"

"Well...yes. Thallas is the far-removed place of my ancestry. But I am a Freeman, first and last."

"But how can you be a Freeman if you're not from Libertas?"

"He is from Libertas, Anek," Brand said. "I told you that long ago, all of the nations except Libertas submitted or fell to Scyllorin. Thallas was one of the nations that submitted. A large group of them, refusing to bow to Scyllorin's reign, fled to Libertas. Ordnance is one of their descendants."

Nivin's mind spun. Libertas sounded like an impossible place—a nation that granted sanctuary and naturalization to refugees, a nation that protected the weak and disabled instead of reviling them. If a man from Rashaan were to set foot in Zerabar for any reason, he would be summarily executed. Her father had told her about his many battles against the dark-skinned Rashaans, saying the color of their skin showed them to be an inferior people. Nivin had never said anything to her father on the matter, but she had privately thought it was the things the Rashaans did that made them wicked, not something as simple as the hue of their skin. What someone looked like made no difference to someone who could not see.

She was surprised Anek had not reacted with fear to Ordnance, if his skin was indeed dark. Horrid tales of the Rashaans were told to terrify children and prove Zerabar's superiority. Perhaps his mother had never seen fit to fill his head with such nonsense.

"You will never find a group of Freemen more dedicated to Libertas than the Thallans," Brand continued.

"Yes," Ordnance said. "It is still something of a personal offense to us that our ancestors in Thallas gave in to Scyllorin's reign. I can't say I relished pretending to be from Thallas, but it served my purpose. I was able to move about and ask questions without drawing too much attention to myself. I inquired regarding the Knights, but most people knew nothing, and those who did were afraid to talk to me. I found almost no trace of the folklore at all— Scyllorin has done well in his quest to silence the stories.

But while I was there, I learned much about dragons. There are few left, and most of them live far in the north.

"Finally, after months of searching, I heard of a village where the Knights of Ardor supposedly came from, a small village on the border of Sardraco and Verderbera proper. The people there were small in stature with a mousy, cowed air about them. Like all the others, they were afraid when I asked about the Knights, but one of them, an ancient woman, drew me inside her house and told me all she knew. The stories she told me, Brand! I learned of things we had never even heard about the Knights of Ardor, though their names have indeed been lost. I thanked her and left, planning to head back to the Council and share all I had learned."

Ordnance slammed a fist on the ground. "I was betrayed!" He stood up and started pacing feverishly. "She told me everything she knew, right before she told the ten spawn who came to the village exactly the way I had gone!" He let out a groan. "They told me as much, using her as their mouthpiece."

Brand gasped softly.

"Their mouthpiece?" Anek asked. "What does that mean?"

Ordnance ignored him. "They took me. There was no way I could overpower them. They surrounded me before I even knew they were there. I thought they would kill me." His breathing became ragged. "I wish they had killed me." He plopped back down onto the floor of the cave and muttered quietly to himself for a long time.

"Ordnance?" Brand said, his voice filled with hesitation.

Ordnance simply continued to mutter for a few

moments, then fell silent. When he finally spoke again, his voice was small and weak and raspier than ever. "They took me to Scyllorin's castle in the heart of Verderbera." He audibly shuddered. "I was...they...they tortured me. No one asked me any questions. They just tormented me. For days." He fell silent again.

Chills shot down Nivin's spine. Despite the fact that torture was sanctioned by King Temere, Nivin's father had always told her in confidence that torture was wrong. He always had possessed a strong dislike for the executioner, despite the fact the jailor and the executioner worked closely together and were both held in high esteem by the king. The current executioner was exceptionally cruel and preferred to torture his charges to death, rather than killing them cleanly. The idea that a person might even survive torture was astounding to her.

After several moments, Ordnance found his voice. "I thought I would never experience worse pain than I suffered at their hands. I was wrong. After days in manacles, hanging from the wall, I woke from half-sleep to see a man in front of me. I knew at once it was Scyllorin, for he bore the staff I have seen pictures of so many times in the Histories. He told me I was sorely delayed in my arrival, and asked why, if I was a Champion, I had not made the futile attempt to slay his wife. I—I tried to be resolute. To say nothing. I tried." Ordnance drew a long hissing breath through his teeth. "I tried to say nothing which would give away the new strategy the Council had hoped to achieve with my mission. But he—he used magic unheard of. Tortured me without even laying a hand upon me. I tried so hard to be resolute, tried so hard...

"But I failed." He took several panting breaths. "I *failed.*

I cracked under the torture and told him my mission. When I told him I'd been sent to seek the knowledge needed to slay dragons, to aid the Council, he laughed. Like a madman. Then he tortured me for days—or hours, or weeks, I don't even remember—and threw me into the darkness of their dungeons.

"The dungeons were nearly as bad as the torture. The sounds alone were enough to drive one to insanity. The sounds of people screaming, crying out in mad gibberish—and a throbbing in the earth itself. Like thunder, in the ground. I thought it would shatter my bones.

"And worse, there was an air of—I can hardly describe it—it was like something ancient slithering unseen through the halls of the dungeon, as though the closer to the deeps it was, the more at home it was. I almost couldn't breathe sometimes. Perhaps I grew mad in my solitude, but I began to think—the presence was Scylla herself." Ordnance shivered when he said the words. "Incorporeally. Perhaps she feeds on the suffering of live souls as much as she does the bodies of her prey. I could think of no other reason for Scyllorin to let me live."

Nivin thought of how some of those who broke the Laws were treated. Her father had said that though it was never done publicly, a select few criminals had been kept alive instead of being sentenced to death, living a life worse than dying.

Was this what her father was facing, even now?

"He did it to break you more," Nivin said, clenching her fists at the thought. "He did it to cement in your mind that your life was pointless, all of your efforts useless."

Ordnance made a small choking sound. "If that was his goal, then he succeeded. I grew intimate with the fact that the mission the Council had given me was the most futile of missions, more pointless than trying to kill Scylla herself. And I was forced to conclude one thing, the one thing the Council would never accept, even after years of failure.

"Scylla is not a dragon. Not truly.

"There is no doubt that dragons do exist—I saw some of them in Sardraco. They are feral beasts, lacking the driving purpose Scylla possesses. I had convinced myself, however, that through some dark arts, Scyllorin had taught Scylla, altered her somehow, in the unholy unity of their marriage. I put all of my heart into believing this. What else has the Council ever allowed us to believe?" His voice sank to a murmur. "What else, what else?"

After several moments, Ordnance cleared his throat. "After my capture, all my faith in this notion was destroyed. There is no way the lurking presence in the dungeons was truly a dragon—that presence shook me deeper than any of the physical torture I suffered at their hands. I wondered if the Champions who had gone before me had suffered similarly, or if I was alone in my fate. The thought that I might be the only one to suffer this way hurt me even more."

There was a long period of silence in the cave, filled only with the sound of the trickling spring and the chaos of Nivin's thoughts. Ordnance's story had turned the aching hunger in her stomach into violent nausea.

At length, Brand spoke, his voice small. "And—and you were there these whole seventeen years?"

Ordnance scoffed. "Seventeen years, seventeen lifetimes—an eternity of darkness and pain and madness. I could not even tell when one day passed into the next.

"I tried so many times to end it. So many times. I

stopped eating and drinking, but once they realized what I was doing, they forced me to eat and drink. I tried to resist, tried not to swallow so I would choke and die, but it is amazing how long a man's reflexes will preserve him even when he has lost all will to live. I started to bash my head against the walls, and they tied me to a chair in the center of the room so I could not. I struggled at the chains until they cut my skin open, hoping infection would take me. But through some conjuring on Scyllorin's part, I never grew ill.

"At some point, I lost awareness. I sank into madness and became one of those voices screaming out in the unholy dark, longing for death, only existing on because I could do nothing else."

Tears stung in Nivin's eyes.

Ordnance said nothing more. He picked up another stone and cast it across the cave. Nivin heard him jump when the stone landed, as if he had not expected the sound at all.

"How did you escape?" Brand said.

Ordnance laughed humorlessly. "I died."

Nivin's mind spun in confusion. "What?"

"Well, obviously I didn't die, at least not in the sense where a man passes from one world to the next, but I died in that my body stopped functioning. My heart stopped, my lungs stopped, everything. For hours—or days—I knew nothing."

"But you…came back?" Anek said.

"I told you, I did not cross from one world to the next. I induced the state of death myself, and I woke from it of my own accord."

The cave was filled with stunned silence for a moment.

"You think me mad," Ordnance said. "Perhaps I am mad. But what I'm telling you is true. In the north of Sardraco, there was a group of men who lived in the mountains. They were violent, cultish men, who worshipped the dragons as gods.

"They practiced human sacrifice, but they genuinely believed you move to a higher plane of consciousness once eaten by a dragon. They developed a way to die without death—in order to wake from inside the dragon itself and be transported to a new holy place through the dragon's belly. I watched with fascination and terror as one man allowed himself to be eaten, dead. In a matter of minutes one could hear screams emanating from inside of the dragon. The men said it was the glorious sound of one world unfolding into the next.

"The men showed me how they induced the deathlike state. It was terrible and fascinating to watch. I could not stop no matter how my conscience pleaded with me to look away. They drew knives across their hands, and sucked on their own blood before they lay down and mumbled their chant until they grew silent. The chant consisted of five simple words in a foreign tongue.

"The men said it was the blood that enabled you to come back from the stupor of this death. I had nightmares of the things I saw for weeks afterward." Ordnance was quiet again, withdrawn inside himself for a few moments. "While I was imprisoned, I forgot nearly everything, forgot who I was, totally lost in madness. But one day, I came back to myself. I don't know what changed, whether Scyllorin's attention was focused elsewhere, but I realized that I was lying on the floor of my cell, unchained. Perhaps I had been without chains for years, held in place by my insanity. Nevertheless, in that moment, I remembered the dragon-worshipers. I imitated their ritual in one last desperate hope to escape.

"Once I had completed the ritual I knew nothing more—it was like a deep, deep sleep, without dreams. I had no thoughts at all, for who knows how long. I started to regain a consciousness of some sort, but it was as though I was reliving every torture I had suffered at Scyllorin's hands, with dragons all around, mocking me. Finally, I woke. I was buried in a shallow grave, with worms and vermin eating me alive. I do not know how long I had been buried—days, perhaps? I coughed and spewed dirt out of my mouth as I dug my way toward the surface.

"I don't know how long I lay there, picking at the lacerations the worms had made in my skin. They were not deep at all, but they itched and burned. I suppose I was so dead even maggots couldn't tell I still lived. Worse, some had crawled inside my mouth and nose." He retched at the mere recollection.

"At some point, the sun rose. And I saw sunlight." Ordnance drew a breath and released it in a sigh of relief. "Sunlight. And I was truly myself once more. Yes. Myself. I remembered who I was, my training, my goal. The mission comes first. There is always time for everything else after.

"So, I determined that I had to complete my mission and bring knowledge back to the Council. Using the rising sun as my guide, I started my journey back to Libertas. I was some distance from Scyllorin's stronghold, in a graveyard that stretched on for miles. As I made my way through the graveyard, I stumbled across something rising up out of the ground—the shield I have with me now. It was good that I took it, because I was able to defeat a spawn that stood in my way with it. Whether or not I killed it, I don't know. But there is a fair chance that Scyllorin is aware of my escape.

"The rest of my journey here was fairly uneventful, until I encountered this accursed spawn building the staircase. It has kept me trapped here, not allowing me to escape. Even when I have been able to knock it down, I can't get far before it ends up herding me back in this direction. And more than once, it has injured me. But I won't let it take me. Never again. I'll kill myself first."

Awkward silence filled the cave. Nivin frowned, thinking of the Zerabari prisoners who managed to commit suicide before being taken to the executioner.

Brand got up and slowly paced the cave. "You said you have been here for two weeks now?"

"Not here, exactly. As the spawn has made its way up the mountainside, I have progressed along with it. It seems unwilling to leave its task for too long, but it is determined to keep me from escaping." Ordnance spat on the ground. "Like prison, prison walking," he muttered. "I won't go back."

"Of course you won't. You are free now."

Ordnance scoffed.

"But you said it built that massive staircase in two weeks?"

"It did. And other spawn have come through, as well as a group of men who were clearly scouts. They ascended the stairs with complete ease. I can only think of one reason for Scyllorin to build this staircase."

Brand hissed through his teeth. "He must intend to mobilize an army against the Freemen. Normally these mountains would cut off troops, but this allows them to cut straight into the heart of our land."

"That is what I thought, too. But why now? Why would Scyllorin send an army to attack us, when for centuries he has only sent spawn to terrorize us?"

"Pock," Brand said. "He told Scyllorin it didn't matter how much sorcery he used to protect himself, the Freemen would win, because we had discovered the secret to their undoing. He said it to distract him, so I could escape. It was only a desperate bluff." Brand was silent for a moment. "Scyllorin must have believed him, after all."

"Who is Pock?"

"My partner Champion. We fought Scylla and Scyllorin face-to-face—just under two weeks ago."

"Partner Champion? They sent two of you?"

"The Council thought it would increase our chances of victory."

"Where is Pock now?"

Brand was quiet for several moments. He could not hide the touch of shakiness in his voice when he finally spoke. "He gave his life for the cause."

"As have most," Ordnance said.

Brand cleared his throat. "Yes. As have most."

Nivin bit her lip. For centuries, the Freemen had been sending Champions, most of whom died—or worse. It made her wonder why the Freemen continued to do something so clearly doomed to failure.

"If so many Champions have died, why keep sending them?" Anek said, as if voicing her thoughts.

"What other choice do we have?" Brand said. "I told you we cannot mount an invasion against Verderbera, but neither can we stand by and let Scyllorin's reign continue unchallenged."

"But surely there must be another way."

"And what would an outsider know?" Ordnance snapped. "How did you come by these new companions, Brand?"

Brand chuckled dryly. "Even you might find our story too outlandish. After I managed to escape Scyllorin, I tried to head south for the gap between the mountains and the sea. But Scyllorin pursued me, driving me to the cliffs that line the coast. Rather than face capture, I cast myself to the sea in a desperate attempt to escape." He was silent for a moment. "I am ashamed that I fled."

"Any fate is better than facing capture at their hands," Ordnance said, his voice a low growl. "How did you escape?"

"I still don't understand it. For a moment, it was as though something pulled me back to the surface, but then something stronger took hold of me and sucked me down. There was the sound of thunder—as if Scylla was approaching—and faint voices I could not understand. I remember grabbing hold of something just before I passed out. When I woke, I was on the ground, surrounded by these two. The sea was gone, as if I was miles away from it. It was night, and when I looked up at the sky to try to find out where I was, I was astounded. The stars we know were gone—and the sky was filled with constellations I had never seen before in my life."

"What?" Ordnance's voice was filled with shock. "Are you certain?"

"Absolutely."

"Do you know what this means? It means the old woman was right!"

"What are you talking about?"

"That woman who told me all she knew about the Knights of Ardor—she said the Knights spoke of being from a different world, a land where the sky was filled with stars completely unlike our own!"

Nivin's mind reeled. Was it possible they had not just been transported to a different country she had never heard of, but a different world altogether? Did the Charybda change everything, or was it simply a portal—a narrow strait between two worlds?

Ordnance turned toward Nivin and Anek. "Have you heard of the Knights of Ardor?"

Nivin ran her hand across the ground, longing for something that might be a handhold in reality. "Not until we met Brand."

"Of course," Ordnance said, a touch a disappointment to his tone. "The Knights of Ardor lived centuries ago. Perhaps they were not even famed in your world. But tell me—how did you come to be back here?"

"We passed through another Charybdon and woke in the mountains," Anek said.

"Charybdon?"

"It is what Nivin calls the portals," Brand said.

"So you have heard of these—Charybdons?"

Nivin's insides froze. "No. I know nothing about them."

"But you told me you had heard of them," Brand said, sounding betrayed.

Nivin swallowed. "I lied. I was afraid of what you would think. I actually know nothing. But it seems I know everything about the Charybda. Nothing and everything at the same time. I don't know how. Even the name just came to me. Everything else is hidden from me."

"They change the people who go through them," Anek said. "Brand looked different in our world than he does here. I was strong there and couldn't think straight, but I am weak here and clear-minded."

"How have the—Charybda—changed you, Nivin?" Ordnance said.

"They haven't." Nivin hugged herself. "It seems I can use them, though. We were all hurt, and I was able to heal us with one—a tiny one. I still have no idea what I did."

"Remarkable. From what I have seen in my travels, I will doubt nothing. Perhaps your hidden knowledge can be of use to the Council."

"I don't know. Something about them seems…wrong."

"Either way, the Council must know of this."

Nivin cringed at the thought of standing before a whole council of people. Her whole life had been one continuous effort to stay hidden in the shadows, away from the eyes of people who would want her dead if they knew her secret. Now she had an even bigger secret, one that made her blindness pale in comparison, one that she herself did not understand.

"Agreed," Brand said. "And we must warn them of Scyllorin's invasion."

"We'll need to find a way around that spawn, first," Ordnance said.

"That sounds like a task for the morning. Anek still needs to rest. We all need rest."

"You go ahead. I'll keep the first watch."

Nivin, Anek, and Brand settled in for the night while Ordnance stood near the entrance of the cave. Nivin kept tossing and turning on the hard cold floor of the cave, shivering from the cool of the mountain night air.

"Are you cold, Nivin?" Anek asked softly.

"Yes," Nivin said.

"Here—come sleep next to me. Murm always did in the winter. She said I kept her warm, and it helped her aching bones."

Nivin thought back to the cold winter nights as a little girl when she would snuggle up next to her own father. Her father had said that Anek was likely as old as forty— certainly old enough to be her father. Now that Nivin was older, though, she had ceased sleeping beside her father in the wintertime. But sheltered as he was, Anek was probably clueless as to any more prurient interpretations of such an arrangement. She hesitated for only a second longer before the cold finally convinced her to accept his offer. She moved over and lay down next to Anek, cuddling up to him for warmth.

"I always wondered what it would be like to have a little sister," Anek said, putting his arm around her. "Now I know."

Nivin smiled, and all fears of impropriety fled her mind. "Good night, Anek."

"Good night."

Soon, both Anek's and Brand's breathing became soft and shallow, reminding Nivin of the way her father breathed when he slept.

Ordnance muttered almost inaudibly under his breath, as if he were talking to himself.

Nivin lay awake for hours, terrified the nothingness would take her again.

CHAPTER THIRTEEN

Sleep did not come easily to Nivin.

Ordnance's constant muttering only ceased when Brand finally took the next watch and Ordnance lay down to sleep. Even then, she could hear him twitching in his sleep, occasionally calling out *no* or *never again* in fevered tones. Once, he shot upright with a panicked shout, breathing heavily, before he lay back down and grew quiet again. Nivin wondered whether he suffered through every night this way, or if it was only because they had forced him to relive the experience of his capture through his tale. The thought of his experiences made her blood run cold, keeping her awake even longer.

Eventually, however, the soft cadence of Anek's breathing lulled her into sleep, and she woke the next morning to faint light and the sound of Brand and Ordnance speaking to each other in low voices. Next to her,

Anek still slept peacefully. She disentangled herself from his grasp and stood up, stretching the stiffness out of her muscles. Despite lying awake so long, she found the small amount of sleep she had was surprisingly refreshing: a peaceful, dreamless sleep, free of the dark nothingness she had feared would find her.

"Good morning," Brand said softly.

Nivin smiled. In just a few short days, the sound of Brand and Anek's voices had come to be synonymous with safety, and to hear Brand so calm put her completely at ease. "Good morning."

"Come sit with us. Ordnance found us some breakfast."

Nivin extended a hand out in front of her and walked toward the sound of Brand's voice. After several steps, his hand took hold of hers. She sat down cross-legged on the floor, grateful the short leggings she wore beneath her dress kept her position from being immodest.

"Here," Brand said, pressing something into her hand. "It's lamb's quarters. Not the heartiest breakfast, but it will keep us alive for now."

She ran her fingers over the long slender stem covered in leaves. Hesitantly, she pulled off one of the leaves and popped it into her mouth. It reminded her of tough, strongly flavored spinach. She thought it would be much better if it was in a stew.

"Brand has been telling me about Zerabar," Ordnance said. "He says you and Anek were fugitives, because of your...abnormalities."

Nivin's stomach twisted. She did not much feel like explaining all of Zerabar's injustices again. "Yes."

"I do not know how anyone could stand by and do

nothing when such unjust laws are being carried out."

"I didn't do nothing," Nivin said, tightening her grip on the lamb's quarters. "I prepared meals for the condemned, even though it was illegal for me to do so."

"Your father let you do that?" Brand said, his voice filled with surprise.

"Yes." Nivin bit her lip. "He is—was—not an evil man."

"I didn't mean you," Ordnance said hastily. "I meant the nation as a whole."

"There was a revolt a few generations ago, called the Teratisma Rebellion." Nivin thought back to sitting on her father's lap, listening to him telling the long tale. "A midwife—a woman who delivers and inspects babies to be sure they are not abominations—started the rebellion after her son lost an arm. She thought it was unfair that infants born without arms were sentenced to death, but those who lost arms due to injury were not. It ended poorly. It was the reason they declared Condemnation on those who are deformed later in life as well as those who are born abominations. You would be surprised at how many think the Laws are just and necessary. The nation doesn't merely stand by while injustice is done. Most people support it. Those who oppose it can do nothing. It's not so different from your history of Thallas, but those who would leave Zerabar have nowhere to go except death."

"I spoke out of ignorance," Ordnance said. "Forgive me."

Nivin sighed. "It's not your fault." She stuffed a handful of leaves into her mouth.

Anek stirred and yawned loudly. "You started breakfast without me?"

"We wanted to let you sleep," Brand said. "Let me see how your back is." He rose and walked over to where Anek was. "Much better. Let's wash the rest of the vinegar berries off and you can put your shirt back on."

Nivin worked on eating her lamb's quarters while Brand fetched water and cleaned off Anek's wound. Anek let out a high-pitched gasp when the cold mountain water spilled down his back, and fabric rustled as he put his shirt on.

"I'll never be warm again," Anek said. "That water was pure ice, and all we have to eat is cold lamb's quarters."

"Sadly, I don't have any hot grits to feed you," Nivin said. Just thinking about a bowl of the steamy, buttery cereal made her mouth water. "My father always said my grits were the best."

"I doubt they were as good as my Murm's." Anek sighed heavily, then let out a laugh. "Why are you torturing me by talking about grits, anyway?"

Ordnance let out a stifled yelp at the word *torturing*.

"What are grits?" Brand said hastily, as if to amend Anek's mistake. "They don't sound appetizing."

"If you've never heard of grits, we really must be in another world," Anek said.

"They are ground cereal grains, cooked in hot water," Nivin said. "You put salt and butter on them. You can serve eggs over the top of them, too."

"When we reach Council City, you can show us how to make them," Brand said, handing Nivin more lamb's quarters. "If we ever make it to Council City. How are we going to get past that spawn?"

"I doubt we can escape it unless we kill it," Ordnance growled.

"No. We'll have to outsmart it. We have no weapons, save your shield and dagger."

"There's an old bow with a few arrows and a hunting knife a little deeper in the cave—they must have been left here by a hunter. But those won't make a difference. Its scales are as hard as rock. I used to have an old sword I found in the graveyard, but the sword shattered when I attacked that thing with it."

"Scyllorin's spawn are not invincible. All of the ones I've ever read about have had at least one crucial weak point—and many of them have been slain with swords or other weapons in the past."

Ordnance scoffed. "Obviously, not *all* of them are vulnerable to swords or other weapons. Is reading the only experience you have with spawn?"

"No," Brand said, his voice cracking at the top of the word. He hesitated for a moment. "But I've never killed one."

Nivin shuddered when she thought of the spawn, how she had been able to sense it so clearly. Something about it had been horribly familiar, but the more she thought about it, the more the answer seemed to elude her.

As if to answer her question, faint thunder resounded through the ground.

The thunder. It was the thunder that pulsed through the earth when the spawn exerted power, the same thunder that Scylla sent cracking through the sky. And though she had not realized it until now, the spawn seethed with the same swirling lights as its mother. It somehow manipulated the forces behind the Charybda to control its power over rock.

The same way she had manipulated the nascent

Charybdon to heal them.

The realization hit her like a punch to her gut. She had used the same kind of forces as the spawn, the kind of forces that had sent her spiraling into the familiar nothingness that had welcomed her like a long-lost child.

The kind of forces that tore portals between worlds.

"The spawn must have started working on the stairs again," Ordnance said. "I don't know how it recovers so quickly."

"Then it's distracted, isn't it?" Anek said. "Maybe we could just walk away from the stairs and continue on our way."

"Don't you think I have tried that? It has pursued me every time."

A terrifying notion wormed its way into Nivin's mind. "Maybe there is something I can do. I don't relish the idea, but it may be our only option."

"What is that?" Brand said.

"Do you remember when I healed us?"

"Barely. I was so delirious that I don't remember anything save waking up to see you healing yourself."

"I remember." Anek's voice was small. "Who could forget?"

Nivin felt a pang of guilt, knowing how much the whole ordeal had terrified Anek. "Well...the tiny Charybdon I used to heal us...it fell off of Scylla."

Silence engulfed the cave.

Nivin swallowed. "As she flew over us, I sensed she was...almost creating them, full of the same strands of light that make up the Charybda. The spawn is the same way, though not as powerful as Scylla. It used those powers to manipulate rock."

Ordnance shifted. "Scylla. Scylla creates the Charybda?"

"Not all of them—I don't think. Scylla was nowhere near Zerabar, and there was a Charybdon there."

"But the Charybdon you used to heal us—that was created by Scylla?" Brand said. He sounded nauseous, and Nivin could hardly blame him.

"I think. I don't know. But I know somehow, I was able to manipulate it, to make it do what I needed it to."

"And you think you might use your hidden knowledge to somehow defeat the spawn?" Ordnance said.

"Yes. If I could use the power that came off of Scylla, then maybe I can use the power from this spawn—even if it isn't as powerful as Scylla was."

"What would you do?"

Nivin's shoulders slumped. "I don't know. Do the first thing my instincts tell me."

"That's far too much risk," Brand said. "What if your instincts fail you?"

"Her instincts haven't led us wrong yet," Anek said, his voice defensive. "Why should they now?"

"Tell me honestly, Nivin. Do you really think you can defeat that thing? Do you trust your instincts that much?"

Nivin hesitated. She did not know what would be worse—being unable to trust her instincts or being able to trust them fully. "I—I don't know."

"Then we can only set you against the spawn as a last resort. There must be something else we can do."

Ordnance huffed. "I've tried two weeks of 'something else' to no avail. If she has a chance of defeating it, I say we let her try."

"No. Not unless we absolutely have to. Think about

it—Nivin is the only one who can see the Charybda. She might be the key to this whole mystery about the Knights of Ardor. If she can see the power Scylla uses, then she might even be the key to destroying Scylla."

"If she can defeat the spawn, then we will know if she can help us destroy Scylla. She might prove to be the only effective weapon we have."

Brand slammed his hand on the ground. "We can't risk anything happening to her—we have to get her to Council City safely!"

Nivin shrank internally. Now Brand thought she could somehow help them defeat that thing that blocked out the sun, and Ordnance thought of her as little more than a weapon. Furthermore, they assumed she would be willing to help them in their quest against Scylla and Scyllorin, without even stopping to consider that maybe she did not want to. No, they expected her to go before a whole Council to explain the powers she did not even understand, and then use those powers to defeat a reign that had gone undefeated for centuries.

"I want to keep Nivin safe, too," Anek said, the slightest edge of a growl to his voice. "But she isn't some weapon you two can argue about. Doesn't she have a say?"

Brand sputtered. "Nivin—I—I didn't mean to—of course you have a say."

Even as he said it, Nivin could hear the silent pleading under his words, begging her to help them. Libertas was a nation worthy of assistance, there was no question of that. When she thought of how in Libertas she would be welcomed and cared for rather than sentenced to death, she wanted nothing more than Scyllorin's defeat. But the thought that she was the key to Scylla's destruction made her stomach toss. Her ability to see and manipulate the Charybda was disturbing enough on its own.

"I don't know if I can actually help you. I don't even know if I could do anything against the spawn. It was just a thought I had. Maybe there is something else we can try."

"I can think of no other way to defeat it," Ordnance said.

"Can we outwit it?" Brand said.

"And how would you go about doing that? Unless we kill it, we'll be pinned here forever."

Pinned. Nivin remembered her father telling a story about how he and several other soldiers had been pinned in a gully by a Rashaan general for days. Her father had recently earned a fine coat of mail for admirable service, which they eventually offered to the general as a bribe. The general had been so delighted with the offering that he let them escape. Her father always laughed when he told the story, telling Nivin she should never underestimate the power of vanity and greed.

"Maybe if we bring the spawn an offering of some kind, it will let us approach," Nivin said. "Maybe we could make a bargain with it." She thought of the horrible screeching sound the creature had made. "Do the spawn understand human speech?"

"Yes, but they do not speak it," Brand said. "And they are crafty—I don't think it would be convinced."

"I don't know," Ordnance said. "It might work. Some of the spawn that terrorized Sardraco demanded to be worshipped."

Nivin smiled. "Never underestimate the power of vanity and greed."

"Hmm." Brand was quiet for a moment. "It is true that

they are prideful. There are records of them demanding worship when they have attacked Libertas."

"I thought you said they couldn't speak," Anek said.

"They can't, unless they use a mouthpiece," Ordnance said.

"You mentioned a mouthpiece before. What is that?"

"The spawn can force a human to speak for them. They use their power to sink their arms into someone—as if they are dipping their arms in water—and then take over the person's voice. As far as I know, it doesn't kill the person—but the spawn usually kill them when they are done, anyway."

Nivin shuddered. The powers the spawn employed—the same kind of powers she herself had manipulated—could be used to take over another person's body. How was it she was able to *see* them? The more she learned about them, the more she wanted nothing to do with them. Even if using the power of the Charybda was the only way they could defeat the spawn, Nivin fleetingly thought she would rather stay trapped in the cave.

It was not until Nivin became aware of the sound of the trickling spring that she realized no one had spoken for several minutes. She finished eating the rest of her lamb's quarters, hoping to quell the hunger that lingered in the pit of her stomach despite the horrors they had been discussing.

Brand clicked his tongue. "What could we possibly offer the spawn that it would be willing to bargain with us? I can't think of anything we have that might appease it."

Nivin thought for a moment, brushing her hand across the rough floor of the cave. Her fingers found a small stone. "Rock. It has power over rock, so if we bring it some, perhaps it will see that as a sacrifice of some kind. We could gather some of the loose stones that are in the cave and pile them up on the shield."

"That's a possibility," Anek said. "And since it can't control the granite in the shield, giving the shield up might satisfy it, too."

"That shield has some property that makes it effective against the spawn," Ordnance said. "It would be a mistake to hand it over. What if we encounter more spawn?"

"If we cannot escape this spawn, whether or not we encounter more is a moot point," Brand said.

"And what if it's not appeased? What then? We'll have no way to defend ourselves from it!"

"If it comes to that, Nivin will have to try to overpower it, and while she keeps it distracted, we can reclaim the shield."

Ordnance muttered something under his breath. He sighed loudly. "Fine. How do you propose we do this? We give the shield and rocks to the spawn and it just lets us go?"

"No. Only two of us take the sacrifice. That should keep the spawn distracted long enough for the others to escape. Assuming the spawn accepts the offering and lets the first two go, then everyone can meet higher in the mountains."

Nivin barely even heard as Ordnance and Brand worked out exactly how they would find each other again. All she could think of was what Brand had said: she would have to try to overpower the spawn if the bargaining failed. She imagined standing by helplessly, her supposed instincts having failed her, while the spawn tore its claws through her companions. It would all be her fault. Both of the options they were considering were her ideas.

It was not until Nivin heard Ordnance say her name that she was able to focus on the present.

"So who will go with Nivin to take the sacrifice?"

"I'll go with Nivin," Anek volunteered.

"No," said Brand. "I should go. Ordnance can't, since it seems to have so much animosity toward him. And no offense to you, my friend, but since you are lacking in strength…"

Anek sighed. "I understand."

"Well, let's not wait any longer," Ordnance said, standing up.

For the next several minutes, they all milled around the cave, picking up as many loose stones as they could. Anek stayed on his hands and knees, since he could not stand up. Nivin crawled around too, using her hands to search the ground. They piled as many rocks onto the shield as Brand said he could carry.

"Do you really think this will work?" Anek said. "Maybe you two should take the hunting knife, just to be on the safe side."

Brand sighed. "I wish we could. After being unarmed so long, it's a tempting prospect. But the knife will do us no good. The spawn will only see us as a threat that way. Nivin's instincts will have to be enough."

"And if nothing else, if the spawn sees the shield it might think Brand and Nivin killed me," Ordnance said. "That might be enough to appease it."

A dark thought crept across Nivin's mind. "Your blood would appease it even more."

"*What?*" Ordnance scrambled away from her. "What are you saying? Stay back!"

"No, I mean—perhaps if you cut your hand and sprinkle some blood on the rocks, it will be even more satisfied with our offering."

The way Ordnance laughed in response sent chills down Nivin's spine. It was a cold laugh, lifeless and flavored with bitterness. "So once again I must cut myself to escape. Why not? Maybe I'll find all the answers to my every problem are just waiting to be cut out of me. Give me that knife."

"Ordnance..." Brand began, an unsettled edge to his voice.

"No, no, she is right. Little else satisfies Scyllorin's spawn better than blood and suffering. After what I've endured, another cut will be of no consequence. I'll do it."

There was the sound of something being picked up. "If you're sure."

"Give it to me."

Nivin cringed at the sound of the knife's quick motion and the hiss of pain Ordnance let out. A faint scent of blood tinged the air as he shook his hand over the rocks. She flinched when one of the warm, sticky droplets of blood landed on her face.

"There. Is that sufficiently gory for you? Or should I make the cut deeper so the spawn *really* thinks I'm dead?"

"That's enough," Brand said quickly. "We should get some more vinegar berries for your hand."

"We can cut off another strip of my skirt for a bandage," Nivin said, wiping the drop of blood from her face.

Brand headed out of the cave to retrieve more berries, while Anek did his best to use the knife to cut off another piece of fabric from Nivin's dwindling hemline. Ordnance paced near the entrance of the cave, muttering under his breath again. Nivin could not even make out words in the low susurrus of his voice. He had said once he saw the sun, he finally came back to himself, but Nivin wondered how much of his prison madness he still carried with him. She squirmed at the thought.

"Don't worry," Anek said, handing the strip of fabric to Nivin. "Once we make it to Council City I'm sure they will make you a beautiful new dress."

Nivin made a half-hearted attempt at a smile.

When Brand returned with the berries, Ordnance fell silent. He said nothing the whole time they applied the berries and bandaged his hand tightly.

"Well," Brand said, "I suppose there is not much sense in waiting any longer."

"There's not much sense in any of this," Ordnance countered. "But I suppose you are right. We should go. Are you sure you can find us?"

"Yes." The pitch of Brand's voice leapt up, as if he was insulted. He cleared his throat. "But don't wait for us for more than a few hours."

As they exited the cave, full sunlight hit Nivin right in the face. She squeezed her eyes shut against the brilliant light, trying to ignore the faint ache in her temples. A shadow fell over her as Anek took her hand.

"Please be careful. I—I don't want to lose you." He sniffed loudly. "Please. If something happens to you—I can't help but feel it's my fault. You were safe before I came to the prisons."

"Safe?" Nivin frowned. "Barely. There is no such thing as safety for an abomination under Temere's reign."

Anek stooped to embrace Nivin, encircling her in his

massive arms. "Friends?"

"Friends." Nivin reached up, feeling every inch of his deformed face. She wiped away a hot tear that rolled down his face and kissed him on the cheek. "Even if we don't meet again, you have to help the Freemen. Libertas sounds good and noble."

Anek gave a soft laugh as he drew himself back to full height. "We'll meet again. You're more powerful than you realize."

Nivin shrank at the thought. Since they had arrived here, Anek seemed to have seen something in her that gave him hope. Perhaps it was her "hidden knowledge," as Ordnance called it. But Anek did not—could not—understand that something about the power she used felt *wrong*. He could not understand how much her hidden knowledge unsettled her, how much her strange abilities filled her with fear. She could find nothing to say to respond to his faith in her, so she simply whispered, "Goodbye."

"We must go now," Brand said. "Strength, friends. We will meet you at the appointed place."

"Strength, brother," Ordnance said. "Nivin." Nivin heard him make a motion of some kind, perhaps waving to them.

Brand grunted as he heaved up the shield. "Let's go, Nivin. Can you help me steady the shield?"

Unease flooded Nivin at the thought of leaving Anek alone with Ordnance. But Brand was right—with Anek's weakness, he would be in greater danger if he came to face the spawn with them. Shaking her head, Nivin carefully walked over to where Brand was and gripped the edge of the shield tightly.

Brand shifted the weight of the shield so that they carried it between them. As they moved forward, Brand warned Nivin about the upcoming terrain nearly every step of the way. Their progress was slow, and the thin mountain air was already growing hot.

When they made it to the staircase, Brand fell silent for a moment.

Nivin tensed up. "What?"

"Nivin, even if it should be for just this short time, I am glad to have known you."

"Thank you for being my friend."

"Likewise."

They proceeded as quietly as possible, Brand whispering to Nivin when she should take the next step up. They had only been on the staircase for a few moments when they heard a throb from deep within the earth. The world became unusually silent. No birds could be heard twittering nearby. An air of dread lingered in the open space. There was no movement. None at all.

"Put the shield down," Brand whispered. "Then we will bow to the ground on our knees, with our arms stretched out on the stairs in front of us."

Stomach tied in knots, Nivin did as Brand said. "Now what?"

"I'll try to call it out." Brand cleared his throat and spoke in a loud voice. "Oh, great and mighty offspring of Scylla and Scyllorin, masters of the land! Proud progeny of great ancestry! How much greater is the scion than his heritage! We have seen your power and we are in awe. We come to offer tribute!"

There was a split second of silence. Then, there was a deep throbbing in the earth and the sound of rocks crumbling.

"Don't move," Brand hissed.

The sound of large footsteps approached them. Nivin felt the creature's movement through the earth, until it came to a stop right in front of them. It was silent for what seemed like a long time.

It screeched—the sound of rock scraping rock, grating and painful.

Brand's voice was barely louder than a breath. "Rise to your knees."

Nivin rose slowly out of her prostration, feeling the spawn's eyes on her as she did. It stared at her intently. Leaning forward, it sniffed deeply and picked up one of the stones.

"Does our offering please you, great one?" Brand said, unable to keep a hint of shakiness out of his voice.

The creature uttered its horrible screech.

"Oh, great one! If you are pleased to accept our worship, give us a sign. We are too frail to understand your speech."

Loud crunching followed. Nivin realized the spawn was eating one of the rocks.

"You honor us!" Brand said.

The creature hissed, then ate another of the rocks.

"We humbly ask you to let your servants continue our journey through the mountains. Will you permit us to leave?"

Turning its gaze to Nivin again, the spawn was silent. A long claw reached out and touched her under the chin, tilting her face upward. Trembling, she realized she might not even have a chance to fight the spawn if it decided to kill her.

The spawn let out a long hiss and withdrew its hand. It turned its back on them and waved them away.

Brand let out a sigh of relief. "Thank you, great one. We will not forget your kindness!" He placed a gentle hand on Nivin's shoulder and spoke in a low voice. "Let's go. Carefully."

They rose from the ground and began to walk away, taking slow steps. Brand took Nivin's hand to guide her across the uneven terrain. They were only a short distance away when a soft throb of thunder coursed through the earth, faint and distant.

Nivin's instincts screamed in warning.

Screeching, the spawn wheeled around and gave a furious kick to the pile of stones. It sprang after them and threw Brand to the ground. Within seconds, strands of energy flickered in Nivin's perception and she knew what the spawn was doing. It sank its arms deep into Brand's back as if melting into him. An anguished scream tore from Brand's throat, only to be cut short. He gagged for a few moments and fell silent. The spawn drew itself to its full height, holding Brand suspended out in front of him like a puppet.

"Deceivers!" Brand's voice was hideously morphed into a screech like the spawn's, painful and grating.

Mouthpiece. It was more horrible than Nivin had imagined. She could almost feel the pain radiating from Brand in the soft thunder throbbing in the ground beneath them.

"You would deceive me!" The spawn swung Brand's body toward Nivin, clubbing her with it.

Nivin reeled as the full weight of Brand's body slammed into her. She fell and hit the back of her head against a stone. The impact sent flashes of light sparking though her perception, leaving her dazed for a moment. She rolled over and pressed her ear to the ground, reaching her senses down into the throbbing beneath the surface. Murmuring voices almost too faint to be heard swelled and faded.

Brand screamed again, his voice his own for a painful instant, then shifting back to the horrible screech. "What is your purpose? What is your intent in letting my foe go free? He still lives, deceivers! My brother has seen him!"

Nivin's mind spun. Another spawn must have been roaming the mountains, and it had found Ordnance and Anek. "Please, we just want to travel through the mountains. We don't want to fight!"

A horrible laugh tore from Brand's throat. As the spawn forced him to speak again, the flickering strands of light seemed to multiply. "You seek to deceive me again? Do you think I am a fool? I know an enemy when I see one! And you—whatever you are—are an enemy. Answer your purpose, or I shall rend your companion in two!"

Swallowing panic, Nivin tried to reach out to the strands of light. She prayed her instincts could tell her how to bend them to her own purpose, how to use them to force the spawn away from Brand, but her mind was blank with terror.

"Answer!"

There was no time to try to manipulate the threads of power now, but she had to do something. The spawn was seconds from tearing Brand apart. With a shout, Nivin leapt up from the ground and launched herself toward Brand. She clasped her hands tightly around his waist and pulled as hard as she could.

"Pathetic fool," Brand's voice hissed. "You think for a moment that this makes a difference?" The spawn swung both of them, slamming Nivin into a tall rock.

Nivin barely let the pain of the impact register. Instinctively, she planted her feet against the rock, reached around Brand, and grabbed the creature by the wrists where they met his body. She pushed against its forearms with all her might. The spawn fought back, somehow drawing on the energy of the flickering lights to keep its clawed hands buried inside Brand. The strands thickened and multiplied.

"You cannot overcome me, weakling," Brand roared. "Tell me your purpose!"

The lights flashed brighter. The faint murmuring of voices grew louder. The Charybdon grew every time the spawn exerted its powers.

Nivin released the spawn's wrists and extended her hands. Foreign words danced inside her mind, and the swirling energy sprang to her hands like bolts of lightning. Drawing tendrils of light upwards like strings, she grasped the spawn's wrists again.

Nivin pushed—and the creature stumbled back, its claws melting out of Brand as it did.

Brand collapsed forward against Nivin. She caught him in a tight embrace. "Brand!"

He did not respond.

As fear for his life took over her mind, the strands of energy slipped away from her grasp. They snaked away down into the earth beneath her, swirling in a rapidly swelling whirlpool of power. Panicked, she groped her hands across Brand's back, feeling for wounds. There was nothing—not even the fabric of his shirt was torn. She laid him down on the ground as gently as she could, at a loss for what to do next.

The spawn screeched so loudly Nivin thought her ears would bleed. And then—

She heard the faint wobbling of something on one of the stone stairs, something round, perhaps...

The shield.

She sprang up and sprinted in the direction of the sound. She tripped over the edge of a stair and fell forward, smacking her brow into the pile of rocks. Groping downward, she found the edge of the shield. As soon as her hands touched the smooth granite, the whirlpool of lights leapt beneath her, drawn to her as iron to a lodestone. The earth trembled. Slides of dirt and rock hissed as they slipped down the mountainside. Nivin tipped the shield over, pouring out the stones that were on top of it.

The spawn took several steps back, gathering to spring. It jumped, launching itself at Nivin and transforming into the jagged rocks.

Nivin heaved the shield up and held it over her head. The sounds of the falling rocks around her disoriented her. Some of the transformed shards ricocheted off the edge of the shield, but a number of them slashed across one of her arms, leaving a trail of deep lacerations. She screamed.

As if in response to her cry, power from the forming Charybdon accelerated. Lightning cracked and thunder sounded. The earth shook. A huge piece of rock broke from the mountainside. The ground sucked at Nivin's feet like mud.

The Charybdon had grown huge. It raged beyond her control—and the voices, the sucking mouth of its presence, resisted her attempts to control or direct it. She called out Brand's name, but she heard nothing. She did not know where the creature was, or whether it had killed Brand. She stumbled aimlessly, crouching under the shield, calling out for Brand again and again.

Everything went black as the Charybdon pulled her down into nothingness.

CHAPTER FOURTEEN

Searing pain wrenched Brand into consciousness. He lay on the ground, held in place by the waves of agony shooting through his ribcage. Sharp, ragged breaths were all he could manage. He remembered his total paralysis and every excruciating word the spawn had forced from his mouth. He remembered the fear and desperation on Nivin's face as she tried to free him.

After that, everything had gone blank.

Slowly, Brand turned his head to look around. He was surrounded by broad-leafed, deep green bushes. The sky above him was clear and deep blue, with the sun moving on toward early evening. He heard the faint sound of cattle lowing in the distance.

He took another shallow, painful breath. The air was humid. After several moments, his breathing became normal and the pain faded to bearable levels. He sat up, his head just crowning over the bushes.

Wherever he was, he was no longer in the mountains. Some hills stood distant on the horizon, but aside from that, green plains surrounded him. Mounds of cow dung dotted the ground around him, and a herd of cattle was not too far off. But the cattle acted strangely, as if they were afraid and might stampede at any provocation.

A Charybdon must have opened after he lost awareness. How else could he be somewhere so far away?

But what had happened to the spawn? Was that what had frightened the cattle, or had it been the Charybdon itself? And where was Nivin?

He turned around and started when he saw a figure walking away toward a stand of trees—a person carrying another person. A large dog loped alongside them. He did not dare call out, in case the spawn was still nearby, so he ran as fast as he could after them. He had only gone a few strides when he tripped over something and fell headlong to the ground. The impact reignited the pain in his lungs. Groaning, he pushed himself up and realized he had cow manure smeared all over his front. He glanced over his shoulder to see what he had tripped on, and realized it was the shield. Without even pausing to wipe the layer of excrement from his clothes and his face, he hoisted up the shield and started running again.

Soon, he was close enough to see it was an old man with wispy gray hair who carried Nivin. Brand was about to risk calling out when the dog turned around and snarled at him.

The man instantly turned around. He started to back away slowly.

"Wait!" Brand cried. "Stop!"

The man hesitated. "Who are you?"

"My name is Brand." Brand slowed his pace to a walk. "That maiden you carry is my friend."

The man whistled sharply at his dog, which stood down, though it still bristled. "Hurry then, she's hurt! I'm taking her to my house, on the other side of that stand of trees." He resumed walking, gesturing with a bob of his head for Brand to catch up.

When Brand finally caught up to the cattle herder, he gasped at the blood that covered Nivin's arm. Her sleeve had been torn to shreds, and an ugly bruise stood out on her forehead. "What happened?"

"I was hoping you could tell me," the man said. "All I know is I hear a sound like thunder, and then some of my cattle're spooked. I look over and see something huge running away, and Cricket starts barking at the thing. Never seen anything like it. Man-like it was, but some evil abomination to be sure. That's when I saw this poor maid on the ground, all tore up. Cricket wanted to chase after the abomination, but I called her off. We've been heading back to the house for a while when she started growling at you, and I wasn't sure if you were friend or foe."

"If you are a friend of the innocent, then I am your friend," said Brand. "That creature you saw—it is more than an abomination. It's a total corruption of nature. It attacked us."

"I see that," the man grunted. "You seem a little barked up too, though I daresay you fared better with that shield, eh?"

Brand shook his head. "No. I fell unconscious before she got hurt. I didn't have the shield then. Please, let me help you carry her."

The herder gave Brand an evaluating look. "You'll get dung in her cuts, boy, and that'll only make her sick. No, I can manage. But if you'll run ahead with Cricket, let my wife know I'm coming. She'll know you're safe as long as Cricket here isn't growling at you."

"But the spawn might come back."

"The what, now? Is that what you call that abomination?"

"Yes. Please, let me stay with you. I already failed to defend her once. I will not leave her now."

"Good man. All right then. We'll just send Cricket ahead." The man whistled sharply. "Crickee! Trouble, Crickee! Home, girl, home. Trouble! Home!" The dog burst into a violent run toward the trees, baying frantically as she did. "She'll let the missus know something's wrong out here. Smartest animal you'll ever see, that girl. Smarter than most folks, too."

"Sir, thank you. I am indebted to you, and do not even know who you are."

"Manasseh's the name. Cattle herder, in case you hadn't noticed." He grinned, then grunted slightly. "And my old age is catching up to me. Not as strong as I used to be. Maybe you ought to take her feet, lad—lay that shield down, we can come back for it."

Brand nodded. He noticed a patch of lamb's quarters and dropped the shield near it before going over to help Manasseh carry Nivin. After a while, they were close enough to the stand of trees that they could see the stone house on the other side. A smaller house, presumably for the help, stood nearby it. Several stables surrounded by a sturdily made wooden fence were visible through a gap in the stand of the trees as well, and a well-trodden and dung-littered path marked the way to it. Already, they could hear Cricket barking hysterically.

A plump, silver-haired woman walked into view in the muddy lane.

"Tim!" Manasseh cried. "We need hot water—there's a girl been hurt!"

The woman clutched at her apron. "Manny! Ah, thanks be, you're all right!"

"Hot water, Tim!"

The woman hoisted her skirts, turned, and ran back to the house. Brand and Manasseh followed after her, and only a few minutes later, made it across the yard and into the house. Inside, a pile of candles had been hurriedly pushed to the floor near the table. A few of them had broken in half. The smell of tallow was overwhelming, and the stout woman was scrubbing the table frantically.

"Oh, bless it, Manny," she sputtered. "Table's a mess—I been working on the candles and fat's everywhere…"

"Never mind that, Tim, she's hurt."

The woman squeaked when she looked up at Nivin. "Bless us, bless us. I'll get a blanket. There are some towels by the fireplace, and the water's on the hob. Oh, bless us." She left the room for a moment, and came back with an aged, stained quilt and spread it on the table.

Brand and Manasseh laid Nivin out on the table.

"Oh, Manny, you're not hurt, are you?"

Manasseh put his hands on her shoulders. "I'm fine."

"Thanks be. What happened to this poor girl?"

"Some kind of abomination attacked her—I found her and her friend here out in the fields."

The woman pointed at Brand. "You go to the well out back and wash, lad. There's a pail with some soap in it by the door. Manny, get me my kit, now."

Manasseh chuckled. "That's me Timbrel, all right." He ran into the other room.

Timbrel immediately set to her task. She tore off the tattered sleeve on Nivin's right arm, revealing deep cuts that oozed blood. Drawing her lower lip into her mouth, Timbrel daubed at the wounds with a towel dipped in hot water. She looked up at Brand. "I mean it, boy. Go out back and wash."

"Not until I'm sure she is all right," Brand said.

"Well then, stay out of our way. You'll do us no good covered in dung like that."

Manasseh returned to the room holding a box. Timbrel went to work with Manasseh's assistance, and they cleaned the wound. The scars on their own hands, arms, and faces, said they had treated many injuries over the course of their long lives. Neither of them spoke, working together as if each knew the other's next move. After Timbrel seemed satisfied that the cuts had adequately been cleaned of dirt and debris, she reached into her kit and pulled out a needle and thread of some kind. She ran the needle through the flame of a candle for a few moments, then waited for it to cool. She stitched the deepest cuts on Nivin's arms closed. Manasseh pulled clean white bandages from the box and wrapped them around Nivin's arm.

"It seems like she must've knocked her head pretty badly," Timbrel said. "She didn't wake the whole time we was helping her."

Brand's stomach tightened. Nivin must have done something to free him, and it was likely she found a way to manipulate the powers like she thought she could. But if doing so had the same effect on her as using the powers to heal them, she might not wake for a long time. "She's been like this before."

Timbrel and Manasseh shot him a peculiar look.

"When she's hurt, I mean. She doesn't wake for a long time."

"How long?" Timbrel said, raising her eyebrows.

"Days, sometimes."

"You better go wash up, now, lad." She pointed to the wooden pail by the door. "We'll keep an eye on her, and Manny'll give you a fresh change of clothes while we wash yours."

Brand nodded. "Thank you." He went outside and scanned the yard for the well. He walked behind the house, passing a large clay oven as he did. A thriving flock of chickens surrounded a well-made coop several yards from the house. It took another moment before he spotted the large wooden square on the ground a few feet from him. He walked over to it, squatted down, and pried up the heavy wooden cover. Laying it on the ground, he set the soap on top of it, then dipped a pail of cool water from the well. After washing his hands and face thoroughly, he replaced the cover and went back into the house. Manasseh handed him a set of clothes, and Brand went into the other room to change.

When he returned, Timbrel pointed to a wooden tub near the door. "Put your clothes in there for now."

"Thank you," Brand said. After he put the soiled clothes on top of an assortment of dirty rags, he turned around to see Manasseh giving him an evaluating stare.

"They seem a little loose on you."

Brand looked down at the borrowed clothes. "Yes, well, I haven't eaten well for the last several weeks."

"Is that so?" Manasseh scratched his scraggly gray beard. "Listen—Brand, is it? I'm powerful curious as to how you, that little missy there, and that abomination came to be in my pastureland."

Brand almost started when he realized Manasseh had called the spawn an abomination several times now. That was what Nivin had said people with deformities were called in Zerabar. If they were in Zerabar, he would have to tread carefully. "You keep calling it an abomination, but it's not. It is not even a person."

"What is it, then?"

"Half-dragon, half-man, bred together by dark magic."

A look of abject terror and disgust crossed Timbrel's face.

Manasseh scoffed. "Dragon, eh? Don't worry yourself, Tim. Dragons don't exist, and if they ever did, they're all long gone." He looked at Brand. "Maybe you got knocked on the head, too."

"No, I'm telling you the truth. We're from a faraway place where dragons still exist. It has been pursuing us a long way."

"Where is that, exactly?" Manasseh furrowed his brow. "Your Zerabari is perfect, and I could swear you have a Central Plains accent."

"The merchant who taught it to me was from the Central Plains."

"So where are you from?"

Brand hesitated for a moment. "Libertas. You won't have heard of it."

Manasseh gave him a sidelong glance. "You're right, I haven't. Where's that, on the other side of Neishar?"

"Yes."

"And they have dragons there, do they?"

"Only one that I know of."

Manasseh narrowed his eyes. "Half-dragon, half-man. All right, then. I'd still say that counts as an abomination."

"I can't say I disagree."

"And that thing has been chasing you?" Timbrel said. "You poor creatures! I'm afraid we don't know much about the world outside our little farm, but bless it, there's an abomination worthy of the Law of Condemnation."

"Tim," Manasseh hissed.

Timbrel jumped. "Of course, all abominations are deserving of the Law of Condemnation." She gave Brand an uneasy smile.

"So that thing's been chasing you for some time," Manasseh said. "How've you managed to survive?"

"Luck, and that shield I was carrying."

"Ah, your shield. Let me go get it for you. You're weary and should stay with your friend in case she wakes. What's her name?"

Brand said the first idea that popped into his mind. "Ana."

"I certainly hope Ana gets to feeling better."

"Thank you, sir, for your kindness to us."

Manasseh nodded. "Be back in a bit, Tim." He grabbed a longbow propped next to the door and slung a quiver of arrows over his shoulder. He went outside, calling for Cricket.

Timbrel went to the door and watched him for a few moments. She turned around and clapped her hands together. "Well, poor Ana is in sore need of a bath, and I need to see if she has other hurts." She walked back over to Nivin and pulled gently at one of Nivin's eyelids, but she did not stir. "Wake up, Ana!"

Nivin lay as still as ever.

Timbrel shook her head. "The poor dear. Do I have your permission, or should I wait 'til she wakes?"

Brand frowned. It could be days before Nivin woke again, and if she had more injuries, they would need treatment immediately. He did not especially like the idea of a stranger undressing her, and he suspected Nivin would not either. Still, it would be better for a woman to take care of the matter. "Go ahead. I don't know when she'll wake again."

"All right. You get out of here, then. Go outside and find a cockerel and kill it. You'll find everything you need in the barn—there's an apron you can use, too. Don't bring it inside until it's completely drained, and knock before you come in, in case I'm not finished cleaning her up yet."

Nodding, Brand walked outside and did as she said. He worried about Nivin the whole time, wondering what would happen if she woke. Would she think he had abandoned her?

Once the fowl had finished draining, Brand returned to the house and knocked. Timbrel opened the door. Nivin lay on the table, covered with another blanket.

"She had quite a few bruises," Timbrel said, "but not any more cuts." She grabbed the pot of boiling water from the hob and carried it outside, setting it down on the ground. She took the bird and plunged it briefly in the hot water before dipping it in a basin of cold water that was sitting out front. She shook off the excess water and handed it back to Brand. "Pluck this. I'm going to see if I have any old clothes I can spare. That dress she has is in tatters, the poor dear. Bless it, what you two must have been through."

She headed back into the house. Several minutes later, she came back out.

Brand was down to the pinfeathers by the time Timbrel returned.

Timbrel beamed. "You remind me of my youngest son. Orren could pluck a bird faster than you'd believe."

"Well," Brand said, "I've been a traveler for a long time. Most game birds have twice as much feather as bird. I'd go hungry before I could cook them if I hadn't learned to pluck them quickly."

"Ah. Well, if Orren were still with us, I'm sure the two of you would make for an interesting contest." She took the bird and held a lit tallow taper near its skin, singeing off the delicate pinfeathers.

"What happened to him?"

"What's that?" Timbrel muttered, turning the bird to singe the feathers on the other side.

"You said 'if Orren was with us.' What happened to him?"'

Timbrel paused, looking at Brand with a peculiar expression on her face.

"Well," she began.

At that moment, Manasseh strode into the yard, pointing an accusing finger at Brand. "You!" He was winded, and his face was red and beaded with sweat. "Go inside, Tim. Now."

"Manny—"

"Now!"

With her lips pursed and eyes narrowed, Timbrel took the chicken and went inside, shutting the door behind her.

Manasseh took Brand by the collar and threw him against the door. "Now, you're gonna tell me the truth.

You're gonna tell me where you're really from."

"I told you—far away. It's difficult to explain—"

"Difficult to explain? I'll tell you what's difficult to explain, you damned whelp! How in blazes d'you explain your being from 'far away' when your shield is made of rock from the quarry less'n a mile from here?" Flecks of spittle flew from his lips onto Brand's face.

"I found that shield on my journeys."

"Of course you did." Manasseh scoffed. "Something that valuable was just lying around, was it?"

"It was in a graveyard."

"A—a graveyard?"

"Yes."

Manasseh looked down at the shield, turned it, and held it up for Brand to see. "Do you see this mark?"

Brand looked at the mark, startled to see that it had changed shape. It was still an ornate letter, and he somehow even recognized it as a *G*, but it was not a symbol in the Common language's alphabet.

"My eldest son left the farm to apprentice with the masons in the quarry. This is his mark. He made very few of these. And you're telling me you found this in a graveyard?"

"Yes."

"And so you desecrated what might have been my son's grave?" Manasseh roared, his face turning purple.

"No! It lay on top of the grave, I swear."

Tears pooled in Manasseh's eyes. "My sons have been gone nigh forty years. Please tell me where you have found their resting place."

Brand stared at Manasseh, completely at a loss for what to say. To tell the full truth was to risk the Law of

Condemnation falling upon both Nivin and himself, and to lie might trap him even deeper in falsehoods. "I wish I could. But I do not know how to get there from here."

Manasseh's face hardened. "I hope for your sake you're telling the truth, lad."

Brand nodded grimly.

"Forty years," Manasseh mumbled, running his hands over the shield's smooth surface.

"I am sorry for your loss," Brand said, "but I am glad the shield has finally found its way home."

"Yes," whispered Manasseh. "Yes."

There was a knock as Timbrel pushed the door open a crack. "Please, I'm sorry—but Ana has woken up and she is very, very confused! She won't even let me near her!"

Manasseh held Brand's gaze with a steely glare for just a few moments longer before waving Brand into the house.

Brand hurried inside. Nivin had clambered down from the table and knocked over many stacks of tallow candles and several of their hosts' possessions. She had found her way to the wall, where she huddled like a cornered animal, sobbing.

And she was naked. In her panic she had thrown off the blanket that lay over her. Now, she clutched her knees to her chest—trying to cover as much of herself with her hands and arms as possible. She shivered miserably. Brand tore his eyes away from her and stared at the blanket on the floor next to the table.

"The poor thing won't even answer to her own name, bless her," Timbrel said. "Who knows what that horrible abomination did to her?"

Horror flooded Nivin's face. "Abom—abomination?"

Brand walked over to the blanket on the floor and

picked it up, holding it out in front of him to block his vision as he moved toward her.

Nivin gasped. "Stay back!"

"It's me, Brand."

"Brand?"

"Yes. It's all right, Ana. You're safe now, Ana. Let me cover you."

"A—all right."

Brand peeked past the edge of the blanket, just enough to see how close to her he was. Once he was next to her, he spread the blanket out over her.

She tucked the blanket tightly under her arms, leaving her shoulders exposed. "Is it really you?" She extended one of her hands, feeling for him.

Brand took her hand and squatted down to her level. "It's me, I promise."

She reached up with her other hand and felt his face, running her fingers along his brow and nose with a delicate touch. As her fingers brushed across his lips, heat bloomed in his cheeks and ears. He wondered if she could feel how warm his face was.

"It is you," Nivin said, letting out a sigh of relief. She folded her arms across her chest. "What happened?"

"I'm not entirely sure. I woke up here, in the fields of this kindly cattle herd and his wife who took us in and helped us. I do not know what happened to the spawn, but the cattle herd said he saw it."

"Ordnance and An—"

"Shh," Brand said. "Calm down."

Nivin massaged her forehead. "I'm so confused."

"It's all right, my dear," Timbrel said, clucking. "You poor thing—all you've been through, waking up in a strange place, having been attacked by that abomination Brand here told us about. It's no wonder you're confused."

"Where are we?"

"You're in our home—I'm Timbrel, and my husband here's Manasseh. We live about a day's journey from Kalaoth."

"Kalaoth. In the Southwestern Plains?"

"Aye," Manasseh said. He shot Brand a distrustful look. "Though I thought you're from far away. How are you so familiar with this region?"

"I told you, I knew a merchant from the Central Plains," Brand said. "He told us a few things."

"What brings you to Zerabar, anyway?"

"Bless it, Manny, leave the poor dears alone," Timbrel said. "Let me finish supper and they can tell us more while we eat." She turned to Nivin. "Oh, let me help you dress, Ana. Come with me into the other room."

Nivin drew her lip into her mouth.

"It's all right, Ana," Brand said, hoping she had caught on by now. "You can trust Timbrel. She has been kind to us."

Nivin gave the tiniest of nods.

Timbrel helped Nivin up, making sure the blanket did not slip. "Manny, get some potatoes out and start peeling them, would you?"

Manasseh nodded.

Timbrel and Nivin disappeared into the other room, leaving Brand and Manasseh alone.

Manasseh dutifully went to a panel in the floor, flipped it open, and pulled out several fat brown potatoes. He grabbed a knife and started peeling them. "You'll have to forgive the light fare. We normally eat much more at midday than the evening. Tim makes a stellar soup, though."

Brand's stomach growled. "I've hardly eaten anything but lamb's quarters for days. Soup sounds wonderful."

"Lamb's quarters?" Manasseh raised his eyebrows. "I'd say you've been doing all right. But—the sheep haven't lambed since early spring this year. Where exactly have you been getting your lambs, Mister Far Away?"

"What? Oh, no. Lamb's quarters is a wild green leafy plant."

"Never heard of it."

"Maybe you call it something different here. I saw some on my way through your land."

"You'll have to show me then. We could always do with easy food around here."

"Of course." Brand watched Manasseh peel potatoes for a few moments. "I can help with that."

Manasseh found another knife and handed it to Brand along with a potato. The two were silent while they worked, but Brand could not escape the feeling that Manasseh was watching him.

After several minutes, the door to the other room swung open.

Brand looked up as Nivin walked slowly into the room. He could see the hesitance in each step she took, the way she put her toes down first before shifting her full weight onto the rest of her foot. She was probably afraid she was going to run into something, and even more afraid their hosts would figure out she could not see. For a brief moment, he understood the panic Nivin's father must have felt every time she was around other people. Brand set down the potato he was peeling and went over to her, placing a hand on her back. Gently, he steered her over to one of the chairs. "Here. Sit down."

"Thank you." Nivin said, smiling.

Brand felt an odd sensation creep over him. She was smiling at him. He had seen her smile before, and thought that maybe he caught a glimpse of a smile on her face when he had gone to comfort her in the cave, but something about this was different. It was as if he was realizing for the first time just how beautiful her smile was—how beautiful she was. Since he first met her, there had been so many dangers on his mind that he had been shoving the realization away. Now, it seemed like the only thing he could notice. Her long, glossy black hair was down and brushed smooth, and the simple brown shift she wore hung gracefully on her frame.

And she was smiling for him. A stupid nervous grin crawled onto his face at the thought. He gave her a reassuring clap on the shoulder. "It's no trouble."

"You just sit there and rest while we finish up supper, dear," Timbrel said, walking into the room. "And don't you worry about the shoes being too small—Manny'll make you a pair that'll fit just right. Won't you, Manny?"

Manasseh grunted in response.

CHAPTER FIFTEEN

It took another hour or so before supper was ready. Brand and Nivin said as little as possible, letting Timbrel dominate the idle conversation. She talked about candle-making and soap-making, telling amusing stories of when she was a girl first learning to do these things. Brand only noticed about half of what she said—his thoughts were preoccupied with worries of Ordnance and Anek's safety. There was clearly another spawn in the mountains, and if it was as difficult to defeat as the rock spawn was, they would be lost without the shield.

The shield. Brand's possession of it had caused Manasseh to distrust him, a distrust Brand could see in every sidelong glance the old man cast his way. It would be difficult to gain Manasseh's trust—but with any luck, Brand and Nivin would be able to leave in the morning. Whether Manasseh would let them take the shield with them was another question, and Brand suspected it was the key to successfully defeating the spawn. Of course the two of them would have to track down the spawn and kill it, or at least take it back to Brand's world. They could not leave it in Zerabar to terrorize the population.

When supper was finally ready, they all sat down at the table together.

"I cannot thank you enough for your hospitality," Brand said, his mouth watering at the rich aroma of the soup.

"Oh, it's just a little soup, it's no trouble," Timbrel said. "We're always glad to aid someone in need."

Manasseh shot Brand a look, as if to say their presence was in fact a great deal of trouble. He picked up his hand-carved wooden spoon and started in on the soup, closing his eyes after the first spoonful. "Ah, Tim—nobody makes soup like you. This's fit to be served in the King's court."

Blushing, Timbrel beamed. "Oh, shush, you old flatterer." She motioned to Brand and Nivin. "Go ahead, eat."

Brand took a spoonful of the chicken soup, and immediately knew what Manasseh meant. Even if he had not been nearly starving, this was by far the best soup Brand had ever eaten. Something about the potatoes and all the flavors were remarkable. Despite his training in table etiquette, he simply hunched over the bowl, eating it as fast as the temperature permitted.

"Ana, you haven't touched your soup," Timbrel said, her face full of concern. "What's the matter, dear?"

Brand looked over at Nivin. She was sitting there with her hands in her lap. For a moment, he wondered why she had not started eating, but then he realized the problem.

The only way she could find her spoon was if she felt around for it. She was probably afraid they would notice something was wrong. Brand reached over and picked up Nivin's spoon and pressed it into her hand. Gently, he took her other hand and placed it on the side of the bowl. "We're safe now. You can eat."

"Thank you," Nivin whispered, relief flooding her mien.

"Ah, isn't that the sweetest thing you've ever seen?" Timbrel said, "You've found yourself quite a man there."

Nivin smiled graciously. "Yes. But my father didn't approve of him. That is why we had to elope."

Brand struggled to hide a smile. She had created a reason for Brand's taking her hands with such familiarity, as well as an explanation for why they might be on the run. It should not have come as a surprise to him, he supposed, that Nivin would be so clever. After all, she had survived for seventeen years without discovery.

"Elope?" Timbrel sighed. "You poor things! So you've been running from your families this whole time?"

"Yes," Brand said.

Manasseh turned and gave Brand a long, evaluating look. "Why Zerabar?"

Brand squirmed internally, trying to keep his face straight and his voice as even as possible. "What do you mean?"

"You say Libertas is on the other side of Neishar. Why choose to come to Zerabar instead of going there? Why come so far south, instead of staying in the Northern Hills?"

"Neishar is overpopulated," Nivin said. She took a spoonful of soup. "There is no work to be had. Since

Zerabar is so careful with their resources, we thought we would fare better here, even if Zerabar is not notoriously kind to outsiders. We *had* hoped to blend in, since we are fluent in Zerabari, but Brand had qualms about lying. We ran into trouble in the Northern Hills when a unit of soldiers learned we were foreigners. So, we have been heading deeper into the country."

"Hm." Manasseh turned his gaze back to Brand, narrowing his eyes. "How did that abomination attacking you come into all of this? You said it's been pursuing you this whole time. Why?"

"That, I do not know," Brand said, unsure of what else to say.

Nivin sniffed as if she was holding back tears. "We think our love is cursed."

Timbrel lightly punched Manasseh on the shoulder. "You've gone and upset her. Just let the poor things finish eating and let them rest. Can't you see they've been through enough?"

Manasseh gave a light grunt and went back to his soup.

*

Once they had finished the rest of their supper, Timbrel set up two bedrolls on the floor in the main room. "It's hot, so you shouldn't need more than a light cover. Let us know if you need anything else during the night."

"We can't thank you enough," Brand said. "We are in your debt."

Timbrel waved her hand. "Oh, it's nothing. Well, Manny, let's you and I get some rest too, hmm?"

"Go ahead," Manasseh said. "I'll be along in a moment. Listen, Brand—step outside with me for a moment."

The two of them went outside into the humid night air, and Manasseh closed the door behind them. He planted a finger on Brand's chest. "Timbrel might believe you, but I don't trust you. I still want answers. I swear if you're not here in the morning I'll hunt you down and wring the truth outta you."

Brand swallowed. "Of course we shall be here in the morning. And I'll answer any more questions you have."

"Good. We'll talk more in the morning." Manasseh opened the door and gestured for Brand to go in.

Brand headed back inside and went to lie down on his bed roll. After a few minutes, Manasseh came in and latched the front door. He went into the other room, gently shutting the door behind him.

Brand waited until he could hear soft snoring coming from the other room, then sat up. Gentle moonlight spilled in through one of the windows, affording just enough light to see. He looked over at Nivin, studying her for a moment. She lay on her back, eyes open wide as if she was staring up at the ceiling. He tried for a moment to imagine what it must be like—to be caught in perpetual night, never knowing colors, never being able to read, and to be despised and condemned for it.

"Nivin," Brand whispered, "do you really see nothing at all?"

"Nothing." Nivin rolled over on her side so she was facing him. "I can usually tell light from dark, but nothing more."

"You've been like this since birth?"

"Yes." She hugged herself. "Timbrel and Manasseh must not find out. They are kind people, to be sure, but Temere's laws are absolute."

"Of course. Why do you think I didn't tell them your real name?"

"We need to leave here as quickly as we can."

Brand massaged the bridge of his nose. "Unfortunately, Manasseh does not believe the story we've told him. When we were outside, he threatened me. He said if we left before the morning he would hunt us down. I would like to avoid that, after how they treated us."

"I agree. They have been exceptionally courteous by Zerabar's standards. Timbrel seems especially kind. But Manasseh..."

"He does not trust us because of the shield."

"The shield?"

"He said his son made it—it's one of the few that were ever made."

Nivin sat up, brushing a strand of her long, loose hair behind her ear. "Then the shield somehow passed through a Charybdon."

"And his sons with it, I think," Brand said, feeling a pang of sorrow for Manasseh's loss. "He said they had been gone forty years. But this shows things other than us are able to travel from your world to mine. Ordnance could be right. The Knights of Ardor might have been from this world, pulled through a Charybdon hundreds of years ago."

"There is something strange about the shield. When I touched it—back in the mountains—the Charybdon that was forming moved beneath me. Almost as if it was drawn by the shield somehow."

"Maybe you had something to do with it, if it happened after you touched the shield."

Nivin was silent for a moment. "Perhaps. Still, I can't

help but feel there's something special about that shield. It seems like I ought to know, but I do not."

"More of your hidden knowledge?"

Nivin scoffed. "My hidden knowledge. I almost hate it."

"Well, perhaps it makes up for all of the things you'll never be able to know."

"What do you mean?"

"You'll never know what a sunrise looks like."

"I'll never know what anything looks like, Brand."

"So you don't even know what you look like?"

Nivin gave an exasperated sigh. "No."

Brand studied her again, sweeping his eyes across her features. After a moment, he began to reach out to push a stray lock of her hair back into place, but caught himself and snatched his hand back. "Your hair is dark. And your skin is light—like porcelain, even though you're sunburned now. And your eyes—your eyes are dark. Dark and beautiful." Heat rose to his face and he looked away.

Nivin said nothing for so long Brand feared he had insulted or embarrassed her somehow. His face grew hotter. Even the tips of his ears were burning.

"My father said as much." Nivin's voice was soft. "He said I was beautiful like my mother was, with fair skin and black hair. He always said my eyes were different, though. He said he didn't know where I got them, since both he and my mother had blue eyes. He thought maybe it had something to do with why I could not see." She paused. "I always wondered what blue was."

"What happened to your mother?"

"She died in childbirth." Nivin drew a deep breath and sighed.

Brand looked down at the floor. He had never known his mother either, nor his father, for that matter. The leaders of the Council of Champions were the only parents he ever had, and they were not gentle. They had served to teach him all he needed to know, and that was all that mattered. Nevertheless, he remembered how sorely Pock had missed his parents. Nivin's voice carried that same longing, that same sorrow and loss—the feelings Brand had never dared allow himself to have. "I am sorry."

"Thank you." Nivin sighed again. "I have often wondered if my father blamed me for her death, somehow."

"I'm sure he did not. How could he?"

"I don't know. I just always...oh, never mind this. What are we going to do about Manasseh?"

Brand cleared his throat, trying to redirect his thoughts back to the situation at hand. "Manasseh is a wise old hawk, to be sure. We need to be careful. We cannot change our story in any way—he will know we lied at the first and be even angrier. And we cannot tell him the truth—even if he believed it, it would put you in danger. But he won't let us leave until we have given him something that will satisfy him. I admit, I don't know what to do."

"And even assuming we do get away, what do we do about the spawn? I do not know how to defeat it, and my 'hidden knowledge' seems not to have helped at all."

"You did manage to save me from the spawn." Brand hesitated. "Nivin, what happened after that?"

"I'm still unsure, myself," Nivin said, sighing softly. "I only remember that when I forced the spawn's claws out of you, it made more of the strands of light—the power that forms the Charybda—appear. As we struggled, they seemed to multiply. They got out of control so quickly…and then I woke up on the table."

"Well, maybe your second attempt to fight the spawn will be better. And even if you don't defeat it here, maybe there will be another Charybdon, and it will at least be somewhere it cannot terrorize people like Manasseh and Timbrel. Maybe, if we have luck, we will even be able to find Anek and Ordnance again."

Nivin was silent for several moments. "Maybe. So what do we tell Manasseh?"

"Improvise, I suppose. You seem to be good at it. I will let you take the lead, since you know more about Zerabar than I."

"What if he separates us and questions us individually?"

"We stick to the story we have already presented. But we should straighten out a few details first—when we met and the like."

The two spent the next half hour or so talking in hushed voices. Brand explained the details of his interactions with Manasseh, and they worked together to invent a believable timeline for their story, as well as making up a few other answers to questions Manasseh might ask them. Once they were satisfied the story was sufficiently convincing, both lay back down on their bedrolls to get some sleep.

It took Brand some time before he could relax enough to fall asleep. His thoughts were a tangled mass of fears— fear for Ordnance and Anek, fear for Nivin. He wondered if she lay awake also, tied up in knots of worry. Brand clenched his fists. He would make sure none of Nivin's fears would come to pass. He would protect her—not just because it was the honorable thing to do, not just because she represented a possible hope for the future of Libertas. No, he would protect her because he cared for her. Though he had known her for a short time, he had quickly come to think of her as a friend—and when it came to his friends, Brand's loyalty was as absolute as his love for his nation.

Even if he had let Pock down, Brand would do everything in his power to keep harm from coming to Nivin.

Somehow, the thought soothed him, and he finally drifted off into a fitful slumber.

*

Brand woke in the morning to the sound of eggs sizzling. He sat up, brushing the crust away from the corners of his eyes and blinking until his vision was clear. Nivin still lay on her mat, but her eyes were open wide. Brand wondered whether she had slept at all.

"I have to say, I didn't have complete faith you'd be here in the morning," Manasseh said.

Brand whipped his head around to see Manasseh standing next to the fireplace holding up bowls for Timbrel, who ladled a thick grain mixture into them. He shot Brand a dark glare.

"Oh, what a thing to say," Timbrel scolded, shaking her head. "Now go set those down—I've got to turn the eggs." She grabbed a spatula and set to work on the eggs.

Brand climbed to his feet and stretched. "I told you we would be here in the morning. I keep my promises."

"I can see that." Manasseh carried the bowls over to the table, setting them down carefully. "You may convince me yet. Come and have breakfast."

Brand went to Nivin's side, reaching down and taking

her hand. She grasped his firmly and he pulled her up to her feet.

"Did you sleep well?" Brand asked softly.

Nivin said nothing, but the faint shadows beneath her eyes answered for her.

Brand guided Nivin to her chair at the table just as Timbrel brought a plate of fried eggs over. Using the spatula, she gently slipped two eggs into each bowl, where the eggs perched beautifully atop the grain mixture.

"Grits," Brand said, realizing what it was.

"And how would you know about grits, Mister Far Away?"

Timbrel huffed. "Bless it, Manny, he's said he has a friend from Zerabar. Grits is as popular in the Central Plains as it is here. Leave him alone."

"No, it's natural to be suspicious," Nivin said, "especially of outsiders. Already you have astounded us with your gracious hospitality—you have been kinder than any we have met so far. But I understand your caution. The stories of Rashaan have reached us even in Libertas—and if we are in the Southern Plains, I can see why you would be especially leery of strangers."

Manasseh smiled wryly. "Oh, Rashaan has nothing to do with it, missy."

"Come now, the eggs will get cold," Timbrel said, pulling a chair up to the table.

Brand took Nivin's hand and put it on the side of the bowl, pressing the spoon into her other hand.

"Thank you," Nivin said, smiling.

Heat surged to Brand's face again. "Oh...it's nothing." He grabbed his own spoon and stared down at his bowl, waiting until Manasseh had started eating before setting in on the grits. They were every bit as delicious as Nivin and Anek had made them out to be. "This is amazing, Timbrel."

Timbrel waved her hand. "Oh, it's only grits. I didn't even have any salt pork to go with it—that's the way it's best. But we haven't raised hogs for a while now, so I'm afraid we're stuck going without." She sighed. "Haven't raised hogs since…well, since…hogs are a lot of work, you know, in addition to the cattle…and without the boys…"

"That's enough, love," Manasseh said, his voice soft and gentle. He took Timbrel's hand in his and pressed his lips to it.

Timbrel nodded, blinking away tears. "Still, our indentured men help us a great deal. We sent them to Kalaoth for supplies early yesterday morning, so they won't be back for a few days."

Nobody said anything else for the rest of breakfast. However, when Timbrel got up to collect the bowls, Manasseh turned to Brand with a calculating gaze. Brand returned it as evenly and calmly as he could.

Manasseh stood up from his chair and stretched. "Boy, come with me. You're going to show me this lamb's quarters you've been eatin' on."

Brand glanced over at Nivin, a thousand disastrous scenarios flashing through his mind.

"Oh don't worry, I'll take good care of her," Timbrel said, a cheerful smile on her face. "Bring back some of the lamb's quarters, and we'll have it with dinner."

Manasseh stomped over to the door, where he began putting on his cured leather shoes.

Brand looked at Nivin again, hesitating. "Will you be all right, Ana?"

Nivin turned her head toward him. "Yes. I can dry dishes for Timbrel."

"Oh, now that sounds like a lovely idea," Timbrel chirped. "You two go along now."

Stomach tight, Brand went to the door and slipped into his boots. He fumbled with the laces, unable to stop thinking Timbrel would somehow find out Nivin could not see. He tried to reassure himself, thinking of how Nivin had survived this whole time—how her father must have taught her how to keep the secret. No, it was Manasseh Brand needed to worry about. Hopefully the lamb's quarters would be enough to convince the cattle herder of his truthfulness.

As Brand stood up, Manasseh opened the door and motioned for Brand to go out with a jerk of his head. Bracing himself, Brand strode out of the house and headed toward the fields. The two of them walked in silence, but Brand could feel Manasseh's eyes upon him the whole time. They had been out walking for some time when panic began to creep in around the fringes of Brand's mind. He knew he had seen the lamb's quarters, but now he struggled to find any.

Manasseh smiled wryly, as if Brand's predicament was amusing him. "Take your time."

After a few more minutes of searching, Brand finally spotted a small cluster of the plants near a post in the ground. "Here! Lamb's quarters."

"Where?"

"At the base of that post."

"That?" Manasseh barked. All traces of amusement slid from his face. "Bittermelde? That's poisonous!"

"What? It's not poisonous, and it's not called

bittermelde—at least where I'm from."

"Where you're from? You must be joking. That's deadly poisonous. Even goats won't eat it!"

Brand's mind swam with confusion. "I swear to you I have lived off of this for days now. Maybe lamb's quarters looks similar to your bittermelde, but—"

Manasseh sprang at Brand, seizing him by the collar. His age and appearance belied the wiry strength of his limbs, made powerful—not brittle—by decades of hard labor. "Don't think because I'm an old man I'm easily fooled. Eighty years' experience has taught me how to smell out a lie." He threw Brand back against the post. "Now you come here, bringing danger into my midst with your spawn. You've endangered my herd, you've endangered my family, and you come here bearing one of my son's shields—and now you expect me to believe you've been living off bittermelde for four days?"

"Not bittermelde, lamb's quarters. It is the truth."

"The truth. Fah! You've not told the truth since I met you. There's no such place as Libertas, and both you and I know it. Sinar's on the other side of Neishar, and beyond that's the sea. But I helped you, because I could see you were in need. And now you're telling me the deadliest poison in all Zerabar is something safe to eat. What're you playing at? Why are you here?"

Brand closed his eyes. "Fine. I haven't told you the whole truth. I didn't know if I could trust you. But please— just let me show you I am trustworthy. I've eaten lambs quarters my whole life—and that is lamb's quarters. Everything down to the shape of the leaf is true. I'll prove it to you."

"What—eat it and die, so I can't get the truth out of

you? Why should I believe you now? Why should I believe anything you say?"

Brand reached down and tore off a handful of the green leaves. Manasseh cried out, trying to stop him—but Brand shoved the whole handful into his mouth and swallowed it without chewing.

The last thing he heard was Manasseh's voice before he blacked out in a fit of convulsions.

CHAPTER SIXTEEN

Unease flooded Nivin as the door closed. She listened as Brand and Manasseh's footsteps faded, trying to decide for whom she was worried the most: Brand, or herself. Brand would be under Manasseh's close scrutiny without sufficient knowledge of Zerabar and the surrounding nations, while she was with sweet, unassuming Timbrel. However, if Timbrel noticed Nivin could not see, all of that sweetness would evaporate in an instant—and if Timbrel told Manasseh about it, the danger would be fully realized.

Nivin bit her lip. In the dungeons, it was dim enough that most people would not have noticed her eyes never focused on anything, so she seldom worried about such things there. She was always cautious in her interactions with the guards, and since they were busy, they did little more than acknowledge her and continue on their way. But to be in full light with a stranger? Nivin had only been in that predicament a few times, and in those cases, her father had always served to distract any attention away from her. He had tried to equip her for such a situation as this, but even the instructions he had given her did nothing to alleviate the fear that crept into her gut like nausea.

Timbrel bustled about the kitchen humming to herself. It sounded as though she was boiling water to wash dishes. "It's so kind of you to offer to dry the dishes for me, but you still ought to rest up. I'll bring the dishes over to you, and you can set them on the table when you're done." She came over to the table and started scrubbing it down. A faint scent of lavender wafted through the air.

Always divert attention away from yourself, Nivin heard her father saying. *People will almost always look at whatever you are speaking of.* "Lavender soap?"

"Oh, yes—I grow the lavender myself. There's a huge patch of it out by the gardens. Such a lovely scent, don't you think? I use it in most of my soaps—plain soap smells so dreary. Orren, my youngest, especially loved it. He used to pick the flowers and bring them to me when he was little—"

Timbrel went still for a moment. Then she slammed her fist on the table, making Nivin jump.

Timbrel stormed back to the fireplace, where it sounded like she took the kettle from the hob. She poured the boiling water into a basin. The wooden bowls clunked loudly as she threw them into the water. She had been silent for a long time, scrubbing away at the dishes, when she whispered something so quiet Nivin could just hear it over the splashing of the water in the basin:

"Cursed be the name of Temere."

Nivin started. Anyone with less sensitive hearing

would have missed it, and even Nivin wondered whether she had heard correctly. But then she remembered something Brand had mentioned to her—Timbrel had said the spawn was worthy of the Law of Condemnation, and Manasseh had immediately amended her statement, saying all abominations were worthy of Condemnation. Nivin had not given it a second thought; she was so used to hearing her father say similar things.

Her father. She always sensed the guilt and conflict inside of him as he both enforced and violated the Laws. The way he spoke of the Laws reflected that conflict.

And Manasseh and Timbrel had spoken of the Laws much in the same way he had. If Timbrel truly had just cursed Temere's name, was it possible Orren—or any other of her sons—had been an abomination? Was it possible Nivin could find an ally in her?

"Here," Timbrel said brusquely, walking over to the table. She set down several clean dishes.

Nivin held her hand out, wincing at the pain that shot through her injured arm as she did. "I'll take one of your towels and start drying them."

"Of course." Timbrel placed a cotton towel in Nivin's hand before walking back to the kitchen to scrub the pots. She sighed. "Forgive my rudeness. I miss my sons terribly."

Nivin slowly reached out to the place where she thought she had heard Timbrel set the dishes. Her hands brushed against the side of one of the bowls, and she quickly found the edge of the bowl and picked it up. "What happened to them?"

"It doesn't matter," Timbrel snapped. "They're gone." She drew a deep breath. "You'll have to forgive me again, dear. But bless it—I can't seem to stop thinking about the boys now you're here. Orren wasn't much older than Brand is, by the look of him."

"What were their names?" Nivin picked up the next bowl and started drying it.

"Well, Gamaliel was the eldest, then I had Garren only a year later. It was three years before we had Orren. The labor was difficult with him—both of us almost didn't make it. After that...well, I wasn't able to have children anymore."

"I'm sorry."

"Well, it wasn't so bad—I had the three of them, after all." She swallowed loudly. "Until Gamaliel was twenty, anyway." She went back to scrubbing the dishes. "Orren was only sixteen when the three of them disappeared."

Nivin's shoulders sagged. She finished drying the stack of bowls and cutlery in front of her just in time for Timbrel to bring over the pots and frying pan. Nivin dried them in silence while Timbrel scrubbed something else.

When all the kitchen work was done, Timbrel went into the other room for a while. When she came back, she was accompanied by the sound of rustling fabric. "I have a dress that might fit you a bit more nicely than the shift you've got on now—and don't you love the color?"

"It's beautiful," Nivin said hastily.

Timbrel chuckled. "I haven't been able to wear this one since before I had Gamaliel. 'Tis what happens when you have children. But I couldn't bring myself to throw it away, not knowing how expensive the dye was to make such a lovely blue-green."

"Are you sure you want to give it away?"

"Well...I'd always planned to give it to one of my

daughters, if I ever had any. And seeing as how you've been rejected by your family, it only seems fitting for me to help you out. Every girl needs a mother, after all."

Nivin's mouth fell open. "I'm honored. I don't even know what to say."

"Oh, shush. None of that. Now, I just have to let the hem out a bit, since you're a touch taller than me."

Nivin sat quietly, listening to the popping of threads as the seam ripper ran along the hem of the dress. As Timbrel worked, she told stories of all the mischief Gamaliel, Garren, and Orren had caused, her voice a mixture of sorrow and joy. None of them had been abominations, at least as far as Nivin could guess from what Timbrel said. In fact, nothing Timbrel said gave any clue as to why she would be cursing Temere. Of course, any reason for such sentiments would be guarded with utmost secrecy.

After Timbrel had been quiet for a while, Nivin decided to take a risk. "What do you think of King Temere?"

Timbrel gave a slight cough. "What do you mean, my dear?"

"I mean, what do you think of Temere as a king—his laws, his character, his rule?"

"Why would you ask that?" Timbrel's voice was harsh, as it had been earlier, but now a note of suspicion was woven in.

"I am only curious. From everything we have heard, he is not a gentle king."

"Well, no, Temere is not gentle, but he is my king nevertheless," Timbrel replied, in measured tones.

"We have heard it said Temere is unjust."

Timbrel exploded up from her chair. "Why are you

antagonizing me with these things? Do you want me to speak ill of my king? I won't!"

Her responses, however, already told Nivin she was not sympathetic to Temere's reign.

Timbrel seemed to realize this, as well. "Please, don't say anything to Manny about this."

"Not a word. I am sorry to have upset you, though."

"Well, it's just—our sons were so foolishly outspoken and opinionated about him." Timbrel made a choking sound.

"Were any of them…well, were any of them—"

"Abominations? Heavens no. We had a midwife come all the way out here to deliver them. We are law-abiding citizens here. But from the minute Gamaliel could understand what the Laws were, he hated them. I think he got some of that from his father, though Manny always knew how to keep it quiet. Gamaliel and his brothers were more vocal, and even argued with some of their friends about it."

Nivin cringed. "They were reported and arrested."

"That's the thing. We don't know for sure what happened. I know it was during a whirlwind that scattered the herd that we lost them—Manny was there when they got separated. Still, I can't help but feel that—oh, I don't know."

Nivin tilted her head. "You think Temere was complicit somehow?"

"Well, it wouldn't be the first time he's attacked using the weather as cover. He hardly even cares about the life of his own men!" Timbrel clapped her hand over her mouth.

"It's all right—I will not tell anyone what you've said."

"It's been terrible, not knowing. Manny said the storm

231

didn't seem powerful enough to carry them away. It was as though they simply vanished. I've had nightmares about them being in Temere's prisons ever since."

"What kind of storm was it?"

"You'd have to ask him to be sure. I wasn't there. The skies were clear all that day, though. I remember hearing thunder in the east, and thinking, 'Bless it, where's that thunder coming from?' Ah! If only I had known!"

Thunder.

A whirlwind.

A Charybdon.

For a moment, Nivin considered telling Timbrel the truth of her tale. By now, perhaps Brand would have softened Manasseh some, and Timbrel seemed as trustworthy as she was trusting. Still, something held her back. Just because Manasseh and Timbrel's sons disagreed with Temere's rule did not mean they would disobey it. And there was no guarantee Timbrel would even believe Nivin anyway.

The door burst open, and someone staggered in, panting. The faint smell of vomit trailed through the air.

"Damned fool." Manasseh's voice was ragged. "Ate bittermelde."

"Maker preserve us!" Timbrel squeaked. "How bad is it?"

"It's bad. He ate a whole handful."

"Oh, preserve us."

"What happened?" Nivin said, swallowing back the bile of panic rising in the back of her throat. "Where's Brand?"

"He's outside. Tim, I don't think I was able to get it all out of him. His heart's flagging."

"Get water," Timbrel said, her voice frantic. "I'll meet you out there."

Still wheezing, Manasseh ran back outside.

Timbrel scurried about the room, collecting various things. Nivin thought she heard the faint chime of glass vials clinking together, then heavy footfalls as Timbrel hastened out the door.

The room was silent save for the violent pounding of Nivin's heart as the word *bittermelde* echoed inside her head like a death knell. She got up and ran after Timbrel as fast as she could, stumbling over something as she did. She picked herself up again, walking with her trembling arms outstretched until her fingers brushed against the open door. Giving it a push, she took a hesitant step forward. Her toes found smooth flagstone, warm with the morning sun.

Its warmth could not touch the chill that shot through every part of her body when she heard Manasseh's voice.

"We're too late. He's barely breathing."

"Hold him up anyway," Timbrel said. "If I can just get him to swallow the gagroot...tilt his head back." A cork popped, as if being taken from a glass bottle. There was a small *glug*.

Silence.

Brand. Nivin clenched her fists. *Brand, please.* Boiling tears stung at her eyes, and her heart pounded in her ears.

Don't leave me alone.

Brand retched violently.

"Quick, Tim—give him the water!"

Water trickled faintly as Timbrel poured water into Brand's mouth. Only seconds later, he retched again. Liquid splattered against the ground.

"Again," Timbrel commanded. She poured more of the tincture of gagroot into his mouth.

Brand gagged reflexively, repeated, horribly—a painful sound that made Nivin's stomach churn. Water trickled again, and almost immediately, Brand vomited it up. The gentle morning breeze wafted the sour smell of vomit toward Nivin's nostrils. Nausea clambered up her throat, and her mouth flooded with salty saliva. Clutching her stomach, she swallowed it back.

Gagroot. Water. Gagroot. Water. Timbrel and Manasseh repeated the process for what seemed like hours. Nivin was held by the door in a daze of nausea and paralyzing fear, silently pleading the treatment was not too late.

Brand vomited one final, gut-wrenching time. Timbrel let out a shaky sigh of relief. "There's nothing left but his own humors now, but there's no telling how much of the poison got in his blood. I don't even know if the treacles will do any good." Another cork popped, followed by several soft *glugs*.

After what could have been moments or years, Brand drew a long, ragged breath.

"Ah, thanks be," Timbrel sighed. "Let's clean him up and get him inside."

Neither Manasseh nor Timbrel spoke while they cleaned the vomit off Brand's face. Fabric rustled, as if they were taking off his shirt, which was probably soiled. Then, with a grunt, Manasseh heaved Brand up and carried him into the house with heavy, uneven footfalls. He bumped into Nivin as he did, knocking her off balance.

She caught herself, but stayed where she was. She could hear Manasseh clattering around inside, his footsteps lighter now that he had set Brand down. Timbrel's feet slapped lightly against the flagstones as she approached the door. She paused for a moment next to Nivin, then went into the house without a word, leaving Nivin completely alone. She could hear them speaking to each other in hushed, tense tones, but she was too overwhelmed to understand what they were saying. Her mind raced, desperately trying to make sense of what had just happened.

Bittermelde. Her father had spoken of it, of how some men would take it to escape the cruelty of torture. Clenching her jaw, she squeezed tears from her eyes. She despised what her father did, how he played his role in Zerabar's twisted justice, but he had loved her. He had protected her and kept her safe, the one person she could trust no matter what. She longed for his protection now, for his comforting arms, for his love, but she knew in her heart he was dead, tortured to death. Would he have been cowardly enough to take bittermelde, to die quickly, without suffering? Or did he scream in agony up to the last second of his life?

Bittermelde. Why would Brand take it? What had he learned that would cause him to abandon hope—Brand, who was so strong and dedicated to his cause?

Why would he leave her alone?

Nivin buried her face in her hands, trying to figure out what to do if Brand did not live. Should she flee? Where would she even go? Could she survive on her own?

Her thoughts were interrupted by Timbrel's voice calmly calling her name.

Nivin turned around and felt for the door jamb, using it as a guide to find her way back into the house. She drew a shaky breath. "Will he be all right?"

"Heavens willing," Timbrel said. "I gave him the best treacle blend I have. Now, you're going to come in here and answer our questions."

Nivin took a few more steps into the house, reaching out with her toes so she would not trip over anything. "Where is he?"

"He's on our bed. Please, sit."

Nivin could not remember exactly where her chair was. She hesitated for a moment, trying to decide whether she should take her best guess or simply stay put.

"Please, Ana. Sit down."

"I prefer to stand."

"Fine," Manasseh said. "Tell me, why would your friend Brand eat bittermelde?"

Nivin's stomach twisted. "I don't know."

"Do you even know what bittermelde is? What it does to a person?"

"Yes. I do."

"So what is your friend so guilty of that he would take bittermelde? Is he protecting that abomination?"

"No!" Nivin clenched her fists. She drew a deep breath, regaining her calm. "No."

"Oh? Well, he told me he hadn't been telling me the whole truth, either. What am I supposed to believe? You've done so much lying—lying about that fake country, Libertas, and probably about the shield, too."

"Brand has been lying to protect me, but not everything he has said is a lie. He really is not from Zerabar."

"And you?"

Nivin drew her lip into her mouth for a moment. "I

am. I was born in Capital City."

"And why is he lying to protect you?"

Sweat prickled on the back of Nivin's neck and the palms of her hands. The truth would be the simplest answer, but also the most dangerous. Even in the farthest parts, word traveled quickly, especially about wanted criminals. As soon as she said her name, they would understand—and either believe her or condemn her. While Timbrel had said they disagreed with the Laws, she had also said they were law-abiding citizens.

"Well?"

Swallowing, Nivin closed her eyes. "Because—because my name is not Ana. It is Nivin."

"Is that supposed to mean something to me?" Manasseh said.

Timbrel snapped her fingers. "Bless it, Manny, don't you remember? That's the name of that wanted girl. From the capital. Bless it, we wondered if you couldn't see..."

"The jailor's daughter? I thought she was..."

"Blind," Nivin said. "She is. I am."

"I was going to say," Manasseh snapped, "she was with some kind of giant. Some kind of abomination! Is that it? Is that what that vile creature is?"

"No! Anek is *nothing* like that creature. And yes, I was with him, but we became separated when the spawn attacked us."

"And why did this—this *spawn*—attack you?"

"It seeks to kill Brand because he opposes its master. Brand befriended Anek and me along the way, and so the creature became our enemy also."

Manasseh was quiet for a moment, as if considering this. "All right, supposing you are telling the truth..." He sighed. "What about Gamaliel's shield?"

"Brand told the truth. It *was* in a graveyard. But he also did not tell you the whole truth—his friend found it, not him."

Manasseh scoffed. "Of course he didn't tell the whole truth." There were a few more moments of silence. "So what country is he from, then? Where did his friend find it?"

"Brand really is from Libertas, but I can't tell you where it actually is. I think the graveyard was in a country called Verderbera. I wish I could tell you more, but I can't. I almost know nothing about them."

"Well, then how did that abomination get here? Where did it come from?"

"It came from Verderbera. A sorcerer, named Scyllorin, somehow bred himself with a beast—a dragon, named Scylla. That creature is their offspring."

"Brand said as much," Timbrel said.

"Did he also tell you Scyllorin is bent on slaughtering his people, down to the last man, woman, and child?"

"All right, all right, so this Scyllorin character is bad," Manasseh said. "But just where are these supposed countries? How've I never heard of them? I'm not an ignorant man."

"I had never heard of them, either. They are in another world altogether, as far as we can tell."

"Oh, certainly. And how does one go about finding this world?"

Nivin hesitated. "There is a strange force that somehow connects them. A whirlwind of power full of thunder and voices."

Timbrel gasped softly.

Manasseh stood up and paced across the room. "You're clever, Nivin. But Timbrel has already told me you asked about how we lost our sons, and maybe she trusted you too easily. And of course, now we see that's true."

"I didn't tell her about the voices, Manny," Timbrel said, her voice pale. "I was afraid she would think we were mad."

"She—she could have heard it from someone else."

"We vowed long ago not to tell anyone about the voices. Do you think I would just break that? I've never said a word to anyone!"

There was a long silence.

"You swear to me you are telling the truth?" Manasseh said.

Nivin stood tall. "Yes."

Manasseh walked across the room and sat down again, the chair creaking softly beneath him as he did. He cleared his throat, and when he spoke, his voice wavered. "So. You are the jailor's daughter. You met this Brand character while you and the giant were fleeing, and the spawn was chasing him?"

"Not exactly. Anek and I were running, when suddenly Brand appeared in one of the whirlwinds."

"These whirlwinds. They have a name?"

"They are called Charybda."

"All right, so Brand shows up in a—whatever you said. Then what?"

"To escape Temere's men who were pursuing us, we found another Charybdon that took us back to Brand's world. Once there, we met Ordnance, a friend of Brand's, who had the shield. He gave it to Brand and me, so that we stood better chances against the spawn. Then a Charybdon sucked us back into this world, in the middle of your fields, apparently."

"I can tell there's a lot of information missing in that story."

"Only for brevity's sake. But I will answer any of your questions as best I can."

"I only care about one thing. How—Ordnance—came to possess that shield."

"Ordnance had been imprisoned by Scyllorin, but managed to escape by"—Nivin wondered whether or not the full tale of Ordnance's escape would be necessary—"pretending to be dead. He found the shield in the graveyard outside Scyllorin's castle and thought it might be useful, so he took it."

Timbrel let out a choked sob. "So they were killed by a tyrant in the end, after all. Just not the one they spoke so loudly against."

"I do not know if they are dead," Nivin said. "Perhaps they only lost the shield."

"You're kind, Nivin," Manasseh said gently.

Timbrel began sobbing in earnest, and Manasseh rose from his place. He walked over to where she stood. Timbrel's weeping became muffled, as if she was burying her face in her husband's shoulder, letting forty years' worth of uncertainty and grief seep into the embrace.

Nivin hung her head, unsure what to say. She waited quietly, feeling like even more of a stranger in their house than before. There was no comfort she could offer them, and all the sympathy in her heart would not be enough to ease their sorrow. Brand could at least have told them more about Scyllorin, but even that would have been no consolation.

"Forgive us," Manasseh said, clearing his throat. "No, forgive me. Timbrel was right to trust you. My accusations must've driven Brand to take bittermelde."

"Your accusations?"

"He said the bittermelde *was* lamb's quarters. I called him a liar, and called him out on his lying about Libertas, too. He wanted to show me he was telling the truth. I guess lamb's quarters and bittermelde must look exactly the same."

Nivin's mind became a flurry of thought. "Maybe they are the same plant."

"How is that possible?"

"Here—in Zerabar—Anek's mind was crippled, but his strength was great. Yet in Brand's world, Anek is sharp-witted, though weak. Anek told me Brand looks different in this world than in his own. Perhaps the plants—lamb's quarters, bittermelde—are one and the same, but are different in each world."

"So what about you? How are you different?"

"I—I don't know. I'm the same, as far as I can tell."

Brand coughed faintly from the other room. Timbrel hurried in and came out a few moments later. "He's still out, but he's breathing and his heart's stronger. He's got a bit of a fever, though—I'll make him some of my mother's tea." She strode over to the fireplace.

As Timbrel bustled about, putting water on to boil, Manasseh came over and stood by Nivin. "I suppose now comes the question of what we do next."

"What do you mean?"

"It seems you and Brand share a common enemy with my sons, rest their souls. Therefore, I'm bound to help you. What do you need?"

Nivin inwardly cringed when she thought of what needed to be done. The idea of facing the spawn again was mingled with the memory of Brand crying out as it plunged its claws deep inside of him. "I wish I knew."

"Well, it's obvious we need to find that thing and stop it from killing people here. Any ideas where it might've gone?"

"Brand told me you said the shield came from a quarry less than a mile from here."

"Yes. What of it?"

"That might be where it went."

"Why the quarry?"

"It has power over rock. It can manipulate it, transform into it..." Nivin frowned. "But it can't affect the granite of the shield. Maybe it went elsewhere."

"The quarry'd still do it a lot of good. There are a couple different types of rock there."

"Then that is where we must start. Once Brand wakes, he and I will have to go there."

Manasseh placed a hand on Nivin's shoulder. "I'll join you."

"You'll do no such thing, either of you!" Timbrel barked. "This poor lad won't be fit for anything but food and rest once he wakes. You'll have to wait till the morning light tomorrow, if then, even."

"It's only midmorning, Tim. That thing will have nearly a full day and night to destroy and kill and do whatever it wants."

"It'll be a small price to pay for all of you to be rested—you'll stand no chance if you're weary. I'll fight you off myself if you try to take this boy into battle, assuming he wakes."

The idea of Brand not waking filled Nivin with dread. "Will you take me over to him?"

Manasseh guided her into the other room, where Brand lay on the bed. She reached out and felt for his hands, but realized he was under a blanket. She could feel him shivering even through the layers of fabric. His face was hot, but not as hot as it had been beneath her touch once. She gently stroked her fingertips across his face, feeling the scarring from where his near-fatal head wound had been—the wound she had healed by torturing him.

The thought of it felt like ice in her heart.

She shook it away. "He's shivering."

"I'm working on that tea for him," Timbrel called from the other room, "a special blend my mother used for fevers—it helps to break the fever sooner. If he can get past this, he'll pull through. Manny, come get the leaves down for me—I can't reach."

Manasseh left Nivin alone by Brand's side, heading out into the main room where Timbrel worked. Nivin listened as Manasseh opened a cupboard of some kind.

"You can't seriously be thinking of going with them?" Timbrel said, her voice low.

Manasseh sighed. "I have to, Tim."

"You're seventy-eight years old."

"And so are you, and we're both hale and strong yet."

"For farming. You're not a soldier."

"It's for Gamaliel. Garren. Orren. They deserve it."

"Dying at the hands of that abomination isn't going to avenge our boys. We decided long ago not to seek vengeance, remember?"

"That was different! We were younger then, we still had hope. What hope is there now? Our sons are gone

243

forever. I won't rest until I have seen this creature pay for the sins of its accursed parents."

Timbrel sniffed. "You might not wake from your rest, love."

Manasseh kissed her. "Someday I will. And there you'll be, Tim, waking up right next to me."

After a moment, Manasseh walked back into the bedroom, dragging what sounded like a chair with him. "I'll make those shoes for you now, Nivin. I'm not really a cobbler—I decided to go back to farming halfway through my apprenticeship—but I've been making our shoes for years. I'll need to measure your feet." He set the chair down next to the bed. "Go ahead and sit down."

"I appreciate your kindness," Nivin said, cringing at the thought of shoes. "But I cannot stand shoes."

"You'll wear shoes or you won't go at all, missy. The quarry will be dangerous anyway, let alone with you going barefoot."

Realizing it was no use arguing with him, Nivin found the chair and sat down. She held her foot up while Manasseh measured it.

"I hope sandals are all right. It takes weeks to make a full shoe." He clicked his tongue. "How've you managed to go without shoes so long?"

"I have almost always gone barefoot. It helps me find my way better."

"Well, your feet definitely look the worse for it."

"Honestly, I usually stayed indoors."

Once Manasseh was finished with all of the measurements, he left her alone with Brand while he went to go make the shoes. Only a few minutes later, Timbrel came in and gently coaxed the partly cooled tea down

Brand's throat. He coughed and sputtered, but did not wake.

"I suppose that's a good sign," Timbrel said. "You don't mind watching over him, do you dear? I've things to tend to."

"Wait," Nivin said. "You said you and Manasseh wondered if I couldn't see. Why didn't you say anything, if you're law-abiding citizens?"

"If we didn't ask, we wouldn't know, and we'd still be following the Laws, wouldn't we?" Timbrel chuckled softly.

"And what about the Laws now?"

"One can only abide something for so long. Now you rest, dear. I'll check back in a bit." Timbrel left the room, closing the door behind her.

A feeling of total aloneness closed in on Nivin. What would she do if Brand never woke up? He had kept her safe from harm so many times. He had reminded her of her mettle, when she felt she had none. He had been the only person, including her father, who ever told her she did not need to be ashamed of her blindness. He had even said her eyes—the dark eyes her father always connected to her blindness—were beautiful.

Her father had always said Nivin was beautiful. But never once had he said her eyes were.

Nivin could hardly have asked for a better friend than Brand. Here he was, fighting off death again—but this time, she could not help him. There was no trace of the powers that formed the Charybda here.

She clasped her fingers together and brought her hands beneath her chin, wondering how to pray for the Creator's favor on his recovery. She remembered her father reading stories about the beginning of the universe, about the Creator who brought everything into being. The people of Zerabar were taught the kings had been left behind to rule in the Creator's stead, but Nivin could not bear to think of a god who would demand the deaths of so many innocents, a god who seemed so different from the Creator in the ancient legends. Her father told her they were only legends—they had been invented long ago to give the kings a reason to claim their power. And yet, Nivin had always wondered if there was a chance—any chance—her father had been wrong, and the Creator of the universe was real, but never intended for the bloodthirsty kings of Zerabar to gain power in the first place.

Even so—how could she dare to approach such a mighty being for one person's life?

She unclasped her hands and buried her face in them.

Please, Brand. Please wake up.

Shaking her head, Nivin rose from the chair, feeling her way to the door. She swung it open, taking a few hesitant steps into the room. Immediately, the sweet-sour smell of yeast overwhelmed her senses. That smell felt like home to Nivin. She had kneaded bread, surrounded by the scents rising from the dough, engulfed in the aromas as it baked in her clay oven. It was a sensation of pure comfort, a reminder of the simplicity of her former life, a reminder of who she was as she lived out her life's purpose.

She took another step forward. "I love baking bread."

"Oh!" Timbrel said. "You startled me. I didn't even see you there."

"I'm sorry."

"There's no need to be sorry, dear. Yes, I always love making bread, too. This batch is for our supper tonight. I'll be busy all day, making a feast for us."

With a sinking feeling, Nivin realized what Timbrel was doing. She was preparing a last meal, in anticipation that her husband would not return.

The thought of it almost sent Nivin careening over the edge into tears. Years of doing the same thing had never affected her this way, not even when she knew the condemned to be innocent. Nivin had done it as an act of mercy, thinking of it as a sort of last rite. Timbrel, on the other hand, did this out of love—the last supper she would ever make for her husband and the last he would ever eat. Hers was a rite far more sacred—a final farewell for the man she had lived with for nearly sixty years, an acknowledgment of the rightness of his sacrifice. She was saying goodbye to her husband, her sons, and the life she had known for decades.

Brand might not recover.

Manasseh would almost certainly die.

Uncertainty swallowed Nivin like claustrophobia. The air inside the house, sweet with the scent of yeast, became too thick to breathe. Panic crept up her spine.

"I—I need to go outside."

"Of course. Let me help you." Timbrel's hand, mealy with flour, took hold of Nivin's. She guided Nivin over to the door and out onto the flagstones. "Here. We have a lovely bench under the trees. You sit here as long as you like—just call when you're ready to come back in."

Nivin sat down on the hard bench and closed her eyes, struggling to regain any sense of calm.

CHAPTER SEVENTEEN

Sitting out in the open air, with the breeze gently whipping stray strands of hair across her face, Nivin finally gained hold of the panic gripping her chest. The longer she sat, the more relaxed she became, and soon found exhaustion overwhelming her. After drifting in and out of sleep for some time, she woke to Timbrel gently shaking her.

"Bless it, child, what're you doing sleeping on this bench? Come inside if you need a bed."

Nivin stretched out her sore muscles. "Is Brand—"

"His fever's gone down some, and I coaxed some more tea down his throat. He's breathing just fine. Come on inside, child. It's getting too hot out here."

Blearily, Nivin followed Timbrel back into the house, where the air was filled with mouth-watering aromas.

"Do you need any help with preparing supper?" Nivin asked.

Timbrel's voice was pure dignity and pride. "No." It was an ordeal she would undertake alone.

Nivin drooped. "Oh."

Timbrel laid a hand on Nivin's shoulder. "But you can help me put together a luncheon. It will be lighter than we usually eat, but since supper will be so big, that's all right, isn't it?"

"Of course. What would you like me to do?"

Timbrel set Nivin to working on lunch, handing her the utensils she needed and guiding her around the small kitchen. Manasseh returned and helped with the final preparations, and then the three of them sat down to eat. They ate in relative silence, and when they were finished and the dishes were cleared away, Manasseh fitted the partly finished sandals on Nivin's feet. Nivin was surprised at how well the curvature of the wooden base hugged the arches of her feet.

"I'll warn you, when these are done, they won't be forgiving," Manasseh said. "Your feet'll get sore until you're used to 'em, and even then they won't be the most comfortable. But that's what happens when a job's done slapdash."

"I am sure they'll be fine, Manasseh," Nivin said, smiling. "Thank you."

"Well, they'll serve, anyway. Can't have you going after that abomination barefoot." Manasseh clicked his tongue. "I oughtn't use the word 'abomination.' People like Temere are the real abominations—but it's easy to fall into the ways of those around us, using words without thinking what they mean. In that way, my sons were stronger than me. But they wouldn't shirk from using the word for its true meaning—things like that—spawn, d'you call it?

That's a thing fitting of the word, just as Timbrel said."

A feeling of warmth spread through Nivin's chest. "I would have liked to have met your sons."

"You'd have liked them. Strong, upstanding lads. Hard workers. I wanted all of them to stay and work the farm, but when Gamaliel wanted to work at the quarry, I could hardly keep him here. Those shields he made were truly a marvel. Only the granite itself's strong enough to really chisel it. The first piece they pulled took months to get loose, and then they found they could use that to chip away the rest of it. Using the granite on itself, it almost works like wood. Gamaliel spent hours sanding those shields with crumbled granite, making 'em smooth as metal. It's strong as diamonds, and surprisingly light. A true wonder." Manasseh chuckled. "Garren and Orren used to say Gamaliel liked the quarry because it was full of rocks, just like his head." He stood up. "Well, I'd best get back to these. I should have 'em done before the sun goes down." With that, he gave Timbrel a kiss and went back outside.

"You go rest up, you poor dear," Timbrel said. "Bed's big enough you can lie down next to your husband."

"Oh," Nivin said. "I forgot to tell you. We aren't married. I'm sorry."

"Oh?" Timbrel's voice was stern.

Nivin blushed. "We've done nothing improper, I swear! We are only friends."

"I see."

"You don't believe me."

"Well, it does explain why he wouldn't look at you when you hadn't any clothes." She sighed. "Go lie down next to your friend, then. You still need rest, and I haven't time to lay out a bedroll for you. But I expect that door to stay wide open."

"Of course," Nivin said hastily. "Thank you. For all you have done."

"None of that. Go rest."

Nivin walked back into the room where Brand lay on the bed. She found Timbrel had pulled back the blanket so he could cool down. Nivin laid the back of her hand against his cheeks and forehead. Beads of sweat covered his skin, and his fever had lessened. She relaxed her shoulders, letting out the breath she had been holding. Still exhausted, she climbed onto the bed next to Brand and lay down, listening to the slow, soft rhythm of his breathing. She took hold of his hand and closed her eyes, drifting off into sleep again.

*

"Nivin?"

Nivin startled awake, sitting bolt upright. "Brand?"

Brand coughed hoarsely. "What happened?"

"You ate bittermelde—I know you thought it was lamb's quarters, but it wasn't. Taking bittermelde is a common form of suicide." Nivin swallowed. "I was afraid you were never going to wake up."

Groaning softly, Brand sat up. "My throat is burning."

"Manasseh and Timbrel had to force it out of you before too much of it made it into your blood. Does your stomach hurt?"

"A little. Mostly my throat." Brand coughed again. "Manasseh and Timbrel—"

"They know everything. Manasseh was angry at first, but it turned out his sons were taken by a Charybdon, just as we thought. After I explained as much as I could, he softened some. Now he wants to help us track down the spawn. We think it might be in the quarry, since there is so much rock there."

"Where are they right now?"

"Timbrel is preparing supper, and Manasseh is making me a pair of shoes. He's been working on them all day."

"What time is it?"

"I'm not sure. I fell asleep."

Timbrel burst into the room. "Ah, thanks be! I thought I heard voices in here—oh, you poor dear. How does your stomach feel?"

"Sore," Brand said. "And empty."

"Well, supper is nearly ready. I made a special soup for you. It's bland, but it should keep you from being sick."

"Thank you." Brand lay back down. "I feel so weak."

Timbrel tisked softly. "Then next time someone tells you something's poisonous, take them at their word, dear. You're lucky to have survived at all."

"I'm sorry."

"Oh, none of that. I'm just glad you pulled through. Now you rest up. Dinner will be ready in a few minutes. Are you up to coming to the table, or should we bring your soup in here?"

"I think I can manage."

"All right then. I'll call when it's all ready." With a rustle of fabric and light footfalls, Timbrel left the room.

About twenty minutes later, Timbrel went out the front door and hollered for Manasseh to come get supper. Nivin offered a hand to Brand to steady him as he climbed out of the bed. He stumbled, but managed to catch himself. Nivin grabbed the chair that had been sitting next to the bed and dragged it along with them.

"Let me get that for you," Brand offered.

Nivin shook her head. "I'm not helpless. Besides, I am the stronger of the two of us right now, anyway."

"Fair enough."

Just as they sat down at the table, Manasseh walked through the door, setting something down on the floor as he did. "Mercy, Tim, it smells like you've made a meal for the king's court." He walked up to her and gave her a loud kiss.

Timbrel laughed. "Oh, you. You say that every time."

"And it's true every time." He pulled out a chair and sat down at the table. "I got those sandals finished for you, Nivin. Hopefully they'll hold up."

A surge of affection ran through Nivin. "Thank you. It means a great deal."

"Enough of that," Timbrel said. "Let's eat!"

They set in on Timbrel's magnificent feast. It truly had been a labor of love: there was bread with plenty of butter and fresh warm wild plum jam; potatoes roasted with rosemary and thyme; roast chicken and rich, fatty gravy; and berry tarts in light, flaky crusts, served with sweet cream. Nivin ate until she thought her sides would burst. She had never baked such soft bread with such a hearty crust, had never made such rich gravy, never made such light pastry. Her father was the one who had first taught her how to cook, and his cooking was paltry compared to this. Anything this good her father ordered — and even then it still paled next to Timbrel's food. Manasseh was right. Timbrel's cooking was truly fit to be served before kings.

Nivin pitied Brand, stuck with his bland soup. But then, as Timbrel had said, he ought to have taken Manasseh at his word.

After they ate, they all sat at the table while Nivin and Brand explained their story more fully. Timbrel and Manasseh were mostly quiet, occasionally asking questions. They seemed to be particularly interested in the topic of Scyllorin. Nivin suspected they were trying to learn as much as possible of what might have become of their sons. When they were finally satisfied, Timbrel rose to clear away the dishes. Brand tried to get up to help her.

"No, sir," Timbrel clucked. "You'll sit there and rest, or I'll tie you down. You're still recovering, and the three of you need to plan the morrow's task, anyway. I'll take care of these." She paused. "It's the least I can do."

Nivin's heart twisted at the sorrow in Timbrel's voice. She imagined Timbrel alone, standing at the door, waiting for Manasseh to come home, yet knowing he never would. Who would tend the cattle for her? Would her way of life simply fall away? Would she die in poverty and loneliness?

"All right, missy," Manasseh said, interrupting Nivin's thoughts. "Let's see if these sandals I've made are worth anything."

Nivin held out her feet while Manasseh slipped the sandals on. The wooden base had been topped with suede, and thick suede straps stretched across the top of her feet and around her ankle. Manasseh tightened the straps, pulling them through snug loops.

"Walk around a bit to make sure they don't fall off."

Nivin got to her feet. Despite what Manasseh had said, they were actually comfortable, even if the base was unyielding. After taking a few steps, she frowned. The sandals effectively blinded her feet and made her clumsy, unable to feel with her toes what lay ahead.

"Are the straps getting loose as you move about?"

Manasseh said, coming over and standing next to her.

"No. But I just don't know if I can walk in these. I can't feel where I am stepping."

"Well, we'll give you a spear tomorrow—you can use that to find what's in front of you. Trust me, you'll not want to be in the quarry unshod. It'll tear up your feet quick. Are those staying on all right, then?"

"They're perfect, Manasseh."

"Oh, I don't know about that. They're apt to fall apart quickly, but they should get you far enough to where you can buy a proper pair of shoes."

Nivin threw her arms around Manasseh, giving him a quick, tight hug. "Thank you."

Manasseh chuckled. "You're welcome, child."

"And to go with your new shoes," Timbrel said, "I finished letting out the hem on that dress. It's as practical as it is lovely, and I can't think of anyone I'd rather see wear it."

Nivin could not even find words. She simply embraced Timbrel, almost wishing she could stay here and live with them.

Timbrel had no words either. One lavender soap-scented hand patted Nivin's cheek, while the other squeezed her hand tightly.

Manasseh let out a heavy sigh. "Just one more thing I want to do before tomorrow. Being as the shield has slots for one, I'll fit a guige on it. It'll make lugging it around a bit easier for you. I already have a cured leather strap that should work."

Timbrel went back to work on washing the dishes, and Brand, Nivin, and Manasseh sat around the table while Manasseh measured the guige and worked on fitting it to the shield.

"Tell us more about the quarry," Brand said, an edge of nervousness to his voice. "What are we heading into?"

"Well, there are two ways down into it," Manasseh said. He picked up something small—possibly a grommet—and pounded it through the leather. "There's the scaffolding and the ramps. It's got three different levels, at present. The deepest one is where you'll find the granite."

"So then all we need to do is drive the spawn into the deepest level, and we'll stand a chance."

"Plus, I have a couple granite arrowheads Gamaliel gave me all those years ago. We'll see what those do to that filthy thing." As he spoke, Manasseh worked several more grommets through the leather. "There. That should hold just fine. Try it out."

Brand's chair creaked as he stood up and took the shield. Leather slid across fabric. "You are a craftsman, without a doubt. This is perfect."

"Good." Manasseh's voice wavered, and he cleared his throat. "Good. Well, I—that is to say, Tim...I'm going to help her with the dishes now."

"Brand could probably use some fresh air," Nivin said. "We will go outside for a bit."

Manasseh clasped Nivin's shoulder and gave it a gentle squeeze. "That's a fine thought. It'll be dark soon, though—don't stay out too long."

Brand took Nivin's hand and guided her outside, pulling the door shut behind them. "That was kind of you, to give them time to talk."

Nivin swallowed, trying not to think of how this might be the last time Manasseh helped Timbrel with the dishes.

"There is a bench under the trees where we can sit."

The two walked over and sat down on the hard bench. Nivin rested her elbows on her knees and buried her face in her hands.

"What is it?"

"Manasseh is going to die, Brand. He is far too old to fight against that spawn, and all of us know it."

Brand sighed. "The thought has occurred to me too. But he is surprisingly strong, and we need all the help we can get. If nothing else, we need him to show us the way to the quarry. If he wants to do more, that is his choice. We can hardly tell him not to."

"I know. But…Timbrel has already lost so much—how can we take her husband, too?"

"You said he wants to do this, didn't you?"

"Yes. And Timbrel seems to have agreed to it. And yet…it does not seem right."

"I know. But the choice is his."

They sat in silence for a long time, uncertainty gnawing at Nivin's insides more and more insistently. The light grew dimmer and dimmer, and the air began to cool slightly.

She jumped when the door opened.

"Come back inside," Timbrel called. "It's time for bed. You'll need your strength."

Nivin and Brand headed back to the house, where Timbrel and Manasseh had set up bedrolls on the floor again. Nivin gave them each a hug good night before stretching out on her bedroll. Brand fell asleep almost as soon as he had lain down, doubtless still exhausted from his ordeal. Nivin lay awake for a long time before falling into a fitful slumber.

*

Nivin woke to the sound of people moving about. Manasseh and Timbrel were in the kitchen, speaking to each other in soft tones. Out of respect, Nivin decided not to listen in. She sat up, shaking her head to clear away the fog of sleepiness that dulled her senses. The room was almost completely dark, and she thought maybe she heard the sound of candles flickering. Fire crackled and something bubbled—grits, by the smell of it.

"What time is it?" Nivin whispered.

"Oh, you're awake," Manasseh said. "It's a little before sunrise, and after a bit of breakfast, we'll be leaving. We were just about to wake you, anyway."

Brand drew a sharp breath and shifted. He sat up, yawning deeply. "Morning already?"

"It'll be light soon. We need to ready ourselves."

"And readying always starts with breakfast," Timbrel said. "Come sit at the table."

They ate their grits hastily and in silence. Afterward, Timbrel took Nivin into the other room so she could change into her new blue-green dress. It was light and comfortable, even over her leggings and snug undershirt. Timbrel was right—it was a practical dress, one that would not hinder her movement or get caught on the ground.

"You are truly lovely, my dear," Timbrel said. She took a hairbrush and smoothed out Nivin's hair, then began to plait it into a smooth, tight braid. "I put a kerchief in your right pocket and some considerations in the left, just in case."

Nivin could not suppress a small laugh. "That will come in handy, doubtless. Thank you, Timbrel." She ran her hands along the braid; not a hair was out of place. "I would have liked to have you as a mother. I never knew my own."

"Fate is a strange thing." Timbrel embraced Nivin and planted a kiss on her forehead. "However briefly we've known each other, 'twas for a reason."

There was a loud knock at the door. "Are you done in there?" Manasseh said gruffly. "Sun's up."

Timbrel cleared her throat. "Time to go."

When they went back out into the main room, Manasseh gave a spear to Nivin. Even though she had held spears before, this one felt curious in her hands. Perhaps it was the knowledge she was going to use it to find her way, something she had never done before for fear of discovery. Perhaps it was that she was going to use it to fight. Either way, a faint sensation of dread crept in as she ran her hands along the spear's shaft.

"You know how to use one of those things?" Manasseh said.

"My father taught me a little, in case I was ever discovered, but I'm not sure what good that will do me."

"More good than if you knew nothing." Manasseh turned to Brand. "Here's one for you. And here's your shield."

"I thought you would want it," Brand said. "It is your son's, after all."

Manasseh slung his quiver over his back. "And what good will it do me? Keep it. I have my bow, anyway." He paused. "Well. We ought to get going."

"Not without food and water, you're not," Timbrel said. She handed a water skin and a pack to each of them. "I don't know how long you'll be gone, but this ought to hold you for a couple of meals."

Nivin gave Timbrel one more hug, and Brand thanked her for all she had done for them. Nivin and Brand walked out into the yard, while Manasseh and Timbrel lingered in the doorway.

When Manasseh spoke, his voice was the gentlest Nivin had ever heard it. "Goodbye, Tim." He gave her a soft kiss.

"Goodbye," Timbrel whispered.

Manasseh waited a moment more, then started walking without another word. Nivin followed after him, using the butt of her spear to feel the ground for anything she might trip on, and Brand fell in step beside her. Cricket, Manasseh's faithful dog, loped alongside them.

Manasseh choked slightly. "Home, Crickee. Home."

Cricket let out a long yelping whine.

"Home!"

Still whining, Cricket turned around and ran back toward the house.

The three of them continued on in silence.

CHAPTER EIGHTEEN

It took them less than an hour to reach the quarry, and by the time they arrived, Nivin's feet were beginning to blister and ache from her sandals.

"Well," Manasseh said, "here it is." His voice echoed out across a huge expanse, the sound reverberating up out of the massive pit in the ground in front of them.

Sweat prickled on the back of Nivin's neck. Just as she had been on the mountainside, she was dizzied by the prospect of that much open space, that much of a fall eagerly awaiting her first misstep.

"It's enormous," Brand said, the anxiety in his voice calling back to him. "There are a thousand places that thing could be hiding."

"No doubt of that." Manasseh was silent for a moment. "Listen. Not a sound but the wind. It's not right. This place's never quiet—there's always the men working and the oxen lowing."

Nivin could take no more. "Manasseh, please. Go back. I can't bear the thought of you risking your life like this for us."

"Don't insult me, child. I'll see this through to the end, whatever that means. My sons deserve that much." Manasseh sighed. "Anyways, that area clear over there is where the men go down—that'll be the easiest way in, unless you feel like flying part of the way. We'll have to go down all that scaffolding, and then down some more into the main area. It'll be much faster than the ramps. Then you can see where the deepest area is—we'll have to go down there if we want to trap the abomination."

In silence, the three of them walked forward along the quarry's perimeter. Nivin found Brand's hand and squeezed it, trusting he would not let her fall into the maw of empty space next to them. They walked for what must have been nearly a thousand strides—Nivin's mind staggered as she tried to comprehend just how huge the quarry must be.

Finally, they arrived at the main entrance. They paused, as if the whole company dreaded their next few steps. Nivin kept wishing Manasseh would turn back and go home to his wife, rather than take that first step down into the quarry where the spawn likely already waited for them.

"Ready?" Brand said, giving Nivin's hand a gentle squeeze.

Nivin drew a steadying breath. They had to do this if they were going to find Anek and Ordnance again. Fixing Anek's voice in her mind, she nodded.

"Can you go down ladders?"

"Of course I can. I'm—"

"Blind, not helpless. Believe me—you have proven to me you are not helpless. I just wanted to—"

"I was going to say I'm used to ladders. Our house had a ladder to the attic where I played as a child."

"Oh." Brand's voice was sheepish. "Sorry, I didn't..."

A smile fought its way past Nivin's fears. "It's nothing. But I am glad you don't think I'm helpless—even when I feel that way."

"But you aren't. You—"

"Let it go, lad," Manasseh said gruffly. "Let's get this over with. I'll go down first, then Nivin, then Brand." The scaffolding creaked as he walked out onto it and started to head down the first ladder.

Brand led Nivin out onto the scaffolding and over to the ladder. The sense she was about to plummet to her death at any second nagged at her. Swallowing, she grasped the rails of the ladder and put her feet onto the first rung. She went down the ladder one step at a time, fleetingly wondering how anyone could easily climb up and down ladders while wearing shoes. When she reached the bottom of the ladder, Brand came down, easily taking half the time she had. They continued in this fashion until Nivin's sandals came down on hard rock. As she turned, the faint smell of rotting flesh pestered her nostrils.

"What is that smell?"

"Dead oxen," Manasseh said. "Over on the ramps. They're just lying there dead—but not a trace of the men. Maybe they fled when they saw that thing—left the oxen behind." Without another word, he went over onto the next level of scaffolding and began to descend the first ladder.

Nivin followed after him, guided by Brand. As soon as

the hard sound of the rock beneath her sandals changed to the hollow clack of wood, the sense she was going to fall shot up her spine again. The scaffolding creaked softly as a gust of wind blew through the quarry with an eerie moan.

The smell of death intensified.

"I don't think the men made it out," Brand said in a low voice. "Come on—we need to keep moving. Just a few more steps to the first ladder."

Holding her breath, Nivin climbed onto the ladder, moving down the rungs as quickly as she could. When she gasped for air, she inhaled the stench of rotting flesh and gagged on it. When her feet came down on the next platform, she pulled out the kerchief Timbrel had given her and tied it over her mouth and nose. In a few moments, Brand landed beside her and took her hand, leading her over to the next ladder. As she was going down, Manasseh cried out several levels beneath them.

She did not need to ask why. Every rung of the ladder brought her closer to the stench, permeating the kerchief she had tied over her face as if it was not even there. The next level only became worse, and the sickening droning of flies echoed inside Nivin's ears. Wings of large birds flapped as they descended into the quarry. Gradually, Nivin's sensitivity to the smell abated, but not enough to alleviate the nausea that threatened to spill into her mouth.

When Nivin's sandals came down on hard rock once again, her nausea redoubled and her stomach tossed. She untied the kerchief and held it wadded tightly over her nose. Flies buzzed in clouds around her.

Manasseh was a few paces ahead of them, weeping softly. "It's not right." His voice was tight with anger. "These were good, honest men. They had families. A hundred men, piled like carrion."

Threads of light flashed at the periphery of Nivin's perception. She tilted her head up, only to realize the spawn was at the top of the scaffolding. Thunder echoed through the quarry as it transformed into the jagged rocks and launched itself toward them.

"Look out!"

All three of them dove out of the way. The rocks hit the ground like massive hailstones falling from the sky, and at once the spawn shifted back into its original form.

It set its focus on Nivin.

Unsure what else to do, Nivin brandished her spear at the thing.

It sprang.

Nivin thrust her spear at it, but the shaft snapped in two. The spawn reached out massive arms and caught her in a vise-like grip, and with a single mighty leap, sprang back up onto the scaffolding. The structure groaned under its weight. She could just hear the shouting of Brand and Manasseh over the creature's growling and the pounding of her heart against her eardrums. There was a faint *twang* and the rushing of an arrow through the air. It hit the spawn, bouncing off it like a pebble thrown against a boulder.

Nivin kicked and screamed against the spawn's grip as it leapt up to the next level, crashing through the wooden planks. The more she struggled, the tighter the spawn's grasp became.

Somewhere, in the midst of the chaos, she heard her father's voice: *Remember, if anyone tries to seize you, do not struggle.*

I know, I know, she remembered herself saying back.

Immediately, she forced her body to relax and went as limp as if she was dead. The sudden shift caused the spawn to stumble back a few steps, its grip on her loosening. Another *twang* sounded and an arrow hissed through the air. Nivin sensed it as the tip plunged deeply into the spawn's upper arm. With a horrendous screech, the spawn lost its grip on Nivin entirely. She fell, clipping the broken planks as she did.

For a few gut-tossing moments, pure emptiness swallowed her whole.

Her body slammed into the level of scaffolding below. The impact pulsed along her spine to her extremities and everything went numb. She felt like she was floating in a sea of nothing—no feeling, no sound. Nothing.

She wondered if she was dead.

An angry tingling like biting ants assaulted her nerves as her senses returned to her. She heard Brand and Manasseh calling her name.

Rock on rock, the spawn screeched again. It leapt after Nivin, landing next to her with a crash. The structure of the scaffolding groaned and the wooden planks fell out from under them. For another terrifying instant, the emptiness swallowed Nivin up again, but then something soft broke her fall. Pure stench assaulted her nostrils.

She had landed on a pile of dead bodies. Her stomach twisted with nausea. Dazed, she tried to climb down and away.

She screamed as something grabbed her wrist.

"It's me, Nivin!" Brand's voice steadied her, holding her nausea and fear in check. She wrapped her fingers around his wrist and he pulled her down from the bodies, catching her in his arms for a brief moment before setting her right on her own feet. "Can you walk?"

Before she could answer, the spawn rose up, drawing itself to its full height, gathering to spring.

Twang. Another arrow hissed through the air, striking the spawn square in the chest. It stumbled over backward and fell to the ground with a *thud.*

Brand ran, dragging Nivin after him. Her heart pounded and she gasped for breath trying to keep up with him. Her feet were clumsy in their sandals, and she stumbled once or twice. They had not even been running a full minute when the spawn rose up from the ground, snapping off the shafts of the arrows sticking out of its arm and chest. Its screech echoed off the quarry walls, causing slides of pebbles to fall to the ground and scatter. Seething with thunder and angry power, it carved a massive chunk of rock from the ground as easily as scooping seeds from a melon. It cocked its arm for the throw.

Brand threw Nivin to the ground and stood in front of her. There was the sound of leather sliding across fabric— Brand must have slung the shield down from his shoulder. She heard the rock sailing through the air, flying straight toward them, propelled by all the spawn's malice and rage.

The rock collided with the shield in a deafening clash. The impact threw Brand over backwards, and he landed on top of Nivin. She winced as his elbow came down on her collarbone.

Manasseh's footfalls ran toward them. He pulled Brand to his feet, then Nivin. "I'm out of the granite-tipped arrows, and nothing else can touch that thing."

"Then we need more granite," Brand said, panting. "We have to get to the deepest section."

Strands of power swirled as the spawn gathered itself

to spring. Before Nivin could even cry out, thunder sounded and the spawn launched itself at them in the cloud of jagged rocks.

"Come on!" Brand snatched her by the hand and started to run again. Manasseh ran alongside them, his breathing raspy and thin.

The spawn shifted back to its original form as it crashed into the ground and surged after them. Each footfall a peal of thunder, the swirling powers augmented its speed. It jumped again, sailing over them and landing in front of them with a menacing hiss.

They stopped short. A chill shot down Nivin's spine as she realized the spawn was trying to cut them off, trying to keep them from reaching the deepest level. It wanted to drive them back, to add them to the heap of decaying corpses.

She had to do something. There were powers swirling all about now, though some of them were starting to flicker out. All she had to do was reach out and call to them, somehow bend them to her will...

She squeezed her eyes shut and stretched out her hands, but the instant the spawn shifted its focus back to her, she froze, her mind blank and helpless.

Brand exploded into motion, rushing forward with a shout. The shield slammed into the spawn's stomach, throwing it back several steps. Brand advanced again, and air rushed around the shield as he swung it upwards, catching the spawn under the chin. The spawn struck back, but Brand shifted the shield in time. Its claws shrieked across the granite shield like nails on slate. Manasseh's bow sang as he fired arrow after arrow. Each one bounced harmlessly off the spawn, but served to distract it just enough for Brand to land one final bash square on the spawn's chest, driving the granite-tipped arrow deeper into its flesh.

The spawn stumbled back with a hissing cough, lost its balance, and toppled over an edge Nivin had not even realized was there. It crashed into the rock below, its screech echoing up out of the pit. Remembered pain of falling coursed along Nivin's nerves, and she took a hasty step back.

The echoes died out, leaving only the sound of the wind and heavy breathing behind.

Manasseh wheezed. "If that didn't kill it…"

"It may not have," Brand said, between gasps of air. "But even if it didn't, now it's surrounded by rock it cannot affect. We need to get down there."

"Scaffolding's this way." Manasseh's footsteps hurried away.

Nivin shuddered at the thought of more scaffolding, but when Brand took her hand, some of her courage returned to her. They followed after Manasseh, working their way down the ladders and platforms as quickly as they could. When they reached the bottom, Nivin started at how different the granite sounded beneath her sandals, how it reflected the sounds differently. It tugged at something inside her, something that shrank with fear. She shook it away, trying to focus on the spawn.

Strands of light still writhed inside it, but the brighter lights from its exertions of power had faded. She suppressed a shiver as she felt its perception focus on her.

Hissing like an angry snake, the spawn rose to its feet. But it remained hunched over, clutching at its chest. Its breathing was labored, and she could sense the waves of pain shooting through it with every motion.

Manasseh swore loudly. "*Nothing* can kill this thing?"

Thunder echoed through the earth as the spawn wove strands of light together, forming something that reminded Nivin of a Charybdon. It took the cluster of swirling powers and placed it over the wound in its chest, screeching in agony as it did.

It was *healing itself.*

This spawn—this *evil creature* was healing itself, just as she had healed her friends, just as she had healed herself. She knew she could see and manipulate the same powers as the spawn did, but to see it use the power in exactly the same way turned her insides to ice.

As it healed itself, the strands of light thickened and multiplied, yet just as Nivin had done, it kept the power metered, never letting it grow beyond its grasp. Nivin realized it had been doing this the whole time, keeping its use of the powers under careful command. It would have done the same with the powers it used to make Brand its mouthpiece, but Nivin's interference with them made them wheel out of control. She had not kept the powers in measured check as she had done with the healing—her panic and loss of instinct had caused them to be wild and more powerful than she could manage. That was why the Charybdon opened so wide, bringing them back to Zerabar.

If they were to get back to where Ordnance and Anek waited, she would have to cause the powers to spiral into a Charybdon again. But here in the quarry, surrounded by the granite, they had a chance to defeat the spawn they might not have otherwise. She would have to wait until the last moment.

"Nivin, what do we do?" Brand whispered.

"I—I don't know."

The spawn ripped the energy away from itself. It had healed most of its wounds, but the granite arrowheads still lay deep inside its chest and arm. It bent down, trying to cut a piece of rock from the ground as it had done before, but the strands of light bounced helplessly off of the granite. The spawn froze, turning its panicked focus back to Nivin.

The spawn burst into a sprint away from them, but it was not fleeing them. It had set its focus on something, something Nivin could not perceive until the spawn took hold of it.

A loose chunk of granite, easily twenty pounds.

"Look out!" Manasseh ran, knocking Nivin out of the way as the chunk of granite sailed through the air toward her. Bones cracked and Manasseh roared out in pain. His body fell to the ground.

Nivin scrambled over to him and laid her hands on his chest. "Manasseh!"

"It's only my leg, I—*run!*"

The spawn was already charging them, razor claws extended. Nivin clambered up to her feet and ran, hoping the spawn would pursue her and leave Manasseh alone. Brand's footfalls fell in alongside hers, and the spawn veered to chase them.

It was too fast. It collided with Brand, knocking him to the ground. The shield rolled away, falling over with a sound like a spinning coin coming to rest. Nivin kept running to lead the spawn away, but this time it did not give chase. It loomed over Brand, hissing.

Too late, she skidded to a halt as the spawn raised its

arm for a lethal blow.

Instinct failed her. There was nothing she could do.

Manasseh groaned and there was the horrible sound of a limb popping out of joint. Something rushed through the air, something Nivin could not perceive until it crashed into the spawn's arm and shattered its bones.

A loose chunk of granite, easily twenty pounds.

"That's for my sons, you bastard," Manasseh wheezed.

The spawn snarled and leapt back toward Manasseh, landing on top of him and crushing his ribcage with a sickening crunch. Its razor claws sank deep into his flesh, tearing through him like a cleaver through meat. Manasseh made no sound other than a strangled cough.

The spawn turned its gaze back to Nivin once more, silently threatening her, promising her the same fate. Letting out a slow hiss, it began to twist the powers so it could heal itself again.

Nivin clenched her teeth. *Not this time.*

She reached out with her hands, and before she even realized what was happening, she had somehow ripped the strands of light out of the spawn's grasp. They swirled away, beginning a slow spiral around the quarry—but they would not sink into the granite.

Screeching, the spawn charged. She turned to run, but her sandal caught on something and she fell. Brand intervened in an instant. He must have retrieved the shield, because the spawn's claws shrieked against its smooth surface.

As she pushed herself up, her fingers found something curious—a thin piece of granite that came to a sharp point, almost long enough to be a knife. Grabbing it, she climbed to her feet.

"Brand!" Nivin held out the fragment.

Without a word, Brand snatched it from her hand. Claws clashed against shield once more, and then—

Brand shouted and drove the spike of granite straight through the spawn's eye.

The spawn made no sound as it collapsed, twitching. She sensed a thick stream of sulfurous-smelling blood flowing onto the ground; the lights seething inside it began to flicker out one by one.

Brand groaned. "Manasseh." Gently, he took Nivin's hand and the two of them made their way to the old man's side.

Nivin fell to her knees, and felt all over his chest. His ribs were almost totally caved in, and blood flowed out of gashes in spurts. "No—Manasseh, no..."

Wheezing, Manasseh grabbed Nivin's hand and squeezed it. "Did you slay the bastard?"

"Yes," Brand said, his voice tight.

Manasseh shifted, groaning. "Then I've done enough. Let Timbrel know—"

"No!" Tears streamed down Nivin's face. "I can help you!"

"It's too late, child—"

"No. No, I can...if I can just..." She reached out with her mind, yearning for the few residual threads of light still swirling around the quarry, praying they would give her enough power to heal him.

"Nivin," Brand whispered. "Just let it be."

No, Nivin thought. *A thousand times no.* Manasseh had been injured because of *her*, because she had opened a Charybdon that had brought the spawn to Zerabar.

If she could heal the others, surely she would be able to

save Manasseh.

Without further thought, she redoubled her yearning for the powers. She stretched out her hands, extending her fingers. Strange words tumbled out of her mouth.

A bright burst of light flared along all the fading threads. They sprang into her palms and thunder cracked through the air as if the world was screaming. The sucking mouth had opened; the voices swelled and ebbed. Already it was out of control. Nivin tried to reduce it, desperately trying to remember how she had manipulated the size of it once before.

The more she struggled to subdue it, the larger it grew.

It was too much, her instincts told her. But maybe—just maybe—she could heal Manasseh's hurts before it swept them away.

She lashed her hands toward Manasseh, engulfing him in the center of the opening Charybdon.

He screamed. The sounds of his anguish seemed to tear her eardrums in two. She was killing him faster than his own wounds ever could. She struggled to command the forces, to make them heal, not injure. The forces were no longer hers to control. They did their own bidding.

The Charybdon seemed to rise into the air rather than sinking into the earth, sucking them up from the ground into its hungry mouth.

Nivin lost consciousness, swept away into the nothingness that waited for her.

CHAPTER NINETEEN

Brand woke to a jarring impact, as if he had fallen from a height. He lay on his back, staring up into a blue evening sky, trying to piece together what had just happened. He had shoved the shard of granite straight through the spawn's eye, and there had been a spray of blood the color of ash as the hideous creature toppled to the ground. He remembered his hands shaking as he slung the shield back over his shoulder, but whether from fear or adrenaline he was not sure. It had not mattered. Once the grotesque thrill of besting the spawn had faded, Manasseh was the only thing that occupied his thoughts.

He sat up, a twinge of panic rushing through him. Where was Manasseh? Where was Nivin?

As he looked around, another question arose: where was *he*? There were mountains all about, but this time he was up on one of the bald peaks. The air was thin and cool, and as it was evening, he must have been unconscious for some time. The remaining question was if they were back in the Guardian Mountains that bordered Libertas or if they were in the mountains in the north of Sardraco. He would not be able to tell for certain until the sun went down and he could consult the map of the stars.

A short scream rang through the air. Several yards away, Nivin jumped up and stumbled around in a panic, calling for Manasseh.

Brand hurried to his feet and ran over to her. "Nivin, it's me, Brand."

"Where is Manasseh?" Nivin reached out and grabbed Brand by the shirt. "Where is he? Do you see him?"

"No, but I didn't even see you until you got up. We'll find him, all right? If he came through with us, he will be here somewhere. Please, calm down."

Nivin squeezed her eyes shut. Gradually, her breathing slowed, and her eyes opened again. Moisture shimmered along her dark eyelashes. With a sigh, she released her grip on Brand's shirt and gave a curt nod.

"Are you hurt?"

She shook her head.

"Good. I was worried after you took that fall."

"Don't worry about me," Nivin said hoarsely. "Let's just find Manasseh."

It only took another moment of looking around before Brand spotted Manasseh lying on the ground a few yards away from them. "There." He took Nivin's hand and the two of them walked over to where Manasseh lay.

"Is he all right?"

Releasing Nivin's hand, Brand stooped down and examined Manasseh. Though his shirt was tattered and torn, all of the cruel gashes from the spawn's claws were now scars. His chest was whole, no longer crushed and blossoming blood.

But it was still. Deathly still.

Brand pressed his ear to Manasseh's breast, only to hear silence.

"Nivin..."

Nivin dropped to her knees and pushed Brand out of the way with a forceful shove. She threw herself onto Manasseh in a panicky embrace, putting her ear over Manasseh's heart for a few silent seconds. "No." She grabbed his shoulders and shook him. "No, no, *no!*"

"Nivin, stop," Brand whispered. "He's gone."

Nivin sat back on her feet and tilted her head toward the sky, tears streaming down her face. She drew a few choked breaths before an eerie, sobbing scream tore from her throat. Her voice echoed off the mountain slopes, strangely magnified.

And the earth answered.

Faint thunder throbbed through the ground as though the rocks were nothing more than the tightly stretched skin of a drum. The ceiling of the sky called back. The trees around them shivered and tiny slides of rock slipped down the surrounding peaks.

Then there was nothing but the deepest silence Brand had ever heard. His every hair stood on end; his heart raced. Nivin collapsed in despair into a heap on top of Manasseh, and Brand was almost convinced for a moment she was dead, as if in the unearthly scream she had given up all her will to live.

Brand was terrified for her—terrified of her, of the thunder that had replied to her anguished cry, of what it could mean. Finally, he mustered the courage to lay his hand on her shoulder. "Nivin?"

She pushed his hand away and sobbed silently.

Brand tried to shove down the competing emotions raging inside of him. His fear of Nivin's hidden, powerful knowledge, his grief for Manasseh's death. The thought of Timbrel's loss haunted him. Timbrel would never know what happened to her husband, only that he had disappeared with the two strangers.

Brand realized with a pang of guilt how jaded he had become in the face of death. He had seen—and come to expect—the deaths of so many, he had learned to put away the sense of loss. It was easier to turn that loss into motivation to fight against Scyllorin and Scylla than it was to face it. However, Manasseh's death rattled him deeply. Was it the thought of Timbrel, alone at home, knowing her husband would never return, having lost every loved one she possessed? Or was it the thought of the faithful dog lying at Timbrel's feet, staring at the door, waiting for her master's return?

The sacrifice of those dedicated to sacrifice—the Champions, the Scholars—it was expected, it was fitting—but an old man, who would leave behind an already grieving, childless widow?

Brand tried to stuff the grief away—but it was so great, and it dredged up so many pains and memories—and guilt. So much guilt. Had he grieved this much at Pock's death? Grieved he had never known his parents? He had been rejecting grief since the massacre during his childhood. How could he deny pain and suffering and turn it into base, spiteful anger—turn it into a quest for vengeance against Scyllorin?

Scyllorin. He was preparing to wipe out the Freemen altogether. It would take many more such sacrifices as Manasseh's, sacrifices far greater than the Freemen had ever made before. Would they be willing to make them? Would Brand be willing to ask it of his own people—the young, the old, and the childless? The thought brought with it a fresh wave of grief.

But he would have to grieve later. He would have to silence the part of him that knew he was still a child. He would have to subdue the sudden longing for the comfort of the mother he never knew. *When everything is ended*, he thought, *I will grieve.*

There would be much to grieve.

But now, there was much work to be done.

His survival instincts kicked in, and he lost himself in focusing on concrete things he could do. He made a quick appraisal of their supplies—of the three water skins, two were missing. The third was badly torn, slashed open by the spawn's claws, and he could only find one of the packages of food Timbrel had made for them. The only thing to do now was to look for signs of water and good places for shelter. Leaving Nivin alone to mourn, he turned away and began scouting out their surroundings. Assuming they were back in the Guardian Mountains, they were now on the west side of the range, judging by the sun. The thought made Brand's heart sink. Anek and Ordnance were still on the east side of the mountains, and who knew whether they had even survived? Shaking his head, Brand pushed the thought away and appraised their situation.

The mountaintop, almost a plateau, was relatively small compared to the grandeur of the peaks soaring up around it. Lichen-covered rocks rose from the earth, and small flowering mosses crept along the ground. On the west side, the plateau dropped off into a slope that would probably be the only way to get down—the other sides ended in sharp cliffs or impassable terrain. Less than a hundred yards down, the forest came to an abrupt stop in a perfect line, leaving the mountaintop bare. Brand focused his attention on the gentler slope. From this vantage point, he could see an indent in the mountainside that might offer shelter from the wind. Near it was a wide clearing which would give him a good view of the night sky. It was far, but not so far it would be dark before they reached it. Satisfied, he started back to where Nivin and Manasseh lay. Nivin sat upright next to Manasseh now, stroking her fingers through his thin white hair.

Once again, Brand thought of Pock, and how he wished he could have laid his friend to rest properly. He shook away the image of Scylla's maw closing and the lump that disappeared down her throat.

"We should move on," Brand said, more roughly than he intended. "I found a place we can pass the night, down the slope."

Nivin bristled. "What, and just leave him?" Something in her tone seemed accusatory, as if she did not think Brand was grieved by Manasseh's death.

The thought stung. "Of course not."

"Then what?"

"We can't bury him—we have no shovels." Brand looked around. Many small rocks lay scattered across the mountaintop. "We can raise a cairn. If I gather the stones, can you place them?"

Nivin nodded curtly.

Brand dragged Manasseh's body next to one of the

large boulders rising from the ground, using the massive stone to form one side of the cairn. Nivin sat by the body while Brand went about collecting rocks, and when he brought them over, she carefully arranged them. They did not finish placing the last few pieces until the plateau was bathed in rosy light and the air had grown cooler. Brand stood back and looked at the cairn, thinking it was somehow fitting for Manasseh to be laid to rest under stone.

A cold breeze blew through, reminding Brand they needed to get to shelter before it became too dark. They were already close to the gentler slope, so they had at least something of an advantage. "We should go now."

Nivin sniffed. "Where is the shield?"

"I have it."

"Give it to me."

"Why?"

"Just give it to me!"

At a loss, Brand shrugged the shield off his shoulder and handed it to Nivin.

"Rest well, Manasseh." She clutched the shield to her chest for a moment, then leaned forward and placed it on top of the cairn.

Brand bowed his head, giving Nivin time to finish her farewell. After a while, he said, "Are you ready to move on?"

She nodded.

"All right." Brand reached out and picked up the shield again.

Nivin caught the shield by the guige. "Leave it! It was the last piece of his sons he had!"

"And he gave it to us to help fight for their cause."

Brand tugged the shield away from her grasp. "This shield is special. I know it, you know it, and he knew it. We need it."

"He deserves to have it with him!"

"He would want us to take it."

"You can't speak for him. He should have at least some part of his own world at his side!" Nivin lunged at Brand, grabbing for the shield.

Brand easily stepped to the side and jerked the shield out of her reach, but she ran past him. She lost her footing and tumbled down the slope with a short scream. Cursing to himself, Brand hurried after her. She came to rest a long way down, finally catching herself on a tree. By the time Brand caught up to her, she was sitting up with her head resting on her knees.

"Are you hurt?"

Nivin said nothing.

Brand sighed. "Nivin, when everything is said and done, I'll find the grave and put the shield on top."

"You're only saying that to appease me."

"No. Do you not think I care about Manasseh? I want to do this."

Nivin raised her head. "Don't make promises that can't be kept. You may not even be able to find his grave when all of this is over. And what does 'said and done' even mean? You said your people have been fighting against Scyllorin for nearly a century. When will everything be said and done? You can't keep that promise."

"If I am at all able, I will do it."

Nivin scoffed. She unsteadily climbed to her feet, wobbling for a moment before catching her balance. "It doesn't matter anymore. Let's move on, since you are so focused on that."

Brand cringed. Her words were like a punch to his gut, but he had no counter for them.

Their journey to the place Brand had seen was fairly easy, though the stony silence between the two of them made it seem arduous. Nivin kept refusing guidance from Brand, and so she stumbled often. She pushed away his hand when he reached out to help her regain her balance. Meanwhile, the sun grew redder and the shadows lengthened. Brand started to fear they might not find the spot before all the light was gone, but they finally made it just as the light became too treacherous for travel.

As he had supposed, the place was a good one. It was against the side of the mountain, with rocks and trees to provide some shelter from the elements. In addition, it was only a few steps from a clearing where he could see the night sky well. Unfortunately, he would be unable to set up the place so they could pass the night warmly. Without a spread of pine needles or leaves, even a hasty one, the ground would greedily siphon the heat from their bodies. Still, they would be sheltered from the wind, so it would be better than nothing.

"Here we are," Brand said, unsure what else to say.

Nivin found a place to lie down on the ground and immediately went to sleep—or at least pretended to sleep. Brand sat down a few feet from her and waited for the stars to come out. The earth was cold and hard beneath him, and the wind was a lonely sigh between the branches of the trees. It took all of his discipline to keep thoughts of fear and despair at bay.

Fortunately, he did not have to wait much longer for the stars. Once they were bright enough, he walked all the way out into the clearing to observe them. As always, he started by finding the Compass, lining up his arms to guess the angle between the bright flickering star and the distant horizon. They were too far south to be in the mountains of Sardraco—but to double check, he found the Swan to get a closer estimate based on that constellation's position. Relief swept through him. They might make it to Council City in less than two weeks, if all went well—and if his calculations were not completely off base.

When he got back, he found Nivin lying supine, her eyes open. Her arms were folded tightly across her chest, and she shivered.

"Well," Brand said, "the good news is we are in the Guardian Mountains—and I think we're even closer to Council City than we had been. Unfortunately, we are on the opposite side of the range from where we left Ordnance and Anek. I would need a sextant to know more."

Nivin turned and lay on her side. "I miss Anek."

Brand nodded. "He was a good companion." He sat down again.

"Do you think we will ever see him again?"

"I do not know."

"The other spawn probably killed him, and Ordnance too. He risked every chance he had to escape safely for me. He is going to die because of me, just like Manasseh."

"How can you fault yourself for Manasseh's death? He made the sacrifice of his own volition. He did it for the memory of his sons. The choice was his."

"I killed him!" Nivin sat bolt upright. "If I hadn't been so—conceited! To think I was capable of healing him—I killed him instead!"

"You were able to heal Anek and me. It made perfect

sense for you to think you could help Manasseh as well."

"That time was different," Nivin sputtered. "I hardly knew what I was doing, and yet I also knew exactly what I was doing. And that Charybdon—it was whole, but small. It had already been created. I just"—she shivered—"used it. It was similar when we first confronted the spawn. It made the powers appear, and when I tried to stop it, that caused the powers to spiral out of control. There was no real Charybdon in the quarry—the powers were fading. I called the Charybdon up, and I don't even know how—those terrible strange words in my mouth, it was like someone else put them there! It happened because I wanted it, wanted it so badly. And I didn't even save him—I killed him!"

"He was already dying."

"If that's the case, then I perverted his death. I took him away from Timbrel. She won't be able to bury him. That is *my* fault!"

"Timbrel also made that sacrifice, in her own way. I think she never expected to see him again."

"It's my fault she never will."

"Nivin, listen. Blame is a cruel overseer. The Scholars used to tell us a story: A young Champion set out before his time had come, proud and determined to stop Scylla. The young Champion, however, came against an obstacle he could not overcome—and one of the Scholars ran after him to save him. The Scholar died in order that the Champion could live to carry on his mission. The Champion, however, blamed himself for the death of the Scholar.

"Was it the Champion's fault? It is true the Scholar would not have had to imperil herself if he had not been so foolish, but the Scholar easily could have let the young Champion die. He overlooked this point: it was the Scholar's free offering to him, not something he had caused. The beauty of sacrifice is that it is done freely, not under coercion. To blame oneself is to make ugly the beauty of the sacrifice.

"When the Champion blamed himself, two things happened: first, the Champion became so obsessed with guilt that he did not continue the mission—the mission the Scholar made the sacrifice for. By doing this, of course, he spurned the Scholar's life and diminished the sacrifice she made for him, rejecting the path she had intended him to take. Second, when he allowed the guilt and blame to consume him, he grew withdrawn and depressed. He cursed his birth and hated himself, thinking himself to be unworthy of life. He believed this so much he took his own life.

"His friends, and some of the other Scholars, blamed themselves in the wake of his death. They thought they should have seen it coming, should have done something differently to help save the young Champion. They were tormented by the guilt of his death—guilt which was not theirs to claim—and it consumed them. Many of them gave up hope in the mission, as well.

"'Blame is a cycle which never ends.' The Scholars always said that to the Champions. They told us that story often. Simply by blaming himself, the young Champion started a cycle which caused damage long after the fact. If he had acknowledged that yes, he erred, and accepted the beautiful gift of the Scholar's sacrifice, then he would have brought honor to her death. But by blaming himself, he not only disgraced her, but he hurt all of the people around him."

Tears streamed down Nivin's face. "It isn't the same, Brand. I killed him, just like—"

"Stop it!" Brand jumped to his feet. "Just stop it. Don't you think I'm sorry he's dead? Don't you think I wish he had stayed behind? But we would never have stopped the spawn without him. He saved us and that's what he wanted to do! Besides, we wouldn't have even been able to come back here if you hadn't called up the Charybdon."

"So it doesn't matter who dies, as long as your mission against Scyllorin is preserved?"

"No! Don't put words in my mouth. I am saying Manasseh wasn't a bystander. He was a willing participant. He wanted to do it! Who was I to tell him no?"

"You keep saying that like the spawn killed him. It didn't! I did!"

"Stop! Stop making this about yourself! You aren't responsible! You tried to save him, it didn't work—maybe he was gone before the Charybdon even whisked us away. It is not worth torturing yourself over!"

Nivin buried her face in her hands and started sobbing.

Guilt immediately swept through Brand. With a sigh, he went over by Nivin and sat down again. "I am sorry."

"So many are dead because of me," Nivin whispered. "All because I insisted on bringing food to Anek. That young soldier died. My father almost certainly died when I was found out. If I had simply listened to him, none of this would have happened, and Manasseh would be alive." She sniffed. "My father would be alive."

"And Anek would be dead."

"He may be dead anyway."

"We do not know that for sure."

"But without the shield—"

"Other spawn have been defeated without a shield like this before."

Nivin said nothing.

"I understand loss. I understand guilt. But it may be providence you are here. Nivin, I need you. My people are in danger. More and more I start to think you might be the key to helping them. You don't have to help me—that is your choice. But I am convinced we cannot win this war without you."

Nivin shivered. "It's cold."

"I'm sorry," Brand said. "I had no time to light a fire—and besides, if there are more spawn about, I would rather not attract their attention. Especially since—"

"Since they may have heard me." Nivin's voice was full of humiliation.

It occurred to Brand that whatever strange power Nivin might possess, she was truly ashamed of it. Had she not tried to tell him as much? She had said she almost hated her hidden knowledge. She had called the thunder evil. Her blaming herself over Manasseh's death went beyond simple guilt. She was afraid of herself, afraid of what she could do.

But blame didn't matter, moving forward did.

Briefly, he yearned for the guidance of the Councilors and Scholars. The keen awareness of his own youth made it even more difficult to put away the blame and the grief. He was silently grateful Nivin could not see him; he was sure the uncertainty and fear were plain on his face.

His training demanded him to be strong. His training demanded him to assuage the fears of others and ignore his own.

No amount of training had prepared him for the complexity of the situation in which he found himself now.

Nivin interrupted his thoughts. "I am sorry. I didn't mean to say you didn't care about Manasseh's death."

"The Scholars always said it is not good to linger on apology. We just have to move forward as best we can, now."

"So what now?"

"We should try to get some sleep. In the morning, we can decide what to do next. I will keep watch."

Nivin nodded. She lay back down on the ground, resting her head on her arms. "I wish we had a blanket. Or Anek. He kept me warm."

Brand chuckled. "The truth comes out. Now I see why you miss him."

Nivin moved over to Brand's side. She curled up into a ball, almost fetal, with her arms folded over her chest and her knees practically touching her elbows. Not wanting to be unseemly, Brand awkwardly put his arms around her, trying to touch as little of her as possible. But she snuggled up close against him, her head on his chest and her knees against his thighs. Irresistibly, his mind was drawn to the image of her nakedness. Even though he had only caught a glimpse, it had etched itself into his memory. The way she clasped her arms across her chest now made him think of her in Timbrel's kitchen, struggling to cover herself. Then, he had been so worried for her that he had hardly noticed; now, all he could think about was how smooth and white her skin was where it had been untouched by the sun. The thought that those barely concealed breasts and those long white thighs were now next to him, only separated from him by clothing, made his pulse thud in his ears.

But nothing about her body could compare to her spirit—her intelligence, her bravery, the depth of her compassion. The thought made his heart race even faster.

Instinctively, he clasped her a little tighter. Without meaning to, he slowly fell asleep with images of her sun-pink and creamy white flesh racing through his mind.

CHAPTER TWENTY

Nivin woke with the same ache in her heart as the one with which she had fallen asleep. The sensation of Manasseh's dead body in her arms seemed as though it would never fade. The sensation she was responsible for his death—whether in part or in full—would never fade. Brand had said she should not blame herself, that Manasseh's death had been of his own choosing, but Nivin was not sure if she would ever be able to accept it. No matter how much Brand was convinced her hidden knowledge would help the Freemen, Nivin was just as certain it could destroy them. The forces that made up the Charybda were powerful, and Nivin had only shown she could not fully control them.

Brand's arms still encircled her, but it seemed he had fallen asleep before he could wake her to keep watch. He was now the only thing she had left. The sound of his soft, steady breathing was an anchor, keeping her sanity from being swept away in the turbulent sea of her grief.

She shifted, and her whole back lit up with pain—horrible, seizing pain that ran along her every nerve like electricity. It was all she could do not to scream. The fall in the quarry as well as her tumble down the mountain had taken a toll on her body, and sleeping on the cold hard ground had only made it worse. With a grunt, she pulled away from Brand's arms and tried to sit up.

Brand stirred, drawing a sharp breath as he woke. "Morning? Oh, no. I'm sorry—I didn't mean to fall asleep."

Wincing, Nivin held in another cry as she finally sat up properly.

"Are you all right?"

"My back hurts—badly."

"Can you stand?"

"I can try."

Brand scrambled up to his feet and gave his hand to Nivin.

Pulling against his grip for support, Nivin slowly stood up. Straightening her posture sent spasms of pain down her spine, and she cried out.

"May I?" Brand's voice was full of concern, but there was an edge of nervousness to it, as if the thought of touching her made him afraid.

As she nodded, Nivin's face went hot with shame. Doubtless, her eerie outburst on the mountaintop frightened him. But it had frightened her too, shocked her that her own cry of sorrow could trigger the thunder—and though she did not want to believe it, she thought she might have seen threads of light flickering in the periphery of her perception. They had vanished as soon as she had perceived them, and the echoing thunder had faded just as quickly.

Gently, Brand pressed his hands against Nivin's back. Nivin held in another scream as he slowly prodded his fingers along her spine and shoulders.

"You are probably bruised badly. I'm sure they go deep into your muscles—maybe your bones, even. You have some swelling, but it does not feel as though any of your bones are broken. Balmwort or willow might help your pain—but I do not think either grow this high in the mountains. " He was quiet for a moment. "I was worried. That fall you took in the quarry could have paralyzed or killed you. You must have landed just so."

"It still hurt badly enough." Groaning, Nivin eased herself back into a sitting position. "Do we have any water?"

"No. I managed to find one of the packs Timbrel sent with us, but the only water skin I found was ruined."

"It always comes down to water."

"Yes." Brand sat down next to Nivin. "But food is what we have, so we might as well eat." There was a soft rustling as Brand opened the pack of food. "Cheeses, dried meat, some dried fruit, and shortbread. We should eat the cheese first—it won't last as long as the rest. Hold out your hand." Brand passed a lump of cheese to Nivin. "Don't throw the wax away. It could be useful."

Nivin began to peel the cheese open, her stomach growling at the prospect of food. She placed the strips of wax in a neat pile next to her, then sank her teeth into the soft, salty cheese. It had a taste unlike any cheese she had ever had before, which was unusual, considering it came from Zerabar.

"Eat slowly. We'll have to make that last for a while."

They sat together in silence, eating the cheese as slowly as possible. Nivin was on her last bite when a loud rustling startled her, almost making her choke. She swallowed the piece whole and caught her breath, but still felt as though she had a lump stuck halfway down her throat.

The rustling sounded again, closer this time.

"Do you hear that?" Nivin whispered

"It's a doe and her fawn," Brand whispered back. "If we are still and quiet, it may come near us to give us good luck or a blessing."

"What do you mean?"

"Don't you have fawns in your world?"

"Yes, but what do fawns have to do with luck or blessing?"

"Well...it's just a myth, but fawns are supposed to be good luck. They told us that when we were young and learning to hunt. I suspect it was just so we would not kill deer that were too young, but part of me never stopped believing it's true. I had dreams of fawns while I was feverish from my cut, even. And they are such beautiful, mystical creatures, it's easy to believe."

"I wish I could touch one," Nivin said, a little too loudly.

At that, one of the deer bounded away, its four hooves snapping sticks and rustling the brush as it went. The one that remained made an odd snort and backed away several steps, as though unsure whether it should flee.

"What happened?" Nivin breathed.

"The doe left, but the fawn is still here."

On a whim, Nivin stood up again, ignoring the sharp pain in her back. The fawn grunted and stamped its hooves nervously, but did not run. Tiny step by tiny step, Nivin walked closer to the fawn. It kept stamping its feet and grunting until she was right next to it. She reached out and placed a gentle hand on the fawn's back, and it flinched, but did not run. Hardly daring to believe it, Nivin ran her hands up and down the length of its body. Its heart beat in a flutter against its ribcage, and its sides swelled and fell rapidly with its breath. She felt its legs and the little triangular tuft of its tail, then turned her attention to its head, feeling the soft ears and its muzzle. To Nivin's surprise, the fawn turned its wet nose into her face, and they stayed there, nose to nose, for a full minute. The fawn grunted softly and licked her forehead. She laughed in response, and at that, the creature bounded away.

"Well, if that doesn't give us good luck, I don't know what will," Nivin said.

Brand sputtered. "How did you do that?"

"Do what?"

"Keep it from running away."

"I didn't. I don't know why it stayed."

"Maybe they are good luck after all. In my dream the fawn licked my nose—and when I woke up, I was with you and Anek."

"If you were feverish, are you sure it was a dream? I've never believed in luck, but I was astounded when Anek was able to find you. Maybe—maybe the fawn had something to do with it?"

"I suppose it is possible. But, there's one thing I do know—if there are deer about, we should not have too much trouble finding water."

At the mention of water, Nivin became keenly aware of how dry her mouth was. The salty cheese had only served to make her thirsty—it had barely even staved off her hunger. "So what do we do now?"

"Well, if we head in the direction those deer went and look for other signs, it might take us to a water source." The pack rustled as Brand closed it up again. "That might take us out of our way, but water is more important than anything else. How is your back?"

Nivin almost started when she realized the pain had been reduced to a dull ache. "Better, actually."

Brand chuckled. "Maybe the fawn gave you a blessing."

"At another point in my life, I would have laughed at the notion." She smiled. "But I've experienced enough to make me question it."

"I know what you mean." Brand stood up from the ground, picking up the shield. Nivin heard the familiar sound of the leather strap sliding across the fabric of Brand's shirt as he slung it over his shoulder. "I begin to wonder how much the Council of Scholars truly knows about anything." He came over to Nivin and took her hand. "Shall we go?"

Hand in hand, they walked together for a spell. The air stayed cold for what seemed like a long time, and it took another hour or so for the sun to hit the slope. Occasionally, there was the sound of rustling as they startled birds and other wildlife.

"Something still confuses me," Brand said, after a while. "How could lamb's quarters and the bittermelde look exactly the same? I have seen several lookalike plants, but there's always some characteristic distinguishing the two."

"I think they are actually the same plant—but just like

Anek changed, it must be different in each world." The thought of Anek made Nivin's spirits sink. "That is the only thing I can guess."

"So then I wonder, is it consistently opposite? We ate potatoes in your world, and we eat them here as well. Though now I think of it, there was something different about the way they tasted. I thought it was something to do with how Timbrel prepared them."

"I'm not entirely sure what determines the changes in character. Anek said your appearance changed, but his changes were extreme. And as far as I can tell, nothing has changed about me at all."

"Not that either Anek or I could see. But I finally caught a glimpse of myself in the water basin yesterday while you and Timbrel were in the other room. I almost didn't recognize myself—my skin was a different tone and my hair was brown. Even though it wasn't that drastic of a change, I can't believe I didn't notice it in my skin color sooner."

"An honest mistake—I didn't notice either."

There was a pause, and then Brand laughed.

Nivin smiled. Her father never laughed at such jokes—instead, he scolded her and told her to watch herself. She had taken to keeping such quips to herself, pursing her lips together to hide her amusement so her father would not ask her what was funny.

"That took me a moment longer to work out than it should have." Brand chuckled again. "But on a more serious note, the changes seem to be completely arbitrary." Brand was quiet for a moment. "I should have listened to Manasseh. Do you know when I first showed lamb's quarters to Anek, he even said he thought it was poisonous? How was it I didn't remember?"

The smile fell away from Nivin's face. "I don't think crossing between the worlds was ever meant to happen. Something—wrong—makes it possible. I can't help but feel the Charybda are aberrant."

"Yet for all that, I can't imagine being able to succeed without everything I've discovered since I first passed through a Charybdon. We may be closer to defeating Scylla and Scyllorin now than we ever have been."

Nivin had nothing to say. Brand still thought she was somehow the key to his enemies' undoing, but the idea filled her with something like nausea.

They pressed on together in silence. After a while longer, they startled a large bird from its perch in a tree.

A bow sang, an arrow rushed through the air, and the bird plummeted to the ground. Brand yanked Nivin down into the brush, pressing a single finger against her lips. Heart racing, she listened as a pair of heavy boots stomped toward them. After several steps, the boots came to an abrupt stop, and there was a tense period of silence. A wooden arrow clacked softly against a bow and a bow-string creaked as it stretched back.

"I know you're there," a deep bass said. "Declare yourself now or I'll shoot."

Brand pressed down on Nivin's shoulder firmly before he stood up slowly. "My name is Brand."

"Why are you hiding, Brand? And who's your companion? I know you're not alone."

"Her name is unimportant to you. We hid because I didn't know if you were friend or enemy."

The stranger scoffed. "You've got a woman up here? This is men's territory."

"I've known women who could split your head in two with an axe," Brand said, a tone of irritation in his voice.

"Is that what you and your little friend are planning to do, then?"

"That depends on whether you are friend or enemy."

The stranger burst out laughing. "Only the Freemen are so concerned about friend or enemy, last I checked." The bow-string creaked again as the stranger released the tension. "Come on out—but I swear if you're in line with Scyllorin's bastards I'll put an arrow in your eye."

Breathing a sigh of relief, Brand took Nivin by the hand. "It's all right." He helped Nivin to her feet, and they walked around the low brush.

"Where's your axe, then?" the stranger said.

"I left it at home with the women."

Nivin struggled to suppress a smile.

The stranger laughed again. "So you two are Freemen, eh? Where do you make camp?"

"Actually, we don't have one," Brand said. "We are trying to find water."

"Now how in blazes did you get up here with no supplies—did you drop from the sky?"

Nivin almost laughed. "That's a fair enough description."

"How about you stop playing games, and just tell me what's what."

"All right," Brand said, "I'm Brand, and this is Nivin. We are lost and separated from our friends. We are trying to warn the Freemen that Scyllorin is planning to attack them by cutting through the mountains."

"Well, you leave a lot of questions unanswered, but you explain why there have been so many of his demon-spawn about. I've lived in these mountains for years and seen one twice before in my life. Now it seems like I see them every few weeks—it's all I can do to keep them from finding me. Damnable bastards.

"Call me Trapper, by the way," the stranger continued, in a more jovial tone. "Why don't you come back with me to my camp, and we'll get you something to eat. For now, here's some water." A water skin sloshed as he removed it from his belt. "Ladies first."

Nivin reached for where she thought the water skin might be, but completely missed. An instant of panic filled her as she realized she had given herself away, but then she remembered she was not in Zerabar. A moment later, Trapper tapped her hand with the water skin, and she took it and drank greedily. Part of her wanted to drink all of it, but she forced herself to stop. With a sigh, she passed it to Brand, listening with envy to the sound of him drinking.

"Thank you, sir," Brand said.

"You just hold on to that as we walk," Trapper said. "My camp's a bit of a ways, still. Let me just field dress this bird first."

Nivin and Brand took turns sipping water while Trapper went about dressing the bird. Once he was finished and had stuffed the bird into his game sack, Brand took Nivin's hand again to guide her, and the three of them set off for Trapper's camp.

After they had been walking for a while, Trapper cleared his throat. "Might be none of my business, miss, but can't you see?"

The fear of having been discovered shot through her again. For a moment, she did not know what to say, but Brand's hand steadied her. "No. I can't."

Trapper laughed in his deep bass. "A blind girl and a lad who doesn't know how to shave, lost up in the mountains. I've seen some things in my time, but that beats all."

"Many of the Champions don't shave, or have just started, when they are sent out," Brand snapped.

"Champions, eh? I've always thought sending out green fighters against Scyllorin was mad. That whole Council is daft. There's a reason most of them never come back."

"We're hardly green. We studied nothing but fighting and survival our whole lives."

"You're Champions?" Trapper roared out in laughter. "You studied survival, and you're the ones up here with no supplies and no water. Ah, the Council gets stupider every year."

"I'm a Champion, she's not. And the Council is full of some of the wisest people I've ever known."

"All right, Champ, settle down," Trapper snorted. "You don't have to justify yourself to me. And I'm sure the Council could split my head in two with an axe. Doesn't mean they're not a bunch of idiots who want to feel like they're doing something worthwhile when they're just sending the next generation out to be slaughtered."

Brand was silent until they reached Trapper's camp.

"During the summer we move around a lot," Trapper explained, "but we have a permanent camp fixed at a much lower elevation. I'm not sure where my companion is, currently. Anyway, there's a small spring down that way, and the water is good and sweet. I'll start on this bird, and you two can go drink as much as you want. Here, take these skins and bring some back with you." He passed two more water skins to them, and Brand and Nivin went down to the spring.

"He has no idea what he's talking about," Brand muttered, once they were out of earshot. "The Council is vital to the Freemen's survival."

Nivin found she had nothing to say, as she herself had questioned the wisdom of the Council's tactics while listening to Ordnance tell his story.

When they returned, Trapper was already cooking the bird. Fat hissed and sizzled as it dripped onto the fire, and the air was thick with the smell of browning skin. Nivin imagined the only thing that could have made it smell better would be a fragrant rubbing of sage. The thought made her mouth water even more.

"Glad you made it back all right," Trapper said. "Been worrying about those filthy spawn. Now they aren't content even to leave the mountains alone." He spat on the ground and wiped his lips on his sleeve before continuing. "You see what your precious Council has done, boy? They have done nothing more than nettle Scyllorin into sending this attack you've told me about. Would have done better just to keep to themselves, the Freemen would."

"You know just as well as I that Scyllorin doesn't work that way," Brand said. "He wouldn't allow the Freemen to keep to themselves. You know he continued to send his spawn to attack our city-states. You know the destruction he wreaked on us."

"That I do," Trapper said, more quietly. "Did the Council's efforts ever do anything to change that?"

Brand faltered. "Well—it—"

"It didn't. After a long enough time, all it did was bring Scylla herself to the Freemen and she wreaked more bloodshed in one day than years of spawn combined."

"Why would Scylla have wiped us out if she didn't see us as a threat? Why would Scyllorin send his armies now to wipe us out if we weren't a danger to him?"

"You ever have a fly that won't leave you alone, boy? You don't feel threatened by a fly. You're annoyed by it. That's all the Council ever was to Scyllorin. A fly. They're coming to wipe you out because they're sick to death of being annoyed by you. Would have been better for the Freemen to just work on the spawn that attacked them and left well enough alone as regards to Scylla and Scyllorin."

"I don't believe that."

"'Course you don't. You were raised not to see it that way. The Council has convinced themselves they do more good than harm, and they've done their best to convince everyone else around them."

"But how do you know more Scyllorin-spawn would not have come if not for the Champions' efforts for all this time?"

Trapper chuckled. "Well, that's part of the problem, isn't it? I guess I can't know how much the Council helped with that—and neither can you, Champ—since almost none of the Champions ever returned to tell the Council how much they helped. For all we know, they might have died from cold, starvation, or dehydration within a few weeks of leaving."

"I have fought against Scyllorin himself!" Brand threw the water skins he had been carrying on the ground. "My friend and fellow Champion died in that fight. I was pursued as far as the sea, and I survived all that time. Hungry. Thirsty. Weary. All of my predecessors were trained to the same degree as I have been! How dare you suggest they were weak and died before they could even face the enemy?"

Trapper chuckled again. "Yet here you are up in the mountains, practically dying except for the help of an old fur-trapper."

Brand launched himself at Trapper.

"Whoa there—!"

But Brand had already knocked Trapper to the ground with a heavy *thud*. The smacking of punches rang through the air, punctuated by grunts.

"You know nothing of what I have been through!" Brand yelled. *"Nothing!"*

"Brand, stop!" Nivin cried.

There was a sudden crashing through the trees as someone burst into the clearing. "What in blazes is going on here?" the new stranger yelled. The sound of more scuffling ensued, then came to an abrupt stop. Nivin could only guess this rough-voiced man had pulled Brand bodily off of Trapper.

"Go easy on him," Trapper growled. "I had that coming, I suppose. Come on now—I'm telling you he's fine. Leave him."

The stranger must have shoved Brand away, because Brand stumbled several steps back toward Nivin. He caught himself and stood still, breathing heavily and exuding anger. Nivin resisted the urge to move away from him.

"What's going on, Trapper?" the rough-voiced stranger said. "I leave you for two weeks and you find someone to brawl with?"

"I just found them today—and we weren't quite what you'd call brawling. This is Brand—a Champion of the

Freemen—and his companion, Nivin." A minor change had come into Trapper's voice, as though being accosted had made him respect Brand somewhat more.

"Champion, eh?"

"Yes. Brand, Nivin—this is Trader. He handles all the selling of our wares."

"I never would have surmised," Brand mumbled.

"Touchy, aren't you?" Trader said.

"I found them when I was out hunting," Trapper said, "and they were in a bit of a bind, so I helped them out. Didn't take too kindly to my opinions on the Council."

"Being as he's a Champion, I can't imagine why." A touch of sarcasm colored Trader's tone. "How'd they get up here?"

"They didn't exactly tell me."

"You trust too easily. That's why you let me do the trading. However, it just so happens on my way back from Respite Height, I came across some strangers myself—a man and big ugly giant. Said they'd lost a couple of young companions."

Nivin's heart leapt. "Anek!" She was too relieved to care that Trader had called Anek ugly.

"As a matter of fact, that's what the giant called himself."

"The other man," Brand said. "What was his name?"

"Wouldn't tell me. But he was Thallan, and looked as though he had seen better days. They said they were on a mission to warn the Freemen of a coming attack, and told me I'd best hurry on, as there was a spawn about."

"Are they well?"

"Little barked up, I suppose, and ill-prepared, just like yourselves. At least they had a water skin. I gave them some food and directions to Respite Height, and told them I'd keep a look out for their friends."

Nivin sighed in relief.

"Well, let's all sit down," Trapper said. "You'll excuse us while we catch up on business, won't you?"

"Of course." Brand's tone suggested he had not forgiven Trapper for his comments.

Trapper and Trader exchanged stories of their last two weeks with each other while they waited for the bird to finish cooking. Trader had left with many furs and come back with none, but had several new goods. They squabbled as they talked, Trapper's smooth bass and Trader's rough growl sounding like an ill-tuned symphony. Trapper would frequently speak as though he were speaking to himself, or no one at all. Trader gruffly commented this was because Trapper was too isolated and had come to rely on his own voice for company, to which Trapper replied it was far better company than Trader was.

After Trapper had finished his lengthy rendition of the past three days, right down to the intimate details of his quarrel with Brand, he started to comment again on the Scyllorin-spawn. "There must have been one about last night. It made the most unearthly sound I'd ever heard. Seemed to make the whole forest tremble."

A crushing sensation went through Nivin's chest. Trapper was talking about *her*.

"As otherwise pointless as I happen to think the Council is—no offense, Champ, just my opinion—as pointless as it might be, the rest of the Freemen do need to be warned. But heaven help them if they don't rally all their people, and just rely on their young pups—brave as they might be—to stand up to Scyllorin."

Nivin waited for Brand's response, anticipating some reaction to the barb against his age.

When he spoke, however, Brand's voice was solemn. "Yes. The time has come for all Freemen to stand together."

"Absolutely," Trapper said. "See, I finally talked some sense into the boy."

"I'm sure you did," Trader said, giving Nivin a nudge.

Nivin attempted a smile, but it was weak. All she could think about was that she had been mistaken for one of Scyllorin's spawn.

Whatever you are, the spawn had said to her, using Brand as its mouthpiece, *you are an enemy.* There was small comfort to be found in the fact that the spawn considered her an enemy. She already knew she was opposed to everything that Scylla and Scyllorin represented—which only left one question:

What *was* she?

CHAPTER TWENTY-ONE

By the time the bird was finished roasting, Nivin had lost her appetite. Nevertheless, she sat down with the others and forced herself to eat. She heard nothing the others were saying—she was too lost in thought about the spawn, Manasseh, and Anek and Ordnance.

What would Anek think of me now? she wondered. What would he think now that she had brought death to an old man and caused thunder on her own? He had placed all his hope in her since they sat by the stream, when he said something about her mysteriousness had saved him from despair. Then, she had thought his hope was misplaced. Now, she was *certain* his hope was misplaced. What hope was there to be had in her knowledge of these horrible forces forming straits between two worlds, changing everything which passed through them? She had always felt something was not right about them—now, she was almost certain they were fundamentally wrong. If anything, her connection to them should be cause for people to fear her.

She was pulled out of her thoughts when Brand, who had been sitting next to her, stood up.

"We cannot thank you enough for your hospitality," Brand said, "but I fear we must be going. There is still half the day left, and I want to catch up to our friends as soon as possible. How far from here is Respite Height?"

"About five days' journey," Trader said, "but you might make it in four if you press hard. You're not going to make it with one measly pack of food, though. Come on— we'll get you some proper supplies."

Trapper laughed. "If I trust too easily, then you're too generous."

"Will you join us?" Brand said. "The more of us there are, the more likely it is that word gets to Council City."

"It's not our battle to fight, Champ," Trapper said.

"But you're Freemen, aren't you?"

"Yes, and we'll give you the supplies you need. After all, somebody's got to warn the rest of the Freemen—but that somebody isn't us."

Brand sputtered for a moment, as though he could not decide what to say. He drew a deep breath. "Thank you. Supplies will go a long way in aiding us."

"All right, then," Trader said. "We have a water skin we can spare, and we'll load a pack with food. I've got an extra hunting knife you can have, too—and we've got a walking stick for this young lady." A few moments later, Trader passed the smooth, sturdy walking stick to Nivin.

Nivin barely listened as Trader gave Brand directions to Respite Height. Her thoughts were with Anek, and wondering if he would still be alive by the time they found him—if they even could find him. Trader had said Ordnance and Anek warned him there was a spawn about. She cringed at the thought of facing another spawn, the thought of how many things could go desperately wrong.

Brand laid a gentle hand on Nivin's shoulder, making her jump. "Are you ready, Nivin?"

Nivin swallowed and nodded, trying to remember the last time she had truly been ready for anything. She clung to her walking stick as if it were the only thing keeping her anchored.

"Good." Brand turned back toward Trader and Trapper. "Thank you again, for everything you have done for us."

"Least we can do," Trapper said cheerfully. "Best of luck to you."

As they walked away from the camp, Nivin could not help but feel the supplies were indeed the least Trapper and Trader could do.

*

Before they pressed on to Respite Height, Brand and Nivin stopped at the spring again to drink as much as they could and fill their water skins. Nivin found the walking stick made her passage much easier; she could lean on it for support, use it to steady herself, and test the ground in front of her. The old latent fear of being discovered was finally gone, leaving her free to fully embrace using a staff. For what seemed like the first time in ages, she was able to walk without somebody holding her hand to guide her. Brand still had to warn her if there was a particularly large obstacle ahead, but for the most part, she managed on her own. The sensation of rediscovered independence was almost heady.

"I can't believe it," Brand said, after a while. "After saying the Freemen needed to stand together, Trapper wanted nothing to do with his countrymen. He called the Council worthless because he thinks it does nothing but hurt the Freemen, but when he has a chance to help, he refuses it. He cares more about himself than his people."

"Maybe that's why he went to live in the mountains in the first place," Nivin said.

"But he went on and on about how the Champions and the Council have failed the Freemen, and it turns out he doesn't even want to help. He just wants to ramble on about how useless the Council is when he has no idea what we've been through—what we have sacrificed!"

Nivin hesitated for a moment, trying to think of what she could say to help Brand feel better. "Some people are more interested in quietly disagreeing than they are in taking a stand." It was something her father had said once, and she had often wondered since then if he was talking about himself.

"Quiet disagreement is none at all. It is the coward's way."

Nivin bit her lip. She saw the truth in what Brand said, yet it was not as simple as he made it. Her father had quietly disagreed with the Laws her whole life, just by keeping her alive. She had thought him a hypocrite plenty of times, but now that her secret was revealed, his disagreement with the Laws was no longer quiet. Her father had almost certainly been executed for that disagreement, executed for *her*. Her father may have been many things, but a coward was not one of them. "Well, at least he gave us supplies."

Brand came to a sudden stop. "What if he's right, Nivin?"

Nivin stopped as soon as she realized he had. She turned back to face him. "What do you mean?"

"The Champions do seem doomed to failure." His voice was small and defeated. "In nearly three centuries, none have succeeded. Most of those who managed to survive were so scarred from their struggle against Scylla and Scyllorin that they didn't live more than a year past their return." He paused. When he spoke again, his voice broke. "What if—what if everything I've done has been worthless?"

Sympathy welled up in Nivin's chest. "I admit your Council's tactics don't make much sense to me—so I understand your doubt. But I do know that doing what is right is never worthless. The Teratisma Rebellion—the one I spoke of—was doomed to fail before it even began, but I don't think for a moment it was worthless. Fighting against evil is always worthwhile, and sitting idly by while evil is done is an evil in itself. That's why I brought food to the condemned." Nivin smiled as understanding swept through her. "Maybe that's why your Council does what it does. Even the smallest resistance is still resistance."

Brand said nothing, but he started to walk forward again.

Nivin fell in step alongside him, using her walking stick to test the ground in front of her. "I don't think what you've done is worthless, and I don't think Pock's sacrifice was, either."

"Thank you—for everything you've said."

They continued on in relative silence, except for Brand's occasional warning to Nivin about upcoming changes in the terrain.

"You've mentioned Pock several times now," Nivin said, after a while. "Were you close?"

Brand was silent for a long time, and Nivin started to wonder if she had gone too far in asking. She was about to apologize when a sudden dip in the terrain caught her off guard. She stumbled forward, barely catching herself with her walking stick.

"Sorry!" Brand said, his voice cracking. "Are you all right?"

"I'm fine. I just missed it with my stick. I guess I'm still learning how to use it."

"I should have warned you."

"No—I shouldn't have asked you about Pock. I'm sorry."

"Well," Brand said, as they continued forward, "you asked if we were close. We were. I thought of him as a brother. He was slightly younger than me, and had spent time with his mother at home before coming to the Council—careful, there's another dip in the ground, take a big step forward—so he frequently talked about her. It was one part of him I never fully understood, but it gave me a greater appreciation for what his mother sacrificed when she let him go—and what my mother sacrificed."

"You never knew you mother?"

"A Champion is given to the Council caretakers as soon as he or she is weaned. But because so many Champions were killed in the attack, the Council changed tactics and decided to send pairs of Champions, people of similar age. Pock's mother was the only woman who was willing to part with her older child, and he was four. Their parting was a sad one, but she told him how proud she was and how brave he was. I always felt, since he was just under a year and a half younger, it was my duty to protect him.

"There was a reason the Councilors always told us that story I told you. It was to keep us from going mad from the guilt. I understand your self-blame for Manasseh better than you think. I felt I had failed to protect Pock, even though his sacrifice was just as valid as anyone else's. But as soon as I started to blame myself, I remembered the story the Council had so carefully planted in my mind. Pock's sacrifice was necessary. Without it I couldn't have survived. I couldn't have met you. I couldn't have met Ordnance and started to unravel all these mysteries. Move to your left, we need to walk around this stand of nettles." He took Nivin's hand and guided her around the stinging plants. "It doesn't ease the pain, but it eases the guilt and allows for honor to be given to the one who made the sacrifice. Pock deserves the highest honor. When we reach Council City I will tell everyone what he gave for the Freemen."

They continued on for a while without conversing. After a few hours, they rested for a meal, then resumed their journey at a stiff pace. As the sun began to set, Brand began to plan ahead for the evening. He found a place that was well sheltered, and they carefully laid out a spread of pine needles and fallen leaves. Brand did most of the gathering and allowed Nivin to spread them out, which she was able to do easily. As the sky darkened, the temperatures dropped rapidly, but it was already too dark for Brand to light a fire. They ate a scant meal, finishing off the last of the food Timbrel had given them. Afterward, Nivin snuggled down into the bed of pine needles and tried to go to sleep.

Despite her exhaustion, Nivin slept fitfully. She tossed and turned in a clumsy dance along the line of sleep and waking, vaguely aware of the sounds around her and the cold hard ground beneath her, yet still being irresistibly sucked down into murmuring voices and the nothingness waiting for her. The voices seemed to grow more insistent every time she dozed off, until she was not sure whether she was asleep or being pulled through a Charybdon.

A vicious snarl ripped her into consciousness.

She grabbed her walking stick and scrambled to her feet in a wild panic. Something was there, huge and radiating maleficence. It let out a steady stream of low growling. It was filled with faint, snaking threads of light, but she could not tell what it was—it reminded her of a spawn, but it was not. Perhaps it was an animal of some kind? Whatever it was, it was in the same kind of pain she had sensed when the spawn had used Brand as its mouthpiece. She shifted her stance, and the creature snarled again. She gripped her walking stick with both hands. Her heart raced. Where was Brand? Had the creature already dragged him away while she was sleeping? Did she even dare call out for him?

A twig snapped in the distance.

The creature sprang. It knocked Nivin onto her back, its weight holding her down. She screamed as its claws tore at her. Her walking stick lay sideways across her chest, slipping up toward her throat. With both hands, she bashed the staff upward. There was a loud *crack* as it collided with the creature's jaw. It snarled louder than ever, and its teeth snapped together inches from her face. She kept pushing up on the staff as hard as she could. The creature made a choking sound—the staff must have been pressing into its throat. Gobs of foul saliva dripped onto her forehead and ran into her hair. She squeezed her eyes shut as the slimy stuff cascaded down the front of her face. Its claws scratched at her more fiercely, and it pushed back against the staff. Nivin screamed again as she felt her arms shaking, ready to give way. The snapping jaws would reach her face in seconds.

A desperate shout rang through the air. "Nivin?"

The staff in Nivin's hands slipped a little farther. "Brand! Brand, help me!" Her own voice sounded foreign to her, wild with a panic that doubled her terror.

Footsteps pounded across the earth. Brand barreled into the creature, knocking it off of Nivin. There was the sound of a knife tearing through meat and the creature roared. Again and again Brand stabbed the creature, until it lay still and the air was ripe with the stench of blood.

Shaking, Nivin wiped her face on her sleeve. She could not catch her breath—each inhale was ragged and shallow. She felt Brand's hands behind her shoulders, gently pulling her upright.

"Are you all right?"

Anger replaced terror. Nivin walloped Brand with the staff. It hit his shoulder with a satisfying *whack*.

"Ow! Nivin, stop! It's me!"

"Where were you?"

"I was trying to check the constellations—I had to go a little further than I thought to see the sky properly."

"Why didn't you wake me?"

"I didn't think you would want me to."

"So you thought I wanted to be left alone and completely defenseless?"

"I thought you would be better off asleep."

"Better off asleep than alert? Why on earth would you think that?"

Brand said nothing, but Nivin heard the answer loudly in his silence.

"Because I can't see? Is that why you never woke me to take watch last night? I'm blind, not useless or helpless!"

"Nivin, I know you're not—"

"Don't you realize I could have died?" She swung the staff again, but Brand caught it in his hand.

"Yes! I understand now. Even I can barely see in this darkness. I was a hypocrite. I was wrong."

Nivin stood up. "By leaving me asleep, you *made* me completely helpless."

"I know," Brand groaned. "I said I was wrong."

"Do you really think I am so helpless and incapable you can't tell the difference between my being awake and asleep?"

"I did not think of it in that way. I only thought—well, you would be better off getting the rest you so clearly needed. I did it because I knew how tired you were, not because I think you are helpless or incapable."

"It doesn't matter how you thought of it. Next time, think better of me before you leave me for dead."

"Nivin, please. I am sorry. I was wrong. Please, forgive me."

Nivin was silent. Anger was more satisfying than forgiveness, a better cure for the tremors of fear still lingering in her limbs. She wiped her face again with her other sleeve, then held her walking stick in the crook of her arm and wiped her hands on her dress. Her fingers found a tear in the fabric.

Timbrel's beautiful blue-green dress was ruined.

She was nearly ready to beat Brand over the head when she realized all of the swirling powers that had filled the creature were flickering out one by one. "What was that thing?"

"A badger." Brand sounded completely miserable.

"I've heard of them, but I don't really know what they are."

"They are an animal that burrows in the ground."

"Are they usually so—vicious?"

"They are very territorial. And if you upset one or get too near its burrow, it will attack and chase you. I've never seen one so big. They're normally mean, but…something was wrong with this one."

"Yes, there was. It—"

A strange rustling sound came from the direction of the corpse as the last of the strands of light vanished.

Nivin jumped. "What was that?"

"I don't believe it," Brand said. "It just shrank. It looks normal now."

"It was full of the lights. The last one just went out."

"Lights?"

"The powers that make up the Charybda—the ones Scylla and the spawn use."

The ones I use.

"Then it was being controlled," Brand said, the pitch of his voice rising slightly. "There are many accounts of spawn controlling animals in the Histories. We need to get out of here—*now*. Tell me the instant you notice anything else."

Quickly, they gathered up their scant supplies and moved on. The sounds of the night seemed magnified a thousand times. Nivin jumped at every rustle of tiny creatures and the swooping down of night birds to seize their prey, but she did not perceive any of the swirling powers, or anything that might indicate a spawn was nearby. Brand tried to warn Nivin of any upcoming obstacles, but since it was so dark, he barely noticed them himself. However, Nivin had become more adept at using her walking stick to test the ground ahead of her, so she had few problems. Brand stumbled more frequently than she did.

It was deeply satisfying—a better revenge than any Nivin could have contrived.

They continued their slow progress all night long, pausing at every sound and hardly daring to breathe. They barely spoke to each other, and when they did, it was in hushed, tense tones. Without a full view of the night sky and all its constellations to guide him, Brand had to keep guessing which direction would be approximately the right one. It was not until the sun finally rose over the peaks that he was able to figure out which way they should actually be going.

"I was afraid of this," Brand said, sighing heavily. "The sun should be to our right, but it's almost directly behind us. We've been veering too far west."

"Can you still find our way to Respite Height?"

"I think so. But we should stop and eat something."

They sat down for a short while and ate a sparing breakfast before moving on. Nivin still jumped every time she heard anything move. Adrenaline, fear, and pain were the only things spurring her on. Her back ached more and more insistently as they progressed. Her shoes rubbed mercilessly against the blisters on her feet, and her toes cramped with a mixture of numbness and pain. She longed to go barefoot, but Brand insisted she would only injure herself even more. Around noon, they paused again to eat and rest. They each took a short nap, but all too soon it was time to continue forward again. By the time the sun began to sink again, Nivin was so weary she was stumbling despite the support of her walking stick. Finally, Brand found them a suitable place to pass the night, and they came to a stop. Nivin took off her shoes and sat on a fallen tree while Brand set up the camp. After everything else was prepared, he started a fire.

"Won't a fire attract the spawn?" Nivin said, even as she shivered.

"There's a chance," Brand said, "but it's not yet so dark that the fire is overly noticeable. Besides, it's cold. Come sit closer."

Stiffly, Nivin rose from her seat on the fallen tree and moved toward the fire. As soon as she sat down, Brand passed her a piece of dried meat and something hard and square. She ran her fingers across it, feeling little dimples in the surface. Nivin nibbled at the corner of the square, and found she could not even break off a piece without using her molars. "What is this?"

Brand chuckled dryly. "Rockbread. Every traveler's best friend and teeth's worst enemy." A loud *crack* sounded; he must have snapped his piece in two. "It's easier to eat if you break it into pieces and suck on it until it's soft enough to chew."

Nivin set the rockbread down in her lap and started gnawing on the meat. "I liked Timbrel's shortbread better. It was soft."

"And it would have been spoiled in a few days.

Rockbread will last for months if you keep it dry."

"Are you used to food this difficult to eat?"

"Yes. Obviously, you look for other food, like plants and game, but this is good when you have no time to hunt or gather. It's not as though I particularly enjoy rockbread."

Nivin laughed. "So the Council did feed you things besides inedible bricks of flour?"

"Of course they did. Our fare was simple, though—probably less elegant than what you are used to eating."

"How would you know what is it I am used to eating?"

"Well—you said your father was highly favored in the court. Surely you had staff who prepared meals for you."

"No. My father let nobody in the house for fear I would be discovered. He did most of the cooking himself—though he did occasionally have meals ordered."

"What was it like for you? Growing up, I mean."

"Lonely." Nivin snapped her rockbread in half. "You and Anek are the first friends I have ever had."

Brand was silent for a moment. "Nivin, I am sorry—about last night."

Something in his tone softened Nivin's heart. She was about to forgive him when she heard something in the trees rustle. "I hear something," she whispered.

Whatever it was, it was moving toward them.

Brand climbed to his feet. There was the sound of him picking up the shield, and the hunting knife gave a short soft ring as he drew it.

The rustling grew louder, then stopped abruptly.

"It's another fawn," Brand whispered, putting the knife back in its sheath.

Nivin smiled at the thought of big soft ears and short coarse hair beneath her fingertips. She stood up slowly, wondering if this fawn would let her pet it, too.

But something was wrong. Faint swirling lights sped toward them and something crashed through the woods.

Before Nivin could even cry out, another snarling badger burst through their camp and sank its teeth into the fawn's neck. The fawn fell to the ground with a horrible sound of pain, and the badger ripped its throat out in one swift motion. Their symbol of luck and blessing lay on the ground, writhing in death throes.

Hissing, the badger turned its focus on Nivin.

Her blood froze.

CHAPTER TWENTY-TWO

Brand's heart pounded in his chest as he tried not to look at the bloody, twitching remains of the dead fawn. His eyes were drawn irresistibly toward its killer. Twice its natural size, the badger turned slowly toward Nivin. White foam and blood dripped from its mouth, and it took slow, jerking steps toward her.

Brand jumped in front of Nivin, holding the shield up. He had failed to protect her before.

He would not fail to protect her now.

Brand's throat was so tight and tense he could barely choke out a whisper. "Give me your walking stick."

Nivin held the staff toward Brand, her knuckles white. He had to tug firmly to get it out of her grasp.

The instant Brand took the staff, the badger snarled and charged him with an unnatural gait. In a fierce downward strike, Brand swung the stick. It smote the badger right between the eyes with a loud *crack*. The badger rolled away squealing, but then it jerked up, sickeningly resembling a puppet. Snarling, it charged again. With an upward thrust of the shield, Brand bashed the badger's lower jaw completely out of joint. Its jaw hung grotesquely from its face. Gobs of foam and syrupy saliva dripped to the ground. It took a single staggering step toward Brand.

"Kill it, please, just finish the poor creature!" Nivin shouted, as though the creature's pain was hers as well.

The badger made one last limping charge at them. In a final crushing blow, Brand brought down the edge of the shield on top of the badger's head. It fell to the ground like a limp rag. Brand quickly dropped the walking stick and pulled out his hunting knife. He plunged the blade into the badger's neck to ensure it was dead. He yanked the bloody knife away and turned back toward Nivin. Her face was as pale as ever.

"Are you all right?"

Nivin gave a shaky nod.

"Are there more? Can you sense anything?"

As if in response, thunder pealed like the warning bell of a sentry tower.

Only a few yards away, the earth burst open and something enormous exploded out in a cloud of choking dust, flinging a spray of dirt in all directions. Brand shielded his eyes with his hand as a shower of pebbles and sandy soil hit him in the face. Unmistakable in its features, a spawn rose up out of the debris. It still retained an ugly man-dragon appearance, but bore some resemblance to a badger, with lengthened forearms and clawed shovels for hands. Its face took on the shape of a snout, and the thin slits of its eyes glinted with anger. It hissed and snarled at them, squatting back on its legs and coiled as though to spring at them. For an instant, it stared them down. It made a horrible, strangled growl. Five more of the huge badgers issued from the tunnel.

Brand shook his head, fighting back the wave of panic sweeping through him. There were so many factors to consider in this fight: there were five of the badgers, he had only Nivin's walking stick as a longer range weapon, and he needed to protect Nivin as well as himself—unarmed and blind, she stood almost no chance.

Or could she see them? She had said they were filled with lights.

"Nivin," Brand said. On instinct, he passed her the hunting knife.

The spawn pointed toward Brand and Nivin with a clawed, spade-like hand. The badgers charged. Slavering, snarling, tormented living puppets, they ran with the same unnatural gait of pain as the first one. Everything about their movements suggested the horrendous suffering the spawn's control caused them. Aberrantly large, stretched beyond their own physical boundaries by the sick arts of Scyllorin's offspring, their appearance and anguish alone was as much of an attack on the mind as their vicious claws and teeth were on the flesh.

Brand smashed the shield's edge down on the badger that was nearly at his ankle. With a sharp blow of the staff, he struck another of them on the head, knocking it on its side. A third badger burst past Brand's defenses and sprang up at Nivin. More panic shot through Brand's chest. The creature's claws slashed her forearm, but she shoved the hunting knife deep into its side. Twitching, it fell to the

325

ground. Nivin pulled the knife out of the badger just in time to meet another oncoming attack—one of the creatures Brand had dazed had recovered and sank its teeth into the hem of her dress.

Brand could not spare another moment for Nivin. Three of the badgers surrounded him, gnashing their teeth. He jabbed the staff at one to his right. It jumped back, still snarling. He made to bash the one to his left with the shield. It too leapt out of the way. The one in front of him took a few steps back, its shiny black eyes glittering.

Brand risked a glance over at Nivin. She had managed to kill another badger. Blood covered her hands, but she held the hunting knife at the ready.

He should not have looked away. The three badgers launched at him. One landed directly against the shield. The others snapped at his arms on either side, their teeth catching his sleeves. He lost his balance and fell to his back, gasping as the hard rocky ground knocked the wind from his lungs. The badgers ripped away the fabric of his sleeves and opened their slavering jaws wide to sink their teeth into the flesh of his arms. Brand yanked the shield closer to his chest. It was just wide enough to shove the badgers aside and protect his arms. All three of the badgers bore down on the shield, scratching and clawing and trying to get at his face. He pushed back against their attack, flinching as a swipe of their claws missed his eyes by an inch. Their breath, rank with the smell of rotting flesh, flooded his nostrils.

"Brand!" Nivin shouted.

Brand looked up in time to watch helplessly as the spawn sprang at Nivin like a feral animal. She brandished the knife, but the spawn slapped it from her grasp and threw her body to the ground. It pounced on her, pinning her down. She screamed.

"Nivin! No!" Brand tried to shove the badgers away, but they pressed down on him like a crushing weight of defeat.

The spawn raised a clawed hand to strike.

Brand clenched his teeth, still struggling to get up, every fiber of his being wanting to interpose. He had failed her. He had failed his mission. He had failed everything.

Again.

An arrow whistled through the air, clipping the side of the spawn's head. With a fierce yowl, the spawn reared back. Thick drops of gray blood oozed from the laceration like tree sap. Another arrow took out one of the badgers attacking Brand. For one moment, Brand thought that Trapper and Trader had come to help them after all. But when he looked over, his heart leapt.

Seemingly out of nowhere, Ordnance and Anek ran into the fray.

The spawn responded to their presence with a hissing shriek. It sprang away from Nivin and ran at them, snarling and yowling. Anek, who was bearing a longbow that was decidedly too small for him, shot another arrow toward the spawn. His aim was shockingly accurate—the spawn sank to all fours to evade the arrow, which landed in the earth inches away from Nivin's side. She yelped and jumped up.

The spawn bounded toward Anek, then reared up on its hind legs. Ordnance leapt in front of Anek, holding out a spear he had fashioned from his hunting knife and a long branch. The spawn stopped, staring down Anek and Ordnance with hatred in its mien. The remaining two badgers attacking Brand backed away from him, still hissing and snarling. They looked back and forth between Brand and the others, seemingly confused. Brand leapt up and smashed the skull of one with the shield's edge. At this, the spawn seemed to remember Brand and Nivin were there. Its eyes darted between its enemies, as though calculating what to do.

It hesitated for a fraction of a second too long. Ordnance launched his makeshift spear at the creature and impaled it through the chest. The spear emerged from the spawn's back in a spray of thick, gray, sulfurous blood. Yowling, the spawn pushed the rest of the spear through its body, then grabbed the shaft from behind and pulled it through its torso like a needle through fabric. It heaved the spear back at Ordnance and Anek. Ordnance dove to the ground as the spear sailed over him, and Anek jumped to the side.

Clutching at its chest and wheezing, the spawn took off running and started to dive for the tunnel. Brand heaved the shield like a discus at the spawn. The shield caught the spawn in the belly and bounced away, landing precariously over the hole in the earth. Only rubble held it up. Brand blinked. He could not have made such a lucky shot had he tried.

Doubled over, the spawn sank to all fours and ran to the hole, but when it saw the shield, it recoiled with a hiss. Its vicious snarling took on a tone of fear. It looked from enemy to enemy like a cornered animal. The gray slime of its blood coated its upper body. It made a wild gesture, and the last badger made a bounding leap at Brand, while the spawn itself sprang at Ordnance one last time. The spawn did not even make a yard before one of Anek's arrows found its throat. It fell to the ground, dead.

Brand had no time to prepare for the remaining badger's attack. It landed on his chest, knocking him over onto his back—but then it started squealing as though tortured and ran off into the woods.

Nobody spoke for a moment.

Delirious with relief, Brand burst out laughing. "It's a miracle you arrived when you did!" He sat up.

Ordnance said nothing. He stared at the ground, his eyes darting around as if he was watching something.

"Ordnance?"

Ordnance shook his head and blinked rapidly before looking at Brand. "Yes, very well met, I should think."

Anek ran over to Nivin's side. "Nivin, are you all right?" He pulled her in a tight embrace.

Nivin let out a muffled squeak when Anek squeezed her so tightly, but she laughed, too. "Anek, I missed you so! I thought we'd never meet again!"

"Me too. Are you hurt?"

"Scratched badly, but otherwise all right."

Brand suddenly remembered to check his own body for injuries. He too seemed remarkably unscathed, only bearing scratches on his arms. He swept his eyes over his companions. Ordnance had deep scratches on his forearms and one across his face, and a swollen purple bruise stood out on his brow. The cuffs of Anek's already tattered pants were shredded even more, and his shins were riddled with angry red marks.

"We need to find bramblevine," Brand said. "But the way those badgers were foaming at the mouth...I worry bramblevine may not do us much good." He suddenly remembered how Nivin's face had been covered with saliva, and knots of worry seized his stomach.

"Possession by a spawn usually causes that in animals," Ordnance said. "I am surprised you don't know that—it's written in the Histories."

Brand's face grew hot. He had forgotten.

"Don't worry, Brand. Bramblevine will do us plenty of good, assuming we can find it soon enough. I have seen none so far, though."

"If things become too bad, Nivin can heal us again," Anek said.

Nivin shrank back and folded her arms across her chest, saying nothing.

Anek frowned. "Are you sure you're all right, Nivin?"

"Yes."

"I'm so glad we finally found you. After four days, we had started to fear the worst."

"Four?" Nivin tilted her head. "It's been five."

"Poor thing, you're confused."

"Wait, no, she's not," Brand said, climbing up from the ground. "It's been five days and four nights; tonight will make five."

Ordnance raised an eyebrow. "Four days and three nights, brother."

"No. We spent two days and nights with Manasseh, and then two nights here in the mountains."

"Manasseh?" Anek asked. "Is that the name of that man who would only call himself Trader?"

"No—sorry, I must explain."

They all sat down around the fire and Brand recounted everything that had happened to them, from how the spawn had made him its mouthpiece to how they had battled the spawn in the quarry. He explained everything they had learned about the shield, how Manasseh's eldest son had made it, and how Gamaliel, Garren, and Orren had vanished. For Nivin's sake, he did not mention her failed healing attempt, nor did he mention her strange mourning cry.

"So the stone is from a different place altogether!" Ordnance said after Brand was finished, his eyes shining. "The Knights of Ardor might have come the same way, hundreds of years ago. The woman *was* right. Wait—you said there were three brothers?" He rose and began to pace feverishly. "What if *they* were the Knights of Ardor?"

"The same thought briefly occurred to me as well," Brand said. "But they only disappeared forty years ago. There is no way."

"But what of the extra day you lived?"

"I cannot explain that—and it wouldn't explain the difference between forty years and three hundred."

Ordnance continued pacing. "Then I wonder if the Knights of Ardor had a shield like this too—if that was what gave them so much success against Scylla and Scyllorin. After all, it was effective against the rock spawn, and the badger spawn seemed to be afraid of it. I wonder if it would stand up to other spawn, or maybe even Scylla herself."

"Manasseh said his son only made a few shields—and the quarry was hardly centuries old. Several decades, maybe, but not even a hundred years."

Ordnance shook his head. "There must have been another quarry somewhere."

"No," Nivin said. "Something so remarkable and precious would have spread all around if it were available in more than one place. I had never heard of such a thing."

Ordnance gave a dismissive wave.

"I have a question," Anek said. "Do you think passing through the Charybdon is what caused you to live one more day than we have?"

There was a long pause as everyone looked at Nivin. It was not until Brand remembered she could not see them that he said something.

"Nivin?"

Nivin sighed. "It's as good an explanation as any. I know when I pass through them I feel unsure of how much time it took. I only feel nothingness." She shuddered. "Perhaps the journey between worlds consumes a day of time."

"Then how did we actually live an extra day," Brand asked, "if the Charybdon was what took up the day?"

Nivin threw up her hands. "I don't know. Why should I?"

An awkward pause indicated just how much trust all of them had placed in Nivin's hidden knowledge, and just how hidden it really was. Brand thought of how much she seemed to resent it, and immediately wished he had not pushed her for answers.

"Well," said Ordnance, in a conciliatory tone, "we seem to be fitting together the puzzle piece by piece. Perhaps we shall discover the answer further down the road. Now, let us tell our part.

"After your departure, Anek and I made for the place we had agreed to meet. However, it hadn't been but a while before we were attacked by the same spawn which we finally finished here tonight. We were able to evade it— perhaps we frightened it some. It was clearly more vulnerable than the spawn which built the staircase. Once we were certain you would not meet us, we were determined to see what the second spawn was doing. It was, along with the assistance of its animal slaves, digging a tunnel large enough for two or three men to walk through abreast. It was a terrible marvel to see. The spawn could even tunnel through rock. The badgers cleared away the debris. Some of them died of exhaustion, but more appeared to take their place.

"When we had found out its purpose, it had already nearly completed its tunnel through the mountainside. Never have I seen anything so astounding. Miles of tunnel, carved out in a ridiculously short amount of time. Of course, how long it had been working already, I cannot say, but my guess is at least as long as the other was building the stairs.

"After we had followed it through the tunnel, we entered into a vicious game of cat and mouse. We sought to prevent the spawn from relaying word that the tunnel was finished to Scyllorin's army. Once it realized we were hunting it—and its stronger companion was gone—we took turns stalking each other. We have hardly had sleep these past few nights."

"The worst part was," Anek chimed in, "once we'd started to follow it down the tunnel there was no turning back. We had to fight those poor badgers as we went, and the deeper we went, it got darker and more uneven. Sometimes, we'd have peace while the spawn was recovering."

Ordnance nodded. "After days of passing through the tunnel—which surely would have taken less time had we not been harried the whole way—we walked out to the rising sun. We had passed through the heart of the mountain. With the aid of the stair, and without having to climb through a pass, Scyllorin's army will gain days, at least. A long day's march would easily suffice to get an army through the tunnel.

"At any rate, we spent the day trying to find where the spawn had gone when we came across a man who dealt in furs—he called himself Trader."

"Yes," Brand said. "We met him. He told us how to find you. Honestly, I thought we would not meet until Respite Height."

"What good luck for us to have found you here instead."

"Luck!" Nivin cried. "Oh, Brand! Our fawn!"

Brand sprang up and ran over to where the fawn's ravaged carcass lay. Nivin followed the sound of his footsteps and knelt beside him, feeling for the fawn. Her hands found its bloody coat; she reached up to the fawn's nose and felt along its muzzle.

"I think this is the same one," Nivin said. "Perhaps your notion that they send blessings isn't so childish."

"Why did it have to die, though?" Ordnance asked, his face plainly stating his horror at the fawn being torn apart. Apparently, even seventeen years of prison and torment had not removed the childhood teaching about fawns from his mind.

"Who knows?" Brand said. "Maybe it had to give up its own life in order to grant the blessing of our survival. Or maybe all of it was coincidence."

"That's a lot of coincidences. I no longer doubt legends of powers or magic."

Brand was silent.

"We should cover it," Nivin said.

"Oh, no," Brand said. "We honor dead animals by letting them serve their true purpose in death. When animals die, they become food for something—be it carrion eaters, or even the earth itself. To prevent an animal from becoming food after its death is to desecrate the order of the world."

Nivin drew a breath as if she was going to say something, but stopped.

"Let's get away from here," Anek said.

"Agreed," Brand said. He stamped out the fire, leaving them with only the last faint glow of the setting sun for light.

Ordnance retrieved his spear. He paused as he walked past the spawn. He squatted down and ripped the arrow out of the spawn's throat, wiping the blood off on the cuff of his filthy pants, then handed the arrow to Anek, who slipped it back into the quiver.

"That was an excellent shot, Anek," Brand said, shaking his head in wonder.

Anek gave a sheepish smile. "Well, I was trying for its head."

"Still, it was well done. Did you know how to use a bow before we came here?"

"No. I'd never even held one."

"It should be impossible for you to be so sharp. How have you become so adept in the few days since we last saw you?"

"I can't explain it. I picked up the bow, and it felt right in my hands. Ordnance showed me how to use it. At first, I was shaky—all my shots went wild. But after two days or so, I started hitting the marks. I've only gotten better since." Anek shrugged. "I don't know why. But at least it makes up a bit for my weakness."

"Well, you just need to account for drop, and you'll be the best shot around."

"You're too kind."

Ordnance turned away from the dead spawn, grimacing. "Badgers. I never imagined in all my life those cantankerous creatures should turn out to be such a ruthless enemy—but that is the way of the spawn and their corruption." He stared off in to the distance for a few moments, his lips forming silent words. He shook his head and smiled wryly. "Still, when we reach Respite Height, I doubt I shall boast of fighting an army of badgers."

Brand laughed. "You have other things to boast of, Ordnance."

The smile slid from Ordnance's face. He looked down at the ground and bit his knuckles.

Anek gave Ordnance a reassuring clap on the shoulder. "Let's move on. Respite Height is waiting for us."

"And Council City after that," Brand said.

Ordnance nodded stiffly, then took off without waiting for the rest of them. He issued a steady stream of incomprehensible muttering as he went.

"He does that a lot," Anek said softly. "Sometimes he seems like nothing's wrong, but then he murmurs like that. He jumps at every noise, too. He's carried more than anyone was ever meant to, I think."

Nivin leaned on her walking stick for balance while she slipped her sandals back on. "I don't think he has left Scyllorin's prison behind. I don't think anyone could."

Brand had nothing to say. He was filled with a sort of cold nausea at the recollection of Ordnance's tale of the past. He could only begin to imagine Ordnance's suffering—living through hours upon hours of agony, drowning in the darkness of that place for seventeen years of lonely pain and madness.

But just as he could not dwell on his own pain, he could not dwell on Ordnance's. There was only the way forward now, and finding justice in the end. There would be time for dealing with the pain after.

The three of them followed after him. Nivin held her walking stick in one hand and clung to Anek's fingertips with the other. Part of Brand felt envious of this arrangement, as he had grown accustomed to holding her hand. Ever since she had gotten the walking stick, she had been adamant on making her way independently, and his hand felt strangely empty. It made sense, of course, that she would be glad to see Anek again, but that same part of Brand could not help but wish he was the one holding Nivin's slender hand, her long clever fingers interlaced with his.

The other part of him was too disturbed by Ordnance's state to care.

CHAPTER TWENTY-THREE

As Nivin walked away with Anek's hand in hers, she felt a mixture of relief and shame. She had been so relieved she had not needed to resort to using the powers once again, relieved there had been no chance of opening another Charybdon. On the other hand, she was ashamed at how utterly helpless she had felt as the spawn pinned her, and how in that moment, she was seconds away from calling out to the powers she already knew to be beyond her control. The twofold shame of helplessness and selfishness twisted inside her. She had almost been willing to risk a situation like Manasseh and Timbrel's again, all in the name of saving herself.

"Nivin," Anek said softly, "you seem different somehow."

Nivin pulled her hand away from Anek's, relying wholly on her staff for guidance. "I feel different.

Something terrible happened. Brand left it out."

"It was kind he didn't mention it, then." Anek gently patted Nivin on the back. "You don't have to tell me if you don't want."

Nivin swallowed. She felt like a naughty child who needed to confess, desperate to know her father would forgive her. "I tried to heal Manasseh. And I did. But it killed him, too."

"It sounded like he was hurt too bad already. It was good you tried, anyway."

"No, it wasn't. I think I already knew I could not do it. I did it out of selfishness." She tightened her grip on the walking stick. "Besides, the spawn we fought healed itself exactly the way I healed us. Watching it made me realize how truly dreadful it is. And I *still* tried to heal Manasseh. His last moments were agony, all because of me."

"Just because the spawn can do the same thing doesn't make the thing itself bad. We would have died if you hadn't saved us."

"Maybe so. But the more I think of it, the more I think these powers—these Charybda—are wrong."

"If it wasn't for a Charybdon, I'd never have found this clarity of mind."

Nivin cringed internally. Anek and Brand had the same conviction that the Charybda somehow were good things despite their fundamentally wrong nature. They would not listen to her fears, they would not acknowledge the truth. Nivin knew she was capable of hideous things— things which were evil at their core, even if something good should arise from the outcome. Anek's clarity did not change the fact he gained it as a result of evil. Manasseh's good and noble death was tainted by the touch of the

Charybdon on his parting. Even the healing done to Anek and Brand—there was a good outcome, but that did not change that she had tortured them in order to attain it. If outcomes determined the morality of the means, then what Temere did was an upright thing. His people even hailed him as savior, since there was seldom any sickness among his cities, and only strength and health.

Yes, good might come from an evil act, but that made the act no less damnable.

"Nivin?"

Nivin wondered how long she had been silent. "What?"

"No matter what, you're my friend. You showed me compassion when everyone else hated me. I'll never forget."

A huge weight lifted from Nivin's chest. She was about to reply when Brand's footsteps came to an abrupt halt.

"*Stop.*"

"What is it?" Ordnance whispered.

"Shh."

Nivin's pulse seemed like a drum in the silence as she strained her ears for any sound at all. At first, she could hear nothing but the sound of her companions breathing. But then she heard it—a faint clink, and what might have been someone speaking in a low voice. If it was a person, they were not speaking a language Nivin recognized at all—the sounds were harsh and guttural.

"Ceyans," Ordnance said, his voice no more than a breath. "Wait here."

"Ordnance, wait," Brand hissed, but to no avail. Ordnance's footsteps, feather light, were already retreating back the direction they had come.

"Ceyans?" Nivin whispered.

"Ceyas is one of the nations that is now part of Verderbera." Even with Brand's voice so quiet, Nivin could hear the edge of worry. "It is where Scyllorin conscripts most of his armies."

Nivin found Anek's hand and held tight. Zings of anxiety replaced the ache in her back. She did not sense any spawn nearby, but then, she had not noticed the badger until seconds before it tore the fawn apart. After several tense minutes, she heard Ordnance coming back.

"Scouts," Ordnance whispered. "Eleven by my count."

Brand drew a sharp breath. "A full decade?"

Nivin frowned. "Wouldn't that be ten?"

"Yes—ten men and their decurion. This is not good."

"What does it mean?" Anek said.

"It means Scyllorin is already making use of the stair and tunnel," Ordnance said. "A decade of scouts usually precedes an army."

"Then the army can only be a few days behind," Brand said. "Maybe as little as two. We have to get to Respite Height."

"Those scouts will be on our heels. They know we were here. They'll be tracking us any minute now."

"Pursued by soldiers?" Anek said. "This is hardly new for us. Let's go."

Ordnance let out a short chuckle. "Good man."

Nivin set her jaw, ready to resign herself to whatever fresh horrors lay in store for them.

They traveled for nearly the rest of the night, and the next few days melted into each other like one never-ending nightmare. They continued on at a feverish pace, eating while they walked and only breaking occasionally. At night, they only rested as long as they thought safe. It seemed once they had been resting long enough to even have a chance of falling asleep, they heard the low sound of voices carried through the quiet night air. Fear, rather than sleep, gave them the energy to keep moving.

The deep, puffy scratches on Nivin's arms itched, and once again she began to worry about infection. After a day, they managed to find vinegar berries—which, Nivin decided, were appropriately named: they stung like vinegar when applied. Still, they only reduced the puffiness slightly, doing little to assuage her fears. Making matters worse, the ache in her back had become almost unbearable, so white-hot and searing she began to wonder if she had indeed broken her spine. The place where the pain was most intense had become swollen, and according to Brand upon checking it, deep purple. Vaguely, she wished there was some source of the powers nearby, so she could heal away the pain, but was immediately ashamed for such thinking. She tried to distract herself by counting her footsteps, but after a while she found herself repeating the same number a dozen times.

"How much longer?" she finally asked on the morning of the third day.

"Not long," Brand said. "There is the stream that feeds the city. If we follow it for a half a day, we should be there."

Once at the stream, they paused to refresh their water skins before moving on. Despite their heavy pace, walking by the stream was almost pleasant. Nivin could hear it widening and deepening as the soft trickling became a loud musical rushing like wind through leaves. Waterfowl honked as they took off, disturbed by the passage of the strangers. Their wings beat like the soft thump of a hand drum. For the first time in days, Nivin felt something that resembled peace—despite the grief still lingering in her soul, despite the pain tearing at her senses, she found a sense of calm. Everyone's spirits seemed to have lifted; while they spoke little, something shifted in the way their feet hit the ground. Nivin's spirits could not help but be lifted alongside theirs.

A harsh and guttural cry shattered the peace like breaking glass.

"Run!" Brand cried. He grabbed Nivin's arm, nearly jerking her shoulder out of joint. "Ordnance, Anek—fall back and guard us!"

Everything was a blur to Nivin as they ran, her concept of distance lost in the number of footsteps she had long ceased to count. Sweat streamed from her brow. Footfalls of at least ten men pounded on the earth. Arrows flew through the air toward them, only just missing. Anek's bow sang and one of the pursuers cried out as the arrow found its mark. It seemed as though they had been running in dizzying zigzags for an eternity when Brand let out a rejoicing whoop.

"Respite Height!"

Nivin thought she heard the sound of something ahead, the sound of rallying shouts. There was the twang of at least a dozen bows and a cacophony of *thuds* as the men behind them fell to the ground. Gasping, Brand finally came to a stop. Nivin's sides burned with exertion her fear had not allowed her to perceive. Suddenly remembered agony flooded into her back as if she too had been hit by an arrow. The pain made her eyes sting with tears, and she fell to her knees, unable to keep herself upright any longer.

Beside her, Brand gasped for breath, and Anek and Ordnance caught up behind them. Anek wheezed and Ordnance drew rattling breaths like an old man.

"Nivin," Brand said, panting, "are you all right?"

Nivin could not even breathe enough to form words. She merely gave a shaky nod.

While they all sat trying to catch their wind, clopping hooves approached from ahead. It must have been at least twenty men on horseback, all armed and wearing jingling mail. They came to a halt a few feet ahead of Nivin and the others. There was a tense moment of silence.

"We have watched your approach, strangers," rang out a clear, commanding voice. "We have seen you pursued by Scyllorin's men. Are you then enemy or friend to the Freemen?"

"I am a Freeman, and so is he," Brand replied, motioning. "Our companions are friends to our people."

The commander shifted his stance, perhaps lowering a weapon. "State your names and your purpose then."

"I am Brand, and this is—"

"Brand?" one of the men in the rear cried. "Champion of the Freemen?"

"The same." Brand almost sounded depressed to admit it.

An excited buzz spread amongst the men.

"A Champion?"

"Here?"

"Pursued by Scyllorin's men?"

Even the commander could hardly conceal the excitement in his voice. "Be welcome in Respite Height, then, Champion of the Freemen! What can we do to aid you?"

"Our needs are too many to name," Brand said. "But our needs are not what matter right now. An army approaches from Verderbera—those men you shot were the scouts that go ahead of the rest of the army. We must get word to Council City as swiftly as we can."

"Come, we will give you an audience with the lord." The commander's voice turned toward one of his men. "Inform the lord of our guests." As the rider took off toward the city in a gallop, the commander dismounted from his horse. "You are plainly weary—you must ride back to the city." His mail jingled as if he was motioning to his men, and at least three other riders dismounted as well.

"My thanks," Brand said. He turned toward Nivin and placed his hand on her shoulder. "Have you ridden before?"

"Yes, but always behind my father," Nivin said. She suppressed a pang of sorrow at the thought of her father. "I've never ridden alone."

"You'll ride with me, then."

"I...*doubt* we have a horse to accommodate your large friend here," the commander said. "But we can bring a cart from the city, if you wish to wait."

Anek let out a wheezy laugh. "I can manage, for now."

A few moments later, Nivin found herself being boosted up to the back of a horse. She put her arms around Brand for support and clung tightly, afraid of the sensation she might fall from the horse. The rocking motion of being on horseback had always disoriented her.

Brand tensed up, as if he was afraid she was so close to him. When he spoke, his voice was unusually high. "Are you ready?"

"Yes," Nivin said, crestfallen. Before the mountaintop,

Brand had never shown any kind of hesitance to touch her—he had carried her on his back before, and had reacted to it with nothing more than determined resignation. But since her breakdown, every time he had to make contact with her beyond holding her hand for guidance or laying his hand on her shoulder, he seemed agitated. He was afraid of her powers, and he *still* was certain she was the key to saving his people. He had obviously concluded she was a necessary evil.

No, Nivin told herself, as the horse jerked into motion. *He seems relaxed enough the rest of the time. It's unfair of me to assume the worst of him.*

Perhaps she only assumed the worst of him because she assumed the worst of herself. She assumed whatever gave her these powers, whatever gave her this connection to the spawn, was filthy and unclean—and by extension, she was something to be feared and hated. Brand obviously did not hate her, and he only seemed nervous when they were close together. The only other possible explanation for his attitude made her blush, especially considering he had probably seen her naked back at Manasseh and Timbrel's. She pushed the thought and her embarrassment away. There were much more important things to be dealt with.

As they rode back to the city, the men plagued them with questions.

"So you are really Brand? The first Champion to set out since the Council was attacked by Scylla?"

"I am," Brand said wearily.

"You must forgive our enthusiasm," said another one of the men. "We have never played host to such a noble guest."

Nivin thought she heard Ordnance scoff.

"Was not your partner a young man? Is he among your friends?"

Brand went completely stiff. "No. He is dead."

The men were all silent for a few minutes.

"Did he die well?" one finally asked.

"Tales of his valor will be told for centuries among our people. But I cannot tell it to you now—I am too weary."

"Of course," the man replied, a hint of disappointment in his voice.

One of the horses sidled up close to Brand and Nivin. "What does he mean, 'since the Council was attacked by Scylla?'" Ordnance said, in a low voice.

"It was the reason they sent two of us," Brand replied, in kind. "I'll explain more later, after we have seen the lord."

Ordnance's voice sank to a total whisper. "Don't tell him who I am. I don't want anybody to know."

"I was not planning to. When we're before him, I will speak for all of us. I will call you 'Loyalty.'"

"Suits me well enough, I suppose."

The horses' shoes suddenly clattered onto cobblestones. The sounds around them echoed differently, as if they were surrounded by buildings or walls. There was a heavy rattling of chains as what sounded like a portcullis fell, followed by the stiff creaking of gates pulling shut. For one thrilling minute, Nivin felt the almost unfamiliar sensation of safety. With the strong gates closed behind them, they truly had respite. But the thrill faded as Nivin realized the streets were lined with people. They shuffled and bumped together, and most of all, they whispered in an excited buzz. Someone had already ridden ahead and spread the word that a Champion had come to

Respite Height, and all of these people had come to catch a glimpse of him.

If they were all staring at Brand, then they undoubtedly saw Nivin as well. Even though she knew she would not be hated for her blindness, panic shot through her at the thought of being under the scrutiny of so many people. How many were there? Hundreds? It was a huge crowd, by the sound of it.

A small child cried out, "Hurrah for Brand, Champion of our people!"

The crowd burst into roaring applause and cheers, as if all of them had wanted to do this, but were unsure whether they should.

Their ride down the street past droves of cheering people was not more than several minutes, however. Soon, they dismounted from their horses.

"These people seem excited you're here," Anek said. Nivin could hear the smile in his voice.

"More than anything else, a Champion represents hope for Libertas," Brand replied, but he sounded unsure of himself.

"Whether or not there is any such hope," Ordnance mumbled, barely audible.

Huge doors swung open and a loud, booming voice echoed down from above them. "Be welcome in Respite Height, Brand, Champion of the Freemen! Be welcome in Respite Height, his noble companions! Come into the hall of Lord Steadfast. He is waiting for you."

"There are steps," Brand said softly. "Be careful."

Slowly, they climbed the stairs. Nivin's shoes had grown looser and were finally starting to fall apart, just as Manasseh had feared they would, so it was hard to keep her balance as they went. As they entered the building, the echoes of their feet became closer and the light changed. Judging from the way sound bounced from the ceiling above them, it was high and vaulted. The air was tinged with the smell of perfumes—a sure sign they were among nobility, not the masses.

"Here he is—our Champion!" a hearty voice said. From the timbre of it, Nivin guessed the speaker was of a solid build, either fat or thickly muscled—or perhaps both.

"Curtsy," Brand whispered.

Nivin immediately did as he said, exactly the way her father had taught her. Briefly, she wondered whether it was the same way women curtsied in Libertas.

After a moment's delay, Brand spoke again, this time in a loud, formal voice. "Lord Steadfast, you know who I am. These are my companions, Loyalty, Anek, and Nivin. I have met them in my travels and must take them to Council City. We bear dire news."

"Yes, I heard supposedly an army approaches from Verderbera," Lord Steadfast said. "Have you seen this army yourself?"

"No, my Lord—only the scouts that precede them. But we know Scyllorin has been preparing the way for an army—he has had his filthy spawn cut a stair into the mountainside and a tunnel through the heart of the highest mountain nearby. The army may be as little as two days behind, and once they are through the mountains, it will be a straight journey across the plains to Council City."

Steadfast sighed. "And doubtless, they will attack any city along the way." He was quiet for a moment. "How did you come by your companions?"

"That is a tale which I must reserve for the Council of

Scholars and Council of Champions."

"Of course." There was a note of disappointment in Steadfast's voice. "Very well, Champion. I am honor-bound to aid your campaign against Scyllorin—what may I do?"

"We are in sore need of rest, but we cannot delay our message to Council City. They must know the army is coming."

"I will dispatch an emissary at once." Steadfast snapped his fingers. "Arbor! Send a messenger and tell the city to prepare its defenses."

"It will be done, my Lord," the man called Arbor said. He ran from the hall, his footsteps heavy with his purpose.

"What else do you need?" Steadfast said.

"Supplies, weapons, and horses," Brand said. "I know it is a great deal to ask of your Lordship..."

"It is nothing less than my duty. Everything you need, you will have. Though I do not think we have a horse that can bear Anek. Our steeds are not so large."

"He should have no trouble keeping pace with us," Ordnance said congenially. "Not with legs as long as his are."

Brand was quiet for a moment. "Anek, do you think you can keep up with us?"

"Not unless I get some rest," Anek replied. "After that—I wouldn't mind one of those carts they mentioned earlier."

Steadfast cleared his throat. "Unfortunately, you will find the passage down the mountainside too narrow for any cart large enough to bear you. Many places on the way require horses to ride in single file. Traders use mules and the like, rather than carts. Besides, what carts we have, we will need to move people into the city. I am truly sorry, my friend."

Anek sighed. "Then I suppose I'll just have to make the best of it."

"You are, of course, welcome to stay in Respite Height if you so wish."

"No. No, I'll stay with my friends."

"How soon will you depart? The day is already half past—will you stay the night?"

Once again, Brand was quiet. He was probably weighing the consequences of continuing on ragged and exhausted over allowing the army so much time to gain on them. "We must leave at first light tomorrow morning, and not a moment later."

Nivin nearly sighed aloud in relief. The thought of continuing anytime soon—even on horseback—made her back ache even worse.

"Excellent," Steadfast said. "Whatever you need, whatever you want—it is yours. My man here will be your servant."

"Thank you," Brand said. From the sound of his voice, he had bowed again. Nivin gave a quick curtsy.

Steadfast sighed again. "You have no idea how much I wish this army of yours was a mere fabrication, Champion Brand."

"You might be surprised, my Lord," Brand said heavily.

"Go. Rest."

Footsteps approached them. "Come with me, masters and mistress," said a man, presumably Steadfast's servant. His voice was a light, cheerful tenor. "I can see you are in need of many things—what can I do for you first?"

Another spasm of pain shot through Nivin's back as

she took a step forward. "I need to see a physicker."

"A...what?"

"A physicker. I'm in terrible pain."

"I can take you to see the apothecary," the servant said, "but I'm afraid to admit I don't know what a physicker is."

"Probably the same thing as an apothecary," Nivin said, hoping she had pronounced the strange word correctly.

"Then I shall take you there straightaway. All of you seem to be in need of care."

They followed the servant to the apothecary's, where an old man examined each of them. He made almost no comment at all when he learned Nivin was blind, for which she was grateful. He did note how well Timbrel had done in treating the wound on Nivin's arm, and recommended she wait at least another week more before removing the stitches. He gave them a terrible tasting tonic, which was supposed to ward off infection, and applied a soothing ointment to all their scratches. Afterward, he deemed Brand, Ordnance, and Anek would make a speedy recovery, and shooed them away so he could examine Nivin's back.

"Lie down here, dear," the old man said gently, "on your stomach, if you please."

Nivin groaned as she stretched out on the bed. The old man quickly unlaced the back of her dress and pushed her undershirt out of the way to examine her injury. His long, spidery fingers probed her back, and she nearly screamed as they pressed down on the sorest spot.

"How did this happen?"

"I fell and landed on my back."

"From how high?"

"I'm not even sure. It was from one level of scaffolding to the next."

"Oh, dear. Well, I do *not* think your back is broken outright, or you would not be able to walk upright. However, a long stretch of your spine and your shoulder blades have been injured. I recommend several weeks of bed rest, and willow for the pain—but I cannot guarantee you'll recover."

Nivin's spirits sank. "I don't have weeks."

"Anything you do besides rest in bed will only make it worse, I can promise you that."

"But we have to leave in the morning."

"Then rest while you can. I will give you a tincture of willow, but it will only help so much."

The tincture of willow reminded Nivin of the horrible liquor her father drank, except the willow was much bitterer. She almost choked as she swallowed it. After that, the apothecary called a maidservant to take Nivin where she could bathe and then rest in bed for the remainder of the day. The bath was hot and soothing, and Nivin felt truly clean for the first time in days. When she was offered a new dress, however, Nivin insisted on having Timbrel's dress washed and repaired. The maidservant promised to take the dress to the tailor immediately, and gave Nivin a simple, soft shift to wear in the meantime. Once Nivin was comfortably laid in bed, the maidservant left.

Nivin sighed. She knew the dress would never be the same—not after how badly it had been torn—but then, Timbrel would never be the same, either.

Somehow, it seemed fitting.

CHAPTER TWENTY-FOUR

Brand lay in his bed, staring at the ceiling. After he had left the apothecary, he had gone to arrange things for their departure the next morning. Two horses had been chosen—one was especially strong, so it would be good for Nivin and Brand to share. The servants had also brought swords for everyone, and there was a sturdy carved walking stick for Nivin as well. Brand and Ordnance were fitted for new shoes, and since Nivin was resting, the cobbler used the shoes Manasseh had made to find a pair to fit her. While the cobbler had no shoes to fit Anek and not enough time to make him new ones, he was able to patch the pair Anek already had. A tailor had also been tasked with making new clothes for all of them. Once all of the other preparations were in place, a supply of food and water was set aside for them, and they were given bedrolls. Brand could think of nothing else to ask for, except the one thing that was impossible: more time. It would take them just over a week to make it to Council City.

Despite his exhaustion, Brand could not fall asleep. The afternoon sunlight peeked around the edges of the curtains, as unblinking as his own eyes. He turned over to see Ordnance completely asleep, breathing through an open mouth. How it was he could sleep was a mystery to Brand—after all, they were both Champions, with the same responsibility and duty to Libertas. The army was gaining on them every moment they tarried.

However, Brand worried about more than just the approaching army. He had spoken with the apothecary, who insisted Nivin's back would worsen unless she was given weeks of bed rest. Yet there was no way they could stay so she could rest—they *had* to get to Council City. The thought of how much pain she would live through made his own back ache. And what of Anek? Would he be able to keep up with the horses? Anek had run for incredible distances before passing through the Charybdon had stripped him of his strength. Was it only his strength that had diminished, or had his endurance been lost as well?

Ordnance gave a sharp cry and turned over, breathing heavily. He whispered something Brand could not understand, then let out a soft snore. Shaking his head, Brand climbed out of bed. He decided to check on Nivin, and then see how Anek fared. As soon as he walked out of the room, a servant who had been waiting by the door spoke to him.

"What can I do for you, Champion Brand?"

Brand cringed at the use of his title. Hearing it without Pock by his side made it feel like an accusation. "I want to go see Nivin, if I could."

"Of course, Champion," the servant said, inclining his head. "She is two rooms down the hall, where Prudence and Ether are standing."

"Thank you." Brand glanced down the corridor and spotted the maidservant and manservant who flanked either side of the door. The room between, where Anek was staying, had no servant attending it. Anek had been given his own room, since there were only two beds to a room, and Anek needed both of them. Brand walked quietly, not wanting to wake Anek—in case he was sleeping as easily as Ordnance was.

When he reached Nivin's door, the maidservant whispered, "She is sleeping."

"I only want to check on her," Brand said.

"Of course." The maidservant quietly opened the door.

Brand peeked in and was surprised to see Anek sitting on a bench by the window. He smiled and waved to Brand, then motioned to Nivin and put a finger over his lips. Brand nodded and went to sit next to Anek. He hesitated for a moment, wondering if the bench would support both of them—but it looked sturdy enough to hold three people, so he decided to chance it. The bench creaked slightly as he sat down, but nothing more.

"I'm glad she's asleep," Anek whispered. "I couldn't sleep for more than a few minutes. I see you couldn't either."

"No," Brand sighed. "Part of me feels we should not stay at all."

"Still, seeing her rest makes me glad we are staying."

"Yes." Brand hated to wait, but if Nivin was indeed the key to all of this, then her welfare was paramount to their success. If she could not rest for weeks, she at least deserved half a day and a night to recuperate. She seemed to sleep peacefully enough, without tossing and turning like she usually did when they had slept on the hard ground. She had the blanket pulled up to her chin, and her glossy black hair was spread out in a mess across the pillow. For a moment, it reminded Brand of how the loose strands had stood on end right before the Charybdon in Zerabar had pulled him in.

After sitting there for a while, he wondered what she would think if she knew he had been staring at her while she slept. He turned to Anek, but the giant had nodded off—his head drooped onto his chest. Brand could not help but smile. Yawning, he realized how pleasant the temperature was in the room. His eyelids drooped.

He awoke later to the sound of the door opening.

Ordnance stumbled in, looking bleary. "They said I'd find you here."

Anek started and sat up, wiping away a string of drool stretching from his mouth to his shirt.

"They've been sleeping for a while," Nivin said. "As long as I have been awake. They sounded so peaceful, I did not want to disturb them."

Brand twisted his neck to loosen the tightness of his muscles. Sleeping upright had done him no favors. "I didn't mean to fall asleep. Did we wake you?"

"Anek's snoring did." Nivin smiled. "What were you doing in here, anyway?"

"We were just checking on you," Anek said. "We're worried about you."

"None of you seemed worried about me," Ordnance said wryly.

Nivin and Anek laughed.

"Anyway, I told the servants to bring us our meals here. I imagined Nivin does not want to go sit at table with her back the way it is."

With a groan, Nivin sat up in bed. "I don't particularly want to sit at all. But I am hungry."

Four servants came in bearing trays laden with food. There was well-seasoned mutton, slow-roasted into tenderness, accompanied by dense, nutty bread served with butter, honey, and a lump of goat's cheese. On each tray sat a generous mug of mead, which Brand found to be much too sweet for his liking. Ordnance had no problem drinking his, however, and the servants brought him another once he had finished the first. Nivin and Anek took light, hesitant sips of theirs, but seemed to prefer the goat's milk that had been brought.

"Do they raise many goats here?" Nivin asked Prudence.

"Goats and sheep, mostly," Prudence said. "Not much other livestock does well here, though there are beekeepers with hives farther out in the woods. Oh—listen, you can hear the minstrels."

Brand's stomach clenched when he recognized the melody that was playing. He hoped everyone would keep talking, but they went quiet. Brand closed his eyes as the haunting, familiar lyrics floated through the open window, as cold as the evening air.

> *The blackened pall of Scylla's wings*
> *Fell on the world in deadly night;*
> *Her jaws spread wide, and fire bloomed,*
> *Its roaring red the only light.*
> *Like ghosts of hope among the flames*

Defenders rushed, raised spears and bows,
But Scylla laughed, for she had bested
More valiant warriors, more deadly foes.

Yet she had great, true cause to fear
The drawing near of her demise;
Why leave the comfort of her den
To rain down terror from the skies?
The Freemen, live or die, are free—
Centuries cannot change this truth!
In our quest to end her vile domain
We were shown relentless, without ruth.

Defenders rose; defenders fell
With each blow from her vicious claws.
Tragedy, fear, and keening reigned—
We bore the price for our great cause.
But resolute, we stood, survived;
Our mission was not cowed, subdued;
From death and loss and all destruction
Our determination was renewed.

The Champions, the greatest threat
She savaged with a cruel greed,
Cherished crushing all their bones,
Destroying all to suit her need.
Yet not one Champion, but two,
will be the ones at last to wreak
Mighty Scylla and Scyllorin's end—
And achieve the justice we now seek.

It was beautifully performed. The woman who sang it

had a clear and piercing voice, and she sang with all the passion of somebody who truly believed it. This was the song that had given hope to Freemen in the wake of Scylla's attack on Council City, the song that took despair and transformed it into zeal with each purposeful note. But all of that hope and zeal hinged on one thing: the Champions' victory over Scylla. Nobody else could ever understand the immense weight it placed on Brand's heart, not even Ordnance. Ordnance was not the first Champion to set out after such a crushing tragedy, with all eyes on him, depending on him to achieve justice for all who died the day Scylla wreaked havoc and murder upon the Council. More than any other Champions, Brand and Pock were the living embodiment of hope for their people—and now that Pock was gone, Brand bore the responsibility alone.

"Brand," Ordnance said, "What does it mean, she savaged the Champions? What happened?"

Brand closed his eyes. He did not want to dredge up more unwanted grief he had no time to deal with. "Ten years ago, Scylla attacked Council City and killed all but two of the Champions. She also attacked the Scholars—only five of them survived. In the aftermath, it was decided two Champions at a time should go."

"Who survived beside you?" Ordnance asked, his eyes wide.

"Ash. He was the youngest. He is eleven now—he remembers nothing." Brand swallowed. "I do not remember much, only bits and pieces. Fidelity tried to lead us all to safety, but she..." Brand almost flinched as he remembered the massive claw that punched through the roof and snatched her away.

"I knew Fidelity. She was only eight when I left."

"She was the eldest Champion at the time. The attack took place a week before she was supposed to have departed on her campaign."

"What about Steel? Or Resolute? Gravitas?"

Brand shut out the echoes of screams racing through his mind. "The three of them went to face her. I never saw them again." He had learned later that they had faced the same fate as Pock.

Moisture glistened in the corner of Ordnance's eyes. "What about little Archer?"

Archer had only been four years older than Brand—he realized she would have been two when Ordnance left. He tried to push away the image of her bright blonde hair dyed red with blood, her rosy cheeks as pale and gray as the ash that flew through the air. He had only seen her body lying on the ground in the aftermath, but it had been branded into his memory like a fiery scar. He could not suppress the thought of her bright green eyes, glossy and staring. "Archer died as well."

"How—"

"I did not see it happen. I took Ash and we hid under the wreckage. The next thing I remember was when Councilor Valiance pulled us out."

"So she survived?"

"Yes. But Councilor Endurance did not. Valiance became the new Councilor of Champions."

"What about Mace?"

Brand shook his head, unable to find words. The supervisor of the male Champions was never found. It was assumed he too had been eaten by Scylla. Of the three leaders, only Valiance lived. The ordeal had driven from her what little gentleness she had ever possessed.

Ordnance stared at the ground. "So—"

Brand stood up. "We should all retire as early as possible, so we can depart the moment it is light." He strode toward the door, but paused when he saw Nivin. Her face was turned toward him, and if not for her unfocused gaze, he would have thought she was looking at him. Tears shimmered in her eyes, too.

Doing what is right is never worthless, she had said. *Even the smallest resistance is still resistance.*

As he looked at her, a thought occurred to him. The hope of the Freemen did not rest solely on his shoulders. Though they did not realize it yet—and perhaps Nivin did not realize it either—*she* was the true answer to hope for the Freemen, an answer that had not been found for centuries. That thought was enough to drive away the memories of blood and screaming. It was something concrete to hold to, something to vindicate Pock's death, something to give him the courage to bury the past and focus on the present.

Brand turned back to face the room. "Good night."

Only Anek and Nivin answered him with a "Good night" in reply. Ordnance stared into empty space, his eyes flicking back and forth as though he was watching ghosts.

Brand hurried from the room, worried if he stayed, his own ghosts might come to visit him. With every step, he refocused his thoughts on the present task, focused on the hope Nivin gave him.

Nevertheless, once he lay in his own bed trying to sleep, he could not keep the haunting melody from playing at the fringes of his mind.

*

The next morning, Brand woke before it was light and finalized all the preparations. All of Respite Height made ready also, bringing in all those outside the wall into the city's redoubt. Men were suiting for battle, and the outer walls were being fortified. As small as it was, Respite Height would struggle to stand against the army. Hopefully, they were not Scyllorin's final target, and the city was well situated for defense, so there was a chance they might survive. Brand thought of Council City, and how they too would prepare for an attack once the message had been relayed to them. Properly warned, Council City stood a good chance of holding off Scyllorin's army—but if Scylla accompanied the army, it would take a miracle for them to survive.

Brand glanced at Nivin. The blue-green dress Timbrel had given her was newly patched and repaired, and looked quite as lovely on her as ever. Her long black hair had been plaited into a smooth, neat braid. His face grew warm, and he looked away. They would be sharing a horse all the way, which would be an extra burden on the horse, but it was impractical for Nivin to ride on her own. Brand was unsure whether this arrangement pleased him or not—he could not afford distractions.

Too soon—or not soon enough—light tinged the sky and it was time for them to depart. Lord Steadfast and a large crowd of people had gathered to see them off.

"Is everyone ready?" Brand asked.

There was general assent, though Nivin seemed less than enthusiastic. Brand and Ordnance mounted their horses, and a servant boosted Nivin up behind Brand. He ignored the way his stomach tossed when she put her arms around him.

"Blessings be upon your journey, Champion Brand," Lord Steadfast said, bowing his head.

Brand bowed his head in return. "My thanks can never be enough. Blessings on your city and your people."

With that, he turned the horse and spurred it forward, leading the way. Anek followed behind him, and Ordnance took the rear. As they departed, those who had gathered cheered. It reminded him of the way Council City had cheered when he and Pock left for their campaign. His spirits sank. He had departed with his best friend at his side, but would be returning without him. He would be forced to tell the whole Council what had happened, to relive Pock's death once again.

At least he had new friends with him, new friends who meant new hope for the Freemen.

They spoke little as they made their way along the winding trails that lead from Respite Height down to the plains. The surrounding landscape was scattered with small dwellings, most of which had been abandoned as their occupants made their way back to Respite Height for shelter from the oncoming army. Several citizens of Respite Height passed them on their way. Many cast a strange glance at Anek, and one or two asked why the party was not heading for the stronghold of the city. Eventually, the houses thinned out and they met no one else. Everyone but them had gone to the city for refuge.

They had traveled a little over half the day when Brand spotted something lying on the ground ahead.

It was the emissary Steadfast had sent, dead and bloodied.

Brand signaled the others to stop. He jumped down from his horse and ran to the emissary's side. A single arrow protruded from his back.

"There must have been more than a single decade of scouts," Brand said.

Nivin leaned forward in the saddle. "What happened?"

"The messenger is dead—killed by Scyllorin's men, most likely." Brand swallowed. "That means bringing warning to Council City rests solely on our shoulders, now."

"It means we might run into them again," Ordnance said.

Brand swept his eyes across the ground. Horse tracks led off the trail into the woods, back in the direction of the tunnel. "I don't think so. I think the scout must have stolen the messenger's horse and headed back to report what happened. Still, we should be cautious." He went back to his horse and climbed back up into the saddle. "We should be on our way."

"Shouldn't we bury him?" Anek said, frowning.

"We don't have the time!" Brand clenched his fists around the reins. "I don't want to leave him here, but we have no choice. We have already delayed too long. He made his sacrifice—we should honor that." He spurred the horse and started forward again, unable to suppress a pang of guilt as he did. Anek followed behind, though Brand could sense his reluctance. Ordnance made no comment.

After another hour or so, Anek spoke again. "Do they have a chance?"

"Respite Height has long been one of the first lines of defense against Scyllorin, even though they are small," Brand said, glancing over his shoulder at Anek. "Any attack from Verderbera would first hit them, and they could send word as quickly as possible to Council City. For that reason, it was built in a highly defensible position—the sheer mountainside guards them on one side, and they have the high ground in all other directions. It has been centuries since Scyllorin has sent an army through the mountains, but Respite Height is still strong."

Anek shook his head. "That doesn't answer my question."

"Respite Height isn't likely to be Scyllorin's target."

"That still doesn't answer my question. I asked if they have a chance."

Brand stared at the trail ahead of them. "I do not doubt any surprise Scyllorin can concoct. If he hits it with everything in his power, the city will be reduced to corpses and rubble and ash." He thought of ashes floating through the air ten years ago. "But as I said, Respite Height isn't likely to be the target. So yes, they have a chance."

"A slim chance," Ordnance said. "No slimmer than ours."

Anek hurried forward until he was walking next to Brand. "We should go back. We should help them. It isn't right to leave them."

Brand shook his head. "The Council has to be informed of what has happened. Respite Height understands her duty."

"But it doesn't seem right! Leaving them as soon as they have helped us?"

"It was their duty to help us—it is the way of our people. The only way we can help them now is to warn the Council, and the Council can send relief and aid. That is *our* duty. You understand, don't you?"

"I still don't like it," Anek grumbled.

Brand looked back. Respite Height had disappeared

from their view. "I know."

*

As the sun blazed on the horizon and the world grew dimmer, they came to a way site. Brand had been told they would find these along their journey—small encampments meant for weary travelers on their way from the plains to Respite Height. Because the city relied so heavily upon trade for access to grain, they had made a point of setting up and maintaining the way sites. This one was a clearing in the trees, about twenty feet in diameter. A small shelter had been erected, made of stone and mortar. There were only three walls, but it was enough to provide shelter from the wind and the rain—Brand guessed four people might be able to sleep in it, if they were packed together snugly. He doubted whether all four of them could fit inside, though, seeing as Anek was nearly twice as wide as a regular person. A hitching post stood next to the shelter, and there was a fire ring lined with stones near the road. As was the custom, the last traveler to use the way site had left a small pile of firewood there for the next person.

Brand decided they would not build a fire, just in case there were any scouts who had come this far ahead. They would only rest for a few hours, and continue their journey once the moon had risen. After a light supper, Brand, Nivin, and Anek spread out their bedrolls in the shelter, while Ordnance sat outside to keep watch. Brand managed to sleep for at least a short while before it was his turn for the watch, but he could barely keep his eyes open until it was Anek's turn. Then, after sleeping a little while longer, they departed, letting silvery moonlight guide their way. When the moon rode low and the sun had not yet risen, they paused to rest again, but continued as soon as the sun's first light blushed across the wispy clouds.

The next day, they maintained a stiff pace. So far, Anek had not had much trouble keeping up with the horses, thanks to his long stride. Though he was becoming winded and needed short breaks more frequently, they managed to keep going at a steady rate for most of the day. They made such good progress they passed the next way site before the sun had gone down. Fueled by fear and not wanting to waste another moment of daylight, Brand insisted they press on until it was dark. That night, they slept under a thick stand of deciduous trees.

Brand woke the next morning to the faint smell of smoke. He sat up and rubbed the sleep out of his eyes, curious as to why Ordnance would have lit a fire when they would be departing so soon—but as soon as his vision cleared, he saw there was no fire. Nivin sat on her bedroll, looking stricken. Ordnance stood stock still, staring back up into the mountains and muttering under his breath. Beside him stood Anek, the dust on his face streaked with tears.

Brand jumped to his feet. In the distance, high above them, a column of dense black smoke rose into the sky.

Respite Height is burning.

Anek's hands twitched before he clenched them into tight fists. "Why didn't we go back to help them?"

"Because we would have met the same fate." Brand quickly bundled up his bedroll and tied it shut. As he loaded their packs onto the horses, he ran over the tale of the Scholar's sacrifice in his mind what felt like a dozen times. "We need to press on, or their sacrifice will have meant nothing."

Blame is a cycle which never ends.

*

By midday, flakes of ash drifted on the wind like deathly snow, and a faint corona shimmered around the red-orange sun like a halo of panic. The fire must have spread well beyond the city for there to be so much smoke. Brand kept looking back. Was it Scylla's work? Had she turned the entire city into one enormous pyre? Or was Scyllorin's army so large they did not even need the dragon's aid?

Even with warning, could Council City stand against such an invasion?

The effects of the fire did not abate for the next two days. The pall of smoke followed them all the way down to the plains, making the air thick and filling Brand's heart with an ever-increasing sense of dread. He continually looked into the sky, half expecting Scylla to swoop down and kill them before going on to destroy Council City once and for all.

Were they not traveling in the shadow of death and fear, their journey across the plains might have been a serene, beautiful experience. The road cut through fields of thick untamed grasses, waiting to be swathed and harvested for fodder. Other fields were golden with wheat where the wind swept across the heavy stalks in waves like a vast sparkling sea. Gentle hills curved the plains, and the occasional stand of trees rose up from the earth in places where water was abundant. Sometimes, a small road forked away from the main like a tributary, leading to another city—another city that might suffer the same fate as Respite Height, depending on how far and wide Scyllorin planned to spread his destruction.

Finally, on the morning of the sixth day since their

departure from Respite Height, the air cleared and the smoke in the mountains behind them had been reduced to a whisper. *Only one more day,* Brand told himself over and over.

It was not even yet noon when thunder sounded in the distance.

"Brand," Ordnance said urgently.

Brand whipped his head around and looked back. A gushing curtain of smoke rose from the plain, thicker and blacker than any he had ever seen.

Ordnance shook his head. "Look at it. It can't be natural."

"It isn't," Nivin said, "That thunder—I think it might be another spawn, but I can't tell."

"Either way, we have to speed up," Brand said. "The wind is driving it."

They went as fast as Anek could manage without breaking into a run, but the fire seemed to be gaining on them anyway. That night, it was a ghostly orange glow crawling after them like a hungry snake. They barely rested. All of them were exhausted, but no one as much as Anek, who looked ready to collapse. Mid morning the next day, they saw in the distance the wall of trees which followed along the Lesser River. Council City would be just beyond the river—but the curtain of smoke was closer to them than ever.

As they moved, they passed a large stand of trees where the Champions had once done a training exercise six years ago. Pock had fallen from a tree and cut his face—it had become infected and left him with an ugly pockmark once it had healed. No one was more good-natured about the change in his appearance than he was. He made jokes about it, saying he put the pock in Epoch. Brand almost laughed—he had nearly forgotten Pock had ever gone by another name.

Brand gave the trees one last look after they had passed by them. Soon they would be burned down, and nothing would remain of them but smoldering ash and his memories.

His panic rose like the smoke behind them. The fire would overtake them in less than an hour unless they sped up, but there was no way Anek could keep up with them. He was already falling behind, step by stumbling step. Brand checked his horse's speed and fell in beside Anek, trying to decide what to do. Nothing mattered as much as getting Nivin to Council City and warning the city of the impending attack. Torn, he looked over at Anek. The giant's eyes were bloodshot. His face was red. He clutched his side and wheezed like an old man.

Brand squeezed his eyes shut for a moment. "Anek…"

"I know," Anek panted. He shook his head. "I can't keep up anymore. You have to go faster or we'll all be killed."

Nivin's whole body tensed. She dug her nails into Brand's shoulders. "Anek, no!"

"You talked about duty, Brand—and it's your duty to get to Council City with or without me," Anek said. "Keep Nivin safe."

"No—we can't leave him—Anek, you can't just give up!"

Brand swallowed. "I'm sorry."

"Go," Anek urged. He reached over and brushed his hand across Nivin's face. She tried to take hold of his hand, but he pulled it away. "Goodbye."

Nivin started to sob. She buried her face in the back of Brand's shirt.

Brand did not know what to say. Any words seemed like they would be too painful. He nodded at Anek, who returned the gesture with resignation. At that, Brand spurred his horse into a gallop.

Ordnance said something to Anek before doing the same, but Brand did not catch what it was.

Behind them, Anek broke into a staggering run. He only made it a few steps before he stumbled and fell to the ground. Anek was going to die. The fact stabbed into Brand's heart like a knife. Every jolt from his horse was another reminder, another blade of regret being driven into him. Did Nivin know Anek had fallen? Would she ever forgive him for choosing to press on without the giant?

But the most pressing question was whether the three of them would even live long enough for Nivin to bear a grudge against him. They seemed to have matched the speed of the fire—it was no longer gaining on them, but it was too close. The horses were tired; their coats had begun to foam with sweat. Brand was not sure how much longer the beasts could bear their terror. Every wild snort from his horse's nostrils made him clench his hands around the reins a little tighter.

They passed a large rock he and Pock had climbed together while on one of their excursions from the city.

Then he realized it.

He was already returning to Council City without Pock—Pock, who had given his life for duty. He could not bear to return without Anek.

Maybe by going back he would be running straight into death's arms, but if there was any way to survive the wall of flame, he would do everything in his power to save Anek. On instinct, he grabbed the shield. "Ordnance— make sure she gets to the Council!"

"Wait, Brand—what are you doing?" Nivin cried.

Ordnance gave Brand a sharp nod, then brought his galloping horse close beside theirs. Brand tossed him one of the reins. He trusted Ordnance to keep pushing on ahead—as long as Nivin made it to Council City, there was hope for the Freemen. Brand pushed Nivin's arms away from him and jumped from the horse, tucking his legs into his chest and rolling onto the side of the road.

Nivin's cry faded into the distance.

CHAPTER TWENTY-FIVE

Brand's words stabbed like a knife into Nivin's gut as soon as she realized what he was doing. One moment he was in front of her, and the next, he was gone. She did not even hear herself cry out—all she heard was the sound of Brand landing on the ground, and the sound of the horse's hooves suddenly lighter on the earth.

There was nothing she could do but desperately reach in front of her, hoping for something to hold on to. She slid forward in the saddle, and her groping hands found the saddle horn.

Once again, she found herself helpless in her circumstances, a ship buffeted by waves beyond her control. But in a way, Brand had also been helpless in this situation. There was no real hope—even the shield he had taken with him would most likely be useless against the fire—yet he had made the choice to go back and try to save

Anek, to fight the helplessness rather than succumb to it. He had chosen to be a sacrifice rather than a victim, because sacrifice was what he had been taught from his youth.

Of all of the things he had chosen to sacrifice his life for, it had been Anek. An abomination. What Zerabar deemed worthy of condemnation, he had deemed worth dying for.

If this was what being a Champion of the Freemen meant—if this was what the Freemen supported and applauded, then Libertas was more than merely good and noble.

Libertas was worth dying for, too.

Nivin had been willing to risk death for her small resistance against Temere's cruel reign. She had defied the helplessness that should have, by all rights, consumed her from her first breath to her last. She had lived her whole life in rebellion against helplessness, fighting and clawing her way past her limitations.

And she would fight now. She would not make ugly the beauty of Brand's sacrifice.

She would fight for Libertas.

The resolution steeled her. It gave her the strength she needed to stay in the saddle. Each jolt of the horse's hooves on the ground was another stab of pain in her back, another nail driven into her resolve. Her feet found the stirrups, steadying her further. She felt for the reins, and found one of them stretched out away toward Ordnance, who must have held it, leading her horse.

Ordnance was silent. Nivin could hardly tell if he mourned their friends—perhaps he had locked the grief into the same cold place in his heart as his dark memories.

Perhaps he was too focused on keeping the horses calm. Either way, she distrusted him, not because she thought he would betray her, but because he was not Brand. She hardly knew Ordnance, though she supposed he must be a good man if Anek had grown to be friends with him. Still, his manner unsettled her. Back at the cave in the mountains, he had seemed far too willing to use her as a weapon, as if she was nothing more than a tool to help the Freemen. Brand at least apologized and said she had a choice.

And her choice was to help the Freemen. She would be their weapon, but not in the way Ordnance thought she would be. She was willing to go before the Council and tell them what she knew, offer as much of her hidden knowledge as she could without actually having to use the aberrant powers. That would be how she would fight for them—by giving them answers, not by engaging in magics as dark as the enemy they faced. She would guide them. She would even fight alongside them. She would risk her life for their cause.

That began with delivering the warning to the Council that an army was approaching.

She fixed that thought in her mind as she rode on, and trusted her horse and Ordnance's guidance to get her to the city. As long as they could continue to outpace the wall of flame, they stood a chance.

They continued on in silence. The fire slowly but steadily grew closer, teeming with hints of the swirling power—but it reminded her of the power that had filled the badgers rather than the presence of a spawn. Nivin could feel her horse starting to falter beneath her, and she began to worry the poor beasts might not even make it to

Council City. But after a little while, she realized it was not only the horses who were running out of strength—she could feel the force and presence of the fire waning. Whatever being drove the fire forward, it had pushed the fire too far from itself, where it could no longer control it fully. It was as if the fire itself said *no farther*.

A glimmer of hope danced through her mind. There *was* a chance they could make it.

There was a flicker of power and a clap of thunder.

The flames condensed and created what might have been almost a miniature Charybdon—and a spawn burst through the tiny portal. Somehow, the spawn that controlled the fire had used it as a passage. The creature launched out of the wall of flame at a breakneck speed, like a stone from a slingshot. Nivin could sense it was manlike, but it ran on all fours as fast as a wolf. Smoke seethed out from around its joints, and a long thick tail trailed behind it. It was almost as though a dragon had taken on the size and shape of a man—the purest form of Scylla and Scyllorin's offspring.

Its appearing filled the horses with new terror, spurring them on.

The creature emanated a kind of hatred beyond what could be called malice. Only something which loathed its own existence could have despised the existence of everything else around it, or taken so much delight in destruction. Destruction, desecration, and murder were its only joy.

Never in her life had Nivin sensed the emotions of someone else so intensely; its spite was palpable to all of her senses. The malice filled her nostrils as readily as the smoke it issued, making her dizzy with nausea. It hated everything. It hated *her*. It intended to douse the internal fire of its hatred with *her* blood.

Ordnance gave a panicked yell. He began shouting incoherently, every unintelligible syllable thick with terror.

Nivin's stomach tightened. "Ordnance?"

He kept shouting. Whether he was ignoring her or he could not even hear her, Nivin was unsure.

"Ordnance, please!"

Ordnance let out a startled cry as if he had just realized she was there. "Nivin!"

"How close are we to the city?"

"I don't know—an hour or two, if the horses don't die beneath us." He cursed. "We can't lead it to the city! Seeing the fire will warn them danger is on the way. We can't—we can't take this spawn right to the city gates."

Nivin bit her lip. Keeping the creature from the city would save hundreds of lives, but it might mean the end of their own.

Brand would have sacrificed his life to save Council City in a heartbeat.

"Then we mustn't go to the city," Nivin said, fighting back a sinking feeling. "What do we do?"

Ordnance was silent. The horses snorted and gasped in terror.

"Northeast," Ordnance muttered. "We take it northeast. We'll lose it at the river, then head back west to the city. Hold on!" With a jerk of the reins, he steered the horses sharply away to the side.

At the sudden change in direction, Nivin's horse rebelled. It reared up to throw her. She struggled to hang on, but the other horse lost its last shred of domestication, and began bucking until it flung Ordnance from its back. It tried to run forward, but its reins had become tangled with Nivin's. In their panic, the horses twisted their legs together and fell to the ground in a mangled heap of terrified flesh. In their final collapse, Nivin flew from the back of her mount. The ground rose up and punched all of the wind from her lungs. Her ears rang from the force of the impact. Her back lit up with pain. Her senses reeled. She was lost in a sea of terror until the sound of Ordnance's vomiting brought her back to a sense of orientation. Still reeling, she stumbled her way toward him, screaming his name. The air became thicker and thicker with the malevolent smoke.

Her own nausea, triggered by the smell of violent hatred in her nostrils, overpowered her. Painfully, she spilled the contents of her stomach onto the ground. Only swirling lights and feral snarling warned her the spawn must have been no more than a hundred yards away from them.

"Ordnance—Ordnance!" she choked.

But he continued to heave, lost to everything around him. He was helpless in the clutches of the creature's nauseating malice.

Retching again, Nivin started to think she too would succumb to the hatred that so fervently desired her destruction. She and Ordnance might as well be dead already. With a groan, she collapsed to the earth, laying her face upon the cool grass. The odor of her own vomit mingled with hate assaulted her mercilessly. As her stomach started to heave again, she tried to reach her senses into the earth below, searching for anything to alleviate the pain of her despair.

A thread of light—still flickering in the distance where

the creature had passed through—called out to her like the faintest beacon of hope.

She reached out for it, but her hand only brought back a clump of grass. The flickering light tantalized her until it seemed like it was the only answer she could ever attain. She reached and reached for it, wanting it so badly she forgot why she even wanted it. She did not know where she was—who she was. The clumps of grass her hand dug up again and again confused her. Frustration made her curse—and then, the sound of cruel hissing laughter brought her back to herself.

The spawn stood right in front of them, radiating heat like a blazing fire. The tangled horses screamed. Ordnance was as silent as the dead. Sulfurous smoke wreathed through the air like tangible hate. All Nivin could do was lie huddled in the pool of her own vomit, tearing up pieces of turf like a traumatized child.

The spawn let out a sickening hiss as it raised an arm to strike.

She was going to die.

Sudden panic triggered instincts deep inside her. She leapt to her feet, reached out both arms, and shouted in pure rebellion against her fate.

The thread of light charged into her outstretched hands, jumping across the distance like a bolt of lightning. Guided by the hidden instincts which had overpowered her actions, she stretched the thread out and multiplied it around her like a spider's web in one smooth motion. The tapestry of light closed in on her for a single moment—but with a shout, she thrust it toward the spawn.

The spawn screeched furiously as it was bodily thrown back. Nivin pulled the strands of light together into a whip and gave a furious lash. The whip struck the spawn, cutting a gash through its hard spiky scales. Snarling, it charged her. Nivin leapt aside, barely dodging the attack. Like a blazing furnace, its intense heat raised blisters across her face and forearms. The smoke was so thick she almost could not breathe. She sensed it as it swiped vicious razor claws at her.

She was ready. She lashed the whip again, coiling the strands around the spawn's wrists. Swinging with all her might, she threw the spawn away from her with strength augmented by the power of the strands of light. Even so, her back screamed with pain at the motion. She lost her balance and fell to her knees. Only a few yards away, the spawn collapsed on its back.

For a moment, nothing happened.

Then, the spawn used powers of its own to break the whip's hold in a crack of thunder. It jumped to its feet and spread its arms wide. More lights flickered and a roaring wall of flame sprang up from the ground, towering high above Nivin's head. It shoved its hands forward, and the wall of flame surged toward her. Nivin flung her arms open wide and her whip became a net of lights, pushing the wall of flame back at the spawn. The spawn flew back several feet and landed on its back. Thunder crashed as the wall of flame melted into smoke.

Reeling with pain, Nivin climbed to her feet. Just a few seconds after her, the spawn stood up with a hiss. She fused the lights back into a whip and lashed at it. It lost its balance and stumbled, arms akimbo. As if she was in two planes of consciousness, aware of both her own mind and the pure instincts that had taken her over, Nivin realized she had created a crucial opening. She snatched the short sword from her belt and flung it at the creature, driving it forward with all the force of the lights behind it.

The blade sank deep into the spawn's belly. Nivin coiled the strands of light and snapped the whip once more. There was a loud thud and the ground shuddered as the spawn collapsed. She lashed the whip again.

Again. Again. Again.

The spawn screeched in agony, writhing with pain so horrible Nivin could feel it.

The earth beneath her feet rumbled. In a crack of thunder, more strands of light materialized and began to swirl beneath her. A tiny Charybdon formed, no more than a seed. It could have fit in the palm of her hand. It was as tiny as the one with which she had healed her companions back in the mountains—the same size as the one which had come into being when Scylla had flown overhead, creating the seeds of Charybda in her wake.

A wave of horror washed through Nivin. She had not lost control of the powers, calling this Charybdon forth from the energies that existed already. Her actions had drawn—or created—the necessary power for it to be born. *Her* actions had brought the embryonic portal out of nothingness into being.

Just like Scylla.

The realization made all of her instincts for survival go blank. She released her grasp on the whip. The streams of light slithered away to join the nascent Charybdon, causing it to swell. For one heartbeat, she thought it might grow large enough to suck them all away, but enough of her innate knowledge remained to tell her the Charybdon would flicker out and die like a candle with no air, as long as there was no further provocation. With all of her groaning heart, she wished she could extinguish the aberration from the face of the world immediately. Even that, however, would not be enough to alleviate her shame, or change the fact she herself had created it.

Like Scylla. Just like Scylla!

What was she even doing using the powers? Had she not decided she would never use them again? How had she gone from that firm resolution to *creating a Charybdon herself?*

No. There was no time for such thinking. She could not let shame and panic overwhelm her. The spawn, grievously injured, had fallen silent. The sheer power of its malice had waned and its temperature was dropping quickly. The strands of energy inside it slowly flickered out as if it was dying, but a chance remained it still might recover enough to attack them again. The desire to leave the horrible creature and the new Charybdon behind overwhelmed her.

"Ordnance! Ordnance, we need to move, now!" A stirring on the ground alerted her to his location, and she ran to him and fell to her knees, feeling for his hands. When she had found them, she tightly grasped them. "Please, get up!"

"Nivin," Ordnance muttered. "What happened?" With a gasp, he sat up. "What in damnation did you just do?"

Nivin blinked back tears. "I'm not even sure. I just know we need to kill that thing and get away from here. I don't know if it will get up again."

There was a pause, during which she imagined Ordnance was surveying the surroundings.

"No, I think it's dead. It's not moving at all." Ordnance let out a soft groan. "Help me up. What did it do to me?"

"It almost did the same to me. Something in the smoke—but hurry. I'm not convinced it is dead yet." She pulled Ordnance to his feet. "Cut off its head."

"I'm not going near that thing," Ordnance spat. "It's finished. If it is not dead yet, it will be soon enough."

"But—"

"I'm not going near it! Never again, do you understand?" Ordnance's voice sank to a mutter. "Never again. I'll die first. Not going back. Darkness. Nothing but darkness." He ran over to where the horses lay tangled. Nivin heard them wheezing, and she almost imagined she could feel them trembling on the ground. Ceasing his muttering, Ordnance spoke soothingly to the horses as he disentangled them from each other. "It's a wonder their legs didn't break." With a little encouragement, he helped them to their feet. "Let us hope the poor beasts won't run at once."

"You can't possibly be thinking of riding them again?"

"Not yet. I think we can afford to walk for a while."

Nivin bit her lip. "But the spawn…"

"The spawn is dead, Nivin. We have to press on to Council City. There's still an army on the way." Ordnance started walking away at a stiff pace, guiding the horses.

Shaking her head, Nivin caught up to him and grabbed her horse's reins. For the next half hour or so, she worried ceaselessly about the spawn they had left behind. Her back felt even worse than it had before; doubtless, being thrown from the horse had done her no favors. She smiled grimly at the passing thought that she could have used the seedling Charybdon to heal herself.

Her stomach went cold. The spawn could easily use the Charybdon she had left behind to heal itself.

As if the realization had struck the spawn at the same time, she sensed a flicker of power behind them. "We have to go back and kill it. Cut off its head, or something. It's alive. I can feel it."

"I'm not going back," Ordnance said, something like fear or shame in his voice. "I told you it was badly wounded enough—it should die soon, if it isn't already dead."

"They can heal themselves."

Thunder rumbled in the distance. The horses stamped their feet and twitched their ears nervously.

"Ordnance, did you hear me?" Nivin shouted. "They can heal themselves!"

"Then we should move," Ordnance said. "Let's see if the horses will bear us. We'll head northeast, just like before, and lose it at the river."

Ordnance came to Nivin's side and guided her foot into the stirrup, then firmly planted his hands at her waist and boosted her the rest of the way up. She realized he must have been taller than Brand, because he lifted her higher—she did not have to work as hard to get settled in the saddle. As she worked her foot into the other stirrup, she listened to him walk back over to his horse and mount it in one easy motion.

If we make it to Council City in one piece, Nivin thought, *I will learn how to mount a horse properly.*

Her shoulders slumped as she remembered both of the people she trusted to teach her were gone.

Ordnance brought his horse next to Nivin's and grabbed hold of one of the reins. "Are you ready?"

Nivin nodded.

Ordnance shouted to the horses and they broke into a

canter. It was not long before Nivin's horse started to limp as it ran. She was torn between sympathy for the animal and the desire to keep riding away from the spawn no matter what. After several more minutes, Ordnance brought the horses to a stop.

"What are you doing?" Nivin asked.

"I still think it's safe for us to walk the horses for a while," Ordnance replied. "That spawn has fallen too far behind. Likely, it is dying, if it hasn't died already."

Nivin could only just sense the strands of power far behind them, but they still sent chills down her spine. "I can still sense it. And the horses are still on edge."

"The horses will be on edge for a while anyway. Let's walk for a ways and see about getting them some rest."

"You don't understand. The spawn—"

"No. *You* don't understand. We can't push the horses any more. They are at their breaking point. If that spawn is really alive like you say, we'll need them to recover."

Nivin dismounted reluctantly. She felt guilty for wanting to spur her exhausted horse into a fierce gallop until she was as far away from the spawn as possible.

Little by little, the horses grew calmer as they progressed, though their limp did not lessen. After they had been walking in the quiet for nearly an hour, Ordnance decided it was safe to rest the horses. He kept muttering to himself that he was sure the spawn was dead, and it must have died of its wounds. Nivin was not convinced. She thought she still sensed the flickering lights in the distance.

While they were stopped, Ordnance checked Nivin's horse to see why it was limping. "It must have pulled a muscle," he said. "There is little we can do for it. Let's give them our water for now. The river is so close the two of us will be fine, but the horses might not make it after such exertion. Hold out your hands."

Nivin held her hands cupped together and Ordnance poured water into them, and the horses sucked up the water greedily, each in turn. It was almost pleasant; the gentle breeze caressed Nivin's aching body and spirit, while the brilliant sunshine warmed her skin. The snuffling of the horses and the tickling of their lips against her sensitive palms made her smile despite her inner fears. The horses had greatly relaxed, an indication that perhaps they truly were out of danger. Surely such embedded animal instincts could be trusted.

Nivin wished her instincts told her the same thing. "How much farther now?"

"Well, it's maybe a mile until we reach the river," Ordnance said. "We'll have to take a less than straightforward route if we're going to lose that filthy Scyllorin-spawn—just in case it is still alive, like you said. I still say you're wrong, but you are the one with the hidden knowledge."

Nivin scowled at the barb. "How long will it take us?"

"It will take another hour, maybe an hour and a half, to reach the northern gates of Council City."

"Should we even bother wasting our time? The spawn seem to have no trouble finding me—I think they can sense me, the way I can sense them."

Ordnance was silent for a moment. "That is a disturbing prospect."

Nivin's ears grew hot with embarrassment. "You have no right to think badly of me for my connection to the spawn—you're the one who wants to use me as a weapon against them!"

"I don't think badly of you. This just complicates things. We should still do our best to shake it from our trail, if we can. If it doesn't work, it doesn't work—but if it does, then we have an advantage." He paused. "We should sit down and rest. We won't get the chance again." He sat down heavily on the ground.

Nivin hesitated for a moment before going over and sitting down next to him. "I'm sorry for jumping to conclusions."

"No matter."

From his tone, Nivin was unsure whether it really was no matter after all, but she decided to drop it. After a few minutes, one of the horses lay down on the ground, breathing heavily.

"I wish we could unsaddle the horses," Nivin said. "They might like to roll around in the grass. My father always told me that about horses. They haven't been free of their saddles in almost two days."

"We don't have time." Ordnance's voice was surprisingly bitter. "We may need to ride again very suddenly. Believe me, I would love nothing better than to curry them and give them a nice hot mash. But our need is too great."

"Will they go lame?"

"If they do, I shall personally ensure they live in the most comfort possible until they die of old age."

"It hardly seems like enough to repay them for their ability to walk and be free of a stall."

"Do you think we have a choice?" Ordnance leapt to his feet. "Human lives are at stake! If you are so worried about the damned horses then call up one of your Charybda to heal them!"

Nivin wanted to lash back at him, but could not find any words. She bit her lip and clenched her fists. Brand would have been more understanding. Even if he was hopeful Nivin would help Libertas, Brand never seemed to be as pushy as Ordnance. Ordnance did not seem to care about the potential wrong of the Charybda—and cared even less about Nivin's hesitance. *But then*, Nivin thought, *what else could I expect from a man who had no qualms about using a deep arcane evil to save himself?*

Almost immediately, she chided herself for such thoughts. Ordnance had relied on the dragon worshipers' ritual to free himself from years of deep dark imprisonment. It had been his last option, the only end in sight to his suffering and madness. She wondered if she herself would not have done the same thing.

After all, had she not just relied on using something fundamentally wrong to save herself from the spawn?

Nivin's stomach turned at the thought.

They rested for about ten minutes and then moved on again. They continued to walk, trying to keep the burden as light for their limping horses as possible. It did not even take half an hour for them to reach the river. Shade from the trees crowding around the river's banks fell down on them, providing relief from the late afternoon heat. There was the faint sound of wind in the leaves, but it was nearly drowned out by the sound of the water.

"It sounds huge," Nivin said, thinking back to the only time her father had taken her to play in the River Tamim west of the capital. That river's loud rushing sound was easily half the volume of this one.

"This is the Lesser River," Ordnance said. "It goes on for thirty miles or so before it feeds into the Greater River in the south, which goes out to the sea. There are some places where you cannot see the opposite shore of the Greater River, it is so wide."

"What about the Lesser River? How wide is it here?"

"We'd be across in five minutes, easily. But we shouldn't cross. We are going to walk in the river for a while—as long as it's passable. It shouldn't be deeper than our waists if we keep to the banks. If we can make it for a mile or so, we will climb out of the river on the north side and head straight to Council City's north gate. That way, the spawn will have a more difficult time trailing us. Assuming it's not dead."

"Assuming it can't just sense me."

"If that's the case, then you will just have do whatever it is you did before."

Nivin pressed her lips together.

They walked in the cold river for what seemed like a long time before Ordnance finally decided to climb up the steep northern bank. Nivin's back hurt even more from slipping on the smooth rocks in the riverbed, and her toes were nearly numb with cold. Even after being out of the water for ten minutes and walking in the early evening sunlight, her toes refused to warm up. She was about take off her shoes to see if that would help when the distinct, horrible sound of thunder throbbed through the earth. Flames roared. The horses screamed.

The spawn had found them.

CHAPTER TWENTY-SIX

Nivin swallowed back the scream threatening to explode from her chest. Panicking would do nothing but make her more susceptible to the spawn's malevolence, giving it an advantage. She had to stay calm so the terrible instincts inside her would not take over again.

Flames sped toward the river banks and leapt through the trees. Thunder thrummed through the earth again and the spawn launched out of the wall of fire, pouring smoke like blood.

But something was different. The smoke was not as thick with malice as it had been, nor was the heat it radiated as intense. Perhaps that would be enough to give Ordnance a chance to fight it, and there would be no reason for Nivin to use the instincts she was desperately trying to ignore. Vestiges of the powers that had created the miniature portal in the wall of flame swirled in seductive patterns of light, calling out to Nivin with the promise of potential safety and strength—if only she would open her mind to the instincts that knew how to control them.

She would not use the powers. Never again. They would have to think of some other way to defeat the spawn.

The spawn charged straight toward them. Nivin dove out of the way, fully expecting to spawn to follow after her immediately.

It did not.

With a screech, it leapt in a single bound onto her horse, sinking its clawed hands into the beast's back. The horse gave a terrified whinny, but then fell into total submission, much as if the spawn were using it as a mouthpiece. The spawn let out an unearthly grating screech and spurred the horse, riding away at breakneck speed.

"It's heading for the city!" Ordnance cried. The other horse reared up and bucked wildly, snorting in terror, desperately trying to escape from Ordnance's hold on its lead. "We have to stop it!"

The city. The place Brand was so desperate to protect. It would assuredly meet the same fiery fate as Respite Height if the spawn made it past the city's gates, spreading flames and death. Brand had given up his life to try to save Anek, and he would have done the same to save the city.

Nivin grabbed at her hair. "What do we do?"

"You're the one who knows how to fight the spawn!"

Nivin froze. The swirling lights danced. It would be so easy to use them, so easy to let her instincts take over.

She could not give in to them. She had decided she

would be willing to help the Freemen, and give her life for them, even. But she had also promised herself she would never use the powers again

"Damn it, Nivin, do something! Don't you know what that thing will *do* to Council City?"

Her instincts rebelled. Against her conscience, she wrapped her mind around the strands of energy and pulled them together. Before she realized what she was doing, she had woven them into a tiny Charybdon. She ran up to Ordnance's horse and plunged the Charybdon into the horse's side, curing it of both its terror and its horrible limp. The horse screamed, just as she had expected it to, just as painfully as hers had when the spawn had taken it over.

Somewhere inside of her, her conscience watched in horror.

Once the horse was healed, she took the Charybdon and coaxed it back down into her hand, then pressed it into her own chest. Her spine was on fire. The pain threatened to make her black out, but the instincts fought against it. Her instincts wasted no time nor energy on her other hurts. She pulled the Charybdon out of herself and pressed it between her hands. There was a deafening thunderclap. The tiny portal collapsed and vanished.

Dizziness spun through Nivin's head. She felt she would faint and the familiar nothingness would close in on her, but she forced it away. No matter how she tried, though, she could not ignore the guilt sweeping through her. Something about the horse was different. It seemed too calm—so calm, it was almost frightening.

She was almost certain it was because of what she had done.

"We have to get on the horse," Nivin said, trying not to choke on the words. "We have to follow that thing."

"What did you do?" A note of fear tinged Ordnance's voice.

"I—I helped it." Nivin blinked back tears. "It couldn't help us pursue that thing otherwise."

"What did you do to yourself?"

Nivin turned her face away from Ordnance as more shame flooded through her. "I healed my back."

Just like the spawn can.

"Why haven't you lost consciousness then, the way the others said you did?"

Nivin started. Normally, anytime she tampered with the powers, she fell into the black nothingness of unconsciousness. But she had used them twice now, and nothing had happened. Was it possible she was building a tolerance for them? That she could tolerate them the same way as Scylla and the spawn?

"I don't know," she said.

Ordnance said nothing more. He untied the supplies from his horse and threw them to the ground with a loud *thunk,* then grabbed her by the waist and boosted her up into the saddle. A moment later, he leapt up onto the horse in front of her and slid his feet into the stirrups. Nivin awkwardly grabbed on to him for support as he spurred the horse into motion. It burst into a furious gallop at once. As Nivin clung to Ordnance, his ribs pressed against the inside of her arms. Her embarrassment at putting her arms around him vanished, replaced by pity. She had never felt a frame so skeletal. While Brand was not well-fed by any standards, Ordnance's body was completely emaciated.

What he had suffered at Scyllorin's hands only

doubled Nivin's resolve to aid the Freemen.

The wind whipping against her face told her Ordnance's horse was galloping faster than it ever had before, and yet it seemed listless. The same inexplicable *wrongness* of the Charybda now emanated from the horse itself. She silently chastised herself. She had to be careful not to let her desire to save Council City overpower her again. How they could fight against the spawn without using the unnatural powers, she did not know, but it was absolutely imperative she did not tap into them again, no matter how desperate.

Nivin was unsure of how long they had been riding before thunder rumbled through the earth again. Fire leapt up out of the plains ahead of them, full of the swirling lights. A cacophony of cries rained down from somewhere above them. The flames licked up against something massive, made of stone—something like a wall.

Ordnance brought the horse to an abrupt halt. "It's attacking the city!"

Another wave of flames crashed into the wall like an ocean breaker against a rock. Men shouted. Nivin was certain she heard the sound of a body hitting the ground.

"How do we stop it?" Ordnance demanded.

Nivin hesitated. Something was wrong with the spawn. Her instincts told her it was not keeping the swirling powers in check—they were growing and multiplying faster than they should have. "I—I don't know what to do."

"Has that stopped you before?"

A chorus of *twangs* sounded. Whistling filled the air as a volley of arrows rained down on them from the parapets above. A throb of power ran through the earth, and the spawn turned all of them to ash in midair. More strands of light slithered to join the others.

Ordnance spat a curse. "Those were aimed at us too! They think we're under the spawn's control! Do something—anything!"

Do something.

Do what?

Panic climbed up Nivin's spine. She *had* to stop the spawn. She had to stop the spawn without using the powers, or fueling them further. They already threatened to swirl into a huge Charybdon. "Attack it. We know swords can hurt this one."

Ordnance scoffed. "Attack it?"

"Yes! Or give me the sword, and I will!"

"Can't you just—"

"No, I *can't*. You don't understand. There's too much already."

"Too much of what?"

"I—the lights! There are too many. A Charybdon will open if I do anything. Who knows where it would take us this time—and half of the city's defenders along with us!"

"I won't go back," Ordnance muttered. "Only darkness."

"You are a Champion! Your people need you. It's the only way. Remember who you are!"

Ordnance let out a crazed laugh. "Death, then. I shall die for the cause like all the others. But I won't go back." His sword rang as he pulled it out of the sheath. "I'll never go back."

Nivin tightened her grip on Ordnance as his horse immediately and fearlessly charged toward the city.

The spawn had stopped a short distance from the city

wall, incinerating flying arrows and sending wave after wave of fire against the defenders. Its focus was purely on the city now. As Ordnance drew up beside it, more blisters prickled across Nivin's exposed skin.

Ordnance swung.

The blade did little more than glance off the spawn's spiky scales, but the force of the blow knocked the spawn from the horse's back. There was a strange sucking sound as the spawn's arms pulled out of the horse. With a terrified whinny, it galloped away in a frenzy.

The spawn recovered from its fall in a heartbeat. It sprang to its feet and thrust a percussion of pure flame straight at Ordnance and Nivin.

Nivin could not stop her instincts. She reached out with a hand and raised a shield of spiraling energies just in time to keep the flames from ravaging them, but it was not enough to keep the force of the spawn's attack from flinging both of them from the horse's back.

The horse fell on its side, unhurt and indifferent to the situation.

Furious with herself, Nivin let the wall of energy drop. Magnified, it slithered away to join the rest of the strands of light, which were now spiraling in the earth beneath them. Whispering voices ebbed and swelled. Surely one more use of unchecked power would tear a full-sized Charybdon open.

She had to be more careful. Somehow, she had learned how to collapse smaller ones, but there was no way she could control one so massive.

The spawn had grown cooler, as if its fire was dying out slowly. But it did not need fire when it had strength. It hissed viciously and leapt at Nivin. Claws slashed across the forearms she raised to protect herself. Ordnance leapt into the fray, swinging the sword so hard it whistled through the air. It broke through one of the spawn's thick scales and bit into the vulnerable flesh beneath.

Another volley of arrows rained from the parapet. The spawn could not react quickly enough to defend itself. An arrow lodged itself one of the scales that guarded its shoulders. The spawn stumbled back, rallying for one final wall of flame.

Nivin's heart pounded. It would be too much. The voices were already too loud.

She bodily hurled herself at the spawn and knocked it to the ground. Sharp spikes punctured her dress and bit into her skin. She fell beside it, raising her hands to shield her face from the smoke.

Footsteps pounded across the earth. In an instant, Ordnance drove his blade down on the spawn—straight through its delicately scaled throat.

There was not even a sound as the spawn vanished from Nivin's intuitive eyes. Its body went cold. Ordnance had snuffed it out entirely.

Slowly, the swirling lights started to fade and flicker out strand by strand. The voices grew less insistent.

Whoops and cheers went up from the city as the defenders realized what had happened. Ordnance let out a triumphant laugh.

Pure relief flooded Nivin's entire being. There had been no Charybdon. They had prevented it.

But then the memories of what she had done to Ordnance's horse rushed to her mind. The beast had not even reacted to a wall of flame. She had somehow damaged it when she used her powers to heal it and keep it calm. Was that truly any different from what the spawn had done to her horse?

Unconsciousness crept around the edges of her mind. She shook her head. Why now? She could not faint now—they had not yet warned the Freemen of the approaching army. She *had* to carry Brand's message to the city he loved so much.

Ordnance knelt down beside Nivin and laid a hand on her shoulder. "Nivin, are you hurt?"

Nivin grimaced as she struggled to sit up and keep the unconsciousness away at the same time. "My arms."

"The apothecaries in Council City are the finest. Hold on."

Ordnance stood back up and shouted a greeting to the city. Nivin danced along the edges of sleep and waking, aware Ordnance was speaking with someone, but unable to understand what anyone was saying.

After a few moments, Ordnance took Nivin's hands. "Let me help you up." He pulled her to her feet and caught her when she stumbled. "They are sending someone out to bring us in."

"What about the horses?"

"I am sure they will do what they can. Yours ran away and I am not sure what your help did to mine. It's just lying there on the ground as calmly as if it were dead."

Nivin suppressed the desire to burst out sobbing.

"Thank you, Nivin," Ordnance said softly. "I would never have found my courage without you pushing me—without you reminding me who I am."

All Nivin could manage was a small, halfhearted smile.

There was a rattle and a clang as what sounded like a portcullis opened. Gates groaned as they swung wide, and soon, a large group of people walked toward Ordnance and Nivin. Nivin immediately recognized the sound of mail—and the sound of hushed, distrustful murmuring. Soldiers were coming to bring them in, and they put her more in mind of Zerabar than of how she had imagined Brand's people.

Ordnance greeted them warmly as they met, but the soldiers said nothing in response. The hands grabbing Nivin on either side were forceful and unsympathetic. The unconsciousness loomed closer.

"Some welcome this is," Ordnance snapped. "We just killed that vile thing!"

Again, the soldiers did not respond. They dragged Ordnance and Nivin toward the gate. Nivin stumbled as she went, relying on the soldiers for support as much as her own feet.

Eventually, they came to a stop.

"Councilor Valiance!" Ordnance said. "What is the meaning of this?"

There was a long pause before a stolid female voice replied, "Prove to me you are who you say."

"My appearance surely hasn't changed so much you do not recognize me."

"Then prove to me you are who you appear to be."

"What proof do you want?" Ordnance snapped. "I kissed your daughter Verity on the mouth when I was ten and she was sixteen. She slapped me for it and nearly broke my nose. You made sure Councilor Mace gave me all of the most unpleasant duties he possibly could. I broke my first wooden training sword when Councilor Endurance told me I wasn't swinging hard enough—I swung it so hard in my next attempt it broke into five pieces." His manner grew more agitated. "Is that enough? Or do you want more?" Fabric rustled. "Do you want to see the scar on my side I got during training, when we were learning to scale a rock face? I fell and landed on jagged rock, and it practically tore my side open. I was on bed rest for two weeks, and it is still the least pain I ever endured as a Champion of Libertas!"

Valiance's tone softened. "Ordnance—can it really be you? You have been thought long dead." She stepped forward, and from the sound of it, gave Ordnance a brief embrace. Her voice became flat again. "You must forgive the harsh welcome. We have endured something of an ordeal here. We were certain you and your companion were in the spawn's service."

"An army is coming from Verderbera," Nivin blurted out. "Brand thought it was coming to wipe you out."

A deep male voice cut in. "Ordnance, what is the name of your companion?"

"My name is Nivin—Champion Brand was my friend. You have to listen, there's an army—"

"Quiet," the deep male voice said.

Nivin pressed her lips together. Heat flared across her cheeks.

"Ordnance," the voice continued, "is this true?"

"Yes," Ordnance said. "There is an army coming from the south, and—"

"Is her name Nivin? Was she in fact Brand's friend?"

"Yes."

"How did you meet her?"

"Wait a moment. You're Councilor Invictus, aren't you? Why are you here instead of your dignitary? What's been happening at this city?"

"Answer Councilor Invictus' question, Ordnance," Valiance said.

"I met her in the mountains, on a large stone staircase one of Scyllorin's spawn fashioned for the use of this very army that approaches."

"They destroyed Respite Height," Nivin said, fighting against the dizziness closing in on her.

"Do not make us ask you to be quiet again," Invictus said through his teeth. "I assure you, you will have a chance to say your part. Ordnance, did you find her on this staircase alone?"

"No. She was with a giant called Anek, and both of them were with Champion Brand."

"Where are the other two, then?"

Nivin could not bite back the words that exploded from her mouth. "They are dead. They were both taken by the spawn's fire."

"Quiet!" Invictus snapped.

There was a pause. Nivin clenched her jaw.

"Is this true?" Valiance asked.

Ordnance gave a despondent sigh. "I don't know. Anek was falling behind and Brand went back to aid him. There was no way they could have outrun it, and there was no shelter which might have protected them."

"Are you sure there is no way? Did they have nothing they might have used to save themselves?"

"Brand had my shield—which *was* effective against other spawn we encountered. But I doubt it was able to save them from the fire itself."

"A shield," Invictus breathed. "What was it made of?"

"Granite."

"Where did you come by it?"

"That too is a long story, Councilor."

"Just tell us where you found it," Valiance said. "Was it in a store? A quarry? A meadow? A stream?"

"A graveyard."

"A graveyard." Invictus muttered. "A graveyard."

"Where was this graveyard?" Valiance asked.

Ordnance was quiet for a moment. "Verderbera. Beside Scyllorin's stronghold."

"And where did Nivin come from?"

"A country called Zerabar. It is in another world—she and Anek passed through a magical portal which brought them here."

"Do these portals have a name?"

"She calls them Charybda. You would have to ask her to learn more."

A long pause followed. Nivin began to feel dizzier and more frenzied by the moment. She took a staggering step forward, not caring if they told her to be quiet again. "The army is coming. You have to be prepared—"

She could hold the nothingness at bay no longer. Unconsciousness closed in around her and she felt herself fall to the ground.

One thought flitted through her last waking moment.

If nothing else, she had carried on the message Brand could not.

End of Book I

ACKNOWLEDGMENTS

I would like to thank all of my wonderful Beta readers: Mary Ellen Carmody, Mirja Conrad, Patty Joy, Stacia Miller, David Sandman, Debra Swanson, Douglas Swanson, Faith Swanson, Laura Swanson, Sara Vossler, M.B. Wallace, and Nathanael Weber. Without you, I could not have produced the same quality of story.

I would also like to thank my editor, Kathy Hendricks. Thanks for catching those pesky mistakes.

Thanks are also due to my map designer Beth Seethaler, who did a beautiful job.

Finally, I would like to thank to my husband Chris Vossler, who held my hand at every step along the way, encouraged me when I felt like giving up, read the first draft, read the final draft, listened to me talk about this book for hours on end, and so much more. You are my right arm.

ABOUT THE AUTHOR

A.L.S. Vossler was born in Denver, Colorado, and has lived in various places throughout the American Midwest. She grew up reading science fiction and fantasy and has a serious passion for the genre. In 2009, she received a Bachelor of Arts in English from Concordia University Chicago. She currently resides in Kansas and spends her days writing, reading, organizing her massive *My Little Pony* collection, and occasionally pretending to clean the house.

You can visit her blog at alsvossler.com.